*Today is success or failure, there will be no in-between.*

"Start the boundary vortex," he ordered. "Bring the field up a little more."

"Chamber pressure coming up," reported the squeeze-field technician. "Plasma temperature is spiking."

"Boundary vortex flow is good," put in the cooling-system tech.

"Plasma loading is complete." The fuel tech checked his readouts. "We have fusion."

The chief engineer nodded and breathed out. "Good, let's throttle up." *We've passed the first test.*

"Field strength is seventy percent. Reaction temperature is twenty million kelvins and rising."

"Good, let's have some throttle."

The chief engineer watched the process, his mind jumping ahead to anticipate what might yet go wrong. "More throttle, and more fuel."

Slowly, inexorably the readouts inched higher. The chief engineer watched in silence now, as his acolytes progressively awakened the furies that would drive *Ark* to another star. The magnetic-field strength peaked at its full rated maximum and slowly they brought the fuel flow up to match it.

"We are running stable," the fuel technician reported.

The chief engineer smiled. *And so, we are under way.*

"Disconnect the cable," he ordered, and was surprised by the sudden applause that arose in the control room. They had cut their link to Earth.

# Baen Books
## by Paul Chafe

*Destiny's Forge*

*Genesis*
*Exodus: The Ark* (forthcoming)

# GENESIS

## PAUL CHAFE

GENESIS

Copyright © 2007 by Paul Chafe

A Baen Books Original

Baen Publishing Enterprises
P.O. Box 1403
Riverdale, NY 10471
www.baen.com

ISBN 10: 1-4165-9163-X
ISBN 13: 978-1-4165-9163-4

Cover art by David Mattingly

First Baen paperback printing, May 2009

Distributed by Simon & Schuster
1230 Avenue of the Americas
New York, NY 10020

Library of Congress Cataloging-in-Publication Data:
2007030471

Printed in the United States of America

10 9 8 7 6 5 4 3 2 1

*For Christian*

For more on the Ark project visit
http://projectark.net

# Prelude

*Let there be lights in the firmament of the heaven.*
—Genesis 1:14

# L–135

Crockery smashed downstairs and angry voices came down the corridor. Josh Crewe woke, eyes staring at the darkened ceiling, afraid. He swallowed hard and listened, carefully gauging the swell of the fight as his parents savaged each other with accusation and recrimination. He didn't understand the words but he didn't need to. What was important was their intensity. If the fight grew bad enough there would be footsteps on the stairs and the lights in his room would snap on so Mother could drag him out of bed to use as a living example of his father's failures before God and man. It would mean no sleep, perhaps getting smacked in the face by his father when the hurt and humiliation finally overcame the man and he lashed out himself. That was minor. Father's anger came and went with a single blow, predictable and so not dangerous, however painful. It was Mother who really scared him. Once she had nearly drowned him in a scalding-hot bath because he'd tracked mud into the hallway, another time she'd made him kneel in the gravel driveway all night, praying for forgiveness for bringing a toy to church. Mother was unpredictable, and therefore dangerous.

The voices rose higher and more crashing came from downstairs. He slipped out of bed and dressed himself, quickly and quietly, then went to the hot-air register beneath the window and removed the grille. He snaked an arm down the vent; the fit was almost too tight now that he was twelve. An adult wouldn't have been able to do it, which is why he used it as his secret hiding place.

He'd grown, and his biceps caught painfully on the sharp-edged metal before his fingers found what he was looking for. He stretched, feeling the metal dig in and ignoring the hurt until he touched something—the end cap of a prescription medicine bottle. He teased it closer with his fingertips until he could grab the bottle and drew his arm out. The bottle was transparent plastic, one of many kicking around the house that bore the white sticky label reading Crewe, Evylin, Primodone, 50mg 3x daily. It was stuffed full of money, coins and bills. He had hoarded it carefully, some saved from his allowance, when his parents remembered to give it to him, more stolen a bit at a time from his mother's cigarette money. His emergency fund.

And the emergency was now. He took a pair of packed book bags from beneath a pile of clothes in the mess that was his closet, picked up his shoes and padded across the hall to his sister's room. She was sound asleep. "Susie." He shook her. "Susie, wake up."

She stirred and her eyes opened. He saw in her face the immediate recognition of the situation. "Are we going outside again?"

Josh nodded. "Yes." He didn't tell her the whole plan.

She nodded and dressed without words, tension in her face as the shouting downstairs grew louder. They went back to his room, slid the window open and climbed out onto the veranda. The jump from there to the maple tree was a frightening one for a twelve-year-old, even more so for a ten-year-old. For a moment Josh was afraid that Susie would freeze there, as she had one night before, tears running down her face as he tried to coax her across.

That night had been bad. They'd been caught, and for the first time Father's anger hadn't vanished with the first hit. Something had snapped in him, and he'd beaten Josh, knelt on his arms so he couldn't protect himself and smashed his fist down over and over, until his nose was broken, his face bruised and bloody. It had been terrifying, more terrifying even than anything his mother had done, because his prediction had been wrong. Something had changed in his father, and there was no telling what that would bring. It would have been better if they hadn't been caught, if they'd snuck back in at daybreak, after the fight had burned itself out. Even if they'd been found missing in the middle of the night, nothing would have been said. Nothing was ever said afterward, it was as if the fights were a secret the Crewe family kept from itself.

He dropped the book bags over the veranda. The tree was there, dark in the chill breeze of an autumn night, and he put a practiced foot on the railing and swung a leg across and felt for the broken branch stub that was the only foothold on this side of the tree. He braced himself against the veranda rail and pushed off, balanced for a brief second only on the foot on the branch stub, and then he caught the tree trunk. At least it hadn't been Susie beaten that night. Josh had been angry at his sister for getting them caught. It wasn't fair that he was the only one punished, and the injustice of it burned deep in him. It was always that way, he was the scapegoat and she the favorite. It was his own fault, he took the blame, protected her, diverted their parents' attention away from her transgressions, because he was older, stronger, tougher than she was. It was what he had to do, he didn't know why, and the knowledge of what he was doing didn't make it hurt less.

He scrambled down the tree trunk, balanced on the fence for a second and hopped to the ground, then turned back to look to see if Susie was following him. She edged out around the veranda railing and stopped. For a moment he thought she had frozen again, but she had learned her lesson and reached her foot out, feeling for the branch stub. She was shorter than he was, and it was a harder stretch for her. Her foot found the branch and then she was straddling the gap, fifteen feet up. She moved to shift her weight to grab the tree trunk, swayed dangerously and clutched at the veranda railing to steady herself.

"I can't, Josh." He could hear the fear in her voice.

"You've done it before."

"I'm stuck." She was on the verge of tears.

"I'll come and get you." He couldn't do anything for her, he knew, but he had to show her he was trying. He climbed up the fence and shinnied up the tree, reached out for her.

"Here, just grab my hand."

She looked at him, her eyes large and frightened. Angry voices came from inside the house, muffled by the walls, and she moved all at once, suddenly motivated. He grabbed her wrist and pulled, and then she was safe in the tree and they were climbing down, the rough bark tearing at their hands until they were on the ground.

"Are we going to the park?" She was calmer now as they walked down the driveway, leaving the scene behind them. The park was where they usually waited out the fights.

"Somewhere else." He picked up the book bags and handed hers to her, then slid a hand into his pocket to verify that the medicine bottle was still there.

"We'll get in trouble when we get back."

"Not this time." He helped her slip the straps over her shoulders.

They walked down the familiar street in silence, past the old, towering trees and the lit windows of the neighboring houses, feeling a sudden nervousness. Getting out when he had to was something he had been ready for, just a variation on the familiar theme of getting out of the way, but as bad and frightening as things were at home, they were also known quantities, and the world opening up before him was vast and unknown and full of threats he could only imagine. He resisted the urge to turn around and look back at his house, knowing he would never see it again. Something tugged at him, the desire for warmth, for comfort, for safety. The house was all those things, when his parents weren't fighting. When they weren't it was even a nice place to live, bright and spacious. Everything he owned was there, his friends lived in the neighborhood. He fingered his cheek, it had been months, maybe longer, though the memory of the flaring pain of his father's fist never seemed to leave it. He blinked back tears that came too easily at the memory. It was dangerous for him to stay now, because next time would be worse. He had to leave, and he couldn't leave Susie behind to face their parents alone.

"Where are we going?" Susie's question was plaintive.

"Far away."

"How far?"

To tell her or not to tell her? They were out of the house now, it was too late for her to go back. "We're going to Aunt Krista's."

"On a plane?"

"On a bus." They turned left to head toward downtown.

He had expected her to balk at that. Her answer surprised him. "Is that far enough?"

"It's far enough," he said, but his confidence that it *was* far enough was rattled just by her uncertainty. What if it wasn't? What if Aunt Krista made them go back?

"I don't like it when they're mean to you, Joshie." She slipped a small hand into his, holding it tightly.

"They won't ever be again." Overhead, the streetlights flickered and went dark, evening blackout. Most people avoided going out after blackout, but Josh was used to it; the darkness was a friend that helped him hide from danger.

"Can we go further? If we had to, I mean?" Susie was looking over her shoulder, worry written on her small features.

"If we have to, we can."

"How far could we go?" The question took him aback and he stopped to look at her. Her face was open and worried and he saw her real question written there. *Can they ever take us back?*

And he didn't know the answer to that, and he didn't want her to see his own fear and uncertainty. He pointed up to the sky, frosted bright with stars and a brilliant half-moon now that the competing city lights were gone. "See that star?"

"Which one?"

"The bright one." He picked one at random and pointed more specifically. "That's Alpha Centauri. It's got a planet just like ours. We could go there. They could never get us back from there."

"Can we really?"

"They could send a ship. I read about it."

"I want to go there now."

"We can't yet. Maybe later."

"If we can't stay at Aunt Krista's, can we go there?"

"Yes." Josh squeezed her hand reassuringly, not mentioning that the book on space in the school library had said it was unlikely people could live on any of the distant worlds discovered so far, or that the ship that could carry them there existed only in a speculative chapter at the book's end. They trudged on in the chill night air, and mentally he rehearsed what he would say at the bus station. *I'd like two tickets for Sacramento please. That's in California.* The bus company wouldn't let children travel unaccompanied, so he'd tell the driver his mom would be along shortly and with luck that would get them on the bus. It was a three-day journey to California. He had enough money for their tickets, enough for food for that time, barely. They had enough clothing in the book bags and they would sleep on the bus or in the bus stations. Three days of fending for themselves, and then they'd be safe. Reflexively he patted the back pocket of the backpack, felt the reassuring crinkle of paper. He'd looked it all up and written it down, the schedules and fares and timetables, maps of the area around each bus terminal, and most important Aunt Krista's full name and address. If they got stopped anywhere, the police would get involved, eventually, and he would tell them that Aunt Krista was their mother. With luck that would get them to Sacramento just as well, two runaways returned to their family, but it would be better, far better to arrive in Sacramento on their own and plead their case to Aunt Krista on her doorstep.

He glanced overhead, at the star he had named Alpha Centauri. Aunt Krista would look after them, he was sure, and if she couldn't, well, they would just keep running, as far as they had to. He squeezed Susie's hand again, was rewarded with her brave, trusting smile and felt a sense of pride overtake the fear and uncertainty. She was his baby sister, and he would look after her, no matter where they went, always.

# Genesis 1

*The Almighty has his own purposes.*
—Abraham Lincoln

# L–95

"Go right in, Dr. Crewe." The secretary was blond, with a stylish reserve. "The chairman is waiting for you." She smiled a less reserved smile than she had been trained to give, enough to hint that perhaps she could make herself available after work, if Josh Crewe cared to ask. He was handsome, with a hint of distinguishing grey at his temples and the casual authority of a man accustomed to being in charge. She watched as he went through the heavy oak doors, still lean in his lower fifties, old enough to be her father but still attractive. The doors closed behind him and she looked out the panoramic windows, far away for a long moment. The lights were bright in the Aerospace Consortium's lobby, and a miniature waterfall splashed down one wall. The power-wasting luxuries were tangible displays of the Consortium's wealth in a world where too many people competed for too little. The luxuries made her own cramped flat with its two puny lightpanels seem even more dingy and rundown. She looked to the doors, imagining what life would be like with a man rich enough and powerful enough that she would never have to worry about material needs again. She smiled, daydreaming. Never being hungry, hot showers whenever she wanted them, the freedom to stay up late reading without worrying about what it was costing her; that was the way things were meant to be.

"Assemblyist Crewe. How can I help the United Nations today?" Harmon Michaud's office was immaculate and expensively appointed, as befitted the chairman of the Aerospace Consortium. His desk held a notepad, a screen and a few models of famous air and spacecraft, nothing else. Michaud dressed in expensive and restrained taste, and his keen eyes assessed his visitor dispassionately.

Crewe took one of the plush leather seats. "You may have heard I'm planning to run for secretary-general."

"There have been rumors."

Crewe spread his hands. "The rumors are true. I need your support."

"Hmmm." Michaud steepled his fingers. "What support can we give you?"

"Money and influence. What else is there?"

"And to ask the obvious question, what is in it for the aerospace industry?"

Crewe picked up a small silver cylinder from Michaud's desk. It had a shiny Mylar parabola attached, a model of one of a sensor-swarm probe. The model was full-sized, except for the solar sail, which would have been miles across. "How would you like to see another deep-space exploration program launched?"

"I wouldn't be uninterested, but frankly, Dr. Crewe, there isn't a lot of money to be made in pure research."

"That could change."

"It could." Michaud stroked his chin, thinking. "It will be difficult for you to convince me that you're the person to change it, given you're the one most responsible for legislating profit limits on government-funded research."

"That puts a negative spin on what I've done."

"And how would you spin it?"

"I would say that I've acted to maximize the amount of research we've been able to do on a strictly limited budget. I've also fought hardest to increase that budget for you."

"My companies are interested in profits, not volume."

"Volume brings profits to efficient competitors. Your industry is a lot leaner and more aggressive now. I'd like to think I've helped set the conditions to make that true."

"And did you do that for us? Or for your own purposes?"

"Does it matter, so long as my purpose overlaps with your business model?"

"It matters."

Crewe nodded. "I'll make you a promise, my first campaign promise. More money for space industry, deep-space exploration revived."

Michaud waved a hand. "Space represents a few percent of the aerospace market, at most, research is a fraction of that. I'd rather see energy credits for commercial air carriers."

"You won't see that." Crewe's voice was flatter than he meant it to be. "That's a mature market."

Michaud arched his eyebrows. "Perhaps I'll see subsidies if I support Assemblyist Plant instead of you."

"Plant is running with the support of the Believers.

Even if he were inclined to give you subsidies, his constituency wouldn't allow it."

Michaud laughed mirthlessly. "Politics is the process of getting money from the rich and votes from the poor by exploiting their fear of each other. I have no doubt Markham Plant will do what he has to do to gain the office he seeks. He may have to be more circumspect about how he presents an aerospace subsidy to the public than you would, but I have no doubt he'll repay loyalty in good measure. What will you do for me if I give you my support?"

"You'll see me encourage your industry to align its efforts with the long-term best interests of the world."

Michaud laughed again, with more humor this time. "You have a certain naïve charm, Dr. Crewe. Still, I don't see how I'll benefit from supporting you."

Crewe paused, studying the other man. "I have something else to offer. You'll have to keep it in strictest confidence."

Michaud leaned forward. "What is it?"

"Iota Horologii."

"What?"

"A class-G0 star. Its second planet has a nitrogen-oxygen atmosphere. There's life there. It may be inhabitable for people."

Michaud nodded. "I remember this now. Proof of life beyond the solar system. Exciting news, five years ago. You won't gain any support with this."

"What about launching a colony ship?"

Michaud raised his eyebrows. "Dr. Crewe, I'm not unfamiliar with your work on interstellar ship design, but this is not possible. We don't have the technology."

"What do you care, so long as your industry gets paid to try?"

Michaud picked up the model probe that Crewe had put down. "These get up to ten percent of lightspeed by the time they leave the system. Interstellar gas comes in like hard cosmic rays. Your seedship will fly slower, I could imagine as much as one percent percent of lightspeed with a speed-optimized design, but even so I can't imagine an embryo surviving that environment, to say nothing of gestating them at the far end."

"I'm not talking about embryos, I'm talking about people. Not a seedship but a colony ship."

Michaud snorted. "You can't be serious."

"I'm quite serious; I've looked at the problem from every angle. You're right about radiation flux, and there are other problems, like braking at the far end, like somehow raising a bunch of embryos into a competent colonization team. Seedships are an impossible dream."

"And somehow sending a person isn't? Say your ship weighs a thousand metric tonnes, which is ridiculously conservative." Michaud looked away for a second while he ran the numbers in his head. "There wouldn't be enough energy in the world to launch that even to Alpha Centauri within a human lifetime."

"Think larger. The ship will weigh one billion tonnes."

Michaud's jaw didn't quite drop. "Impossible."

"Trip time is on the order of ten thousand years, assuming we still want to go to Iota Horologii by the time it's ready to launch." Josh Crewe smiled, appearing to enjoy Michaud's incredulity. "We may decide to change the destination. We're sure to learn a lot more by then. There may be closer worlds, and better."

"It would take a hundred years to build such a thing."

"Again, does that matter to you? The Aerospace Consortium will be a thriving concern for your great-grandchildren."

Michaud considered. "No, perhaps it doesn't matter." He paused, contemplating his steepled fingers. "I have a question for you."

"What is it?"

"Why?"

Crewe paused, choosing his words carefully. "Because humanity's destiny is in the stars."

"No doubt. But what I want to know is why you in particular are committed to that destiny." Michaud leaned forward, his eyes locked on Crewe's. "I know your history, Dr. Crewe." He slid a piece of paper out of a folder on his desk and read from it. "Parents divorced, raised by your aunt. Your sister died at age nineteen . . ." If Michaud caught the momentary tightening of Crewe's expression at those words he gave no notice. ". . . no other close relatives. Top honors at Caltech in aerospace engineering, seven years at Boeing, five at Aerospatiale, left there for academia and taught at Oxford for four years, then Samara State Aerospace University in Russia for another four, fluent in English, French and Russian, with a passable knowledge of Arabic and Chinese. Five years ago you abandoned the ivory tower for politics, first regional and now global. As UN secretary of transportation you have been, if I may be frank, a persistent thorn in the side of the aerospace industry. You remain unmarried, despite occasional attachments, and you show no signs of settling down anytime soon. You have little contact with your aunt, none with your parents, and your sister is dead. With no impediments you've been free to do as you choose, and you've made good use of that freedom. Your achievements show you're an intelligent man, your life shows you to be a driven one too. You are accordingly a man to be reckoned with." Harmon leaned back steepling his fingers. "Before I throw my support to such a man I want to know where that drive comes from, the better to predict where he will go."

"I will go to the stars."

"Again, why?"

"Because we can, because they're there. There are no more frontiers on Earth, not mountains, not ocean depths, not even the solar system anymore. We have solved all the great problems of science and as many of those of humanity as I believe are solvable. We must have challenges, something to inspire us outward, or we will turn inward and collapse."

Michaud cocked an eyebrow. "If you were still a scientist I might believe you believed that, but not now. Those words will play too well on a newsfeed for me to give them credibility."

"Why do you think I left science for politics, if not to see this ship made?" Crewe's eyes searched the other man's face. "I see you still doubt me. I'll give you the best proof I can. Five years ago we found a habitable world at Iota Horologii. Five years ago I left my research for politics. I did that to gain the power I needed to make this voyage real."

"You'll never live to see this ship launched."

"King Cheops never lived to see his pyramid completed. He still made building it his lifework."

"Is this what you want? Your memory carried down the generations through this vast project?" Michaud snorted. "A pyramid won't buy you immortality."

"Not for me. It will for the human race. If we're going to survive we need to leave this planet. Our civilization can't last forever."

Michaud shook his head. "Your thinking is fuzzy. Every generation thinks it's the last one, death by a comet or an ice age, greenhouse gases or nuclear war or global plague. Death by divine decree if nothing else. A life in politics has rusted your scientific method, Dr. Crewe. Those challenges have all been faced, and conquered. There's no evidence that the world is about to end."

"I don't think our generation is the last one, that's not the same as realizing that civilizations have a lifespan. There have been hundreds of civilizations since the dawn of history. They last four hundred and thirty-five years, on average. We're already living on borrowed time."

"That average doesn't apply to us. We aren't Easter Islanders or Hittites, building idols of stone and temples out of logs. We aren't even the Greeks or the Romans. There's never been a civilization even a tenth the size of ours, never been one that includes every nation on every continent. We command technologies our ancestors couldn't dream of. We can avert comets, cure plagues, adjust the thermal balance of the globe as we need to. War is a memory. Humanity has come into its adulthood, and our childhood afflictions are behind us."

"Which doesn't exempt us from resource depletion. Most civilizations die of starvation. We have twelve billion people, chewing through more power and resources in an hour than most of humanity's civilizations used in their entire history. That simply can't last."

Michaud shrugged. "So if civilization must fall, it must rise again. History shows that too, and certainly neither you nor I nor our children will have to deal with it."

Crewe shook his head. "No, this is where our civilization really is different. We've exhausted all the easy resources, coal and oil and uranium, even copper and iron and tin. What's left takes high technology to extract. If the technology is lost, there are no more stepping-stones out of the stone age—and when the end comes, it will be the final end. We mark the ages of humanity by the raw materials they use, the stone age, the bronze age, the iron age. The industrial revolution began the fossil fuel age, though we don't call it that. We're in the energy age now. Power is the most basic raw material we have. With it we can do anything, without it we can do nothing. We've had power shortages in North America since I was young, now they're severe. The rest of the world has caught up in power consumption per capita, but now the number of available kilowatts per person is falling. World population is still going up. You do the math. In a few years those shortages will be worldwide. This planet can't support twelve billion people without high technology. We've used up our world, and sooner or later, a lot of people are going to die. If our species is to survive, we must claim the stars."

Michaud nodded. "You've convinced me, Dr. Crewe. I

don't think your hypothesis is true, but I think you do." He smiled without humor. "You don't want to build your pyramid for personal glory but because you truly believe it will bring the favor of the gods. You are an idealist, and more dangerous than I thought."

Crewe spread his arms wide. "When Cheops built his pyramid, his quarrymaster became a wealthy man. Harness me then, for you own ends, or oppose me to our mutual sorrow."

"I'll present your case to my board." Michaud nodded slowly, contemplating his guest. "You understand the final decision on whether to support you or not will be theirs."

"What will your recommendation be?"

"I will have to consider that."

"While you're considering it, consider this." Crewe tossed a thick folder onto Michaud's desk. "Thanks for your time." He rose to leave and shook Michaud's hand. "I hope we'll be working together."

Harmon Michaud watched him leave and then picked up the folder and looked at it. The title page read "Engineering Design Considerations for a Multi-Generational Interstellar Colonization Ship." He opened it, saw on the first page an outline drawing of the ship itself, a long cylinder with spherical fuel tanks clustered around its forward section. Something caught his eye and he raised his eyebrows. The outline itself was unsurprising; a generation ship would need to spin to simulate gravity, and so would inevitably be configured as a disk or cylinder. What was unusual was the scale marker in the lower left-hand corner, which marked not in tens of meters or even hundreds of meters but kilometers. *Thirty from end to end, by far the largest thing the human race might ever build. Why so large?* The brief descriptive note at the bottom answered his question. *To ensure ecological stability over a ten-thousand-year voyage.* Ten thousand years, longer than all of recorded history. *The man is mad, stark raving mad.* The next page unfolded to show the internal details of the vast habitat, a ring-shaped lake twelve kilometers long at the aft end, a cliff city built into the forward wall. The whole habitat was to be filled with twenty meters of rich alluvial topsoil, land to sustain successive generations of colonists on the centuries-long voyage, and mass as a shield against the hard radiation of deep space. *Crewe is not just driven but insane.* There was no way such a construction could ever be built. It would require the up-orbit transfer of millions of tons of material. It would not only take generations to reach its destination but generations to build; a hundred years was an optimistic guess. It was like some great medieval cathedral, a grandiose monument to the glory of God and the vanity of Man, immense and beautiful and pointless. The cost would be beyond comprehension, and several nations' worth of roads and power plants, schools and hospitals would go unbuilt to see its completion. It would be politically unsellable to a world population growing restive beneath the inevitable restrictions that occurred when twelve billion people tried to share a medium-size planet. The human sacrifice implicit was incredible, if not directly measurable. He looked again to the door, as though expecting to see Crewe still there, watching for his reaction. *A brilliant mind unhinged.*

He looked back to the folder and flipped through the

section headings: Drive Design, Ecocycle, Technology Roadmap, Radiation Management . . . He scanned through the documentation on the drive, saw the fusion tube running down the long axis of the vast habitat cylinder, saw heat-transfer equations and superconductor specifications, and realized that the waste heat from the drive would be dumped to a quartz-shielded tungsten sheath to heat it incandescent and make an artificial sun. There was a huge transparent dome at the forward end, cast as a single vast lens of amorphous diamond, a window to provide sunlight in the years, *decades* of construction, to establish the ecology before the drive could be turned on. The dome would serve another purpose during the voyage, dumping internal heat to space. Water vapor evaporated from the ocean at the aft would convect up the axis to condense against the dome, forming ice, clouds, and a perpetual gentle rain that would fall to percolate back through the soil to the ocean, nourishing it along the way. It was a working water cycle built on a vast scale with no moving parts. *He may be mad but he's no fool.* He moved to another section that listed target stars with the characteristics of their known planets, another full of calculations of thrust and drive efficiency, boost gravities, cruising velocities, turnaround points. More figures—an initial crew of ten thousand, with room to grow to a hundred thousand in the course of the journey. There were eight million tonnes of hydrogen tankage to fuel the drive, a fifteen-centimeter-thick shell of steel, the first layer of a radiation shield that included the ten meters of soil and water that formed the biosphere. Crewe had chosen steel because it was cheap, but the design was sophisticated, each plate faced in nickel-chromium stainless steel, backed by successive layers of high-tensile alloy. There were calculations that showed that the hull, exposed to water, would lose five centimeters of thickness in that time despite the almost nonexistent corrosion rate of the alloy. To prevent that, there was an inner shell of amorphous diamond on a silicon-nitride substrate that would float inside the outer shell on a cushion of carbon fiber. It was a design meant to absorb failures gracefully, with no single weak point. It was a design meant to endure.

Michaud pushed the document away and leaned back. *What arrogance the man possesses, to design such a thing.* It was insanity, a masterwork perhaps, but insane nonetheless. He closed the folder, saw that Crewe had not put his name on it. *He wants this built, he doesn't care about the credit. He leaves his name off so I can't use it against him if I decide to oppose him.* No question Dr. Joshua Crewe was smart. Smart and rapidly growing powerful, and that made him dangerous. He was the kind of man who would stop at nothing to realize his dream, and devil take the consquences. *And what is it that drives him to this vision?* Not the answer he'd given, but the real answer was important, and unknowable. Michaud drummed his fingers on the closed folder, contemplating possiblities. The best thing would be to avoid such a man, by the widest berth possible, but Crewe's ambitions precluded that. Perforce he must choose sides, for him or against him. It was true the final decision would be up to the board, and of course the board could only in turn make suggestions to the myriad companies that made up the Aerospace Consortium. Nevertheless the board's suggestions carried as much weight with the organization's members as his own did with the board, which meant that, ultimately, the decision he made would be the decision that was implemented. Crewe would see, or not see, tens of millions of euros and a huge amount of political support based on Michaud's word. Crewe knew that, of course; it was why he had come in the first place.

So the plan was a practical impossibility, but was that any reason to oppose it? Harmon Michaud wasn't afraid of making an enemy of Josh Crewe if he had to. He hadn't risen to the position held now by avoiding conflict. More to the point, Crewe's primary argument was right. If the UN set out to build the ship it would divert a substantial fraction of Earth's talent and treasure to the aerospace sector, which would grow accordingly. Michaud's own power and prestige couldn't fail to grow along with it, and a person with foreknowledge of the program could invest intelligently and make a fortune. He thought about that for a while, turning the idea over in his head. Aerospace was a commodity industry now, growth was flat, the moon base as developed as it was ever going to be, the grand adventure to Mars over and done and unlikely to be repeated, the satellite industry was limited not by boost capacity but by orbital slots, and commercial air transport was hard up against the energy wall. This project, this vast, grandiose project, would change the basic economics of his business for generations to come. Michaud picked up the folder again and flipped through it, reading chapter headings and musing. Aneutronic Fusion Ignition.

Ecocycle Considerations. Extreme Lifetime Technology Design. Crewe's research was exhaustive if nothing else. He flipped back to the diagram of the vast ship and considered. Starting the wheels in motion to launch this project could secure his posterity. He leaned back and opened the folder again. The last chapter was Life Aboard *Ark*. Michaud stroked his chin. *Ark. That's exactly what it is, the Biblical parallel is exact.* He saw now how the project could be, would be sold to the masses. For the largely Christian West, the appeal was direct, but even for the non-Christian part of the world the emotional appeal was powerful. *Humanity does have a drive to explore, and this will play into that as much or more than the Mars mission did.* The public would applaud the great adventure.

*And yet the cost will be staggering. The public will not applaud that.* A project so large carried a large risk of failure, and a failure so grandiose would destroy the ability of the Consortium to influence the government for decades, certainly for the rest of his career. *Risk and opportunity, opposite sides of the same coin.* The full scope of the project would be kept secret at first, the required infrastructure built on other pretexts. When it later turned out to be useful for *Ark* as well they would be seen as simply prudent for taking advantage of investments already made. *Even so this is tantamount to the construction of the Pyramids.* Sooner or later they would have to come out and ask the public to shoulder the economic burden. *Which side to pick?*

He keyed his intercom. "Miss Dorian."

"Sir."

"Call a board meeting. We have a decision to make."

# L–93

Snow was falling, lending a superficial layer of purity to the dingy streets of midtown New York. The power was off to the subway, and perforce Abrahim Kurtaski had to take a rickshaw through the streets to the UN Secretariat. Kurtaski smiled to himself at the pedestrians bundled against the cold and the way the pedcars slid and skidded in the slush. New Yorkers weren't used to such weather. In Moscow this much snow wouldn't rate a scarf.

There was a prayer group on the steps of the UN building, singing a hymn while their leaders beseeched Heaven to intervene on some political issue. Abrahim skirted around them and went up the stairs to the main entrance. The Secretariat was not a particularly impressive building, lacking both the sheer scale necessary to compete with the towering spires of the Manhattan skyline and the historical weight of power centers like the Kremlin or Whitehall. Nevertheless he paused to breathe deep before he continued in the doors, because the UN did not need grandeur to convey its power. The Secretariat ran the world, and though national governments frequently balked at its rulings, none dared defy it.

And if they did not, who was a junior professor of engineering to defy a summons from the secretary-general? That he was an old friend seemed to make no difference; it was a daunting prospect. He breathed out and walked forward, into the impressive lobby where Foucault's pendulum swung to mark the turning of the Earth, to the main desk where his appointment was confirmed, through a security checkpoint and into a private elevator, through another checkpoint, past oak-paneled offices and meeting rooms and finally to the door of the man who ran the world.

"Abrahim! *Zdras'te!* Come in." Josh Crewe smiled with real pleasure. "How is Samara doing without me?"

Abrahim laughed. "*Pri'viet, muy droog.* It's much the same, as is your Russian."

"By which you mean to say not as bad as it might be."

"I would never say that out loud." At the sight of his old mentor all Abrahim's misgivings vanished. It was the same face, more lined perhaps, made more patrician by the weight of his office, grey now streaking his beard, but still the same quick eyes, the same ready smile he had shown at the university. They shook hands warmly. "Mr. Secretary-General. You've done well since you've left."

"I would rather have stayed. Politics isn't research."

"I don't envy you that." Abrahim laughed and sat down as Crewe waved him into a seat. "Is this your daughter?" he asked, indicating a picture of a pretty, dark-eyed girl on Crewe's desk. "Surely not your wife."

"My sister."

"She's beautiful. In all these years I didn't know you had a sister."

"She died. I don't usually talk about her . . ." A flash of pain appeared in Crewe's eyes and was gone.

"I'm sorry." Abrahim paused, not sure what to say. He had caught Crewe's brief expression and knew it as a rare openness. "She was ill?"

"In a way . . . She died because she couldn't escape any

other way. It's been thirty years now, longer." For a long moment Crewe looked away, and Abrahim feared he had said the wrong thing. The silence stretched out and then Crewe looked back. "I have a job for you, Abrahim, if you want it."

"What's that?"

"I want you to build the *Ark* for me."

"The *Ark*?" For a moment the Russian looked confused.

"The senior design exercise, I'm sure you remember. I had you working on fusion enhancers for the drive." Crewe took a thick folder from a drawer and passed it across. "That's the complete design package."

Abrahim looked at the folder, read the words on the cover. "You want it built? It couldn't be built! It was a tremendous design problem, but the technologies don't exist, the resources required . . ."

"I'm secretary-general now. You tell me what resources you need and you'll get them."

"But—"

Crewe held up a hand. "No objections."

"Half the systems are pure speculation!"

"So you will lead the research teams that make them real."

"Josh, I can't do that. I'm a junior engineering professor, nothing more. I give exciting lectures about automated assembly systems and stay late in the lab only to save power at home. This isn't even my field."

"You're the world's leading expert on sky cables."

"Only because nobody's managed to build one. That was a history paper, nothing more. I can't . . ."

Crewe stood up. "No! Don't say you can't do it. I need

you for your vision. I've taught a hundred graduate students in my time, and none ever saw as deeply into a problem as you, not one."

"I'm complimented of course . . ."

"It's no compliment, that's a simple truth. This is not a job for some tenured fossil who puts his name on his students' papers. This requires youth and energy, someone with the *yajtza* to get it done, if only because he's got nothing to lose. You're the one I need."

"Josh, I can't just quit and move to the other side of the world. I have classes to teach and a mortgage to pay."

"The university will find someone to take over your course load."

"Someone to replace me, you mean. I don't have tenure, I'll have to start all over again somewhere else, and what about my house?"

"The salary I'll give you will more than compensate for what you'll lose in moving, and there's enough in this project to occupy you for the rest of your career, for the rest of your lifetime. You won't be starting over again anywhere else."

"And if it fails?"

"Even to fail at this would be to fail attempting greatness. You'll have director rank within the UN. If we can't make this work you'll have your pick of positions at any university in the world."

Abrahim shook his head. "I can't build this ship, it's too big, too . . ."

"I don't need you to build the ship, the ship will take generations to finish. I need you to build the organization that will build it." Abrahim started to object again but

Crewe cut him off, leaning forward. "Abrahim, listen to me. I have made it the focus of my life to see the *Ark* become real."

"Why?"

"Because . . ." Crewe looked away, his eyes distant before they fell on the picture on his desk. "Because we all need to escape, one way or another." He was silent a long moment, then looked back to the other man. "I want to build it myself, you understand. I always planned it that way." He looked up to meet Abrahim's eyes. "I can't, that's a reality that comes with this office. You're the best I can find, Abrahim, and you're a friend."

Kurtaski considered the thick folder. *Even to fail would be to fail attempting greatness . . .* "If I were to do this, and I emphasize the *if*, when would we start?"

"Immediately. Time is what we don't have. We need to have significant progress inside of two years."

"Haste is risky."

Crewe nodded. "We'll do it in stages. We need the sky cable first. That has to go up fast, and that's all the public needs to know about at first. It's going to take years to get enough steel up there to even start building the hull."

"How are you going to explain building a sky cable to ship steel into orbit and not explain what you're going to use the steel for?"

"International Metals has been exploring the idea of building a cable for an on-orbit solar aluminum smelter. Venezuelan bauxite is cheap and high-grade, so they can make aluminum oxide for almost nothing, but SouthAm power is too expensive to process it into aluminum economically. They ship it to Africa now, and that's almost as costly. We'll build the cable for them, and then when it's ready we'll use it to get our steel up there as well, maybe even ship the bauxite itself up. It's got a significant fraction of iron oxide as well. We process it all, ship the aluminum back down to pay International Metals' profits, keep the iron to make steel for the *Ark* and save the oxygen to make her atmosphere when we're ready. All the work on the ship will be pure research until then. Once I have a second term secure we can announce the full project."

"I can't believe it takes less power to smelt a pound of bauxite on the ground than to ship it into orbit, even if sunlight is free."

"It won't be, but with us building the cable, IM will just have to pay the incremental cost and that will turn loss into profit for them. We need an equatorial site for the base tower, on a mountain if possible, and they own rights on Mount Cayambe in Ecuador. It's close enough to Quito to make logistic support easy, and IM is owned by Lundstrom, who have a construction subsidiary based there. Lundstrom will make money on building the base tower even as IM makes money using the cable; they'll know a free lunch when they see it. The Aerospace Consortium will be on board, because they're going to see all the contracts for the on-orbit construction, and they know they're going to see all the business for *Ark* as well. We're going to see a lot of support on this."

"You think a base tower is necessary? The cost . . ."

"It's essential. Cost isn't going to be an issue."

"And the General Assembly will accept us subsidizing private companies like that?"

"The General Assembly does little other than subsidize private interests, I've learned. I entered politics with a certain amount of idealism." Josh laughed. "I've since learned that cynicism is more realistic, and pragmatism gets better results."

"I'll let you worry about the politics." Abrahim looked away for a moment, thinking. "It's the engineering that concerns me. Even trying to build the cable is risky. As for the ship . . ." He ticked off points on his fingers. "We don't even know if building such a large fusion drive is even theoretically possible. We have no idea how to build a sealed ecology that will function for thousands of years. We can't even imagine how the society inside it will evolve, but it will be hard to maintain the technical knowledge within the limited population it could carry. That means that not only do our systems have to be able to last that long, they have to be built to run entirely maintenance-free. I could go on . . ." He looked up to meet Josh's gaze. "What's the target star?"

"Iota Horologii."

Abrahim nodded. "It would have to be. You know, we only *think* it's got life. There's not enough data to say it's habitable."

"There's enough to start. We'll know more before we launch it. If we build it for a fifty-light-year range, that gives us three thousand stars we could go to, most of which we know nothing about yet. The important thing is to start building now."

Abrahim nodded, leafing through the folder. "The scale of this is almost too large to contemplate."

Crewe got up and walked to the broad windows,

looking out into the snow falling over Manhattan. "You're right, of course. This is an enormous venture. You have to understand that if we don't undertake it nobody will. The world has enough problems, enough other priorities that will always come before unchaining humanity's fate from this planet's." He turned back to Abrahim. "There will be problems we can't even imagine right now. I'm not asking you to finish, neither of us will live that long. Just get it started. We need to entrench this in the public consciousness and the economy so deeply that no future administration will be able to kill it."

"That sounds more cynical than pragmatic."

"Abrahim, you have no idea . . ." Josh paused, considering his words. "There's an old saying. 'Those who enjoy sausage and respect the law should never watch either one being made.' I can add something to that. You can't be a butcher without getting blood on your hands. Politics is the same way."

"Hmmm." Abrahim paused to flip through the design section on the space-cable portion of the project. "We start with the sky cable as necessary infrastructure and build from there. We have two problems, as I recall from when we studied this. One is that we can't spin continuous cable anywhere near fast enough. The other is that the base tower is going to be exposed to the ozone layer, and to monatomic oxygen as well. It's going to get eaten alive."

"There's some data now about fully fluorinated nanotube fibers. We'll use those for the tower structure. Above the ozone the monatomic oxygen partial pressure is low enough that we won't have to worry so much."

Josh nodded. "How much time?"

"Offhand, five years for the tower, five years to spin the cable. We can do both at once, but that's only if we can solve the problem of spinning cable fast enough. If we can't solve it . . ." Abrahim shrugged. ". . . maybe never."

"How about a cable-only solution, even one that won't carry loads?"

"What's the point of that?"

"It's a political thing. The general public won't know the difference, and once the project is a fait accompli it'll be that much harder to kill."

"That could be done in two years, or three, given that we didn't build a tower, and it would be useless for any practical purpose. A minimal cable might mass ten tons, but the ozone layer would erode it fairly quickly, and it wouldn't support a spinner so we could never repair it or strengthen it."

"It's probably not the best plan, just something to consider if all else fails." Crewe paused, meeting his ex-student's gaze. "I need you, Abrahim, to make this happen. I need your vision, but more than that I need someone I can trust. Will you do it?"

Abrahim hesitated. "I'll do it. I'll try."

"Good man. Just tell me what you need and you'll get it."

"Time." Abrahim pursed his lips. "It's time that will make or break us. We don't have much of it, if you want this done in time for your second term, quite possibly not enough. Frankly, I don't think you can do this as fast as you want to."

Crewe nodded. "I know the problems, but it has to be done. Politics is a far less certain game than science. We can't announce *Ark* until the cable is up, and we need to be able to announce it, to get the establishment committed to it. The project has to be well under way before the next election."

"I'll do my best." Abrahim stood up and they shook hands. He was glad he didn't have to deal with politics, and with luck the world would continue to not ask him to. Questions of resource allocation were beyond his scope, but it was clear Josh Crewe was under a lot of pressure. As if to underscore the point the lights of New York started going off outside Crewe's office window. *When I was young this city never slept.* There had been time when power didn't have to be rationed on a continental scale. *Every civilization is limited by its resources. If we don't build this ship now, it might never get built.*

"Come on," said Josh. "I'll show you your new offices. Tomorrow you can meet Eric Smithson, he's chief engineer for International Metals."

Abrahim laughed. "You were so sure I'd agree."

"If you'd been able to turn down the challenge, then you weren't the one I needed to run this project."

Half an hour later Abrahim's head was spinning as he tried to coordinate the details of his resignation from Samara, a completely unexpected transoceanic move, and the workings of his new office suite on the thirtieth floor of the Secretariat building. The entire floor had been given over to him, proof of Crewe's serious intent to realize his dream. It was already furnished and supplied with an administrator and receptionist, the frosted lettering behind the reception desk read "United Nations Initiative for Space Exploration" and the nameplate on his own door said "Abrahim Kurtaski—Director." Everything was ready for him to start, the administrative machinery was there, all he had to do was pull the levers. He sat down behind his new desk and looked around, taking in the incongruously utilitarian furniture and the sweeping view of New York City. It was a far cry from his cramped office at the university, where his shelves were overflowing with papers and journals and the air smelled of ancient chalk dust, where students and colleagues would drop in and talk and argue over engineering problems and political points with equal passion, often into the small hours of the night. He pried the nameplate off with his fingernails and handed it to the administrator. "Here, get me one that reads 'Chief Engineer.'" Josh Crewe had abandoned design work for administration as a necessary precondition of realizing his dream. Abrahim Kurtaski didn't intend to make the same compromise.

Over the next weeks he found he had to make compromises enough, as he struggled to come to grips with the demands of forging a multibillion-euro government agency. As he did, he began to realize how ambitious the undertaking really was. Even the sky cable was a grand vision, dreamt of for a hundred years, attempted twice before, but never actually completed. It would start with a base tower on the equator a hundred kilometers high, built of truss sections made of wound carbon nanofilament and pressurized with nitrogen to trade their incredible tensile strength for compressive strength. From the top of the base tower four nanofiber strands would stretch forty thousand kilometers into space, cross-linked to form a locally rigid structure to support the boost tracks. At the upper end the platform that spun the cable would counterweight it, defying gravity like a child's ball whirled on a string, with the Earth's fifteen-hundred-kilometer-per-hour rotation doing the whirling. When it was finished it would serve as a railway to space, with boost cars sliding on an eight-day journey to orbit, driven up the cable by immense launch lasers.

*And even those lasers are an engineering challenge, and they're the simplest part of this project, which itself is just a prelude to the real effort. How can I even dream of building a ship to fly light-years?* Abrahim pushed aside a pile of paperwork at the end of his first week in office and rubbed his eyes. He had been working no less than sixteen hours a day, and every problem he solved seemed to create two new ones. He was starting to doubt that they could possibly meet the aggressive schedule Josh Crewe had laid out for him. He switched off his desk and went to grab a nap in the small dayroom attached to his offices. He went to sleep only to dream of monumental failure, and woke up to spend the next day dealing with the thousand administrative crises that seemed to spring up every time he turned his back.

Over the next week his core team began to arrive, chosen from a short list of colleagues. They had all jumped at the chance to work on the ambitious project, though he told them only of the sky cable portion of the plan. *Ark* itself was to remain a secret held within the walls of the secretary-general's office. They all came needing laboratories, administrative assistants, technicians and equipment, and it seemed that none of those things could happen without paperwork and frustration administered in equal and heavy doses. As the first month slipped past, the pitfalls seemed endless, but so too did the resources available for dealing with them. As people and equipment began to pour in, the once cavernous office space filled and became bustling, the impossibly tight deadlines feeding an infectious energy. The lights of the thirtieth floor burned around the clock as engineers brought breakfast to work and stayed long after dark to tackle unexpected problems. With some amazement Abrahim realized that it was he who was responsible for that, that his choice of people, his direction and leadership were what was driving the process. The sky cable became known as simply the Cable, capitalization implicit, and its realization became the single-minded goal of an organization that seemed to be exploding in all directions.

Even given boundless energy being applied, at first it seemed that the effort was doomed before it began, with too many essential problems not only going unsolved but seeming unsolvable; however, as the weeks stretched into months and more and more of his colleagues rallied to the cause the outlook began to improve. He was well acquainted with the capabilities of a first-rate engineering team given a really challenging problem, but he hadn't understood how unlimited resources would accelerate the process. Within a month they had test samples of carbon-bonded-carbon nanotube matrix that would serve as the Cable's material, within two months they had confirmation that the material was physically strong enough to do the job, and six weeks after that they had a fluorination process that would protect the base tower's trusses from the chemical ravages of ozone in the upper atmosphere. It remained to find a cable-spinning process that would produce a single cable strand thirty-eight thousand kilometers long, with the required exponential taper over its entire length. *But that's just an engineering problem, we just have to figure it out.* For the first time Abrahim began to believe his mentor's grand dream might actually succeed. *We will do this.*

He looked out over the Manhattan waterfront, the still darkness interrupted here and there by the lights of hospitals and other essential services. UNISE itself was gifted with the power credits to work all night on a whim, and the lights were usually on twenty-four hours a day. Sometimes Abrahim wondered if that was wise. The citizens would see the lights burning from their candlelit apartments. Those who could not afford light and heat could not help but resent what to them could only seem like government wastage. *Thus the world is divided, no longer into the nations of race or language and geography but into nations of rich and poor.* He looked up from the darkened city to the star-dappled sky. *And perhaps it's wrong to commit the world to this project while people go without lights, without heat, even without food, but we do need to go to the stars if we're going to survive.*

"This project is an abomination in the eyes of God." The True Prophet raised his arms on the word "God," as though summoning lightning from heaven. The camera panned around, showing the jammed arena and the cheering crowd on Joshua Crewe's screen. The Prophet lowered his arms, waiting for the crowd to quiet before continuing. "We are entering the end times. People are sleeping in the cold and in the dark while the secretary-general builds monuments to his own greatness. We have to, we *must*, save them. This is the will of our Lord." Riotous cheering flooded the arena as the camera view panned around to take in the Prophet's supporters screaming their approval. "God struck down the Babylonians for trying to build a tower to heaven." The Prophet was tapping into a fundamental energy, and the crowd was lapping up every word. "Now they are building another one. They are trying to bring God's wrath down upon us all. Are we going to let them?" He threw the words at the crowd, and it roared back "NO!" until the stadium shook. Most of the people in the audience belonged to the Believers, the Prophet's core group of followers. He was saying exactly what they wanted to hear.

Josh Crewe made a gesture and the newsfeed froze on a frame with the Prophet pumping his fist in the air in triumph. *People turn to their gods in time of crisis.* The True Prophet's name was Norman Bissell, and he had clawed himself from obscurity to power purely on the strength of his oration, playing on popular desperation with a ready-made set of divinely inspired solutions, and then with consummate skill he had blended the twin appeals of pragmatic self-interest and religious fervor into an unshakable constituency. A cynic might wonder if he believed what he said, but his voice carried the passion of the true believer. The speech was the throwing-down of a gauntlet, his castigation of the government a direct challenge to the authority of the secretary-general. Crewe studied his opponent's face as though through close enough inspection he could divine his thoughts. His incom chimed and he pointed the call up to the screen.

"The True Prophet is here."

"Send him in." Crewe blanked the display and turned in his chair to greet his visitor. "Mr. Bissell." He nodded as the man came into the room and took a seat. You could not be in the same room as Norman Bissell without being drawn to his eyes. He was not an otherwise memorable man, surprisingly young for someone who commanded such a following, of medium height and medium build. He was the kind of man you could imagine living a life of quiet desperation, never quite failing in life, never coming close to his dreams. His eyes told you that wasn't true. They were sharp and compelling, the eyes of a man convinced of his own rightness, and they held a subtly veiled cunning.

"Secretary-General." The Prophet kept his gaze locked on Crewe's. He was not about to be impressed by any office on the planet.

Crewe leaned forward. "I'm pleased to meet you at last."

"Untrue, I'm sure. You'd ignore me, if you could." The Prophet pursed his lips.

Crewe conceded the point with a slight nod. "Then let's get down to business. What can I do for the Believers?"

"You can cancel your grandiose plans for space exploration until the cold and hungry right here on Earth are looked after."

"You make the assumption that the two are mutually exclusive."

The Prophet made a dismissive gesture. "They are

mutually exclusive. Every euro that goes to your pet project is wasted, every kilowatt you consume could be used to improve someone's life."

"I heard your speech."

"You'll hear many more like it, if you don't redirect this government's priorities where God wants to see them."

Crewe leaned back, regarding his opponent. *Does he realize that amounts to a direct threat?* The Prophet sounded sincere, but then he would not say anything that might alienate his faction anywhere where he might be recorded. "The cable project has barely begun, and its costs are tiny in the overall budget. I can't believe you have no higher priority than to end it."

"Your lack of belief tells against you, Secretary-General. I know your background. You worship at the altar of technology, and its brass temptations have led you to create this Tower of Babel."

"This isn't a tower to heaven, it's a ladder to space. This will be of incalculable benefit to people worldwide. The world doesn't have the resources to support our current population. We have to turn to the solar system, first for the raw power to process raw materials, then for the materials themselves."

"So you say. My supporters say otherwise." The Prophet held up a hand to forestall Crewe's reply. "Our salvation isn't going to be found in asteroid mining, it's to be found in prayer." He held up a hand as Crewe started to interject. "There is no point in arguing with numbers, I know the numbers. I speak for people who are afraid. They don't want you tempting the wrath of God."

"A fear that exists because you pander to it."

Norman Bissell shrugged. "I am just the voice for ten million people."

Crewe laughed without humor. "And God, evidently."

"God's will is written for all who care to read it, I am only his servant. The Book of Genesis, Chapter Ten, tells us that God forbade the construction of a tower to heaven. You are creating an abomination in his eyes."

"I doubt the Bible explicitly forbids space travel."

"God struck down the first Tower of Babel. It is not for man to know the heavens. And the ship you plan to build with it." The Prophet's eyes narrowed. "Noah was commanded to build an ark. Were you?"

*How does he know about that?* Crewe bit his lip. For a moment he considered saying "Yes," just to see what the Prophet would do with that answer. Instead he said, "What are you driving at?"

"I mean this vast colony ship you're planning on building to violate Heaven."

"There's no such plan." Crewe's voice was flat.

The Prophet laughed. "Come now, Dr. Crewe. Your research on the subject is on record." He took a sheaf of papers from his briefcase and held them out. "You even call it *Ark*."

Crewe leaned back in his chair, keeping his expression neutral. *It was inevitable that news of* Ark *would leak out. I didn't think it would happen so soon.* "When I was a researcher I studied the question. Interstellar travel is a challenging technical problem. I left research for politics and now I study other problems." *I should have found some other name for the ship.* Except what else would you call such a ship other than *Ark*, and he hadn't been thinking of the political ambitions of hard-line religious sects when he'd first conceived the project, some twenty years ago.

"And you appointed your protégé to head UNISE."

"UNISE is simply continuing our current space exploration program."

"And participating in building this tower for International Metals, at public expense."

"International Metals is paying the UN for research and consulting. They're subsidizing our research and development, not the other way around."

"That's not how I do the math. Let's not play games, Secretary-General. I may not have courtroom proof of your intentions, but I've heard about your ambition, and the evidence that you're putting your plan into action is there for anyone to read. Why are you building this ship?"

Crewe paused a moment before answering, choosing his words carefully. "I'm committed to space exploration because of the long-term benefits it will bring to the human race."

"My ten million Believers do not want to see man violating God's Heaven."

"And canceling the Cable won't make a material difference to any of your ten million followers, nor can I imagine how God would care one way or another. He seems to have tolerated satellites and the moon base and star probes alike without much concern."

The Prophet smirked. "The man in the street sees nothing but blackouts and an economy in free fall. His job is at risk, if not already lost. He's scared, and he wants someone to blame. This is a high-profile undertaking. If you keep going against my opposition, that blame is going to land on you. I'm sure you know the political risk you're undertaking in opposing me."

Crewe leaned back in his chair. "Let us go deeper than that. Your opposition is based on your personal political ambitions."

The Prophet kept his voice flat. "I don't expect a man like you to understand what it is to serve a higher calling."

"Is that what you call it? If you wanted me to cancel the Cable project you would have come to me beforehand. You have instead made your stand, and your demand that it be canceled, very public. You've cast it in religious terms, which will allow you to claim credit if we do cancel it and to claim divine guidance if we don't."

"I don't intend to make it easy for you, I intend to make it embarrassing." The True Prophet narrowed his eyes. "Very embarrassing."

"In order to weaken my position so you can dictate terms to the government. So you can prove your political strength to your followers, and thus gain more followers."

"And thus save more souls, Secretary-General. The wider world is the Devil's Playground. I work to save the common man from temptation. Simplicity is the proper approach to life, and humility before God is the proper attitude for man. I will not see Heaven defiled with your creation."

"Right now there's only your assertion that I intend to build such a ship. I have yet to hear any proof."

Bissell leaned forward. "I know what I know. I've told you I don't have any proof, not direct proof. That might change, but it also doesn't matter. If I tell the public that you plan to squander countless trillions on this colony ship, they'll believe me. What will you say then?"

"I'd say that right now there is only basic research going on, with no plans to go beyond that stage. *Ark* is only a design concept, years old now, one of dozens UNISE is working on, nothing more."

"And you would be on the defensive in having to say that. You'd be better off to call me a liar directly."

Crewe shrugged. "I think that engaging in direct confrontation would only give you a credibility you don't deserve."

"I already have all the credibility I need." The Prophet spread his arms expansively. "You've seen the level of support I have. Religion is a powerful motivator. People will go to great lengths to prevent the sacred from being assailed by the secular." The faintest hint of populist exhortation entered his tone, a low-key version of his pulpit voice. "This sky cable is the Tower of Babel, and you will violate Heaven itself."

Crewe snorted, refusing to be drawn. "I can't bring myself to believe you mean that literally."

The Prophet lowered his arms and leaned forward, his gaze intense. "But I do mean it literally, and more important for you, my followers mean it literally."

Crewe observed the Prophet carefully. *Does he truly believe this, or is his faith a matter of expediency? Either way he wants me to know that he's doing this quite deliberately. Even a true believer can act strategically.* He leaned back. "Your constituents are a fraction of the population of one continent. Most of the world doesn't subscribe to your philosophy." He put enough emphasis on "your" to underline the fact that he understood that Prophet's expressed beliefs were not his private ones.

"My Believers have influence well beyond their numbers. Your hold on the North American bloc is shaky. You would be wise to make a deal."

"I wasn't aware you were offering one."

"Cancel the sky cable now, and I'll be your political ally."

Crewe shook his head. "You'll be my political master, once you've proven you can force your will on me."

The Prophet tightened his lips. "I will be anyway. You can accept that gracefully or oppose me and have me destroy everything you've worked for."

"Come up with a policy I agree with and I'll support it with everything I've got. I'm not going to derail humanity's future so a few pampered Westerners can avoid some long-overdue belt tightening."

The Prophet snorted. "Humanity's future. Are you expecting a flood?"

"The Bible predicts Apocalypse, doesn't it? The Bible may be right." The Prophet's eyes widened, just a fraction, and Crewe leaned forward to press his momentary advantage. "Perhaps now you think we should have a colony ship after all."

"And who is going to decide who gets to escape the end of the world in this lifeboat you're building? It's God's place to choose those who will survive the Apocalypse, not yours."

Crewe put on a politician's smile. "You asked me if God had ordered me to build an Ark. How do you know I'm not the next Noah?"

The Prophet looked at him, his momentary uncertainty resubmerged. "Because I know what God commands." His eyes were intense, and Josh Crewe found himself revising his estimate of the man. *He believes, however expedient that may be.* That only made him more dangerous, because a cynical operator would take a good deal if it were offered him. A zealot would have no choice but to go down fighting, and devil take the consequences.

"You take your orders from the Aerospace Consortium," the Prophet went on. Crewe raised his eyebrows and his adversary smirked. "Oh yes, I know where your support comes from. Let me warn you, Dr. Crewe. God will not allow his will to be turned aside."

The Prophet got up and left, and Crewe breathed out, feeling the tension of the interview leave his body. *That one will be trouble.* How much trouble remained to be seen. He pointed his phone line up and gestured for Janice Jansky, head of Interpol.

Her face appeared in his screen. "Do you know the True Prophet?"

"Which one?"

"Norman Bissell, leader of the Church of the Believers movement, mostly active in NorAm."

"I know of him."

"I need you to find out what makes him tick."

"Has he broken the law?"

"I doubt it. Don't do anything active, just pull in all the information we have on file, plus what's available open-source. I want to know who it is I'm dealing with. I have a feeling he could be a problem."

"A problem how?"

"I don't know yet. I just had him in my office and the interview didn't go well."

Jansky nodded. "I'm on it."

Crewe waved the connection closed, and gestured to dial again. Thom Pelino appeared, under a logo that read United Nations Directorate of Communications.

"Josh, what can I do for you?" Thom was a gift from Harmon Michaud, once the Aerospace Consortium's chief spin doctor, more recently the architect of Crewe's drive for the secretary-general's chair.

"We need a public awareness campaign about the importance of space industry to the economy. Something about jobs today, hope for tomorrow. You know the kind of thing I'm looking for."

"Target audience?"

"Middle class and lower in NorAm. I'm specifically looking at the demographic that's likely to follow evangelical fundamentalism. I want to steal that audience, or at least inoculate them against the True Prophet's message."

"The leader of the Believers of God?" Thom looked puzzled.

"Right. He's on widecast. Tune in, find out who he's talking to and sell them on the idea of space exploration in general and space industry in specific."

Thom nodded. "I've already got the pitch. Something about how the superiority of NorAm technology and know-how uniquely position the continent to lead the world into the next century. Jobs are the carrot and xenophobia is the stick."

"You're going to want to put something in there about how it's going to make everybody's life better too."

"You know it. Leave it with me."

Crewe cut the connection. Thom was a wizard of public opinion, and technology was always an easy sell in NorAm, despite the back-to-basics philosophy of the Believers. Still, there was only so much spin they could put on the current situation. The reality was the world didn't have enough power and the global economy was stalled because of it. NorAm, with the most advanced economy, was inevitably suffering the most. The True Prophet was simply doing what demagogues did best, giving the masses someone to blame for their troubles. A public-relations offensive would buy some time, but at the end of the day he was going to have to do something substantive about the problem or lose the next election.

*And I can't allow that to happen, not when I'm this close. But we still have some time.* Putting up the Cable required solving daunting technical challenges. Satisfying the world's insatiable demand for energy was incalculably more difficult. That required either convincing people to make conservation a permanent way of life or a miracle.

Josh steepled his fingers and looked out his window at the vast expanse of the New York megalopolis. Of the two a miracle seemed much more likely.

Norman Bissell left his car at the top of the lane and got out. Only machines driven by muscle were allowed on his farm, in keeping with strict Believer creed. He would have rather done without the car at all, but it was a necessity if he was to obey God's command to go out into the world and proselytize. *So much of what I have to do falls outside the life I want to live.* He did it willingly,

uncomplainingly, as Jesus had borne his burdens, but still
. . . *It's good to be home.* He paused a moment to inhale
the rich, earthy scent of the apple orchard, feeling the
stresses of the secular world drain away, then started up
toward his house, through the simple wooden arch with
the word BELIEVE engraved on it, a reminder to remain
faithful to God, and humble before the glory of His
creation. There was a heavy mist and the air was warm
and still, the legacy of a tropical storm battering the coast
some hundreds of miles south and east. He walked up the
gravel drive, avoiding puddles as he went. The jingle of
harness bells sounded in the distance; on the other side of
the trees Jacob Eby was plowing his fields. Bissell's own
fields needed attention, and he was looking forward to a
good few days with horse and plow, away from the devil's
playground and all its temptations. It was a heady thing to
walk the corridors of power, to command the loyalty of a
movement millions strong, but such power bred arrogance.
*I am only God's servant, a tool he is using to remake the
world as he meant it to be.* It was important to remember
that, and to remember how very long the road ahead was.
Only a small fraction of his followers lived on the land,
most of them Mennonites and rejectionist Mormons who
were already living that way before adopting the Believer
creed. The bulk of his flock were evangelical Protestants,
who accepted the idea of simplicity in theory, but who had
little idea what it meant to live it in practice.

*And that is my fault, and so leading them to the true
path is my burden.* With enough followers he could force
the government to impose change from above, he could
stop the headlong rush to damnation the world had set

itself upon. There was strength in obeying God's will. He came around the corner to the house to find Marta waiting on the doorstep. She greeted him with open arms and a kiss, her smile and the warmth of her body healing his doubts.

"Where's the baby?"

"Sleeping. Come in, Beth's making dinner."

He kissed her, then went into the kitchen to embrace his second wife. Her belly was straining against her plain blue dress, swollen visibly over the week since he'd gone. Her child was due in just a month now, her third, his sixth. A large family was both a privilege and a duty, but the miracle of new life seemed nearly wondrous every time. *All miracles belong to God.* It was important to remember that.

"North America, the future is ours." The woman's voice was pitched as though she were about to make an indecent proposal, and her megawatt smile seemed to suggest the same thing. It faded from the screen to be replaced by a glowing image of the continent, a visual suggestion that the present might again see the casual wealth of the past. Abrahim smiled to himself. *Sex sells everything.* Of course the commercial spots weren't actually selling anything physical. They were selling a vision, a dream, for the working masses of the North American population. The reality was that NorAm was no longer the center of global economic power, no longer the place to be if you wanted to have a hand in forging the future. First to achieve universal wealth, it was now leading the world into decline as more and more people competed for fewer and fewer resources.

It no longer had more opportunity than anywhere else in the world. What it did have was a disproportionate number of seats in the General Assembly, and that made it important to make the population feel that what had once been true still was.

"Dr. Kurtaski, we'll be landing in Quito shortly." Abrahim raised his vidgoggles. The flight attendant was an attractive woman of thirtysomething, and her professional smile was more genuine than the one that had just faded from the screen.

"Thank you." He moved his seat upright and fastened his seat belt without making her tell him to. On charter jets they never asked you to do anything right away, they gave you the chance to do it yourself first, in order to preserve the illusion that the high-ranking passengers were more than just self-loading cargo. *In order to preserve the illusion for the passengers.* Abrahim was sure the flight crew themselves were quite comfortable in their own minds about who was in charge of the flight. He wasn't entirely comfortable with the subtle deference, but he'd grown used to it. *As long as I don't come to expect it.* All his life he'd found the self-important to be laughable. He didn't want to pick up that particular governmental infection. The attendant had a nice figure and a wedding ring. He looked away from her and out the window, trying to spot the snowcapped peak of Mount Cayambe, but there were a lot of snowcapped peaks in the Andes, and without knowing exactly where he was it was impossible to tell which was which from altitude.

Twenty minutes later he was on the ground, and in thirty he was in the backseat of a diesel-powered Land

Rover, heading north through the bustling streets. The driver pointed out Mount Cayambe, just visible over the tops of the shorter peaks that formed the high mountain valley that cradled the Ecuadorean capital. The cab was diesel, because Orinoco heavy crude was cheaper in SouthAm than hydrogen cracked with electrical power imported from NorAm. Kurtaski's eyes stung with the gritty pollutants of five million belching internal-combustion engines, the heavy air held hanging between the mountain ridges that flanked the city to east and west. *North American cities might have trouble turning the lights on reliably, but at least the air isn't palpably toxic.* He found it hard to breathe too, though that might have been due simply to the city's ten-thousand-foot elevation. The altitude was not the deciding factor in selecting a site for the Cable base tower, but every kilometer above sea level helped.

It was a two-hour drive over rough roads to the small farming community of Cayambe, named after the volcano that overshadowed it, jutting up to dominate a landscape that was already two kilometers high. Cayambe was a world apart from bustling Quito, where everything was new and modern, crowded and dirty. Here it looked like nothing had changed in a hundred years. *And quite possibly nothing has.* The UNISE team was set up in a small hotel that looked as if it had been built by the conquistadores. He dismissed the driver, checked in with the liberal use of sign language to compensate for his minimal Spanish, and dumped his suitcases in his room. His phone went to satellite mode for want of a usable ground signal, and he mused that UNISE would have to install the most basic of infrastructure before they could start building the tower. The peaceful town was about to undergo a lot of major changes.

Eric Smithson, International Metals' engineer-in-charge of the build site, was staying in the same hotel but wasn't in his room when Abrahim knocked on the door. He tried to call but couldn't get an uplink. Finally he went back down to the front desk to borrow the phone there. The proprietor was happy to loan it to him, but his sign language proved inadequate to the task of learning the appropriate international dialing codes. *And it says something about the world we live in that I can't talk to a man in the same hotel without placing a transcontinental call.* He had just resigned himself to wait when a white utility truck pulled up in front of the hotel. A woman in a white hard hat got out and came in. She was looking for something, and when her eyes met his he realized that she was looking for him.

"Dr. Kurtaski?"

"Yes. And you are?" Abrahim assessed her. She was in her mid-twenties, with blond hair and blue eyes that were tougher than he might have expected. An attractive young woman in a leadership role in a rough-and-tumble industry that was still very much a man's world, she would be strong and she would be smart. Whether she was good remained to be seen.

"Daffodil Brady. Eric sent me to take you around." She offered her hand, gave him a solid handshake. "I go by Daf."

"Eric couldn't find time to come down himself?"

"He didn't think you'd want him to slow down surveying just because you're here."

Kurtaski nodded. *And no doubt Eric knew I wouldn't mind being shown around by a pretty woman.* Smithson was a shrewd man. Daf smiled a smile that would melt ice at ten paces, and unlike the flight attendant she wasn't wearing a ring. Abrahim reminded himself that it would be a mistake to pursue her. She doubtless spent too much time fending off unwanted advances to appreciate even the most well-meant compliment, and it would only complicate the project to get involved with one of the engineers. *The responsibilities of office lie heavy indeed.*

Daf was still speaking. "My time is more expendable." She turned and said something in Spanish to the proprietor, who nodded, smiling, and answered, and then she turned back to Abrahim. "Eric's gone up to the base camp on the volcano. I can take you there if you like."

He nodded. "I would." He paused. "I'm glad you're here. I have to admit my Spanish isn't as good as I thought it was."

"The dialect here is difficult. I grew up speaking Spanish and I still have to work to follow it." She laughed. "At least in town most people do speak Spanish. A few miles out from here the primary language is still Quechua." She led him out of the hotel and opened the passenger door of her truck for him.

"I didn't even know there was such a language."

"You already know the important words." She climbed in her side of the truck.

He raised an eyebrow. "I do?"

"'Cocaine' and 'quinine.'" She started the engine and pulled away from the hotel, carefully steering around a tired-looking mongrel asleep at the curb. "Quinine.

Mosquitoes aren't a problem above fifteen hundred meters, but if you go down in the valleys make sure you take your antimalarials. Cocaine. It's everywhere, so if you see someone guarding a field with a Kalashnikov, just walk the other way. That's all you need to know to be safe in Ecuador."

"I'll keep that in mind."

"'Cacao' is another important Quechua word, especially after a long day up on the mountain. Our cook isn't the best, but this is where they invented chocolate. He does it with scalded whole milk and nutmeg, no sugar." She smacked her lips. "It gets cold up on the mountain." She gestured to a canteen on the dashboard. "Try some."

"Give me a chance to get cold first. What can you tell me about the site?"

Daf frowned, guiding the truck around a farm wagon laden with produce. "Logistics is the big problem. We've got work under way on a class-one road, and we're going to be starting on the rail yard as soon as we can get heavy equipment up to the site. The geosurveys are in. There's no significant ground movement, and the tremors are small enough to be manageable—as long as they don't get any bigger." She paused. "I'm not a geological engineer, my specialty is carbon fiber, but it seems to me that this might not be the best site for the base tower. We've got major active volcanoes within forty kilometers on every side, and Cayambe itself blew up just three hundred years ago. That's not long enough that we can really call it dormant."

"Where would you put the tower?"

"In Africa, Mount Kenya." Her tone showed she'd

considered the question already. "It's been quiet three million years, and the ground geology is better. It's close to Nairobi, which can provide better support than Quito, in my opinion, even discounting the volcanism."

"And without the risk of being ambushed by a trigger-happy coca farmers." Abrahim nodded. "I agree with you, but there are deeper considerations."

"Like what?"

Abrahim paused, choosing his words carefully. "If we want to get this project built, it's essential we have the support of the North American public. That isn't right, but it is the way the world works. The equator doesn't run through NorAm, so we simply can't build it there. With a little coaxing they'll get behind a sky cable built in SouthAm, because at least that's in their backyard. Most of the NorAm public see Africa as a great rival. If we build it in Africa, we'll get no support there. If we get no support in NorAm, Secretary-General Crewe won't get reelected. If he doesn't get reelected, this project won't get finished."

"If Cayambe erupts it won't get finished either." Daffodil Brady pursed her lips. She started to say something, then stopped. After a moment she said something else. "All right, politics aren't my job. The area looks acceptable, given that the volcano doesn't go off. We've got an idea of how we want to set up the build site." She pointed at a file folder on the dashboard. "My preliminary layout is there, along with an assessment of tasks."

"Good." Abrahim took the package and leafed through it. It wasn't a polished report, just a collection of working documents and scribbled notes. That made it harder to read, but he preferred to see the raw data before it had been massaged into a presentation. It often contained truths that didn't make it into the final draft. He nodded approvingly. Daf Brady's work was thorough and well put together even at this early stage. He leafed through the section about infrastructure, noted a problem. "We're going to need to put in a high-tension line and a substation. That's going to have to go all the way back to Quito. Cayambe only has forty-kilovolt service."

"Actually, I had an idea about that," Daf said.

"Oh? Tell me."

"We put in our own power plant. It'll be cheaper in the long run, and we'll be independent of the SouthAm grid."

"Cheaper? It'll take us ten years just to get the permits, and we've got no easy source of water." He pointed to the looming white bulk of Mount Cayambe. "Running a line seems a lot easier to me."

"Not geothermal, solar." She held up a hand before he could object. "I know the usual arguments, but we are in a unique environment here. We're right on the equator, above most of the atmosphere. If we put it up on the peak we'll have better than three hundred cloud-free days in a year. You can't get more solar flux anywhere on the planet."

"There's still no easy water source."

"You're thinking of solar steam generation. I'm talking about direct photovoltaic conversion."

Abrahim raised an eyebrow. "The cost . . ."

"Won't be a factor. There's a company I've been following, they make photocell sheet out of semiconductor plastic. They can give you acres of it for pennies a square meter. Twelve percent conversion efficiency."

"And we'll still need to put in power lines for the cloudy days."

"We'll need to put in the power lines to sell the power we generate. We could pay for this thing just selling the power."

"I've worked with plastic solar cells before, they don't stand up to weather well." He saw the disappointment in her face at his dismissal, and modified it. "Look, do the detailed math on it for me, will you? You're right that we're going to need a lot of power to get this thing built, and a lot more once we start sending payloads up the Cable. It's worth a look."

"I've got a question for you, actually, regarding the math on this project." Daf's voice was cautious.

"Yes?"

"The best aluminum refineries here on Earth use ten kilowatt-hours of power for every kilogram of aluminum they put out. It's also going to take ten kilowatt-hours of energy to get a kilogram of anything up the Cable to geostationary orbit."

"And so . . ."

"And so it takes two kilograms of alumina to make one kilo of aluminum. That's twenty kilowatt-hours of energy just to get it up-orbit. Even given that the power cost for on-orbit smelting is zero, this just doesn't make economic sense."

"Except we can deliver it anywhere in the world when we deorbit it. That twenty kilowatts includes worldwide transportation."

Hmmm. "Which wouldn't amount to ten kilowatts per kilogram, no matter where we sent it. Even if it did, we'd just be where we started, in terms of production costs, except with this huge orbital infrastructure inserted into the middle. Aluminum refining isn't rocket science, or at least it shouldn't be. I've run the numbers in some detail, and under the most optimistic assumptions I can make this is barely a break-even project. Factor in the technological risk . . ." She shrugged. "Don't get me wrong, I'm all in favor of the Cable, I love the concept, and for a carbon-fiber structural engineer, let's just say that this will make my career. I just don't understand why International Metals is doing this, or UNISE."

Abrahim nodded slowly. *It's a pity she can't be told the real reason. Ark* remained a closely held secret. "IM is doing this because UNISE is covering their capital costs. They get an orbital refinery for free, so all they have to pay is that twenty-kilowatt-hour boost fare. It's a win-win situation for them."

"And for UNISE?"

"For us, we get a high-capacity railway to space. Their usage pays for all the maintenance and ongoing operational costs. We get to piggyback on that essentially for free."

"For free, after we pay the ten-billion-euro capital cost. That doesn't sound like win-win for us."

"We're the government. We don't have to win; our role is to invest in primary research and new capacities."

Daf nodded, absorbing that. "I also saw some International Metals documents that talked about shipping bauxite directly into orbit, rather than extracting the alumina on the ground first. That's even less efficient; you're sending the iron ore fraction into space for no good reason. Granted you could get the steel out as a by-product, but there's no way it would be cost-competitive with a ground-based refinery."

Abrahim looked at her. She was concentrated on driving, seemingly unaware of the impact her questions were having. *She's very close to unraveling the whole cover story.*

Daf was still talking. "I've heard a rumor that the secretary-general wants to build a colony ship. If that were true I could see a reason for all that steel going up the Cable."

Her voice was musing, conversational, but Abrahim felt adrenaline surge through his system. *She has all the pieces she needs to put the puzzle together.* That probably wouldn't be a problem with a UNISE engineer committed to getting the Cable up. *But if she's so close so soon, other people will not be far behind, and not all of them will want us to succeed.* "Right now all the options are on the table," he said, trying to keep his tone casual. "I can't say if the secretary-general has a colony ship in mind." *Which is true in that I can't say anything about the* Ark *project. I'm learning to speak like a politician.* "But any on-orbit infrastructure we want to build is going to take materials in orbit. We ship up bauxite and get back not just steel and aluminum to use up there, but oxygen as well, which we'll recover from the smelting process. This cable is half-experimental; the whole project is. We're going to wind up using it in ways we can't even imagine yet." He watched at the window in silence for a minute as the looming white peak of Mount Cayambe grew larger. *Change the subject.* "Talk to me about carbon fiber. What's the biggest risk we're going to face?"

Daf began to talk about her specialty, distracted for the moment from the economic realities of the Cable project. Abrahim listened with interest as she went on enthusiastically about the tremendous material properties of long-fiber nanofilament. It was important information, but he couldn't still the little voice in the back of his mind. Daf had nearly figured out the secret behind the sky cable, and if she had others would soon. *This is all going to become public before we're ready, and if that happens the Ark will never get built.*

As the truck took the grade up the mountain the main cone of Mount Cayambe loomed so high in the darkening sky that it seemed it must already reach all the way to space. The farms that surrounded the town crowded close to the volcano's skirts, climbing up the lower slopes to cling there at improbable angles. Every square foot possible was under cultivation, taking advantage of the rich volcanic soil and the twelve-month growing season. The road grew steeper and narrowed as they approached the mountain, changing from asphalt to gravel to dirt. Their progress slowed as Daf maneuvered the truck around potholes, pedestrians and a small herd of llamas being shepherded by a pair of young boys. They climbed past the highest fields and onto a track so twisting and rock-strewn it would have challenged a mountain goat. The sun was slipping below the horizon by the time they reached their destination. Cayambe base camp was a collection of inflatable shelters, hidden from the constant wind in a small valley on the mountain's southeastern flank. A crude helipad had been hacked out of the rocky valley floor, its corners marked by flashing red strobes in the twilight.

Farther up the hillside an array of solar sheets glinted darkly, thick cables running down from them to power the camp. A pair of heavy walkers were parked by the main structure, awkward mechanical camels resting with their legs folded. Abrahim looked around at the rugged terrain. Movement past the base camp would have to be by walker, or on foot. *All this effort to save just five kilometers of tower height.* Building at sea level had been one of the options in the site search, but gaining those first five kilometers avoided most of the lower atmosphere and saved a significant amount of the construction cost. *Everything is a compromise.* A third walker heaved itself over the crest at the upper end of the valley and lumbered toward them. Daf pointed.

"That'll be Eric. We might as well go down to dinner and meet him there."

At the mention of dinner Abrahim realized he hadn't eaten since his plane lifted out from La Guardia. As they turned to go down there was a deep thud, felt more than heard, and the ground jolted hard enough to make him stagger.

"Just a tremor," Daf answered the unspoken question on his face. "Nothing to worry about."

Abrahim nodded. "Everything is a compromise." He paused and looked up to where Smithson's walker was still making its way down the slope, its steady gait unaffected by the bump. "I just hope we're making the right ones."

Josh Crewe met Janice Jansky over lunch on the top floor of the UN building in his private dining room. His predecessor had installed the room and a personal chef to go with it. Crewe didn't like the elitism that implied and preferred to eat in the general cafeteria. *But this needs more privacy than that would allow.* Jansky had brought her newly opened file on Norman Bissell. They talked over inconsequentialities over the curry, and when they were done she pushed the dishes aside and laid a folder on the table.

"It's all there." She patted it. "Everything is public-source. We did some interviews to fill in details."

Crewe nodded and flipped the document open. "Good." He scanned it briefly, riffling through the pages. *We can transform a man's life into an open book, but it's what's not written here that may be most important.* "Give me the highlights."

Jansky pushed her chair back from the table. "Bissell himself was originally a fundamentalist Mormon, born to a farm family in Plentiful, Utah, seventeenth of thirty-eight children. He joined a Mennonite sect in—"

Crewe looked up. "Did you say *thirty-eight* children?"

"That's correct. The group in Plentiful is polygamous; his father had nine wives. That's why Bissell left. He was the ninth son, so he didn't have much hope of inheriting land or getting married by staying at home."

"Explain."

"Polygamous groups work by sending the young men away and keeping the young women in the community to become brides for the elder landowners. Somewhere between sixteen and eighteen a woman's father declares her marriageable, at which point the Church will assign her to a husband. It's called 'placement.'"

"I see. Go on."

"He left at seventeen and worked as a carpenter's apprentice building houses. He joined a Mennonite sect in South Dakota, age nineteen, by marrying Bridget Klassen. He became a bishop at twenty and was evidently passionate about converting outsiders to the faith. That put him at some odds with the Mennonites—they aren't big on converting other people—but he was evidently well liked in the community, at least at first. He stayed there four years, then left."

"Why?"

"He was shunned, cast out. The Mennonites refused to discuss why. We spoke to his former wife, and all she would say is that it was difficult for outsiders to truly live their faith. These are horse-and-buggy Mennonites, no power, no datagrid, no fuel cells, hand-pumped wells for water, hand labor for building and farming. It would be hard to adapt for anyone not raised in that culture. They had no children."

Crewe raised an eyebrow. "So why did he go there in the first place?"

"You'd have to ask him." Jansky shrugged. "If you want my guess . . . Mennonite teenagers sometimes go out and live in the wider world before they settle down, as a part of what they call *rumspringa*, running around. That's part of their culture too. If he met this girl during her rumspringa, it wouldn't seem too big a jump from his own background, raised in a strictly religious farming community. He didn't stray too far from home." She smiled. "And of course he was in love."

Crewe nodded, pursing his lips. "But then when he

has to give up all the pleasures of the modern world it's harder than he thought it would be."

"That's my read. He worked as an assistant to a cabinet-maker with the Mennonites, building on his carpentry experience. According to them he was good at the trade, he had a talent for woodworking. After he left them he tried to start his own handmade furniture shop, but it failed. He drops off the radar after that, nobody seems to know where he went or what he did. The next place we see him is a year later in Alabama. He's got a little church and his own congregation, and he's preaching what's now the Believer creed, although at the time he called it the Baptist Church of Believers."

"Which is?"

"A blend of Mormon fundamentalism, Mennonite simplicity and Baptist evangelicalism. The most radical stands the Believers take are for polygamy and against technology, but in reality those elements aren't strong in the Believer Church. They preach it, but most don't practice it."

"Why not?"

"They couldn't. It's a mass, evangelical movement. No mass movement in our civilization is going to turn its back on technology in any real sense; it's too powerful a force in our world."

Crewe nodded his head. "And polygamy?"

"Polygamy is official Believer doctrine, and it's a big driving force behind the Church's growth."

"How does that work?"

"Church doctrine is that all marriages must be approved by the Church. It also holds that good Believers evangelize, go out and spread the word and win converts. If you bring in a lot of new members to the Church you get rewarded with the Church's blessing for more wives." Jansky chuckled dryly. "Evidently that's a powerful motivator for ambitious young men. In six years he's gone from nothing to over ten million Believers, with a hard core of probably a million who believe he's literally speaking for God, and maybe as many as a hundred million who wouldn't call themselves Believers per se, but would certainly take seriously anything he said."

"And why would the women go along with this?"

"For the most part they don't. Actual polygamy is limited to a very small percentage of Believers, mostly high up in the Church hierarchy. For everyone else it's more of a goal than a way of life. The fundamentalist Mormon groups make it work because they're small and very tight-knit, so young women have a lot of social pressure to do what they're told. In the great, big, wild world . . ." Jansky shrugged. "Getting Church approval to marry two women is one thing, convincing two women to marry you is something else."

"This small percentage includes Bissell himself, I imagine."

Jansky nodded. "He's still legally married to Bridget Klassen; the Mennonites don't recognize divorce and he never filed for one. He's had a string of lovers, but since founding the Church he's settled down. He has two wives—not legal marriages, of course, but recognized by the Church."

"The most important question is, what's making them so successful?"

"It's a cult, nothing more or less, just a very effective one. A cult is really an emotional pyramid scheme. People are sucked in at the bottom with the offer of social support and a ready-made community. That's an attractive proposition nowadays. The future is uncertain and people feel scared and alone. Once you're in, you're kept in by the chance of advancing to the next level, which offers more power and privilege. Of course, most people don't advance to the next level; it's their effort and labor that serve to give the next level the very power and privilege they covet. The polygamy angle serves to motivate young single men to go out and sell the product, but the product itself is a sense of belonging and reassurance. I doubt Bissell himself would describe it that way, but that's what it amounts to. If you Believe then the future will get better."

"Which is why he's had such success in NorAm." Crewe looked away, contemplating. "There's despair enough to go around on this continent."

"Mostly in NorAm. He's got some traction in Europe, nothing serious in Africa, yet, and nothing at all anywhere else."

"Not yet. Right now the standard of living is still improving for most of the world, but that's not going to last. He's built this in four years, from nothing. He's put himself in direct opposition to us and in a position where we can't simply ignore him. What do you have on his organization?"

"He's at the top, and below him is the Elder Council. They take care of the practical running and organization of the Church. He appoints them from the bishops, who are the next level down and run districts, which vary in size. Below that it gets a little fuzzy. Districts have their own Elder Councils, and individual congregations are run by committees. It's a very populist structure. Open at the bottom, closed at the top."

"Can we penetrate it at the top?"

"Covertly? It would be difficult. And illegal, unless there's a crime I should know about?"

"No. No crime." Crewe picked up the folder and stood up. "Keep on this, please, Janice."

"I've done as much as I can without at least due cause to suspect a crime. You're stepping close to the line yourself here, Josh, asking me to investigate a private citizen. Interpol isn't the right tool for this."

"Norman Bissell has power and the ambition to have more. He started out attacking the Cable project. Since we started building he's got a loud minority of NorAm assemblyists to stand up in opposition in the General Assembly, and he's broadened his attacks to take in the whole of the government. He's gaining adherents in the public, and the politicians are sensing which way the wind is blowing. He has the leverage to do a lot of damage, and I believe he's starting to think of entering politics directly. He claims to speak for God, and I think he believes that himself. He's dangerous."

"I think you're probably right, but I still don't have anything to justify an investigation."

"What can you do, legally?"

"I can look at open sources, gather what's already out there." She laid a hand on Bissell's dossier. "I've already done all that."

"What about doing the same for his organization?"

"How soon do you need it?"

"Let's say thirty days. We'll schedule a meeting of the executive council, maybe get Michaud from the Aerospace Consortium in on it as well. Bissell's major problem seems to be the Cable project, so he has an interest."

Jansky nodded. "I'll see what I can get."

The blackout went on at ten p.m., and decent citizens in New York made it a point to be in bed by then. By that measure the Believers were not decent citizens, their rally had begun at sundown, and it would last until sunrise. Harmon Michaud's plane had been delayed getting into La Guardia, and when his car finally emerged from the Midtown Tunnel the streets thronged with Believers. Despite the hour they didn't seem dangerous. They were all well dressed, well scrubbed, generally urban middle class, and the streets were lit up with dozens of portable floodlamps, power cables snaking through the streets to trailer-mounted fuel cells, venting steam. Michaud raised his eyes at that. This rally must be costing them a fortune. The easy route to UN headquarters was blocked, and so his chauffeur threaded them carefully through the jammed streets trying to find an alternate route. The Believers were in a state of high arousal, carrying lit torches and chanting prayers or singing songs. Animated peelsigns had been slapped up on every horizontal surface, alive with glowing messages. *With Faith You Will Live Forever! He Is Risen! The Blood of the Lamb Shall Be Spilled in Resurrection!* The Believers didn't seem dangerous, but Harmon was uneasy. He knew how fast a crowd could become a mob, especially when emotions were running high. If that happened the last place he wanted to be was caught in a limousine, an obvious outsider and an obvious target. With sudden decisiveness he pushed the intercom button to talk to the driver.

"Pull over here, I'll walk the rest of the way. Bring the car around when you can."

"As you wish, sir."

Michaud climbed out into the warmth of a midsummer night and made his way north.

"It's a beautiful night, brother." The speaker was a large man with a large smile on his face. He offered his hand to Michaud. Michaud shook it, somewhat amused. "His spirit is with us. Tonight we have the power." The man's voice was eager, enthusiastic, his grip strong on Michaud's hand.

Michaud nodded. "His power is with us," he agreed. He went on his way before the man could engage in further conversation. He proved to be only the first of many; it seemed to be expected among the Believers to greet complete strangers as if they were long-lost friends. He was called brother, was invited to join with groups singing, or praying, or listening to inspirational speakers preaching from improvised pulpits set up in the street. Fireworks burst overhead, their reports echoing among the office towers, and long thin streamers drifted down from them, colorful snakes undulating in the bright light of the full moon. The streamers fragmented as they fell, until they were rain of confetti-like strips a few inches long. He picked one up and looked at it, found an inscription.

*Rejoice! Rejoice! He Is Coming in His Glory!* Another, more ominously, said *Rise up Ye Believers and Smite Down the Enemies of the Lord!* He looked around at the crowd. The Believers seemed an unlikely group to riot, but they thronged in tens of thousands and any call to action seemed dangerous.

Moving through the rally was an unsettling experience, but at the same time exhilarating. Michaud had lived a long time in circles of power that prevented him from having to mix with street crowds. Normally his authority sped him through airports and checkpoints, at public events he enjoyed VIP seating, and he traveled in private aircraft. He had intended to walk the few blocks to UN both to save time and because of his fear of standing out as a target. Once among the Believers he found himself irresistibly drawn deeper into the gathering. He wound up walking away from the UN, toward Times Square, where the True Prophet was going to address the faithful at midnight.

"Be one with the Prophet! Be one with the Prophet, right here!" The voice lacked the semi-rapture of a Believer; it was hard-edged, huckstering. A fat man stood behind a wheeled booth laden with images of Jesus Christ and the True Prophet. Holograms showed moving images of the Transformation and the Resurrection, or the Prophet delivering a sermon in full three-dimensional color. "Hey buddy." The voice was directed at him. "Show your faith, be one with the Prophet." Michaud looked around, noticed that most of the Believers were wearing holographic medallions or bracelets. He went over to the booth.

"How much for one of these?" He picked up a bracelet, protective coloration.

"Twenty euros."

"That's steep."

"Take or leave it, buddy, I'm almost sold out."

Michaud looked around. A middle-aged couple with their teenage daughter had already formed a line behind him. "I'll take two," he said. He picked a pair of bracelets, one with Christ, one with the Prophet, and thumbed for the charge.

"You won't be sorry, buddy, it's a once-in-a-lifetime experience." The huckster was already moving to serve the couple and Michaud walked on, slipping on his bracelets. The crowd thickened as he got closer to Times Square, with more of New York's ever-eager entrepreneurs hawking their wares from sidewalk stalls and pushcarts. The crowd's mood grew almost euphoric as he moved toward the center. Some families had brought their children, many had brought blankets or lawn chairs and had set themselves up little squares of territory in what they judged to be an advantageous place. There were a few police circulating in the crowd, including some on horseback, but they seemed relaxed. They too had judged it an unlikely crowd to riot.

"He is coming, brother, He is coming." A well-dressed man clapped him on the shoulder, full of cheery enthusiasm.

"Amen." Michaud tried to put enthusiasm into his voice, even though he felt oddly uncomfortable. There was no reason he shouldn't be on the street, no reason he shouldn't watch the rally. It was a public gathering, after all. Nevertheless he felt like an impostor, an outsider whose impersonating ruse might be detected at any moment. He was not one of the Believers, and in fact he represented all that they opposed. *I'm late for my meeting, if I had any sense I'd go to it.* He couldn't deny the reasonableness of the thought, but he didn't change his direction. Instead he took out his phone and called Josh Crewe on his private line.

"Crewe."

"It's Michaud. I'm held up by this demonstration. Better to start without me."

"Do you want me to send an escort?" The tone in Crewe's voice was not quite concern; that might be taken as an insult to a man as powerful as Harmon Michaud. Nevertheless his readiness to take action on Michaud's behalf was clear. The Believers were just citizens, but their leader had declared himself an enemy of the secretary-general, and by extension of the Aerospace Consortium. Michaud felt that hostility even though nobody in the crowd could know who he really was, and it was clear that Crewe felt it too.

"No. No, I'll be fine. My car couldn't get through, I'm coming on foot. I'll be there shortly." He disconnected and walked on. Michaud strode ahead. *They aren't actually dangerous.* The True Prophet was a man of God, after all, though he preached the dissolution of the General Assembly and a return to religious basics. The Believers were strongly against technology, a position that they somehow found not at all at odds with the demand that the foremost political priority had to be solving the energy crisis. He could learn a lot here, walking among his adversaries. It was not in Harmon Michaud's character to dirty his hands with such things. He was a power broker, the eminence grise behind the aerospace industry, a man who other men feared without even knowing his name. Chance had made him a spy of sorts in the house of his enemies. There was something heady about the sudden switch in roles, and he felt alive, charged with adrenaline as he hadn't been in years.

Another volley of fireworks boomed overhead, and he looked up to see the word BELIEVE picked out in sparkles and slowly descending toward him. The sparkles exploded, and BELIEVE vanished, the letters replaced with larger, more diffuse ones that spelled S-A-C-R-I-F-I-C-E. The S-A and C-E were dimmer than the other letters for some reason. He watched the word fall and fade. There were more bursters in the volley, and more streamers floated down, breaking up into individual message slips as they dropped to join those already littering the sidewalk. Something tickled his neck and he fished out a slip that had fallen down his collar. It read simply *You Are Chosen*. He looked up and found himself on the outskirts of a small crowd gathered around a man preaching from atop a box.

". . . and I tell you, brethren, He is coming, and I tell you, brethren, He is the Lord, and He is angry with this world!" The man stopped and swept his gaze across the crowd. For an instant his eyes met Michaud's, and Harmon felt himself transfixed, as though the man were looking into his soul. "He is angry with the waste, He is angry with the sinners, He is angry with those who challenge His power in their arrogance! And He will smite them in His mighty wrath, He will strike them down and

He will consign their souls to burn in eternal hell! Do you hear me, brethren!?"

"Amen, brother!" chorused the crowd.

"DO YOU HEAR ME, BRETHREN!?"

"AMEN, BROTHER!" The shouts echoed from the buildings, momentarily drowning out the constant chatter of the larger crowd. The energy was contagious, and Michaud had to suppress the urge to scream amen with them. He felt an irrational surge of anger at those who might oppose the righteousness of this group. Some still cool part of his brain smirked at himself. *I'm the one they're talking about, I am the Prince of Sinners, the evil God of technological capitalism.* Emotion was not thought; it would be good to remember that.

He moved on, past another huckster selling hot sausages. Despite various wayside distractions there was a definite current to the crowd as people moved steadily in toward Times Square, where the main event would take place. The crowd density grew in the darkened streets, faces made strange by the glare of the floodlamps. More fireworks boomed overhead, and he felt his pulse quicken. He passed a side street blocked off by police cruisers, red and blue lights flickering. Beyond the cruisers he saw cops in what might have been riot gear. The sight was at once relieving and worrisome—relieving because it showed the authorities were ready to deal with problems, worrisome because it showed they took the possibility of problems seriously. For a moment he considered heading back, but something drew him forward and the unease passed. A few blocks farther on, something was different, and it took him a while to realize that the streetlights were on.

The city was making concessions to the demonstration—probably a wise precaution from a safety standpoint, but a bad precedent to set. It was not a good idea to give a group like the Believers the idea that they had power to force their will upon any level of government. He passed a couple more side streets blocked off with police troops held in readiness behind the barriers, and then he was forced to slow his pace as the crowd compacted into Times Square itself. At the far end a platform had been set up, with enclosed tents behind it. Floodlights lit the stage, illuminating a forty-foot hologram of Christ dangling from the cross, bleeding from violated wrists. The image's face was full of the death rapture as it twisted against its torture, and the breeze rippled the holographic film to lend it a ghostly unreality.

The night was warm and humid, and Michaud found himself sweating. He moved forward again and found himself a face-to-face with a young woman in a white hooded robe.

"Have you been saved?" She had dark hair, and impossibly huge eyes that locked on to his and drew him in.

His instinct was to say yes, to dodge her as he had dodged the rest of the brethren throughout his exploration. Somehow that instinct never made it to the surface.

"No . . . No, I haven't . . ." Michaud was uncertain.

The girl reached out and took his hand. "Come with me." Her touch was electric, and Michaud found himself suddenly unable to think. He followed her unquestioningly, being led by the hand toward the floodlit stage. As he went he noticed other figures in white robes moving through the crowd. She led him around behind one of the tents, and through a flap. The inside was lighted, and he could see a fuel cell and tanks in one corner. A table had been set up with a row of computers, and power cables snaked across the floor to the fuel cell. Unlike the affable chaos of the crowd outside, the people in the tent worked with serious purpose, intent on the thousand operational minutiae necessary to stage the rally.

"Are you nervous?" the girl asked him.

"I'm . . ." Harmon found himself unsure what to say. In the light he could see that she was heartbreakingly beautiful. *I'm married, I love my wife.* A distant part of his brain tried to push the words past his lips, as though that would break the spell he found himself under, but his lips wouldn't move.

"Don't worry, everybody is at first." She smiled at him. "I'm Holly, I'm a Virgin." He could hear her put the capital on Virgin the way that the secretary-general put the capital on Cable.

"Don't worry about anything," she went on. "The True Prophet is wonderful. You'll be saved by him, it's a tremendous privilege." Michaud could see the rapture in her face when she spoke of the True Prophet. "Brother Michael will take care of you."

She led him to the end of a line of six other awkward-looking people, presumably other candidates for salvation. "I'll be back in a while." She squeezed his hand and went back through the tent flap into the crowd.

Brother Michael was a man of about twenty-five, with shoulder-length blond hair and intense blue eyes. He too wore a white robe, and he was entering people's names

into one of the computers. The line moved quickly, and
then he was asking Harmon for his name. He hesitated,
then gave his first and middle names, Harmon Bernard,
and let brother Michael think that Bernard was his last
name.

"Go through there and wait," Michael said, pointing to
a flap leading to another section of the tent, where he had
sent the others. "You will be saved."

Michaud went through, wondering what he was getting
himself into. He considered just leaving but didn't. *I may
never get another chance to meet the True Prophet.* Some
part of his mind realized that that wasn't important, that if
it were necessary that the Aerospace Consortium make
contact with the True Prophet, he had access to people
who were trained in intelligence and infiltration work, as
he was not. At the same time, he realized that being
saved would be a very public spectacle on the stage in
the full glare of the floodlights, and almost certainly on
widecast media. It wouldn't do for a man in his position
to be seen in such circumstances, the repercussions
would be far-reaching. He fought off the fog in his head and
was about to leave the tent, when he saw the other initiates
being dressed in hooded robes like the senior faithful, only
green and not white. The hoods were large, leaving the face
inside in shadow. A matronly woman with her own white
hood thrown back touched him on the shoulder and offered
him a green cloak. Wordlessly he put his arms into the
sleeves and shrugged it on, pulling the hood up and over his
head. He had a vague sense that events were proceeding
beyond his control, but he did not consider that his
motivation for staying might really be the hope of seeing

Holly again, pleasing her with his transformation, impressing her with the status that would accrue in her eyes if he was saved by the True Prophet. *Surely I'm too old to be led into this by a girl.* But he wasn't.

There followed a period of waiting. For the most part the other initiates stood silently, and he stood with them. There was a large sound and light board hooked up to another computer on a raised platform, arranged so that the operator could see the stage. After a while the presentation began, not with the True Prophet, but with a lesser preacher. The stacked speakers on either side of the stage were facing in the other direction, and so, though the volume was loud, Michaud could not make out the words clearly. From the wild responses of the crowd, the shouted echoes of "Amen!" and "Praise the Lord!," he could tell they were being whipped into a frenzy. *Classic mob psychology, put them into an emotional state, a receptive state, build their anticipation and then introduce their master. Harness the crowd's power and use it to take control of them.* It was nothing that Hitler hadn't done, nothing in fact that any talented demagogue didn't do, or even any half-decent politician—Joshua Crewe, just for example. The principles were well understood, but Michaud still found himself fascinated by the process being demonstrated so masterfully here.

*And what am I doing here?* He still couldn't properly answer that question. He felt giddy, energized, nervous in a way that he hadn't felt in years, perhaps a way that he had never felt. Another volley of fireworks burst overhead, invisible through the tent roof, but close enough that he felt their concussion as much as heard it. The volleys were

going up more frequently, punctuating the words of the
speaker as the time for the True Prophet's appearance grew
closer. The operator at his raised console was whispering
into a headset microphone, controlling the spectacle with
the precision of a general orchestrating a battle. Michaud
knew that his own role in the show would be as a prop, a
living puppet to dance his way into enlightenment at the
command of the Prophet in order to prove the Master's
omnipotence to the crowd. *I should leave now.* The voice
in the back of his brain was insistent, but somehow he
didn't want to obey it. He looked around to see if Holly
had returned, but he didn't see her. Outside there was a
sudden lull in the performance, silence from a crowd that
had been madly cheering a second ago. The silence
stretched out, and then the new voice rolled out over
Times Square, deep, powerful, confident in its control.
The True Prophet had taken the stage.

Again Michaud couldn't make out the words, but he
felt their impact, felt a nameless thrill building up in him
as they rolled over the crowd. *They're doing something
with the sound system, infrasonics to create an emotional
response.* He knew it had to be true, because his own
response was completely divorced from any content the
words might have, but the knowledge did not lessen the
result. He found himself almost childishly eager to get
onstage, to be in the presence of this great man face-to-
face, to receive his benediction. Then he was being led
onto the platform with the other initiates. Four red-robed
figures stood guard at the corners—*inquisitors,* he'd
heard someone call them—and he saw the True Prophet
for the first time, intense blue eyes and long hair, his

gaze skewering Michaud before it moved on to the other initiates. Hands behind him removed his hood, and he found himself unable to protest though he knew that his image was being widecast, that his anonymity had been compromised. And then the Prophet was standing before him, and a hand on his shoulder urged him to kneel as the other initiates were, and he did so. The Prophet touched him then, his palm on Michaud's forehead, and his touch seemed to burn its way into his flesh. For the brief moment he felt a powerful connection to the man, and through him to the entire universe.

"Believe in the Faith!" the Prophet commanded, and Michaud believed. The experience was rapture, purer than love, more powerful than sex. When the contact was broken he yearned for nothing more than the man's touch again, but the moment was gone and the Prophet moved on to the next initiate in line, and the next and the next, and then returned to his speech.

"My brethren!" The Prophet raised his arms, arching his back as if to open himself to heaven. "You see here before you the newest lambs of our flock. You see those who have been called to the way of Christ, our father. You see those who have chosen to deny themselves to those who defy the word of God." The Prophet brought his arms down, locking his gaze on the crowd. "This city, this nation, this world lives in darkness. Look around you! Those who claim to rule you cannot even bring light to your lives. They talk, they argue, they plead for patience, but they are powerless in the face of global collapse. They take your money and send it to the godless masses, that they may enjoy the wealth that you have earned. Look at me!" Instinctively, reflexively Michaud moved, as though the command to look was a command to prostrate himself, and he felt the other initiates do the same beside him. "I am the voice of God, and I alone speak for you." The Prophet was yelling now, his voice thundering through the square. "God has told me He will strike down the Tower of Babel, and so I prophesy to you. Listen to me! I alone can bring light into your lives. For God has said, 'I shall strike down all those who defy me, for I know the heart of every man, and I am coming in my holy wrath to smite the enemies of the Word.'" He paused, as if inviting anyone to challenge him. "God has spoken to me again, God has directed me to lead His legions on this earth. God has ordered me to be His shield, God has commanded me to be His sword, and I bow in obedience to the will of God." His words grew to a crescendo, his eyes sweeping the crowd with his piercing gaze. "And believe me, my brethren, God will wield me without mercy. I shall strike terror into the hearts of those who oppose His mighty power! I shall slay His enemies in the certain knowledge of the righteousness of His cause." The Prophet's words shook the city, and Michaud shook with emotion at their power. The Prophet advanced to the edge of the stage. "And you, my children, you shall be my sword as I am God's sword! You shall be the cutting edge of a new world order. You will show no mercy to the unbelievers, as God shows no mercy to those who would deny Him. You shall rise up against those will oppress you, shall overthrow those who deny you the birthright that was your parents'. You will unshackle yourselves from the bondage of a government which counts you no better than those who do not know God." The Prophet raised his fist in the air, hitting the words hard. "You are the Chosen, and your will, my will, God's will, shall be done!"

The Prophet brought his fist down, and silence crashed down on the crowd, the vast audience staring up at him spellbound, as enraptured as Michaud himself was. For a long moment the silence stretched out, and then there were shouts from the edge of the square. Michaud raised his head to see their source, saw a ripple of commotion spread through the crowd. More shouts rose, and then a gunshot split the night. Galvanized, he leapt to his feet. The Prophet was speaking again, screaming into the microphone with wild eyes. "Smite them! Smite the enemies of our Lord! Strike them down . . ."

There was a hand on Michaud's shoulder, and he turned and found himself looking into Holly's eyes. She spoke quickly, her voice low and urgent. "Come with me, we've planned for this."

Wordlessly he followed her. The other new initiates were also coming. She let them down through the tent and behind it, through a barricaded area free of people, through a less thick section of the crowd, to a street at the edge of the square. Ahead of them a phalanx of police in riot gear were moving toward the square. Behind them a volley of shots rang out, and screams of pain and fear rose over the commotion.

"Link arms!" It was a new voice, another woman. Holly moved him, put him in line with the other initiates, put his arm through the arm of the man next to him. He found himself part of a human chain facing the oncoming wedge of ballistic shields. Behind him more bodies were lining up, forming a solid human wall to prevent the police from entering the square. The True Prophet's voice echoed from the buildings. "Resist them, my children! You have the strength of God behind you." A bottle arced over his head, thrown by someone several ranks behind him. It shattered in front of the police, spreading flame. Some of the Believers had come prepared.

Michaud looked around to see if he could spot Holly, but she was gone. The police advanced past the flames, truncheons raised above their shields. Another bottle flew over, but this one failed to ignite when it shattered, spreading just the pungent smell of gasoline. He felt fear and for an instant he considered running, but the crowd was pressed tight behind him and there was nowhere to run. The police line stopped in front of him, close enough that he could have reached out and touched the nearest shield.

"Faith, brother, faith." The man next to him tightened his arm against Michaud's, his voice mixing determination and ecstasy. A six-wheeled armored vehicle growled forward behind the police line. An array of spotlights on its roof switched on, the blinding beams dazzling him. He squeezed his eyes shut and averted his face from the glare. Sirens rose in the distance.

"Disperse at once, or we will use force!" The voice was bullhorn-magnified, drowning out the Prophet, and as painful to Michaud's ears as the light was to his eyes.

"Faith!" His neighbor yelled the word with the same kind of rapture that Michaud had been feeling minutes before in the presence of the Prophet. Now he felt only fear and confusion.

"Disperse now, this is your last warning!"

Some of the Believers began singing a song, but seconds later it cut off and in that instant an invisible fist slammed Michaud in the face. He reeled back, suddenly soaked from head to toe. He barely had time to register what had happened when the water cannon hit him again, driving him back against the people behind him and then throwing him bodily to the pavement. Pain burned where exposed flesh was abraded raw. Instinctively he rose to his hands and knees, and a truncheon came down on his shoulder. Bone crunched and pain flared anew, hard and bright, and he went down again. Somebody stepped on him, and then somebody else grabbed him from behind, forced his hands behind his back. Plasticuffs zipped around his wrists, cutting off circulation; another set went around his ankles, immobilizing him, and then he was alone with his pain. He opened his eyes, and ahead of him he could see the police line advancing into the crowd. The armored vehicle ground past, looming huge from his prone position with its water cannon still jetting into pockets of resistance. He watched as the follow-up squad efficiently secured other fallen brethren, leaving them as he was, to be collected when they had the situation under control. He could no longer hear the voice of the Prophet. The square was alive with shouts and screams and the bullhorn commands of advancing police squads.

Reality washed over him, replacing fear as quickly as fear had replaced the rapture of the Prophet's presence. *What am I doing here?* He was Harmon Michaud, senior director of the Aerospace Consortium. He was supposed to be in a government meeting of the highest level, plotting strategy with the secretary-general to advance the Cable project against the opposition of groups exactly like the one he was part of now. Instead he was lying soaked on dirty pavement, trussed like a hog for slaughter in the robes of an initiate of the Believers, with his shoulder broken, having allowed his face to be widecast receiving salvation from the True Prophet. He groaned, the anticipation of humiliation overshadowing even the pain of his shoulder. He could do nothing but lie there and wait for the police. Suddenly he felt very old and tired. The sounds of the fight intensified, though he could see little, and another volley of gunfire broke loose, automatic this time. The distant sirens grew closer, and he knew he would be lying there for a long time.

He was still lying there when the Believers rallied and broke through the police line, the mob surging forward behind a barrage of Molotov cocktails, swarming over the water-cannon vehicle, setting it on fire. Those cops not overrun turned and fled back to the safety of their barricades. The mob pursued them, screaming for vengeance, coming at Michaud like a living tidal wave as the scattered police ran past him. In sudden terror he tried to roll out of their way, trying to make it to the edge of the street, to the edge of the buildings there where the crush might be less intense. His shoulder crunched with blinding pain every time he turned over, and a dozen lesser hurts assaulted his body as rough pavement dug into his flesh. He ignored them all in his panic, vaguely aware that the other trussed prisoners were doing the same. It was an impossible task; there was not enough time and the mob was coming too fast. They thundered over him like a herd of cattle. The first ones jumped his body, and for an instant he thought he might survive, but those behind the leaders couldn't see him in time to avoid him and feet kicked him, stepped on him, tripped over him. He screamed as his injured shoulder was broken a second time, and the adrenaline was such that he barely felt the ribs shatter when a heavy man who was already falling drove his boot into them.

It took the police until dawn to restore order, but Michaud had been dead for hours by then, his broken body lying in the dirty street in a pool of blood vomited from his internal injuries. His last thought had been of the girl named Holly, but no one would ever know that.

Abrahim Kurtaski's ears popped as his jet descended once again toward Quito. A year ago, having his own jet at his service had seemed the height of privilege; now the twice-weekly journey was more of a chore. Out the window the sunrise was blood-red, the legacy of last month's eruption of Nevada Cumbal, one hundred kilometers north of Cayambe. The pillar of dust and ash had climbed to the stratosphere and forced aircraft to deviate around it, and the plume had already circled the globe. Cumbal had given Abrahim some worry, because the heavy tremors that presaged its eruption had shaken Cayambe as well. For a while he had fretted that perhaps Cayambe would go up instead.

But it hadn't, though Cayambe's seismic instruments had become more active than he'd have liked to see them. He went to the other side of the plane to see if he could spot his mountain. He found it almost at once, not because of his growing familiarity with Andean topography but because the growing spire of the sky-cable base tower made it impossible to miss. The tower climbed for the heavens from its southwestern flank, not one structure but three, set in a triangle four kilometers on a side. Each subtower was a tripodal open latticework of trusses, three hundred meters at the base, the highest almost seven kilometers up now. The trusses were made of wound carbon nanofilament, nitrogen-pressurized to trade the material's tremendous tensile strength for compressive strength. Even the lowest was over five kilometers high now.

He gestured to the flight attendant. "Ask the pilot to take a spin around the tower, if he can."

His request went forward to the cockpit, and Abrahim heard the copilot asking air traffic control for a deviation from their planned approach. A couple of moments later the aircraft banked and swung around. Even from the plane Kurtaski found the base tower impressive, given scale as it outstretched the towering peaks around them. The latticework subtowers stretched down ten thousand feet from their flight altitude, up at least another ten thousand to the point where they disappeared in the cloud deck overhead. They would meet and unify twenty kilometers above to form a tripod, with interties every five kilometers to maximize the strength of the structure where the atmosphere would batter it hardest. Each subtower carried a boost track, a superconducting magnetic levitation carrier system that took cargo climbers full of construction materials to the automated assembly heads at their tops. The heads would build a level, then jack themselves up another ten meters. It took two hours or so for the robots to complete the cycle, and their surefooted grace as they moved around the latticework was something to behold, a carefully coordinated mechanical ballet of construction.

As they banked closer he could just make out multi-jointed rigger robots moving over the latticework at the first intertie level, building the cross braces that would link the three towers into one. Automation was the only way to achieve the required build rate, and human workers would have had to work in pressure suits. The cost of such specialized labor would have been prohibitively high even for the open-ended budgets of the Cable project.

Abrahim frowned. Not that the project was on schedule at all; far from it. Translating research into reality was proving frustratingly slow. His eye found the rail line snaking away from the base of the tower. Far below, a freight train loaded with prefabricated structural elements inched its way toward the railhead. At full throttle the assembly heads could handle a trainload of nanofilament beams every twenty-four hours, but the steep and winding transandean rail line rarely managed to deliver that many. They'd lost train time to volcanic-ash falls in the highlands, to storm-induced washouts in the coastal jungles and to derailments on the treacherous Nez de Diablo switchback that carried the trains between them. *And of course we aren't the only traffic on the line.* Daf Brady was right; Kenya would've been a better site.

But Kenya wasn't the site, and rail delays were not even his biggest challenge. Standard carbon nanofiber was sufficient to build the lower levels of the tower, but it was vulnerable to chemical attack by ozone in the upper atmosphere. The UNISE team had devised a method of fluorinating the fibers without destroying the ability of the binder resin to hold them together, but the fluorination process was tricky, and it took time and it took power credits, and the political situation was making it difficult to get enough of either. *Josh told me not to worry about the politics, and now I tell other people not to worry about the politics while I fight political battles for resources we can't do without.* It was not the role he had envisioned for himself, but it was what he had to do if the project was to have even a chance of success.

The plane banked steeper and for a single terrifying instant Abrahim thought they were going to collide with the structure. The pilot knew his business, though, and while they skimmed close to the red flashing warning lights that studded the latticework, there was no danger of collision. He looked up, his eye again following the towering spires as they reached for the clouds. *Even to fail in building this would be to fail attempting greatness.* Those words had been true when he'd accepted the project from Josh Crewe, but now that he'd committed his life to it, Abrahim Kurtaski wanted very much to avoid failure. The jet leveled out to continue its descent and the towers vanished behind them. Fifteen minutes later they were on the ground and he was climbing into one of the two UNISE Kamovs that were assigned to the Cable base. He had consulted on the helicopter's automated assembly line back in his Samara days, and he felt a twinge of pride as the pilot spun up the rotors and pulled them into the air. *There will again be a day when I am an engineer, when I design things and don't just supervise other designers.*

Shortly they were coming in to land at the build site helipad. The primitive base camp Daf Brady had shown him a year before had been transformed into the most advanced construction site in the world. A semiautomated loading gantry was taking bundles of prefabricated structural subassemblies off a long line of flatcars and loading them on to the stream of dedicated haulers that would carry them to the tower bases. Each subassembly was coded with an embedded identification chip that specified its place in the final structure. The control computers in the prebuild shed would read the codes and assign robotic work teams to put them together into structural units, and then each unit would be boosted to the tower-top assembly heads. Eventually the boost tracks would connect to the cable-climber system that would take ten-tonne loads of high-grade bauxite into space in under an hour, though the trip all the way to geostationary orbit would take the better part of a week.

The skids touched down and Abrahim clambered out, instinctively ducking beneath the rotor blades. Just as instinctively he looked up at the soaring north subtower, the closest to the landing pad. He felt awe and frustration in equal measure. *We're so far behind schedule.* A group of four men with a widecast camera and a zap mic went past to get on the helicopter he'd just vacated; another documentary. The tower project had been a media circus since its inception. The publicity had been helpful at first, but now they were documenting delays, shortfalls and missed schedule dates. The knowledge that the schedule was politically imposed and practically impossible did not remove the stress. An immense heavy hauler rumbled past with its cargo deck loaded high with wound monofilament truss sections. A four-by-four utility truck pulled in from behind it and Daf Brady waved to him from the driver's side. He went over and got in, aware all over again of how lovely she was. *It isn't that I didn't remember, it's that memory is not presence. I should find more reasons to come here.*

And it wasn't reasonable to even consider a relationship, no matter how many reasons he found to come to the tower site. He shook her hand professionally, and kept his eyes on hers. "So tell me all your problems. What's the biggest obstacle right now?"

She pointed to where the news crew was strapping into the Kamov. "There's a documentary team sticking their cameras in my face every time I turn around."

Abrahim laughed. "I share your frustration, but if that's your biggest problem I'm paying you too much."

A faint tremor shook the ground. Daf pursed her lips. "Our mountain is restless. We're lucky Cumbal has taken the pressure off the system. There are a few other issues. The operation is well tuned right now. We're getting materials from manufacturing at a good pace, and we're getting them up the tower as soon as we get them. We can go faster; we have ample spare handling capacity here on the ground, ample prebuild capacity at the tower bases, and the assembly heads are working at only half-capacity. To take up the slack we need to speed up the pace of delivery from manufacturing, but that would just create a bottleneck at tower base unless we boost our upship tonnage, and that will take more power."

"It all comes down to power." Abrahim sighed.

"It's probably above my level to suggest this . . ." Daf hesitated while she maneuvered the truck around a series of deep ruts gouged out of the hardpack by the heavy haulers. ". . . but if we had our own power plant . . ."

Abrahim nodded. "It would make a difference, I know . . ."

"We could double the amount we upship, more than double it, if we had the power to run the boost tracks at full throttle." There was a suppressed eagerness in the young woman's voice. She believed in the project. She wanted to see it finished.

"Yes, if we had the power available we could do that. You've suggested we put in our own plant, but as you said the system is well tuned right now. Rail capacity would be the bottleneck then, and it would take months, maybe a year to get a plant running anyway."

"Actually, sir . . ." Abrahim winced at the word "sir." Daf went on, oblivious of his reaction. "I've worked the numbers pretty thoroughly. We aren't using the trains we've got as well as we could be, and we've got the handling gear at railhead to boost throughput. I know I can double the efficiency at prebuild. Manufacturing is the real key, but I've spoken to the fab plants and not one of them is running at more than half capacity. If you can get us more trusses faster, I guarantee we'll get them up-tower and installed. If we use a photovoltaic plant we can have it up and running in two months from the word go."

There was a certainty in her voice that went far beyond her years, and Abrahim looked at her with new respect. "Smithson always sends me his best, doesn't he?"

"Of course." Daf Brady took the implied compliment

matter-of-factly. "You're the chief engineer, what else would he do?"

She pulled the truck up in front of the field office attached to the north tower's prebuild shed and they got out. The heavy hauler they had been following had run up under the unloading gantry, and automated hydraulic arms were already grabbing sections of truss from its cargo deck and carrying them into the building. Abrahim followed her inside. Inside the office she handed him a hard hat and a set of safety goggles, then took him onto the assembly floor.

The floor was a beehive of activity. Automated arms took the truss sections coming in on the gantry and, with motions both powerful and precise, rotated them into position so that multijointed assembler robots could pin-seal them into a completed subsection. As they watched, the assemblers swung into position like so many mechanical spiders, walking along the extending truss as each new beam section slid into place. Abrahim allowed the oddly compelling display to distract him from his various concerns, caught up in the mechanical dance. He had not designed the system, but he had contributed several key ideas to the team that put it together. The protective gear was a simple formality. In contrast to the mud and dust surrounding the build site, the prebuild shed was almost surgically clean, and humans weren't allowed into the robots' operating area. It took twenty minutes for them to complete the assembly as it grew to extend the length of the shed. Another set of gantry arms at the other end of the building took the completed truss and slid it out to another waiting heavy hauler and on its way to the boost track. Already the assemblers were working on the next subsection.

Abrahim looked at Daf. She had promised she could double the efficiency of this operation but from where he stood it seemed there wasn't enough slack in the operation to achieve such gains. *But of course she doesn't intend to make them busier, she intends to make them more efficient.* It still seemed an ambitious task.

He chose his words carefully. "Power is the key to manufacturing too. The fab plants are running below capacity because we can't get power credits for them."

"Well, the UN is going to have to make up its mind. We have no hope of getting this thing done on schedule if they won't give us the resources to do it." There was some frustration in Daf's voice. "Thirty meters a day is just ten kilometers a year."

Abrahim smiled paternally. "Politics is like engineering: Everything is a trade-off. The secretary-general would like nothing more than to see this project completed. He's taken considerable political risks to give it the resources it has now."

Daf nodded. "I understand. At the same time he has to understand . . ." She looked him in the eye. ". . . and you have to understand that we will not be able to meet our schedule unless we can increase material flow to the assembly heads. I can show you the math."

"I don't need to see the math." Abrahim turned his gaze back to the busy robots on the build floor. "I know the realities. Besides . . ." He hesitated, but there was no reason not to tell her. "Besides, we still don't know how to fabricate the Cable. It would be a tremendous embarrassment to get the tower finished and have nothing to connect to it."

Daf's reply was cut off by a sudden deep thump, felt more than heard over the whine of hydraulics in the build shed. A distant rumble followed it, and it took a long moment for Kurtaski to realize what it was. Explosion! They traded a glance, then instinctively turned and ran for the door.

Kurtaski's first thought was that one of the high-capacity nitrogen tanks used to pressurize the truss sections had ruptured, but the scene outside seemed completely normal, except that the workers around the tower base were also looking around as if trying to find the source of the detonation. For a long moment he wondered if he had imagined it. There was no expanding cloud of smoke, no shattered metal, no wreckage, nothing, but then there came a sound. It was faint at first and far away, a low-pitched rumbling that grew steadily louder and higher, like the wind noise in an accelerating race plane. He couldn't understand what might be making it. Then a worker yelled, "Run! Eruption!"

He looked up and saw in horror the entire top of Mount Cayambe exploding upward into a boiling mass of black and grey, fountaining red-hot lava in jets hundreds of meters high. Workers were running frantically downhill in a vain attempt to outrun the catastrophe. Abrahim instinctively grabbed Daf's hand and turned to run as well, glancing over his shoulder to see a wall of ash avalanching down the slope toward them. Pyroclastic flow! The ash would be searing hot, and though distance made it seem almost stationary it loomed visibly larger even in the two-second glimpse he took. Pyroclastic flows could move over a hundred kilometers an hour, which gave them . . . he visualized the distance to the peak . . . two minutes, maximum. There was no point in running. *We need shelter.* Except the base tower complex was an industrial worksite, its buildings made of nothing more substantial than sheet metal, not nearly enough to protect them from the onrushing conflagration. A chunk of rock the size of a truck fell out of the sky and landed on a parked walker, obliterating it and spraying fiery gobbets from its still molten interior like an exploding bomb. Flames rose where they landed, and more rocks began to rain down, most smaller than the first, some even bigger.

*And even the smallest is big enough to be lethal.* A second glance back showed the ash wall looming closer. With luck they might evade the falling rock, but when the pyroclastic flow hit them, they would die. *We need shelter, now.*

"Tower coming down!" A worker was yelling and pointing. Abrahim followed his fingers, looked up to see the towering structure swaying, starting to topple. Key support elements had been taken out by the flying boulders. His throat constricted, the pain at seeing his creation destroyed overwhelming for an instant the peril of their situation. *All that work.* His dream was destroyed. Josh Crewe's political enemies would use this to destroy him, and with it humanity's single opportunity to unshackle its fate from Earth's.

*No time to worry about that now.* The added danger of falling tower debris seemed insignificant in the disaster unfolding around them. Shelter was the priority, and there was none to be had. The ash flow would scrub away the construction camp's flimsy buildings like a fire hose turned on a sandcastle. He looked around desperately. There! The base tower's leg footings were solid concrete, thirty meters on a side and ten high. They offered no cover overhead, they would still be vulnerable to falling boulders and chunks of tower, but their downslope sides would at least be protection from the direct impact of the scalding ash.

He glanced up to see a jagged array of black carbon-monofilament struts falling toward him seemingly in slow motion. He was still holding Daf's hand, and he hauled her toward the tower footing. It went against every instinct to run toward the looming ash cloud as it thundered toward them, a decision made psychologically harder because everyone else was running the other way. The footing was upslope from their position, two hundred impossible meters of rock-strewn ground away. A boulder slammed down twenty meters in front of them and a fist-size chunk of still glowing rock hit him in the chest, hard enough to knock him down. He lay there for a second, too stunned to even feel pain, and then Daf was pulling him to his feet and they ran again. The ground was shaking now, hard enough to make the rocks underfoot dance, and it became impossible to run properly. Their progress slowed to an awkward, broken half-shuffle. More boulders rained down, intermixed now with chunks of carbon-fiber truss. Above them the onrushing ash cloud enveloped the base of the upslope subtower. They were rapidly running out of time.

It seemed to take forever to reach the dubious protection

of the tower base, but they made it before the pyroclastic flow arrived. The main section of destroyed subtower landed first, its impact hard enough to noticeably shake the already rocking ground. The force of the impact drove the wreckage deep into the moist earth, spraying dirt and blotting out the view. Abrahim threw Daf prone behind the heavy concrete support block and threw himself down on top of her. The onrushing ash cloud reached them at the same moment, blotting out the sun as it swept over and around their hiding place, the blasting roar of its passage droning out even the explosive rumble of the eruption. It began to rain gravel and ash hot enough to scorch whatever it touch, and he was overwhelmed with the burning stench of sulfur dioxide. *If you can smell it, there's not enough to be lethal.* That removed only one of a dozen ways the mountain might yet kill them. A few other souls had been running for the tower footing, and Abrahim looked up to see if he could see them, squinting to keep the ash from his eyes, but he couldn't even see the wall he was pressed up against. The burning dust was agonizing where it touched bare skin, and each breath he drew seemed to be coming from a blast furnace. And then something struck the back of his head, and there was darkness.

"What in hell was Michaud doing there?" Josh Crewe stood at the front of his executive council, his anger palpable. "He called me and said he was walking the last few blocks. The next thing I know his face is on all the widecasts as this cult's latest member." He directed his gaze at Janice Jansky. "What do you know about this?"

Jansky swiveled her chair to face Crewe. Her eyes were red from lack of sleep as what should have been a routine meeting had turned into a twenty-four-hour emergency session. "I have no idea why he chose to get out of his car, but once he was out he was vulnerable. Whoever put those fireworks together for the Believers put in a few extra ingredients."

Crewe raised his eyebrows. "Explain."

"Those message streamers they dropped from their fireworks were laced with a mood synergizer, Ceranine. If he happened to pick one up to read it he would have absorbed the drug through his skin."

"What would the effect have been?"

"It would have made him excited and suggestible, responsive to the crowd's mood. I would put odds on that being exactly what happened. He picked up a slip out of curiosity. Ceranine works fast but not for long, and while he was under the influence one of their recruiters picked him up."

"Right. You were wondering about a crime, now we have one. Let's pick up the True Prophet and anyone else in his organization we can get for this."

"Wait a second." Jansky held up a hand. "We don't have anything strong enough to make arrests on. This needs some more work."

"More work? You must have traces of the drug in his blood, traces on the streamers."

"No. Ceranine metabolizes very quickly in the body, and breaks down in the presence of oxygen."

"So how do you know they used it?"

"It's all circumstantial, based on the behavior of the

crowd and the presence of certain breakdown products in the message slips."

"Are those compounds unique to Ceranine?"

"Normally yes, but not this time. They were clever, they also soaked the strips in a catalytic compound that degrades Ceranine-breakdown products but not Ceranine itself. We can prove the presence of the catalyst, but there's nothing illegal about that. We'll get them in the end, though. I've got a team working on this. Those streamers didn't come from nowhere, and it wasn't a ghost that laced them. We'll get evidence, and we'll get convictions." There was hard determination in her voice.

Crewe nodded. "Do that." He looked around the room. "This is getting out of hand. We have a serious problem with these hard-line fundamentalists here in North America. I've been hoping we'd get ahead of them in our programs and the problem would evaporate, but I can see now that was a mistake. We need a strategy and we need it now."

Thom Pelino finished scribbling a note on his datapad. "I think ignoring them remains the best strategy. Responding tells them that they have power. It will only encourage them."

Jansky shook her head. "These people already have power; they've taken it and they demonstrated that they're willing to use it. It would be a mistake to fail to recognize that reality."

"They represent a fraction of a percent of the people on this planet. We can't let them blackmail us."

She gave him a look. "Neither can we let riots go unchecked."

Crewe raised his hand before the argument could go further. "What about the True Prophet, can we pick him up on general principles?"

Pelino shrugged. "I'd be amazed if his hands were dirty on the Ceranine issue. We'd be courting trouble if we locked him up and couldn't make the charges stick."

Crewe's face darkened. "We need to shut this organization down."

Jansky pursed her lips. "We don't need any Ceranine evidence to take the True Prophet off the street. He was clearly inciting the riot, and we have that on video. We have that on widecast. No one would fault us for picking him up on that basis."

Pelino leaned forward. "What we saw last night would be nothing compared to what the Believers would do if we made a martyr of him."

"What we're seeing with this movement is the start of an avalanche." Crewe paced back and forth at the head of the conference table, then shook his head. "No, we can't pull him in until we have him dead to rights. Does anyone know what started the fighting?"

Jansky dropped a folder on the table. "I have the NYPD preliminary report. So far as we can tell everything was peaceful until someone started an altercation with one of the mounted units. An officer was pulled off his horse and beaten. His partner fired a warning shot and the crowd charged them both." She paused, looking away for a moment. "Of course, the official report isn't going to point the finger anywhere but squarely at the Believers. What really happened . . ." She turned her hands palm up.

". . . we'll see if we got it on surveillance video. If not we'll probably never know."

Pelino pulled the folder over in front of him, glanced at it. "It's really irrelevant who started it. The important thing is that we prevent it from happening again." He held up a hand before Jansky could interrupt him. "Not by locking up the True Prophet on a minor charge."

The Interpol chief turned to him. "Incitement to riot isn't a minor charge. A lot of people died last night, Thom."

Pelino shook his head. "It isn't big enough. These people are very good at propaganda, and you know the Prophet's team will take that and run with it. They'll turn him from a prophet into a saint, a crucified saint. We'll be buying ourselves problems we can't even imagine now."

Jansky looked angry. "A hundred thousand people just rioted in midtown New York." She took the file back from Pelino, glanced at it. "Four hundred people are dead, there's at least half a billion euros in property damage. This wasn't an accident; the Believers planned for this to turn into a riot. They drugged people, used infrasonics and God only knows what else to get the crowd pumped up. They came with gas masks and body armor, they used firebombs. They expected to fight, they were organized to fight, and they fought." She stood up and made a gesture to bring the widecast footage of the riot onto the screen. "This was supposed to be a peaceful religious gathering to raise awareness on the energy crisis, and it wasn't. They didn't say a single thing about the blackouts, they spoke about holy war and smiting enemies."

On the screen the churning chaos of the riot replayed

itself once more, and Crewe could see the corner near
Broadway where Harmon Michaud had died. Harmon
had not been a friend, exactly—the realities of high-level
politics denied them that kind of relationship—but he had
been an ally, and for his own reasons he had shared
Crewe's dreams. Crewe felt a chill run down his spine.
*Dreams come with costs. I didn't think the cost would be
blood.*

Jansky was still talking. "We cannot allow this to go
unanswered, and it must be answered publicly. I don't
know what we'll buy if we start breaking this organization
up, but if we let this self-styled prophet get away with this
. . ." She looked around the room, meeting everyone's
gaze. ". . . we're buying ourselves a civil war." She sat down
again, and the silence stretched out in the wake of her
words.

"Other than incitement to riot, what do we have on the
True Prophet?" Crewe asked.

Jansky's fingers made quick symbols in the air, and data
flowed across the surface in front of her. "Nothing. He
doesn't maintain bank accounts, stays completely off the
transaction net, handles everything through flunkies. He's
always had a small following; it's only started to snowball
in the last six years or so."

Crewe nodded. "Six years ago. That's when people
started to get scared about the future." *And I know my
own election hinged on that very fear. Opportunity and
crisis were two sides of the same coin.* "How many followers
does he have?"

"It's hard to know. There's a small core group of a few
hundred that've been with him from the beginning,

essentially cultists though they wouldn't use that term themselves. Probably three or four million would identify themselves as belonging to the Church of the Believers, or following the True Prophet. His widecast channel brings in well over ten million people daily, and he's reached a hundred million for his Easter service. As for the amount of support he enjoys, probably half of North America agrees with him in principle on issues like the economy and power distribution, and the role of the UN. Probably more than half. Maybe a third of those would go along with him on religious grounds as well."

Pelino leaned forward. "The fundamental issues are what counts. There's always going to be a minority who will follow some self-appointed messiah. The vast majority are getting on his bandwagon because he tells them what they want to hear. People are scared—they're scared of losing their jobs, they're scared of seeing their families go cold and hungry. The world is changing. NorAm is losing its place. The citizens don't like that; they aren't used to it and they want it to stop. They don't want to hear complicated reasoning, and they don't want show patience. They want things to turn around, immediately and at no cost to them." He spread his arms. "That isn't rational, but that's what people want. We can go after this guy, we can shut down his organization. And then some other messiah will come along and do exactly what the Prophet is doing now. We're not actually going to change anything until we change the underlying reality. The Prophet has his faction in the General Assembly and they will use those votes to win the next election. The back-to-religion movement is going to keep growing until we change the economic fundamentals."

"So what about the fundamentals?" Crewe looked at Ira Roberts, the minister of finance and economics.

Roberts shrugged. "The basic problem is that NorAm industry has lost its leadership position. The continent has become a cash-crop energy exporter, because SouthAm and Africa and Eurasia can pay more for NorAm power than NorAm citizens can. That can't be fixed until the energy problem is fixed globally. I defer to Minister Dudek for the answer to that question."

Crewe switched his gaze to his resources minister and raised an eyebrow.

"In the short term there's not much we can do." Dudek tabbed his datapad and the vidwall displayed a graph showing power production and demand curves. "Our installed capacity is climbing worldwide, actually faster than it ever has before. The problem is demand growth is so high right now, and it's going to keep right on growing."

"Could we stop that, or throttle it back?"

"We have the option, but it won't help North America to put barriers in the way of its biggest export. Force the producers to sell to the local market and the citizens will be able to afford power, it'll be food they can't buy." He shrugged. "That's just an economic reality. Africa is the fastest-developing part of the economy right now. The bottom line is, they can do more with a kilowatt than NorthAm can, and they pay more for them. It's a working market and we interfere with it at our peril."

"What if we did interfere?"

"We'd have to force the producers to sell at below-market prices to meet NorthAm demand, and the African assemblyists would certainly invoke the Free Market laws.

The legal battle would take years. And if we did manage to force the issue the power generators are going to scream loud and long. Africa has almost as much influence in the General Assembly as the North American Union. They'll point out quite rightly that NorthAm still gets more power per capita than they do, and does less with it in terms of productivity gains."

"How long until we turn the situation around?"

"At the current rate of power capacity installation, we've got about five years." He smirked sardonically.

"Not soon enough."

Dudek spread his arms. "The system has gotten so far behind the curve that there isn't the flexibility to do it faster. The limit is how fast we can grow our installation capacity." He shrugged. "It takes time to build a reactor, that's all there is to it."

Crewe nodded, then stood up to address the room in general. "The True Prophet put a shot across my bow on the *Ark* project. The Believers are getting a political foothold. That's what concerns me, far more than this riot."

Pelino snorted. "It's not a foothold they've got, it's a stronghold. Soon it'll be a stranglehold."

"How can they be against technology and still protest against the energy crisis?" Jansky asked the question of no one in particular.

Dudek looked annoyed. "It's purely an emotional response. Surely they can read the numbers as well as anyone. Yes, we have problems, but North American power production is catching up with demand. The current situation is purely temporary."

Crewe nodded. "It's the emotional response that matters. Our support numbers are slipping badly, and the True Prophet is building a swing constituency to make himself the kingmaker in three years. A lot of assemblyists are going to go where the wind blows, and anger linked to fundamentalism is a powerful wind. We need a coherent plan in place to turn the North American demographic around and peak our support to get us back into power."

Pelino shook his head. "It isn't right that NorAm has this much power."

"It isn't right. It *is* the way the UN is built. Give me another five years in office and I'll start changing that." Crewe looked around the room, meeting the eyes of his key advisers. "We know what the problem is, we need an answer. Let's work on that, ladies and gentlemen."

The meeting adjourned and Crewe went back to his office. Dudek followed him back. "Can I steal a couple more minutes, boss?"

Crewe waved him into a seat and sat down behind his desk. "Talk to me."

"Listen, my power grid construction priority list puts the Panama link upgrade on top, at your direction."

"I know that. I put it there."

"That's a lot of transmission capacity, and it's all outbound from NorAm."

Crewe shook his head. "I know that too, and if you're going to—"

Dudek raised a hand. "Hear me out, boss. I know I've said this before but I would be remiss in my duty if I didn't say it again. All these fundamentalists believe the rest of the world is stealing power from them. Putting in another outbound transmission line is—"

"—only going to worsen the situation." Crewe sighed. "I know. The *Ark* project needs the power to speed up construction, and then to boost steel up-orbit."

"Can't that wait? You don't even have a final design yet."

"Design isn't the issue. It's going to take decades just to get all the material into space."

"If it's going to take decades then another year or two won't matter to the project. If we held back a year or two it would make a huge difference, politically. This project is beginning to extract a measurable percentage of the economy, and power costs are certainly not the end of it. Maybe now isn't the time—"

"No!" Crewe slammed a fist down on the table. "Now is the only time. We have to get it done. I don't care what it takes."

"You may be handing the election to the Prophet and his Luddites. Have you considered that?"

"We have three years to get this project so entrenched in the economy they won't be able to stop it even if they tried. I don't care what happens then."

Dudek shook his head. "I was talking to Kurtaski. He doesn't think the major research and development for *Ark* is going to be done in five years, let alone three."

"It doesn't matter. Getting iron into orbit for the hull is most of the effort right now, iron and carbon that's it. We're paying good money for power and raw materials. If we keep that spending up and increasing for three years a lot of people are going to have a vested interest in seeing it continue."

"Josh." Dudek paused, choosing his words carefully. "You put me on your team because you trusted me to make the right decisions. Trust me now. I know you're hoping to make this project unkillable, but this won't be enough. Harmon Michaud just died."

"The Aerospace Consortium will still be behind me. Even without Michaud."

"I'll wait and see on that—but even if they are, this is going to take more than money and power, it's going to take votes. You got into office because a lot of NorAm people are unsatisfied with the way the world has been working."

Josh shook his head. "The world isn't working, and it's beyond anyone's power to save it at this point. We can check the tide, maybe, for a generation or two. I hope we can, because the only hope our civilization has is to get this ship launched. Right now we're worried about power, but sooner or later we're going to run out of food. There's too many people, and too few resources." He spread his hands. "I wish I had better news for you, but unless you can find a way to stop people from having babies, that's it."

"That's a cop-out, Josh. Maybe we are doomed, but it doesn't matter. What matters is, the people of the world chose you to turn the situation around for them. If they don't see you delivering you, *we*, are finished. And as for your pet project, realistically you need the *Ark* itself well under way before you leave office, not just tonnes of steel in orbit. You need to have every aspect of the economy getting a slice of the *Ark* pie. This is politics, this is reality. The True Prophet's people aren't the only ones who don't like your priorities. You need another term, and to get another term you have to address the concerns of the North American public. It doesn't matter what you think of their beliefs, it doesn't even matter if those beliefs are completely constructed by the True Prophet for his own purposes. It only matters that you have three years to convince them that you are making their world better."

"They already have it better than most of the world."

"The public doesn't have to care about that, and they don't." Dudek hesitated, then continued carefully. "There's more to this than the pursuit of your own personal goals. The electorate have a right to good governance. Maybe we really need to get a colony ship out there, maybe we don't. That's a question bigger than I can answer. It isn't going to happen if we don't turn public opinion away from the True Prophet."

"Okay." Crewe breathed out slowly, his eyes far away for a long minute. "Okay, so what do we do?"

"We need to solve the energy problem. Get more power into NorAm, throttle back Afro-Eurasia. Find a way to do it subtly so AE doesn't realize what we're doing, and move the Panama link priority down. That's a flash-point issue in the making." Dudek held up a hand to forestall Crewe's objection. "I'm not saying stop building the Cable. I'm just saying use South American power and resources. Put a few high-profile contracts here in NorAm, let the people think they're gaining from SouthAm hubris. Give me some of those resources to get generation capacity online faster."

"How much can we grow power production?"

"If we do all that? I can keep up with NorAm population

growth. The citizens won't see more kilowatts but at least they won't see less."

"Africa will see less. Eurasia will see less."

Dudek shrugged. "It's a zero-sum game. Worldwide the population is growing faster than production. Somebody's going to win and somebody's going to lose. NorAm has the swing bloc and that means we have to win their approval if we want to win the future. It isn't what's best for the whole world but if we want to have any influence it's what we have to do now."

Crewe nodded. "I'll take it under consideration." Dudek got up to go and Crewe called after him. "Jack!" The other man turned around. "Thanks."

"It's my career too, Josh. It's all of our careers." There was concern in Dudek's voice. "And it goes farther than that too. A lot of people died last night. We knew one of them. The decisions we make have real consequences." He paused. "Just keep that in mind."

Crewe nodded. "That reminds me. I need to know who's replacing Michaud with the Aerospace Consortium." The secretary-general's eyes were intense, but his voice was mild. "That's a resources question. Find out for me, will you?"

Dudek opened his mouth to protest the callous dismissal of a man's life, then closed it without saying anything and went out. It took a driven man to become secretary-general, driven to an unhealthy degree. The *Ark* project was a symptom of Josh Crewe's disease. It would serve no useful purpose to challenge him on it. What Crewe's obsession would cost them all was another question.

Crewe's desk chimed as Dudek left, and he pointed the

call live. Eric Smithson's face appeared on the screen. He was haggard and wild-eyed, and the picture had the jumpiness of a handheld phone.

"Eric, what is it?"

"Cayambe is erupting. The base tower has collapsed. We're . . ." He suddenly looked off-camera for moment, his eyes widening in horror, and then the screen went blank.

Daf Brady woke to the brilliance of dawn cascading through tall, white-curtained windows. At first she didn't know where she was, and then vague memories came back, corridor lights flashing overhead, concerned voices, a helicopter, hands lifting her onto a stretcher. Why? More images, the searing grey wall of Cayambe's pyroclastic flow thundering toward her, Abrahim's hand on hers, pulling her toward the base-tower footing. She had run with him, knowing his judgment was right, though it went against every instinct to run toward certain doom. *And his body over mine, and the heat.*

"Good morning." The nurse's words came with a heavy overtone of Quechua-laced Spanish.

"Good . . . good morning." Daf found it hard to form the words. Her throat was throbbing sore, and for the first time she became aware of the IV drip attached at the crook of her elbow, the oxygen mask on her face, the dressings that wrapped her forearms. The nurse's accent suggested she was still in Ecuador, but there were blanks in her memory. *Where's Abrahim?*

"I'll just look you over. You're in Hospital Metropolitano, in Quito, in case nobody's told you." The nurse bustled about, took Daf's temperature, checked the pulse monitor by the bed and adjusted her mask. She wore a crisp white uniform and starched cap of a kind that had been out of style for a hundred years in NorAm health care. "You're doing well. You were very lucky."

"And Abra—Dr. Kurtaski. How is he?" There was a screen on the wall at the foot of Daf's bed, showing some SouthAm drama series with the sound off.

"I'll check for you." The nurse tapped her pad. "He's here . . ." She paused, reading, and Daf saw the sudden shadow come into her eyes. "He's in intensive care."

"I want to see him." Daf sat upright, then fell back, suddenly short of breath. The nurse sat down beside her to check her oxygen again. "I need to see him."

"We're keeping him asleep for now. You can see him later, right now you need to rest. You inhaled a lot of sulfur dioxide up there and your airway is still swollen." She pulled a styrette from her duty pouch and slid it into the IV's injection port. "I have to change your dressings now, you have a few burns. This will make it more comfortable for you."

*We're keeping him asleep for now.* That was a gentle way of saying he was in a medically induced coma, which meant his condition was grave. Daf wanted to ask questions, at least get the information, but the drug, whatever it was, quickly slid her into a state of blissful relaxation and it became hard to translate thought into speech. The nurse went to work. The pain was still sharp, but she wouldn't have cared even without medication. She had seen the nurse's expression when she'd called up Abrahim's information. *A medically induced coma.* He had been on top of her, his burns would be worse . . . She remembered the chunks of rock that had rained down around them and prayed that none of them had hit him. *Please God, let him be safe, let him survive and heal.* Somewhere in the process she drifted off into a deep and dreamless sleep.

She awoke a long time later, unaware of how much time had passed. It was dark outside her window. At least twelve hours then. There was someone with her, a man, with a face she felt she should recognize . . .

"Ms. Brady, I'm Josh Crewe."

"Mr. Secretary, I . . ." She struggled to sit upright.

He held up a hand. "Call me Josh." He helped her, pushing the bed-adjustment buttons that she couldn't with her swaddled hands, and arranging her pillows behind her back. "I understand you're the one who kept saying we should build in Kenya."

"I was. I didn't think Cayambe was stable enough."

"You were right. For the record, Abrahim pushed your opinion forward in very strong terms. I overrode him, for purely political reasons. I was wrong, and I'm paying for that now. Not as much as you are, or he. A lot of people have paid for my error with their lives." Crewe looked out her window and over the darkened city. "I'm sorry, for what it's worth."

"I . . . I don't know what to say."

"You can say that you'll step up as the chief engineer until Abrahim is able to step back into that role."

"Chief engineer?" She looked at him in disbelief. "Of what? There's no project left."

"We're starting again. In Kenya. I need you to oversee

the site selection. You're going to have to drive the project hard."

"I can't, I'm here."

"It's your brain I want, not your body. You'll have to dictate memos until your hands heal, but that won't be long."

"Eric Smithson . . ."

"Dead at Cayambe, though we probably won't find his body."

Daf swallowed hard. Eric had chosen her, mentored her, shown his confidence in her. Now he was gone. *How many more friends have I lost today?*

"Will you take the job? I need someone who can make things happen, make the right decisions, now more than ever. Cayambe has been a setback, to say the least. I'm sure I don't need to tell you there's a lot of opposition to this project."

"I'm flattered. I don't know if I should accept. There must be dozens of people on the project with more experience than I have."

"None better than you, in Abrahim's judgment."

Daf's eyebrows went up. "Abrahim said that? He's awake?"

Josh shook his head. "No, he's told me that often in his reports."

"He barely knows me."

"He knows your work. That's his job. I need you, until he can do that job again." He saw the look in her eyes and put a hand on her shoulder. "He will be better. You can have faith in that."

Tears welled up in Daf's eyes, springing from some

emotion she couldn't even describe. She blinked rapidly to clear them and nodded. "This is very sudden. Can I think about it?"

He tossed her a fat file folder. "Here, you can think about this."

She opened it, saw the title: "Engineering Design Considerations for a Multi-Generational Interstellar Colonization Ship." She looked up to meet his gaze. "So you are going to build this thing."

"It's still a secret."

"Not a good one. There are all kinds of rumors. Why make it secret at all?" She leafed through the document, scanning. "Why not just come out with it? It's a fantastic vision."

"A lot of people would oppose it. Their support is growing steadily. They have a lot of seats on their side in the General Assembly, mostly in NorAm, but also now in Eurasia."

Daf raised an eyebrow. She'd expected to discuss rebuilding the tower. "I didn't know. I don't follow politics too closely."

"The True Prophet is using the average citizen's fears to his own advantage." Crewe looked out the window. "And he's right. Things have gone downhill in the last five years, and when people are scared they turn to religion."

"You mean when they're scared and ignorant."

"It isn't ignorance, it's the very human desire for a simple explanation, and for hope. If we can't provide that then we can't succeed." Crewe paused. "I'm really still an engineer. Politics doesn't come easily. I haven't managed to show people that I have an answer as good as the True Prophet's."

Daf spread her arms as though she were beseeching Heaven for its indulgence. "We live in a complex universe. There are no simple answers, and surely people are responsible for creating their own hope. God helps those who help themselves."

Crewe laughed without humor. "You're an engineer too. I've learned in politics that people don't want complex long-term solutions. They want simple answers, and they want them right now. And yes, they want to be given hope, they want to be given a lot of things, and given that they pay the government to provide them, they have a right to expect that we do our best to give them what they want. What they don't want right now is a fantastic vision that won't pay off for generations. Their concerns are more immediate."

"So if they don't want the *Ark*, why are we giving it to them?"

"Because humanity needs it. Because we're either going to escape this planet or die on it." There was a sudden venom in Josh Crewe's voice. "I won't see us bound to this sorry globe through glorified superstition."

"Excuse me for saying so, but that seems . . ." *Arrogant.* Daf wasn't going to say that to the secretary-general. She let her sentence trail off instead.

Crewe seemed to understand what she had been about to say. "I have a dream, Daffodil. I want to see humanity make it to the stars. I don't give a damn about being secretary-general except as how it aids that dream. The best I can do is start it on its way. That's something I believe in, something that's good for the whole world. I've fought for that, sometimes I've fought dirty, but just imagine your grandchildren, your great-grandchildren, growing up under another star. That's worth something. Norman Bissell isn't interested in anything but his own power".

"People have to be free to make their own choices, even bad ones. And they have to be able to believe what they want to believe, right or wrong. That's the way people are."

Josh nodded. "You're right, of course." He sighed. "I'd just like to be able to take action without worrying about those who hold the True Prophet to be some sort of higher power."

Daf smiled a sardonic smile. "As long as you don't aspire to that higher power for yourself. Dictatorships are efficient. That doesn't mean they're good for people. I believe in this project, too, but it isn't up to us to decide what's right for the world."

Crewe gave her a look. "I can see why Abrahim speaks so highly of you."

"Why's that?"

"A lot of people might not speak their mind to the secretary-general. Your point is taken. I'll let the True Prophet make his speeches."

Daf laughed. "Once again the Church serves to restrain the ambition of the state."

Crewe gave her a look. "You aren't a Believer, are you, Daffodil?"

She shook her head. "I'm a Catholic. There's no love lost between us and them."

"And yet it's the same God, isn't it?"

"God is a He, not an it. And yes, He is the same God. We don't worship Him in the same way."

"Hmmm." Josh looked away, musing. "When you think about it, there only can be one God, can't there?"

"How do you mean?"

Crewe sat back in his chair. "Really, all monotheistic religions have to have the same God. The universe only has room for one all-powerful deity. Jawah, Jehovah, Allah, the Holy Trinity, whatever you want to call it, or him, or her even. Any all-encompassing God is the same as any other all-encompassing God, by definition."

Daf shook her head. "That's true only so far as omnipotence and omniscience go. We can still imagine different Gods who want different things from humanity, or who act in different ways. Religions can differ on these points without disputing the fundamental nature of God." She looked at Crewe for a long moment. "What do you believe in, if I can be so bold as to ask?"

Crewe shrugged. "I believe in science. I believe the universe follows fundamental rules, and that if we ask the right questions we can learn those rules. Perhaps there is some great awareness out there with the power to alter those rules on a whim. Maybe some vast, sentient being created the universe through sheer force of will. Science can't prove that *didn't* happen. All science can say is that whatever or whoever it or he or she is doesn't seem to intervene in the operation of the universe in any statistically recognizable way."

Daf looked at him. "Do you believe in life after death?"

The secretary-general's face showed pain for a second. "I'd like to."

"But you don't."

"No."

"Then why live, if it's all going to be erased?"

"That's a question I don't have an answer for."

"Doesn't that make life pointless, not knowing what you're here for, believing that you're going nowhere?"

"I think we're here because our parents had children. That doesn't mean our purpose is procreation, it just means that all of our ancestors managed to reproduce. Life is a gift for us to do what we want with. As to where we're going, if I have anything to say about it we're going to the stars."

"A belief you hold as dogmatically as any priest or bishop."

Crewe smirked. "A goal I pursue as relentlessly as Norman Bissell pursues power."

Daf pursed her lips. "And you have no room for God in your universe?"

"I don't have an answer for that either. Physics tells us the universe began some twelve billion years ago. Physics doesn't tell us how that happened, or why. Perhaps some vastly powerful being set the wheels in motion, perhaps we simply haven't figured out enough physics yet." Crewe leaned forward. "I can tell you I've got no room for the kind of God Norman Bissell is pushing. I believe man created that particular God in his own image, which is why we see a vengeful, capricious God who plays favorites among his creations, punishes them on a whim and rewards them for groveling at his feet. I couldn't imagine a less worthy God if I tried."

"You sound bitter."

"My parents believed in that God, and justified everything they did with the Bible." The secretary-general looked away, his face distant. "They did a lot that was unjustifiable."

Daf Brady watched the secretary-general for a long minute. *I've seen his public persona, his tremendous strength and his resolve. Now he's letting me see his weakness, and perhaps where all that ambition comes from.* It was a rare privilege, but not a comfortable one. *Change the subject, but not too drastically.* "Perhaps the problem is that Norman Bissell chooses to use his power to oppose your own."

"The problem is, he sells power from heaven." Crewe shook his head. "Just send him money, and he'll invoke the might of God for you, but look what that means. At the behest of this God's priests, our supposedly kind and generous deity has sanctified mass slaughter and gross persecution. Intolerance is raised to holiness through the imprecations of those who claim to preach peace and acceptance."

"Priests are only human, and it's true some have misused God's word. There are also those who have worked to improve the human condition. Religion can be a great force for good."

"Marx said, 'Religion is the opiate of the masses.' I think it's a far more dangerous drug than that."

"Marx did his masses no favors in weaning them from their drug of choice. People need faith, Josh. They need to believe in something bigger than they are."

"I believe in this project." Josh's voice grew intense. "It's bigger than I am, bigger than this whole world. When we reach the stars it won't be because God has brought us there, it won't be because some priest has prayed that we'll reach them. It will be because you and I and people like us have invested our thought, our sweat, our lives in making it happen. The tools we're using have been developed by all of humanity, through our own ingenuity over thousands of years. Prometheus didn't bring us fire and God didn't give us the wheel—people figured out how to work with the world around them, and then other people built on those innovations. The True Prophet wants people to believe in him. I want people to believe in themselves."

"I'm not arguing. I'm an engineer too. I'm just saying there's more to the universe than we can encompass with math and science. Prayer has its place."

"Prayer." The secretary-general slid open the side-table drawer by her beside, pulled out the Gideon Bible there. "I'll tell you what I believe. I believe that if I drop this book, it will hit the ground. I believe that no matter how many times I pick it up and let it go, it will hit the ground every single time, without fail. I believe that because I believe in physics, and if you give me a few minutes with pencil and paper I'll work out how fast it will fall and how hard it will hit and any other detail of its trajectory that you care to ask me for, and I'll guarantee those predictions will be more accurate than any prophecy written inside it. And they'll keep right on being accurate as long as there's a book to drop and a planet to drop it on. But!" Josh met Daf's gaze. "If you can, through the power of prayer, just delay that fall a single second beyond what I predict it to be, I'll be a believer."

"It doesn't work like that, Josh."

"No, I didn't think it did." Josh put more sarcasm into

his reply than he'd meant to, and Daf didn't answer him. They sat in uncomfortable silence for a minute.

"You want me to fill in for Abrahim." Daffodil changed the subject "What's the main effort going to be?"

"The engineering is well in hand; we're ahead of the game there, if only because it's going to take time to recover from Cayambe. What I need is popular support, some way to sell this project, not as a great scientific endeavor, not as the exploration of the final frontier, nothing so poetic. We need a way to sell it to the average citizen, to make them embrace it as something which will impact their lives in a positive way, something that's worth what it is costing them."

Daf shook her head. "That's the wrong approach. People are scared because they see shortages. Build power plants. Energy is the bottleneck in the economy right now, not enough power for manufacturing, for heat and light. Let them see abundance and they won't care what grand visions are built with the public purse."

"We're building them. We just need more time to get ahead of the population-growth curve."

"I can build the Cable for you. The growth curve doesn't have an engineering solution."

Josh nodded. "I know, I know." He turned to look out the windows. "Just keep it in the back of your mind. And work fast. If we get enough momentum into the project the fundamentalists won't be able to kill it when they get into power."

Daf took a deep breath. There was a subject she didn't want to discuss, which didn't mean it didn't need to be discussed. "Which brings up a current problem. I'm sure

Abrahim was about to bring this to your attention, if he hasn't already."

"What's that?"

"The required time frames. There is absolutely no way the Cable can get done in two years. Even five years is seriously pushing the envelope."

"It has to be done."

"Josh, you're thinking like a politician." Daf held up a hand, to forestall Crewe's answer. "I know you have to, I know that's the name of the game, but the engineering reality and the political reality just don't match up. We can build the Cable, but there are limits to how fast we can get it up."

"We can build a new tower faster than the original. Whatever limits there are we have to overcome them. If it's more money . . ."

"It's not more money, it's the basic physics of cable synthesis. We can get as many factories as we want building tower struts, but the cable has to be spun in one continuous strand, from orbit. That alone is going to take two and a half years, but we're not even going to get the platform launched for another three months, if we're lucky. International Metals has been in charge of the spin platform design and building, and frankly they've been a bottleneck."

"What's their problem?"

"They want a complete orbital refinery complex. That's a lot of extra design work above and beyond a bare-bones spin platform."

"It's supposed to be modular."

"It isn't modular enough. They've got some internal

power play happening and it's making a hash out of the design process."

Crewe waved a hand. "That's easy to fix. We'll take them off the project. The original concept is obsolete anyway, we aren't going to be shipping Ecuadorian bauxite up a Cable based in Kenya."

Daf raised an eyebrow. "That will completely strip any pretense that this thing is being built with private funds, for a commercial purpose."

"We're beyond that now. Just get the Cable up."

"People are going to want to know what we're putting it up for. And we won't be able to evade that question, because no matter what we do, this project is going to overlap the next election cycle."

"Now *you're* the one talking like a politician."

"It's what we're up against, like it or not."

"We'll find a reason. In the meantime, focus on the spin platform. We should be able to get faster production as we gain experience with it."

"First we need to get the new tower site confirmed."

Crewe nodded. "Whenever you're ready. Say two weeks from today, you should be well enough by then." He pulled out his datapad and tapped it. "You've got my personal line now. Call me."

He left her alone with her thoughts then. *Two weeks from now.* She looked at her bandaged hands, lifted one to touch the oxygen mask over her nose. *I won't be fit to get out of bed for a month.* She opened the design folder and began reading. *Ark* was a grand design, no doubt, and she immersed herself in its details, marveling at the sheer scope of the project. Hours later she finished, not having read everything, but having gained a good understanding of the entire concept. *At least now I understand why the bauxite economics never made sense. They were never intended to.* The economics of the colony ship were something else entirely. Whatever dividends humanity would reap from it would never be seen on Earth. A tremendous act of faith, or a tremendous waste of resources.

She became aware that the hustle and bustle of the hospital had faded. She pointed the screen at the foot of her bed live, just in time to see the time flick over to three a.m. *Wide awake in the middle of the night.* She was more upset than she cared to admit over Josh Crewe's rejection of her ill-defined religious beliefs. *It isn't as if I'm devout.* Catholicism had been part of her childhood, but the last time she'd been in a church had been for her father's funeral. She'd been seventeen, and she'd left for university a week later.

Her hand went to the small gold cross she wore on a chain around her neck. *I'm a trained engineer, I have as much faith as he has in physical equations. I know there's nothing below us but rock and molten iron, nothing above but endless space and countless stars.* The cross was a gift from her mother for her confirmation; she wore it to feel close to her family, not to affirm her faith. *But I prayed to survive in the Cayambe eruption, and I pray for Abrahim's recovery now.* What, exactly, did she expect her prayers to do? It seemed unlikely that God had altered the flight of a boulder that might otherwise have killed her at Cayambe. *And if he did it for me, why didn't he do it for the hundreds who died?* "The Lord works in mysterious ways," her mother had said, the first time she'd asked

"Why . . ." *Why did God let my father die?* It was all supposed to be part of some grand plan, but it seemed random and arbitrary to her. Of course God's plan was supposed to be too intricate for mere humans to understand. *But science exists to explain the world.* If science could let her understand the inner working of stars and the DNA helix, why couldn't it reveal God's mind? Science was simply a way of understanding that which was systematic in the universe. If A then B. If God's will was truly unknowable, then it must truly be random, and that could hardly be considered a plan. *Even random events bow to statistical analysis.*

And if religion lost every time it collided with science, as it had with the shape of the Earth and the paths of the planets, as it had with the location of Heaven and Hell and the origin of humanity, why should she put any stock in it at all. "You must have faith," the priest had told her after the funeral, and given her Saint Paul to read. She'd read it in between the textbooks of first-year engineering. To her, faith was simply belief in the absence of evidence. *And perhaps I believe because I don't want to know my father is really gone.*

With nothing better to do she gestured up the channel menu, relieved that the screen could read her hands even with bandages on. There was one English-language channel and she selected it, saw to her surprise an image of the base tower in the first moments of the Cayambe eruption. It was shot from an aircraft, with the sound of rotor blades for accompaniment—*that news crew that got on the helicopter when Abrahim arrived.* She watched with a combination of horror and fascination as the whole top of the mountain exploded. The boiling ash cloud soared skyward as the helicopter banked around to better frame the event. She watched as the pyroclastic flow formed at the edge of the crater rim and thundered down the slopes toward the tower. *Abrahim and I are down there.* At first she thought the helicopter was too far away for people to show up in the image, but then the camera operator zoomed in on the build site, and she saw running figures, still too small to identify as individuals. The camera panned up the mountain to show the onrushing cloud of hot gases and ash. Someone yelled something offscreen that she couldn't understand over the sound of the rotors, and then the view jerked suddenly sideways and back, recentering on the tower, which was now coming down, support elements fractured by boulders blown out of the crater by the eruption. The camera followed the fragile structure through its collapse, and as it fell the pyroclastic flow came back into view, now almost to the build site. She saw then how it was she had come to survive the disaster, how the main force of the flow had been diverted into a valley uphill from the site and channeled around and past it. What had washed over the build site itself was just the debris thrown up from the sides of the main event. The camera switched views again to show a second subtower falling, and then the third. The scale of the disaster was awesome. *I'm down there, in that somewhere.*

The view on the screen panned back, to show the images she'd been watching projected on a huge vidwall on a large stage. A well-dressed man with a microphone was there, gesturing at the display as though he'd just completed a magic trick.

". . . and God has struck down this Tower of Babel, exactly as I have prophesied! Brethren! It is up to us to make sure that it is never rebuilt . . ." The True Prophet's voice was sonorous and sincere, full of passion and conviction in the truth of what he said. "Hear me, brethren! See how God is angry at the secretary-general! Mankind was never meant to violate the sanctity of Heaven—"

Daf pointed the widecast off in disgust. Perhaps her faith was belief in the absence of evidence, but the True Prophet's creed was faith in the face of the evidence, faith not hopeful but defiant. There was something poisonous there, though she couldn't put her finger on it. She would take Josh Crewe's offer, if only to prove to the world just how wrong the True Prophet was. She fell asleep with images of carbon-fiber lattice dancing in her head.

The wind was cold in the cemetery, and Josh Crewe kept himself from shivering through an effort of will. The day was right for a funeral, grey and blustery, with a cold mist enshrouding the barren trees. Harmon Michaud was gone, and a priest was chanting words over his grave, promising the mourners that their friend and loved one had gone to a better, happier place. The words were meant to comfort, but they left Josh feeling empty. He scanned the faces of Michaud's family, etched with grief and tears. The priest's blessing was mercifully short, and then he raised his head. "Amen," he said, and the crowd echoed him.

The cemetery keeper pushed a lever and the coffin slowly sank into the grave. Harmon Michaud was gone, vanished into the embrace of the Bordeaux countryside that had sired a hundred generations of his ancestors. One by one his family filed past the grave, his mother and father, both in their eighties, his brother and sister, his young wife and two young children, all crying, his mother barely able to walk. After they had gone by, the dignitaries went past in order, Josh in front, the movers and shakers of the Aerospace Consortium behind him. He remembered the first time he had met Michaud, how urbane and confident he had been, assessing the upstart assemblyist with his wild-eyed project. They had become allies after that, almost friends. For such a man to die in the way he had died . . . Unconsciously Crewe set his jaw. *This didn't just happen, and the answer must be found.*

Behind the dignitaries came the public. It was not a large funeral, for all the high-ranking people in attendance. Harmon Michaud had been very much a power behind the throne, his name unknown outside of the rarefied circles in which he walked. There were perhaps a few hundred, dressed in black, heavy overcoats warding off the cold, folded umbrellas carried in case the mist turned into rain. Josh quickened his step and caught up to Mme. Michaud as she ushered her children into the waiting limousine. Her stylish black dress looked inadequate against the chill, but Harmon's wife looked beyond caring, beyond crying, her expression somehow disconnected, as though she were only a puppet being worked by some poor apprentice of a puppeteer. Perhaps Parisian society had made assumptions about the nature of the relationship between a man of wealth and power and his young and pretty bride, but she had clearly loved her man.

*And why did he choose to get out of his car?*

"I'm sorry for your loss." The words seemed inadequate.

*"Merci, M'sieur."* She gave him a brief smile, a mere formal acknowledgment of his merely formal condolences, but it showed for a brief instant the vivacious beauty she must have radiated on any other day.

Another man stepped forward. "He's with God now." Crewe looked up to meet the eyes of the speaker. Norman Bissell. "I can't tell you how sorry I am about the way he died."

*"Merci, M'seur."*

The driver was ushering the rest of the family into the vehicle, and Crewe stepped back, and found himself standing next to Bissell.

"It was a terrible thing," Bissell said.

"It's under investigation." Crewe tried to keep his voice level, to speak as a diplomat should. *My anger won't serve any purpose here.*

"This man died having accepted God into his heart." Even speaking softly, Bissell's voice carried the intensity of one of his sermons. "He died in a state of grace. God will punish the guilty, you can rest assured of that."

"I'm surprised you came."

"Why? Because I oppose you, because he was your ally? Harmon Michaud died in sacrifice to the glory of his Lord." Bissell paused, reflecting for a moment. "Such sacrifice must be honored, that's why I came. The Lord asks a great deal of his Believers. In return he gives eternal life."

"Some might say it was you who asked for his sacrifice."

"I am only the Savior's servant, I do as I am called to do, as your friend did." The Prophet pursed his lips. "I sense you suspect my motives."

"No. Your motive is power. It's a common enough drug."

"Power is your drug, Dr. Crewe, but it doesn't surprise me that you see it in me. We all see ourselves reflected in those around us. I do seek power, but only because I seek the salvation of mankind. To me it's only a means to an end, nothing more. I would rather not fight for power, for position." Bissell laughed. "You don't believe me when I say that. Your doubt is obvious. Come and visit me in my home, and see how I live. I use the tools of power, yes, but I do not yield to its temptations in my private life."

Crewe considered his adversary for a long moment. "Perhaps we have more in common than you or I might believe."

"How is that?"

"I don't want power either."

"Really? Then why do you have it?"

"As with you, it's a means to an end."

"And what is your end?"

"This isn't the time or place to discuss it."

"Not your starship?" The True Prophet cocked his head questioningly. "Surely you've abandoned that madness."

"This isn't the time, Mr. Bissell."

"God has struck down your tower, as he struck down Babel's tower. You trifle with forces you little understand, Dr. Crewe."

Crewe turned to look in his adversary's eyes. He kept

his voice low, but his words carried a vehement force. "The tower will be rebuilt."

Bissell looked genuinely surprised. "And how do you intend to justify it this time?"

Crewe didn't answer right away. Instead he turned to watch as the funeral procession pulled away, and other cars began to follow it. He looked over to where his own motorcade was waiting, smartly turned out gendarmes on motorcycles ready to clear his way through the streets to the airport. "I have to go. I appreciate your coming here today." *A political truth, necessary to say, impossible to disprove, and absolutely valueless because of that.* There was a time when Josh Crewe had disdained such empty words. Since taking office he had come to master them.

"I am obedient to God's command." The True Prophet's voice grew intense and the evangelical light flashed for a second in his eyes. "There's still time to be saved, Dr. Crewe. Jesus loves all his children, he asks only for your love in return."

Crewe didn't respond at once. Here and there, on high ground, at chokepoints, his security detail had positioned themselves unobtrusively, quiet figures dressed in black for the service, noticeable only in their unusual alertness as they scanned the area for potential threats. The trappings of power came with the job of secretary-general, and for good and sufficient reasons they couldn't be forgone, no matter what his personal preference. *And I really wanted none of this. I have no desire to struggle for power with this man.* He returned his attention to Norman Bissell. "Perhaps we'll meet again."

"Good day, Dr. Crewe."

In the car Josh Crewe called his secretary to set up a meeting with Janice Jansky on his return. *I need to know where we stand with this man.* He spent the remainder of the trip studying briefs that had nothing to do with *Ark.* It amazed him that the business of running the world could be distilled down to a series of executive summaries that one man could, with effort and diligence, absorb, consider and make some sort of coherent decision on. *And every decision must be made right.* It was a fearsome responsibility, but one he couldn't avoid if he wanted to get what he wanted.

*"Sloochylovs."* Abrahim's eyes flickered open, just for a moment, but it was enough. "What happened?" By his bedside Daf Brady smiled and pushed the button to call the nurse. By the time the nurse arrived Abrahim was waking up. She took his hand, as well as she could with the cast he was wearing. He tried to speak but the effort was obviously painful and she put a finger to her lips. "Just rest. You're doing fine."

He tried to speak again, his lips moving gently. She leaned forward to listen, made out the question. "The tower?"

"It fell, but we're building a new one, in Kenya. The secretary-general—Josh is already getting that started." She squeezed his hand. "You saved my life, did you know that?"

He shook his head. The nurse bustled about, reading his vital statistics off the monitor, checking his IV. "I'll go let the doctor know he's awake." She went out again.

Daf went on, grateful for the temporary privacy.

"When you pushed me down beside that wall. A girder section came down almost on top of us. It grazed you, but if you hadn't done that it would have hit me, much harder." His eyes registered surprise. "I owe you," she said, and suddenly found her throat constricting. She blinked back a tear before he could see it.

"How long?" His lips formed the words.

"You've been unconscious over a month. Your mother will be glad to see you awake, she came in from Russia."

"And you?"

"I come here whenever I can."

"Thanks." The word was a whisper, and he squeezed her hand almost imperceptibly. "Where is 'here,' exactly?"

"You're back in New York. Josh wanted to make sure you were looked after." She hesitated. "He's under a lot of pressure right now. The True Prophet has thrown his support behind Assemblyist Plant. The NorAm bloc is calling for his resignation."

"Believers." Abrahim rolled his eyes. "They're Luddites, throwing their shoes in the machinery because they're afraid of it."

"Abrahim . . ." Daf took his other hand so she was holding both of them. "I'm going to space. We're starting the spin platform, I'm going to oversee that." Daf bit her lip, unsure of how he'd take the news.

"You're doing my job?"

"Just until you're better."

Abrahim nodded. "Do it right." He seemed to think about something for a moment, then smiled. "Make me proud."

"I will." Daf released the breath she hadn't realized she'd been holding, feeling tears well up. "Abrahim . . ."

"Yes?"

Daf opened her mouth to speak, but the words wouldn't come. Instead she leaned forward and kissed him, gently, on the lips. She took her time, and when she leaned back his eyes met hers.

"That's a nice surprise." There was a bit of the old twinkle in his eyes.

"It was." She smiled, surprised at herself as much as he was. "It's to help you get better."

The nurse came back carrying a styrette. "Your vital signs are good. The doctor will be in this afternoon." She turned to Daf. "I need to give him his needle. He needs more rest."

"Yes, of course." Daf got up, but kept holding Abrahim's hand while the nurse slid the needle into his arm and slowly pushed the plunger down, kept holding it until his eyes slid closed again. She watched him for a while, then kissed him gently on the cheek. "I'll go tell his mother he was awake. She'll want to know."

"He's going to be better," said the nurse. "The scans don't show any permanent brain damage. It's all been edema, no structural injury that we can see."

"That's good to know."

Daf went out, down the hospital corridor, dialing Mrs. Kurtaski as she walked. Abrahim's mother was out, so she left a message. *He's going to live.* The doctors had assured her that he would, but she hadn't been quite willing to believe until she saw him awake for herself. *He saved my life.* He'd pushed her down and thrown himself on top of her. It was only when the ash and dust cleared and she'd looked up to see daylight shining through the twisted wreckage that had nearly buried them that she'd understood. She'd been afraid he would die before she could thank him for that. *I kissed him.* She felt giddy suddenly, like a schoolgirl who'd kissed her teacher. *Enough of that, Daffodil, you've got a lot of work in front of you.*

Fall in New York, and the evening air was chill in the vents as Josh Crewe guided his volanter down to the landing pad on the top of the UN building. The demands of office had kept him away from New York, and allowed him to forget the challenge posed by the True Prophet and his Believers for the duration of the journey. He was reminded as soon as he opened the door of his flier. There was a crowd of demonstrators gathered in UN Plaza below, several thousand strong, dressed warmly against November's chill. A line of uniformed New York City police held the crowd back from the steps to Secretariat building. They carried signs that read God's Power to God's People, and Crewe Out, Lights On, and God Is the Power, He Struck Down the Tower. They had a projector rigged, and there was a thirty-meter image of the True Prophet up on the wall of the opposite building. He was in midsermon, but his amplified words were being drowned out by the chanting of the crowd. Crewe listened, but couldn't quite make out what they were saying. *Nothing important.* As long as they were watching the sermon they weren't rioting. There had been more Believer riots since Times Square, none so large or so devastating, and none that showed the same evidence of central organization. The True Prophet had demonstrated his power once. Now he had as much interest in keeping it harnessed as the UN did. Crewe stood and watched the sermon, finding it increasingly difficult to reconcile the Prophet as he appeared in public with the Norman Bissell he had met.

Crewe went in to the elevator and down to his office. Janice Jansky was waiting and followed him in.

He waved her into a chair and sat down at his desk. "What have you got for me?"

"Good news and bad news."

"Bad news first."

"It doesn't run in that order." She smirked. "The good news is, we have arrests on the Ceranine question. They're Believers."

"Good work. And the bad news?"

"It looks like they were working for Assemblyist Markham Plant."

"The True Prophet's main puppet in the General Assembly. I'm not surprised, though I don't see how that's bad news."

Jansky pursed her lips. "We don't have hard evidence to link them to Plant, and they aren't naming names. This is going to become a very risky investigation if we continue with it. If we start pursuing Plant and don't come up with hard evidence, he could make this very uncomfortable for us."

Josh Crewe nodded slowly. "We need to get this taken care of. This amounts to a very direct challenge to UN authority."

The Interpol chief raised an eyebrow. "Do you want me to manufacture evidence?"

"I want you to find the evidence you and I both know

must exist. This took organization and support. Those bursters were an integral part of his rally. We're not dealing with a few fanatics who took the Prophet's imprecations too far."

"Oh, I'm quite sure he's behind it, ultimately. Certainly, he's the one who pulls Plant's strings. Nevertheless, going after Plant is risky. This could blow up in our faces."

"Hmm." Crewe put his hand to his chin, pondering. "Have they done anything similar since?"

"We've been monitoring every public event he's held since then. They use bursters a lot, usually with message streamers, but they've been clean."

"Are you sure?"

"Of course. We have people at every one of those events, testing the air, testing the water, testing everthing that might be a delivery vehicle. I don't think we'll see that tactic used again. They applied it when it really counted to generate chaos and attention. The violence at the Times Square rally set the Prophet up as a defender of the common man, and set us up as the repressive and incompetent government. It's what boosted him out of the merely religious sphere and into the political arena. It was a very carefully planned, one-off event designed to achieve a certain effect. That effect has been achieved. He has nothing to gain by repeating it, and a lot to lose."

Crewe leaned back in his chair with his hand on his forehead, pondering. "We can still use the fact that the culprits are Believers. The public will infer the link."

"That might not be a good thing. A broad swath of the public sympathizes with them. They're gaining a lot of adherents." She gestured to the window and by implication to the chanting crowd on the street below and the millions of True Prophet supporters out in the world.

Crewe shook his head. "I can't understand why."

"He offers certainty in uncertain times. People are angry, Josh. They're scared. He's giving them someone to blame for that, and that someone is you. If we try to smear him without pinning the crime, he's just going to have something else to throw back in our faces. You can bet that Assemblyist Plant and the NorAm faction will make an issue of it if we do. I have to be careful. There are probably a few Believer sympathizers on my own staff. I don't want to give anyone anything to leak."

"If you have any loyalty risks, fire them." Crewe's words were emphatic.

"For what? Holding religious beliefs?" Jansky raised her eyebrows. "Are you sure you want to open that door, Josh?"

"No, you're right." He paused, thinking. "What are the details?"

"We still don't have the whole picture, we still have to link our culprits to the actual modification of the bursters. It seems unlikely they were tampered with in transit, the bursters are sealed at the factory. We've checked with the shipping company anyway. Their records are complete. According to the paperwork they were handled in accordance with the appropriate dangerous-goods shipment regulations, which includes secure storage."

"According to the paperwork?"

"Paperwork can lie, of course."

"Is it in this case?"

"We're still verifying that, comparing the freeway log

times of the trucks involved, verifying who had warehouse access, and so on. So far it checks out."

Crewe nodded slowly. "What about the breakdown catalyst? Is there something we can link there?"

"Markham Plant owns a big stake in Pharmacorp, who make it. Again, there's a link but not a case. We can try to make something out of that, but it won't be a strong argument, and if it fails . . ."

"The True Prophet will be able to make it seem like persecuting him for being a Believer."

"Exactly."

"I don't want to see them getting away with murder, Janice." Crewe stood up and went to the window to look down into the chanting crowd on the street. "I don't care if Plant is an assemblyist." He turned back to face her. "We can't let these people take over. It would be the dawn of a new dark age."

Jansky shook her head. "We'll get them. I can guarantee that."

"How can you be sure?"

"He might get away with the Ceranine. We've got his people linked to it now though, and I'm betting that if we keep pulling that thread, we're going to start rolling over people higher in his organization. Maybe someone will take the fall for him. That doesn't matter, because someone like that, someone who feels he's above the law, is going to keep right on breaking it. Sooner or later he'll slip up, and when he does I'll be there waiting for him." Jansky's voice had a hard edge to it.

"That's the bottom line, isn't it?" Crewe smiled. "I'm glad you're on my team, Janice."

"That is the bottom line. The progress report is here."
She pointed his screen live, and gestured up the document.
"You don't need to read it. You already know the important
part."

"How long is it going to take to finish this?"

"I can't answer that. It'll happen, mark my words." She
gave him a terse smile in return. "You've just got to have
faith." She smiled a predatory smile. "Not in God, in me."

"I will."

Crewe watched her leave before turning his attention
to her report. It contained nothing of import that she hadn't
already told him, but he had to know the facts when he
met the press. He grimaced. He would rather be reading
progress reports on the status of the Cable project, but the
best way he could serve its interests was to pay attention
to the minutiae of government and not let his merely
personal preferences dictate how he spent his time. He
drummed his fingers on his desk as he read. The work was
thorough, the report detailed, but there was nothing there
that could stop the steamroller of the Prophet's popularity.
*The people want certainty. They want someone who tells
them what they want to hear.* Crewe pointed his vidwall
live, called up the True Prophet's widecast channel. The
Prophet's face filled the screen, the same widecast the
protesting crowd outside was watching. Crewe guestured
to mute the volume and watched the performance in
silence. *His power is growing, and I'm running out of
time.*

He sat for some time contemplating the image. The
chants from the demonstrators in the street below
occasionally grew loud enough to faintly penetrate his

office. Finally he gestured to dismiss the image and called up the latest reports on the tower construction. They were not encouraging. It would take six months to get back to where they had been before. That wasn't as bad as it might have been, because problems with the spin platform had put that part of the project over two months behind already. The extra time would let them catch up with the on-orbit part of the project, but still . . .

He pointed up his scheduler. The Cable-project time-line was a stack of multicolored bars, each bar indicating the estimated time required for each of the project's many critical subtasks. He waved a hand to scroll the display to the left. After the end of the Cable project came the start of the *Ark* construction program. Some of *Ark*'s subtasks were already in motion, concurrent with Cable construction. Right now they were mostly research programs and none were officially connected to each other. But nothing on the sheer scale of *Ark* could be kept truly secret. The space-technology press was full of speculation. *And I'm neglecting the duties of my office, and I can't allow that to happen either.*

Crewe drummed his fingers on his desk. Somehow the mundanities of running the world couldn't compete with the urgency he felt over the *Ark* project. The loss of secrecy was a bad thing, for *Ark* had to be born in secret if it was to be born at all. Another bad thing was the political time-lines laid out beneath the engineering charts. There just wasn't enough time until the election, and it looked like the Cable wouldn't be finished until after that was over. The Cayambe disaster had pushed them past the critical point. He had intended to make the Cable a showpiece, and now it threatened instead to drag him down. *God has once more struck down the Tower of Babel.* The way the Prophet said the words it sounded as if God had done so on the Prophet's command. *Why does anyone believe this?* It didn't matter. Norman Bissell's popular following had gained him growing support on the floor of the General Assembly. He wouldn't run for secretary-general himself, of course, but he would control the agenda of the Secretariat. Space would be shut down as a visible sacrifice to the demands of the people. It would take years, decades to restart, if it ever did it all, and nobody else would ever have the strength of will to get humanity off the planet. He looked at the picture on his desk. *No, I will not fail.*

Which meant he had to take action. He keyed his intercom. "Get me a connection with Daf Brady."

The African sky was brilliant blue, and Daf Brady marveled at the contrast with the surrounding green jungle spreading out below the trail leading up the slopes of Mount Kenya. Josh Crewe led the way up, his long stride making it hard for her to keep pace beside him. Her lungs were still recovering from the hot gases she'd breathed during the eruption at Cayambe, though she was no longer coughing up sputum made gritty by ash. The burns on her hands weren't yet healed but they were healed enough, the doctors had admitted when she pressed them. They'd wanted to keep her another two weeks, but Daf hadn't let them. She smiled to herself. *You take your victories when you find them.*

Behind them the town of Nanyuki was waking up,

streetlights winking out as the sun rose into the clear Kenyan sky. Nanyuki had once been a British garrison town, in the days when Africa had been sliced up into colonies by competing European empires. It had become, through a painful history of exploitation, poverty and privation, an exclusive resort. Now the newly wealthy elite of Africa came to play at the Safari Club, to hike and ski the high slopes of Mount Kenya, but Josh had no time for either recreation or history, and with all her efforts devoted to keeping up with him, neither did Daf. The mountain loomed above them in the thin air, sloping steeply upward, beckoning them higher.

Josh pointed up at the peak. "This is the place." Daf caught up and followed his finger. "We should have built here from the start."

She nodded. "Politics . . ."

"Politics." Crewe made a slashing motion with his hand. "I should never have let that sway my judgment." He paused, considering. "I knew this project might cost lives. It's a big industrial operation, that happens. I just never thought it would be my fault, directly my fault."

"You played the odds."

"No, I played political games. I knew Cayambe was a gamble. The whole area is geologically active. I bought off the NorAm assemblyists, I bought the support of International Metals, and those decisions took me to Cayambe. I took the easy solution, and I paid for it."

"It might have been five hundred years before the next eruption. You couldn't have known."

Crewe gave his acting chief engineer a look. "I could have guessed. The volcano was due, the seismography said as much. I took the risk. People died." He pointed up at the distant peak again. "This is the mountain we should have been at all the time. We've lost a year's work at Cayambe. Starting over will be that much harder, but we'll do it." He looked back down the trail toward Nanyuki, hidden now by the lush forest. "We'll need to upgrade that rail line."

Daf Brady nodded, musing. "We're going to have to ship every last strut over from NorAm now. That's going to increase our transportation costs."

The secretary-general shook his head. "No. There are perfectly good carbon fabs on this continent. We'll build everything right here." He looked up at the peak above them. "Let's go, we've got a lot of climbing in front of us."

They hiked higher, the exertion of the climb preventing further conversation. Eventually they came to the first survey camp, high on the mountain's northern flank, and then they borrowed a walker to cover the ground more efficiently. There were survey teams everywhere, getting the detailed data needed to lay out the footings for the new tower, but it was important to get a feel for the area. Finding the right location for the base tower required balancing the competing demands for altitude and ease of access. Daf Brady rode in the back while Crewe gave the driver directions. She listened to the whine of the walker's servomotors as it negotiated the difficult slopes.

The walker turned downslope, and the sunglare made her squint. She looked away and rubbed her eyes. *And why are they damp? Abrahim should be here.* She forced her thoughts to the task at hand, refusing to show tears in front of the secretary-general. Power was once again going to be a problem, even more at a premium in Africa than in SouthAm. Once the Cable climbers were off the tower boost tracks and on the Cable itself they would depend on power beamed up to them with lasers, and the energy coupling efficiency of the laser/receptor system didn't amount to a quarter percent. A farm of solar sheets on the mountaintop, well above most of the clouds, would go a long way to feeding the voracious power beams. It was a shame they couldn't extend the boost tracks all the way to orbit. Then they could put solar sheets in orbit, arrays a kilometer on a side if they wanted, and power the tracks from the other end. *Power from heaven indeed!*

She paused. *And why can't we do that?* Carbon nanotubes could be made to superconduct. The necessary doping would cost them tensile strength, but not so much that a carbon-superconductor power line couldn't carry most of its own weight while hanging from a central support cable. No, *four* support cables, with the boost tracks strung like rungs on two sides and the superconductors in the middle. She felt the thrill of new understanding, visualizing the configuration. There would be no need to beam power to the climbers . . .

Suddenly the details of the new base tower's foundations seemed like a trivial concern. She needed her computer to run simulations, she needed to talk to the space engineering team, she needed . . .

"Take us back to Nanyuki."

"What's wrong?" Josh Crewe turned around in his seat, speaking loudly over the din of the walker. Briefly, Daf outlined her concept. Crewe nodded and motioned to the driver to turn around. On the way down the mountain they discussed how the Cable could be reconfigured to carry the boost tracks all the way to orbit. The superconductor concept might not be viable. *Cooling will be a problem in sunlight outside the atmosphere.* But even uncooled already carried power a thousand times better than copper, and perhaps that would be enough. Daf did rough calculations on her datapad, while Josh pulled figures and formulas out of his head. By the time they were back at the Safari Club they had a rough concept, a cable that would allow transport both up and down, and recover almost all the launch energy of a climber on the downward trip through regenerative braking. There would be problems in development, of course, there always were, but the only real concerns were cost and time. The redesign would take time, and reconfiguring the spin platform would take time, and doing those things fast would take money.

"Don't worry about money," said Josh. "I'm done trying to placate anyone. Let the NorAm bloc complain, we're going to do this or die trying." He gave her a smile. "How do you feel about going to space?"

"To space?" Daf looked at him, incredulous. "Are you joking?"

"The spin platform is going to be the key component of the project. You don't have to go, but it would be—"

"Of course I'll go." Daf cut him off. "Try to stop me."

The peaches were ready, and the farmhands were working hard to gather them at the peak of ripeness. Norman Bissell worked with them, picking, sorting, driving wagonloads of overflowing baskets to the end of the drive where the distributor's truck would come to pick them up. Handpicked and organically grown, Believer-grown produce commanded a premium price in city supermarkets. He wore a broad smile as he worked, encouraging the hands, praising God for the bountiful crop. Farming was far more satisfying than political power games, though he did what he had been Called to do, as any dutiful Christian should. Nevertheless he looked forward to the time when he could hand over the reins of the Church to some worthy successor and spend all his time celebrating God through a life of hard work and humility. The only problem was finding a worthy successor, someone capable of guiding the Church in these turbulent times, someone capable of bringing the word of Jesus Christ to the masses so their souls would be pure on Judgment Day. He didn't worry overmuch about that problem. The day would come when his successor arrived, when a new Prophet arose to lead the Believers forward until every man on Earth knew the glory of God in his heart. God would reveal the new Prophet to him, just as he had revealed the Calling of Norman Bissell. Until then, he would serve as his visions had foretold.

Norman guided his wagon team between the ranks of trees, stopping here and there to heave a full basket up onto the wagon bed. When the wagon was full he climbed up onto the buckboard, stirred up the horses and went out to the end of the drive. There was a shiny black limousine waiting for him there; a portly, round man, his hair grey, his face jolly, was waiting beside the car. Assemblyist Markham Plant.

"Blessings, Prophet." Plant extended a hand in greeting as Bissell climbed down.

"Blessings, Markham. What brings you here?"

"We have an opportunity, if we play our cards right."

"What's that?"

"Our support has reached a critical mass. We have leverage now, if we choose to use it."

"Are you sure?"

"We have enough of a margin in enough assembly districts to take control of the General Assembly."

"God has been kind to us."

"We have worked hard, very hard, for a very long time."

An expression of distaste came across the True Prophet's face. "You went too far with the Ceranine, Markham."

"The Lord's way is written in the blood of the Lamb. It was necessary. Our victory depends upon the populace seeing the government as the enemy, and that's what we achieved that night. And the results have proven me right. How many souls will be saved, for the sacrifice of those few we lost?"

"Perhaps." Norman Bissell's expression showed he remained unconvinced.

"You don't understand power. What we did was necessary."

"Necessary. The dead won't come back to life."

"They'll know eternal glory in heaven." Plant's smile was almost convincing.

He turned to face his orchards, away from the assemblyist, and his car, and the secular world. "Well, if we are ready then we must move. God has been kind to us. May He guide us now to victory." He turned back. "I'll prepare my next sermon to open the way for you. Once it's delivered, you can act."

"Yes, Prophet." There was nothing more to say. The assemblyist got back in his car, motioned for his driver to take him away. Norman Bissell watched him go, then remounted the wagon and turned it back toward the orchards. He would have the rest of today to spend with his farm and his family, and then he would have to return to the wider war for human salvation.

To Daf Brady, Baikonur Cosmodrome seemed to have been dropped onto the trackless Kazakh desert from outer space. Beyond its borders there was nothing but windblown desert, a desolation that was as alien in its relentless emptiness as the Cosmodrome itself was in its advanced technology. At Baikonur, so the joke went, even the phone calls had to be flown in. That wasn't quite true, but certainly everything else was. Even the delicious strawberries served in the communal mess hall came in on cargo flights from Georgia. When she'd first got off the plane herself the wind had nearly knocked her off her feet, so hot she'd thought she'd accidentally stood in the jet exhaust of another aircraft. Nighttime saw wind and temperature fall together, until the desert was wrapped in an icy stillness, with air so clear the stars were diamond-bright, and the Milky Way spilled across the sky with undiminished brilliance.

Perhaps it had been as bright at Cayambe, but there the mountain had always dominated the sky. Here the sky overarched the land with nothing to challenge it but the skeletal frameworks of the launch pads.

She was given the obligatory museum tour on the

first day, but the artifacts on static display were nothing compared to the living history of the launch complex itself. *Here is where Sputnik went up, where Yuri Gagarin became the first person to leave our world. And here is where I will leave it.*

She had to go through three months of training at Baikonur before she could go to space. She had to qualify in the vacuum suit and on all the orbital process facility's systems, had to prove she could function in zero g and that she could withstand the six g the crew shuttle would subject her to on launch. She was poked and prodded and assessed by platoons of medical people, who wanted to make sure she was carrying no contagious pathogens into the closed environment of the spin platform. Failing any of the tests would end her long-held-secret dream of spaceflight. The injuries Cayambe had inflicted on her body had healed, but she was weak from the time spent in hospital and recovery.

She took to running every day to bring up her fitness level, something she had enjoyed in university but hadn't had time for since. *Something I haven't made time for since.* The distinction was important, because it let her know she was in control of what she did with her life. There was satisfaction in the feel of sweat on her body, in the pull and stretch of muscles pushed to a goal, of the pounding of her pulse in her ears as the kilometers slipped past beneath her feet. She found a stark beauty in the arid emptiness, and learned to carry extra water in case she got caught in one of the ferocious dust storms that could whip up in minutes and make it impossible to do anything but find shelter behind a rock and wait.

On top of the training were the demands of her new position. Baikonur didn't work on weekends, so she would use that time to fly down to Africa to monitor progress and troubleshoot at the Mount Kenya site. Fortunately, with the experience gained at the Cayambe site, the African installation went quickly and with no more than the expected snags.

After her first month the workload abated, as Abrahim recovered enough to take over his old position again, leaving her free to concentrate on the spin platform. She ruthlessly sliced away InterMet's sophisticated additions until there was nothing left but the cable spinner itself, and just enough habitat for the skeleton crew who would oversee it. The design was still modular, but now the modules would be self-contained, flown into orbit as they were finished and not all at once to form an interdependent whole. The vast thin-film melt mirrors that were the core of the on-orbit smelter concept, and that had been giving so many problems in development, she simply canceled. Officially there was no change in the mission, but nobody in UNISE still thought that there would be an on-orbit smelter, or that space industry was going to show a profit in primary-resource extraction. The mirrors would still go up, when the bugs were worked out of them, but they would be used to forge *Ark*'s diamond and steel hull from the carbon and iron the Cable would bring into orbit, not to wring aluminum out of bauxite. In the meantime the thin-film inflation technology that was still inadequate to narrow their focal point sufficiently would work just fine to stabilize the huge arrays of polymer solar cells that would serve to power the Cable's boost track—if hard ultraviolet didn't destroy the polymer, if local charge buildups didn't short out, if they didn't get tangled, if . . . if . . . if . . .

Using carbon fiber to conduct power was nothing new, but a thirty-six-thousand-kilometer superconducting power line was. The new Cable design required six strands instead of one, and all of them were significantly larger than the original design had planned for. That change radically altered the spinner design, and the new design also required spacers to hold the cables apart and in the proper relative positions.

And there was never enough time to get done all she wanted to get done in a day. She spoke to Abrahim almost daily, but their conversations were strictly professional. Was there a desire for more behind his eyes, a reluctance to terminate the calls? Perhaps she was only imagining it. She wanted very much to take time off to fly down to New York to see him, but her schedule forbade it. She did wonder about him, in particular what had made him shield her body with his when the tower came down. Maybe nothing more than reflex. He wouldn't have had time to think about what he was doing, only time to react. Of course it was reflex. That was all it could be. *And why did I kiss him? He's too old for me to be having those kinds of thoughts.* But she couldn't deny that she found him attractive, had done so from the first time they'd met. She sent a card and flowers when he came out of hospital, idly wrote out mash notes to go with them that she crumpled and threw away. *You're not a teenager anymore, Daf.*

By then she'd been at Baikonur for a month, training hard at International Metals' simulators. She had to learn every one of the orbital smelter's systems well enough to repair them in case of emergency. It was a challenge she hadn't had since graduate school, and she found herself enjoying the mental exercise as much as the physical.

They solved the cable rate production problem by developing a method of annealing monofilament strands together, making the entire cable into a single carbon molecule. It was not crystalline, despite the repeating hexagonal pattern of the atomic-scale carbon tubes that made it up, nor was it truly a polymer, since the microtubes that made it up did not bind to each other in predictable repeating patterns. They dubbed the new thing a macrotube, which was only slightly more accurate than the competing term "macromesh." They were breaking new ground, and the old guidebooks were out of date. They tested constantly, of course, building strands of monofilament with different lengths and taper profiles and stressing them until they snapped, firing dust grains at them at orbital velocities and then examining the impact points to see how the material behaved. They exposed the strands to high-flux proton radiation to simulate what would happen in the Van Allen belts. They shot them full of micrometeorite craters and then ran the self-heal annealers over them, to see if the heat of annealing at the weakened spot would cause the cable to fail before it could be fixed. They did steady pull tests and jerk tests and oscillation tests. *But ultimately we can't be sure the Cable will work until we get it up.* It could not be tested at small scales; it was all or nothing.

And then there was the glorious day that the spin platform got launched atop a heavy Proton V booster, and the whole platform team stood at the back of the control room in nail-biting silence, awaiting nameless disaster, until finally the ground controllers reported it was safe in geostationary orbit, floating right where it was supposed to be. It would still take a little nudging to position it right over Mount Kenya, but that was a mere detail. There was a party that night, where she drank too much champagne and stayed up far too late, singing and laughing and shouting. She spent the last half of it kissing a dark-eyed cosmonaut named Konstantin, and woke up late the next day with a headache and the realization that she was taking off herself in two days, and she very much wished to see Abrahim before she left.

He was in the crew room on the day she was to take off, and he called her aside after the preflight briefing.

He embraced her and stepped back, smiling broadly. "You're doing what I've always dreamed of doing. Thank you for the flowers."

"They were the least I could do." She smiled. "I still owe you my life."

He waved a hand. "You owe me nothing. Get *Ark* started up there and we'll both be happy."

She nodded. "I'm glad to see you're better, Abrahim."

"I'm a Russian, we're known for having hard heads."

She laughed at that, and he pulled a flask from inside his jacket. "Here, a toast to a good flight." He unscrewed the cap to reveal two thimble-size shot glasses, and poured each full.

"I can't drink that," she protested. "I'll be flying in two hours."

He laughed and handed her one of the glasses. "Just as a passenger. You're in Russia now, and we aren't so concerned with such rules. This is fine paper vodka, Lavochkin, and there isn't enough there to get a mouse drunk."

She took the glass, and didn't point out that Baikonur was in Kazakhstan, which hadn't been part of Russia for a very long time now. They clinked glasses and drank, and in truth there was barely a mouthful of alcohol. That was good, because although Lavochkin was doubtless a premium brand to a connoisseur of vodka, to her it tasted like nothing more then unadulterated jet fuel. She swallowed hard to down the burning liquid and managed to avoid grimacing.

"Good flight!" he said, and embraced her, kissed her on both cheeks, and then just when she thought he was going to let her go, he kissed her the way she had kissed him in the hospital, slowly and thoroughly and long enough to make her dizzy. "Perhaps I'll follow you up there one day."

He let her go before she had a chance to recover and held the door open so she could catch up with the rest of the team. The dusty, dry heat of the Kazakh summer rolled in, beading sweat on her brow almost instantly, and she reflected that it was the last time for a long time that she'd have to worry about weather. *And the last time I'll see Abrahim for a long time. I want time with him, just to talk, to get to know him more.*

She pushed the thoughts out of her mind as the countdown ticked away the minutes and seconds. There were more immediate things to think about. She ran over her checklists in her head as they taxied, made sure she knew what she was going to be doing once she got on station.

And then the turbines spooled up and the g-forces pressed her back hard in her seat as the carrier jet thundered down the runway, and hauled itself into the sky so steeply that she wondered if somehow the rockets had fired out of sequence. That doubt was erased sixteen minutes and sixty thousand feet later. There was a sudden lurch and momentary weightlessness as the carrier dove away beneath them, and then the main engines ignited with a roar that vibrated her entire being. The roar rapidly faded as they left the atmosphere. The engine's power was transmitted through air but not through the shuttle's frame; the craft was too well tuned for that.

The sky outside faded from purple to black and the stars shone hard through her window. *I'm in space.* The realization felt strange; the ride was too short for such a momentous change. The acceleration eased, then stopped, and they went weightless. It was the same sensation she'd had in training, but it went on and on. Occasionally there were surges as the pilots maneuvered them into their rendezvous orbit, and then she just had to sit there and wait while they caught up with the spin platform to dock. Sixty-seven minutes in all, from runway to geostationary orbit. Flying home from the UNISE office took longer.

Docking took a while, and so she experimented with the gravity, letting her pen float in front of her, trying the now impossible task of juggling the three squeeze balls of orange juice that came in her meal pack. Eventually she settled down and brought out the well-thumbed copy of *Anna Karenina* she'd been reading. *How quickly the fantastic transforms itself into the mundane.* It would have been different if she'd been able to look down and see Earth down below, but her window looked out only into endless night.

More surges, gentler this time, and then the pilot got on the PA to tell them they were docking. There were six other passengers on her flight, including Konstantin Khondovsky. The others were riggers from the Baikonur team, experienced experts in spacewalking and specially trained to run the robots that would connect the subsequent modules that would expand the spin platform into a functional on-orbit construction facility. They were the ones who would deploy the melt mirrors and her solar arrays when they arrived. *And perhaps I should have taken a later flight, to make sure those deployment problems were solved first.* Except she couldn't be everywhere at once, and the cable spinner was having its own issues, and she was the expert on nanotubes, and they had eight months to solve the mirror problem before it became a project-delay issue.

The riggers were all Russian and Ukranian, and though they all spoke the English required by global transportation standards for aircrew and spacecrew, they spoke Russian among themselves for convenience. That left Daf out of the conversation, but she didn't mind. The docking module had a viewport that faced down, unlike her seat window, and with not a trace of guilt about hogging the view she pulled herself over to it and floated there, watching the planet as if seeing it for the first time. *Which in a way I am.* She'd heard that floating weightless while the globe slid past underneath felt like flying, but in geostationary orbit the planet was fixed underneath her and there was no sensation of motion. Earth was the size of a fat grapefruit, and it looked like she could just reach out and pick it up. *I don't feel like a bird, I feel like a goddess, dwelling up here in the heavens.* Africa was directly below her, and she strained her eyes to see if she could pick up the base tower in Kenya, but of course she couldn't. Below, the terminator line was creeping across western Asia. She found France and then England, and imagined she could see London. Somewhere west of there was the town she grew up in. In the twilight zone around the terminator it was easy to find the cities, outlined with their own lights like jeweled frosting. She picked up Saint Petersburg, where Abrahim had grown up. Later at night they would be impossible to see as the blackout followed the terminator around the globe. On the dayside she could find them, but it was a challenge. *There once was a time when the cities were so bright they lit up whole continents.* She shifted her gaze to the spin platform. The cable spinner had already spun thirty kilometers of leader line, and she followed its path until it vanished against the atmospheric haze. Once the leader line was anchored the spin platform would start spinning the four-stranded main transport cable with its two superconductor conduits. Perspective made it look like it already stretched to the planet's surface, though in fact it wasn't even being spun down but forward—"prograde," in the parlance of orbital mechanics. When it was complete the far end would be deorbited with a thruster firing a long, gentle retrograde burn, and flown into the atmosphere to mate with the tower. *Another technology we can't even test until we try it.* It had worked in the simulations, but . . .

Something jostled her, and Daf became aware of the shuffle of people and baggage around her. The experienced platform crew were treating her like an obstacle. *I'm just another spacestruck space tourist to them.* She smiled to herself as the commander turned and went up the hatchway to the passenger deck. *But here I am in orbit looking down on my beautiful planet. Nothing can take this away for me.* Taking over the role of chief engineer disallowed her much of the work that she loved to do, but it had opened the door to space. This time it would only be temporary, but if—*no, when*—they started building the colony ship she would be moving to orbit permanently. She didn't allow herself to consider the future if the project was canceled. *One step at a time, Daf. First you have to finish the Cable.*

"Beautiful, yes?" Konstantin smiled at her as she pushed herself away from the viewport to make room for the rest of the passengers to come through the docking tube. "You never forget the first time seeing it. Never."

"It's like a jewel." She scooted herself and her meager ten kilos of baggage through the docking tube and into the spin platform itself. Khordovsky and the others followed.

"A busy jewel. Too many people, not enough space. Not like up here."

Daf looked doubtfully around the confines of the spin-platform habitat. It was a large space, but crammed full of equipment and ultimately meant to accommodate twenty people living and working. The only privacy anyone would get was behind the cloth screen of their sleeping bunk. "I can only imagine we're going to be pretty crowded."

"Not in here, out there." Konstantin pointed out the viewport. "You and the stars, nothing else. I built the second Mars ship, twelve hours in the suit every day. Out there you are alone with God. Truly, up here we live in heaven."

Daf turned her gaze back out the viewport, drinking in

the brilliant, fragile Earth against its star-dappled black background, and let the beauty of the universe fill her soul. *I'm not just living in heaven, I'm living as a goddess.*

Josh Crewe frowned as the monorail slid into the Nanyuki station. A belt of rainy-season thundershowers had forced his plane down at Nairobi, and though the journey by train itself was just half an hour, the entire detour had cost him three hours, most of it spent negotiating traffic from the airport to the station. That delay was the least of his worries, but it was a frustration he could do without. There was a car waiting to take him up Mount Kenya to the new base tower. *And really, I should be happy.* The site had been transformed in six short months, the rough-cut roads now paved, and the heavy hauler convoys replaced by a continuous rail conveyor system, linked to the bustling logistics yard at the mountain's base. The delay in relocating the project from South America was frustrating, but the experience gained there had been put to good use in creating the new installation. The new assembly heads could build height at twice the rate of the original ones, and the new towers were going up as fast as the trains could deliver structural materials. The bottleneck now was manufacturing capacity, but with money not an object new fabrication plants were being qualified on an almost weekly basis. Everything was going as well as it could have been. *But four kilometers a month isn't fast enough.*

A car and driver were waiting for him at the station, along with an Interpol escort. Thom Pelino was waiting in the back of the car.

"Have you heard the news?" Pelino looked upset.

"What news?"

"The True Prophet is on the air every day now calling for you to be thrown out of office over this project."

"That's nothing new."

"It's new that he's doing it in every sermon, every day. It's new that the newsfeeds are covering it in detail. Most importantly, it's new that Assemblyist Plant just proposed a no-confidence vote on the floor of the General Assembly. The NorAm faction is solidly behind him."

"What!? Why haven't I heard anything about this before now?"

"You've been wrapped up in the Cable, Josh. The increase in Believer rhetoric is in your weekly public-opinion status report. The vote . . . it just happened. I tried to get word to you in the air, the storm had the secure channel shut down, and I didn't think you'd want to hear about this on the air-traffic-control frequencies."

"Damn." Crewe was silent for a minute. "What have you got?"

"They've pulled off a coup, gathered their support without a ripple. They're counting the votes now, but you can be sure Plant wouldn't have made his move without being positive of his support."

Crewe picked up the car's phone. "I'll get the jet turned around."

Pelino shook his head. "Don't do that, Josh."

Crewe's face darkened. "What do you mean, 'Don't do that'? I'm the secretary-general. If my government is going to be challenged like this I have to be there."

"It's too late for that. The motion was moved, the vote

is in progress. They have a majority on the floor. They are going to win, and there's going to be an election. We have to start getting ready for that."

"How do you know? How did they get a majority?"

"The Believers have been building their political base for years now. They've finally gotten it to a critical mass." Pelino shrugged. "As to who they've gotten on their side, we'll have to wait and see who votes on their side."

"I should be there. At least I can show my face." Crewe ground his teeth.

"All you'll accomplish by coming in now is to make yourself look desperate, and it'll be worse because we're going to lose. The best thing we can do now is prepare our response, have it out to the media the instant the vote is done."

Crewe nodded, breathing heavily. "There's something wrong here. We've had our own counterpropaganda running. I don't see how they could have come up so quickly."

Pelino nodded. "Something very wrong, boss. We've dropped the ball somewhere, and I'll take responsibility for that. In the meantime we have to get a grip on this."

"This is too soon." Josh looked out the window to the bustling hive that was the build site. "I need more time."

"We have to play the cards we're dealt."

"Right." Crewe inhaled, exhaled slowly. "I'll be back tomorrow. Call a general staff meeting and we'll work out how we're going to handle this." He met Pelino's gaze. "Losing this isn't an option. There's too much at stake to hand the world over to a bunch of religious fanatics."

Pelino smirked. "Losing is never an option. Losing is

what happens when you run out of options. Don't worry, boss, we'll win or go down fighting."

"You're right about that. I need to think about this for a while." Crewe turned to watch out the window as the car took the grade up the mountain. He could see the thunderheads building up out on the plain, soaring, billowing masses of pure white cloud, and he envied the ease with which they climbed to the edge of the stratosphere. If he could command his world as Cheops had commanded Egypt he would not have had to worry that his vision might not be realized, but Cheops' people had not found fulfillment in hauling stone for his glory. *I am not a tyrant, and I will not allow myself to become one.*

Abrahim Kurtaski was waiting for them at the control center at the base of the northernmost subtower. He sent Thom Pelino back in the car to fly back to New York and start working on the election campaign, and went to greet his old friend.

"Abrahim, *z'draste*, are you well?"

"Better than the last time you saw me." Abrahim smiled. "Come and see what we've done."

For an hour Josh toured the site with his chief engineer and lost himself in the details of the vast construction project, issues of politics forgotten while he took in the scope of what had been accomplished there. The towers were soaring skyward so quickly their tops were already far out of sight, and almost out of the stratosphere. The assembly building, using advances Abrahim had gleaned from his experience at Cayambe, was pure poetry in motion, and the organized chaos that was the logistics yard was crowded and busy, keeping raw materials flowing up-tower at the optimum speed. Initially the tower struts had all been prefabricated and shipped in ready-to-assemble form, but there was a huge nanofilament spinning plant going up to custom-build the struts on-site and save the delay in shipping. Another building housed a facility that made the boost cars, each one a twenty-meter spacecraft without engines. The complete system would use hundreds, and though they were still years from completion, that much lead time was required to make sure the Cable would have a full complement of cars when it was finally up. It was hard to believe that had been only an idea a year ago. It was harder to believe that it might be undone in just three months. *We are so close to making this happen.*

When they had finished the tour they went back to Abrahim's spartan office, where the chief engineer poured thick Russian coffee and laced it with vodka.

*"Budmo!"* Abrahim raised his cup. "We've come a long way, *muy droog.*"

*"Budmo!"* Josh raised his own cup, and they both drank deep. He hesitated before he spoke again, not wanting to ruin the mood. *But silence will not change reality.* "I have some bad news."

Abrahim cocked his head. "What is it?"

Josh outlined the political situation, and the no-confidence vote. ". . . and if Markham Plant is secretary-general, this entire project will be over."

Abrahim considered that for a while before speaking. "So what are your chances of winning another term?"

"I still have support on the assembly floor, but not enough. Plant has the True Prophet behind him, and the True Prophet can swing a lot of critical votes. It's going to be an uphill battle." He drummed his fingers on Abrahim's desk. "I need to show progress on something, particularly something that's going to make a difference in NorAm."

"What about the Aerospace Consortium? International Metals? We are providing a lot of work for a lot of people."

"We'll have them on board, but I don't think it will be enough this time. I got in with their backing, and with the dissatisfaction of the public with the previous government. Their backing isn't what it once was; we lost a lot with Harmon Michaud. More important, public dissatisfaction is now Plant's weapon, not mine. That's the source of the Believers' strength." He looked out the window at the bustling logistics yard. "If we could at least finish the Cable and hand it over to private industry, it would be beyond the ability of the General Assembly to take it down." He looked back at Abrahim, the question he didn't dare ask written in his face.

Abrahim read it, and answered it. "I'm sorry, Josh, it's impossible. Three months is another twelve kilometers of tower, no more. If I cut quality control and some safety margins I could make that twenty kilometers, maybe. That would mean accepting some fairly large risks." He spread his arms. "More than that just isn't physically possible."

"I know." Josh leaned forward, rubbing his forehead. "I just need something, anything, to create at least the appearance of success here. I need something to give people faith in civilization, or they're going to turn their backs on us and embrace the True Prophet."

"And vote in Markham Plant." Abrahim furrowed his brow, then looked up. "Give them power."

"Power?"

"Power, electrical energy, to heat their homes, and light their lives. People are pessimistic. Why is that? Because they see their children will live less well than they do. And why is that? Because too many people compete for too few resources. There is no more fundamental resource then energy. Give the people energy and you give them hope. People don't want a great project like the *Ark* if they don't have hope first."

"Nobody knows about *Ark*."

"Josh, everybody knows, it's an open secret now."

"There's been some speculation, but . . ."

"Speculation that everyone believes, and belief is more important than reality."

"So people know." Josh Crewe's voice held an edge of irritation. "This project makes no material difference to the global economy, it takes no food from anyone's mouth."

"No, but the True Prophet has turned it into a symbol, a symbol of government indifference to the needs of the common man, of the official decadence. Symbols are powerful things."

Josh stroked his chin, considering. "I thought we had that countered. Obviously I was wrong. You're right about the need for hope, and you're right that energy is what it's going to take to restore it for the world, but I can't create power plants from nothing."

"No, but you can turn the Cable into one. We are already putting solar foil in orbit to run the boost cars. We can't finish the cable to carry cargo much ahead of schedule, that's a reality. Maybe we can just get a pair of leader lines down in time to tie them to the grid. It won't be a lot of power, but . . ."

Josh nodded. ". . . but it will be a symbol. More important, it will eliminate their symbol." He stood up, reenergized. "That's brilliant, Abraham. Let's make it happen."

"Of course it's brilliant. That's why I'm chief engineer."

For Daffodil Brady, zero gravity had evolved from an exciting novelty to a frustrating challenge to a simple fact of life. The view of Earth and the stars through the viewports was still breathtaking, but she found that life on-orbit allowed little time for sightseeing. The cable spinner had worked fine on the ground, but it had been impossible to test it fully under zero-gravity conditions, and the process needed refinement and tweaking. Experiments that would have been trivial on Earth were greatly complicated by the requirement to go EVA just to make an adjustment or collect a sample of extruded cable. A lot of care was required to prevent longer samples from snarling into hopelessly tangled balls of braided monofilament. It took a month before the process was running the way it should be, and another month of careful testing to prove that the material properties of the Cable were what they should be. And then came the order to change the spin configuration, eliminating both the four main load-carrying strands and the boost-car guide tracks, and spinning only the power conductors. What that was about she couldn't guess, and Abrahim refused to tell her on an open circuit. He would be coming up-orbit to help with the deployment of the solar array, and he would tell her then.

In the meantime, they had to completely reconfigure

the spinner head. The new template was shipped up on the next shuttle, and installing it meant yet another EVA. She volunteered for it, not because she wanted more work, but because she wanted to get better at working in space. She went out with Konstantin Khordovsky, and they started the delicate dance, first removing and securing the old spinner head, and then installing the new one. It was tricky work to position them properly in zero gravity while wearing pressure gloves, and every movement had to be made slowly and carefully.

Which was only typical of her EVA experience. Earth floated above her, a brilliant blue orb, and she realized that once more she would not even have time to glance at it. In reviewing the design for the spin platform she had never considered that such a change might need to be made, and so it was a difficult and painstaking job, complicated by the sensitive X-ray diffraction cameras used to monitor the quality of the extruded strands. They had to be carefully removed first, and then, once they had a replacement template installed, the cameras had to be replaced and carefully realigned.

And then finally they were finished. She reattached her connection tool to her tool belt and gave Khordovsky a thumbs-up. He returned it and she turned to find the airlock, only to hear him come over the radio.

"Platform, this is Khordovsky. We're almost done, we'll be inside in thirty minutes."

"Thirty minutes—" Daf was about to protest, but he put a finger to his faceplate to warn her to silence, then pushed his helmet against hers so he could talk to her without using the radio.

"We have oxygen left. Let's enjoy the view." He swept his arm to take in the Earth and the stars. She nodded and he pushed away gently, to float gently at the end of his tether. Daf breathed out and looked down, aware only of her own breathing. Earth looked so small and fragile, a grapefruit-size beacon of light and life set in infinite empty blackness. *Alone with God*, Khordovsky had said on her first day in space. She put out her hand as though to pick up the blue-white sphere. *Twelve billion people down there, and only a few thousand have seen what I'm seeing now.*

She had thought that thirty minutes would be a long time to float alone in space, but when Khordovsky tapped her on the shoulder to say it was time to go in it seemed as if he had only just left. A line from a poem came to her. *For I have slipped the surly bonds of Earth, and danced the skies on laughter-silvered wings.* Neither said anything on the way in, nor as the lock cycled. They didn't have to.

They stripped out of their suits in the postlock chamber, and he took the opportunity to kiss her. It was gentle, almost casual, a natural extension of the experience they'd just shared. He was a good kisser, and Daf felt herself responding to his well-muscled body, hard against her softness through the thin fabric of their suit liners. *And why shouldn't I have a fling up here if I want one?* Konstantin was handsome and intelligent, and he would know enough to be discreet. *And what about Abrahim? You're too old for crushes, Daffodil.* She and Abrahim had no established relationship, and their respective positions stood in the way of one ever developing. His hands were on her hips, pulling her close, but the postlock chamber wasn't private enough for anything more. She let her lips linger on his for what seemed at once a long time and a short one.

"Later," she whispered, finally.

"Will you come to me?" He didn't let her go.

She gave him a look. "There's no privacy here."

"If you want something enough, you'll find it." He moved to kiss her again, then stopped, just short. "Will you come to me?"

"Maybe," she said, and smiled.

He smirked "'Maybe' means no, but I think you'll change your mind."

Without waiting for a reply he kissed her, hard this time, and broke away before she quite realized that he'd started, winning a small gasp from her throat. He turned to pull on his jumpsuit, and Daf just watched him, the scientist in her already analyzing the contents of the brief encounter. *He's so sure I'll change my mind. He's cocky, that's for sure.* She smiled to herself, admiring his lean, muscular form. *He might also be right.*

"Markham Plant. Because he *believes* in your future." The image cut to a profile shot of Assemblyist Plant with an expression of resolve on his face, backdropped by the darkened silhouette of New York. The voice-over faded and the music rose while the lights across the cityscape winked on one after another until the scene blazed with light. Crewe made a gesture to freeze the display on the last frame. The most effective thing about the advertising was the emphatic way it drove its point home. Plant's endorsement by the True Prophet was never stated, simply underscored by the emphasis the voice-over put on the word "believes." That told the Believers all they needed to know, while doing nothing to alienate those who might disagree with a blatantly religious political agenda. The lighting up of New York implied that Plant would solve the energy crisis, but by making the claim nonverbally it spared him any questions on how he might accomplish that. The NorAm faction's unrelenting attacks on Crewe's government on the energy issue were enough for a public hungry to lay blame for the current state of the situation.

He made another gesture and the True Prophet's most recent widecast replaced the commercial spot. It was an outdoor rally, and the crowd was angry, shouting and carrying signs denouncing the government. The scene cut back to the Prophet, arms upraised as he exhorted the cheering throng of Believers. His speech was on the Cable project, castigating the government for defying the will of God while people went cold and hungry on Earth.

Crewe blanked the display. The election was still a month away, and a lot could change in that time. *But if nothing changes, then they are going to win.* The fact was there, black and unpleasant but undeniable, written in poll numbers that bespoke the frustration of the world's public with the status quo. The Believers had expanded far beyond their NorAm base now. Eurasia had come to support their position, as the inexorable laws of supply and demand drove the price of energy out of reach of the average citizen in the nations of the Old World and the East. All told no more than five percent of the world's population would swing their vote to the True Prophet's command. The built-in inequities of the General

Assembly gave them a voting bloc of perhaps ten percent of the floor. A small number, but in a world where every region voted for its own agenda it made the Believer faction the largest single voting bloc. Their voices would override the rest of the world.

*And more people will start to follow them.* Whatever humanity's long-term future, in the short term there could only be more power shortages, less resources, higher prices, less opportunity. That was a reality beyond the ability of any mere politician to change. In the long term the energy crisis might yet be eased, but that would come too late to save Josh Crewe. Or the *Ark*.

And the Cable project was spinning power leads down from orbit as fast as it could, but there was no guarantee the system would be in place in time to sway the election. Crewe waved his hand angrily to bring up his contact list, pointed live a call to a number he'd had for a while but never used. The other end rang and a man answered, and he spoke. "I need a meeting with Norman Bissell."

In politics you learned fast or you failed. Josh Crewe had enough experience to know when it was time to cut a deal.

A week later he found himself on his way to Norman Bissell's private residence. He would rather have flown his own volanter; instead a UN jet flew him into Richmond, Virginia, and then he went in a ground car with an escort. It was not a publicized media event, but neither was he trying to keep his visit secret. As Thom Pelino pointed out, it would do his public image no harm in NorAm to be seen visiting the True Prophet. *Such are the times we live in.*

Bissell's home was on a large farm in the rolling hills of rural Virgina, set in tilled fields and extensive orchards of apples and peaches, and surrounded by well-built barns. Bearded men in plain blue serge shirts worked the fields with horse-drawn plows and wagons. The house itself was large but plain, clapboard-sided with big windows. He left his escort outside and went in to be greeted by an attractive young woman waiting outside the door. She introduced herself as Beth, and he wondered if she was one of the True Prophet's wives. Inside, the house seemed to be a step back in time, with oil lanterns hanging on walls and hand-thrown rugs on the waxed hardwood floor, wood stoves in the rooms to provide heat. Beth showed him in to Bissell's inner sanctum. The True Prophet's study was surprisingly spartan. *In this I have something in common with him.* Crewe filed the observation as potentially useful. *I'm here to find common ground.* With their positions so diametrically opposed, even the smallest shared characteristic might prove to be a useful lever. The desk was wood and looked handmade. The prophet might well have made it himself; he had started out as a carpenter. The vidscreen on the wall seemed jarringly out of place.

Crewe's reverie was interrupted by the arrival of Bissell himself, who came in and shook his hand with restraint. *So he will not pretend we are friends, which may be good or bad.* His host waved him into a plush leather armchair by the glass-topped coffee table, and he took one himself. "And how is Dr. Kurtaski?" Norman Bissell's tone didn't hold the concern that his words expressed.

"He's recovered, and back working." Crewe clenched his jaw unconsciously with the effort of remaining cordial with his adversary. *He's telling me this to let me know that he knows my friendships, knows the details of my life, knows me.*

"Good, good." The Prophet's smile was almost genuine. "The eruption was such a tragedy. An act of God . . ." The smile broadened. ". . . although not unforeseen. I had hoped you might act to avoid further tragedy."

"Meaning what?"

"Isn't it obvious? God has sent you a message. You would be wise to listen."

Crewe met the Prophet's gaze and held it. "If you think I'm going to shut down the Cable project, you're wrong."

"Mr. Secretary-General." Norman Bissell spread his arms expansively. "You defied God, and God struck you down. How many times will you try His patience?"

"As many times as necessary. The world needs this project, and I am going to see it finished." His words carried the force of angry conviction, and he pushed himself back in his chair as a physical reminder to retain self-control. *If he can goad me to anger he wins.* He took a deep slow breath to calm himself.

The Prophet shook his head. "That's where you're wrong, Dr. Crewe. The world does not need this project. The world needs hope, the world needs faith, and the world needs a government that understands those values." He walked over to look out the windows and out over the harbor. "The world needs a leader, not a deluded visionary with stars in his eyes." He turned back and gestured behind him. "It's dark out there, Dr. Crewe. There are riots in the streets, there is hunger and there is fear. Thirty percent of the NorAm crop was lost this summer because the farmers couldn't get the power credits to harvest it. Thirty percent. We are living in the end times, Dr. Crewe. The people understand that."

"We won't solve today's problems by turning our back on technology."

"Simplicity and devotion to God are the way to salvation, and we are going to need salvation soon. The Four Horsemen of the Apocalypse are saddled and waiting. Famine is only the first to ride. War is not far behind, and where War and Famine scythe souls, Plague follows close. And Death, Dr. Crewe . . ." Bissell's eyes burned demon-bright. "Death will stride high over the land and strike down the ungodly in their millions. Your *Ark* is no salvation."

Crewe snorted. "My *Ark* is our only salvation."

Norman Bissell smiled a nasty smile. "So you admit your true goal at last."

"Perhaps you've convinced me that it's the only way to save our civilization."

"You say that because you have no faith in your heart. I don't fear the Apocalypse. The Messiah is coming and those who have accepted God into their hearts will be saved." The Prophet's eyes burned with the zeal of the true believer, almost frightening in their intensity. "Those who don't will be condemned to burn in Hell. No starship can save you from that."

Crewe looked at him. "You know, Mr. Bissell, I can never decide if you are the most cynical and manipulative man I have ever met, or simply the most deluded." Even as he said it Josh Crewe regretted the words. *I am goading him for goading me.*

The Prophet just laughed. "So if I believe what I say

I'm deluded, if I don't I'm simply fraudulent. It seems I have no way to gain your respect, Dr. Crewe." He stood up. "Of course, it is more complicated than that. You didn't become secretary-general without understanding the dynamics of power, or the power of ambition. Let me be perfectly frank with you." The Prophet pointed at the ceiling-high figure of Jesus Christ on the cross that hung on the wall across from his desk. "The Bible commands that we do not worship graven images, and yet we do. The Bible tells us that the meek shall inherit the Earth, and yet it is the strong who rule it. People have always worshipped lifeless stone made into the shape of their gods, and people have always elevated men strong enough to command them into living Gods on Earth." He paused and met Crewe's gaze. "I am such a man, Mr. Secretary-General. I have wrought myself into a form that other men will worship. I have shaped myself with care, because I aspired to become God's Voice on the earthly plane, to rule the world as God intends it to be ruled. I have anointed myself as Prophet to command the spiritual obedience of my followers. That has required more than just simple faith, that has required tactics and strategy. You might call that manipulative, but I would say I simply understand the realities of power. You see how I preach against technology and yet use the tools of civilization to advance my goals, and you might call that cynical." He shrugged. "I would say I use the tools of Satan to do God's work. I will bend the General Assembly to command the lawful obedience of everyone else. Humanity will face the End Time in a state of grace under my leadership."

Josh Crewe looked at his adversary with more than a

little awe. *His arrogance is total, and yet . . . Coming from anyone else such a grandiose ambition would have seemed ludicrous. Coming from the True Prophet it seemed . . . prophetic.*

The Prophet sat down again. "Look in the mirror, Dr. Crewe, and tell me that your vision is any less arrogant than mine. You're as much a true believer in your vision as I am in mine, maybe more. The difference between us is that your faith is built on secular sand, while mine is founded on the rock of the Word."

"Perhaps. That doesn't mean we can't find common ground."

"You're forgetting one thing, Dr. Crewe."

"What's that?"

"God has ordained my victory." The True Prophet paused, considering. "It's true that He helps those who help themselves, I don't expect to win without fighting, without sacrificing. I do think I can expect to win without making a deal with Satan."

"Is that what you believe?" Crewe looked at the Prophet with disbelief.

"That you are the devil incarnate?" Bissell laughed. "No, of course not, Dr. Crewe, but in defying God's will you ally yourself with His Adversary."

"I notice your obedience to God's commands seems well allied with your own personal interests."

Bissell's face darkened. "Are you implying that my motives are less pure than yours? Look around you. I live simply, not in splendor. The earthly power I claim is used in the service of God, and in the service of those who suffer here on Earth. My followers are real, live people who are suffering every day, Dr. Crewe. They are real, live people whose immortal souls are at stake in the coming Judgment."

*And now is the time to apply the pressure.* "Interpol is investigating the use of Ceranine at the Times Square rally."

The Prophet nodded and smiled a tight smile. "A regrettable incident. We've cooperated with the investigation fully, of course."

"They've made linkages to Believers, and more to Markham Plant."

The Prophet raised an eyebrow. "I think you're angry with me, Dr. Crewe, but I wasn't the one who struck down your Tower of Babel, it was God."

"It wasn't God who laced those streamers with Ceranine."

"Neither was it me. You tread a dangerous line, Mr. Secretary-General." The Prophet's expression hardened. "That riot was caused by the police, not the Believers."

"There's video of you inciting the crowd to riot. There's enough evidence there to see you in prison."

"You underestimate the power of belief, Dr. Crewe. Those who have pledged to follow me through Heaven and Hell will surely rise up at my arrest." Bissell leaned back in his chair, contemplating Crewe as though he could measure his soul through sufficient scrutiny. "Perhaps you could attain a conviction, but it would cost you all you've labored for."

"According to you, I've lost it anyway." The Prophet's eyes narrowed, and Crewe took a deep breath. *I must not lose sight of my goal here.* "I haven't come here to argue,

I've come to find how we might find our own interests aligned. We don't have to be enemies."

"And how would that work?"

"I need you, I need your people."

"You won't buy my support, not at any price."

"I don't want political support, politics are just a means to the end. What I need is your faith, and your commitment, and your way of life. Not for any political ambition of mine, I have none beyond seeing *Ark* built. The voyage will take thousands of years. The major ship systems can be designed to last that long, the ecology will be self-sustaining. The society is another question. It will have to be built around hand labor and basic farming. Your people are almost unique in having preserved those skills. It will have to be built around faith and tradition, to keep alive the memory of Earth and the vision of the future. Who better than the Believers to do that?"

Bissell stood up. "You dare to suggest—"

"Hear me out. You say we're living in the end times, and I think you're right. We have too many people and not enough land, not enough power, not enough food. Our civilization can't last, our species may not long survive it, at least not in its present form. You say my sky cable is the Tower of Babel. What if it's really Jacob's ladder, a stairway to heaven. What if *Ark* is really humanity's last hope?"

"You aren't the next Noah, Dr. Crewe."

"I know I'm not. Have you considered that perhaps you are?" *Appeal to his ego.*

"An interesting idea." The Prophet sat down again and stroked his chin. "Where are you going with it?"

"*Ark* won't be a ship, it'll be a world, a world with its

own sun, its own sea, its own soil. I can build it to run for ten thousand years, give it power to reach the stars. What I can't do is give it all the resources of Earth. It won't have minerals to mine or hydrocarbons to pump. Whoever lives there will have to build their own tools of wood and sinew, grow their own food with their own hands."

Bissell's face hardened. "You want to exile me."

Crewe shook his head. "It will be decades before the ship is ready, and you'll be here on Earth for all that time. You're a young man, you might live to see it launched. I certainly won't. My goal is simple: I want to see humanity reach the stars. I'm offering you the chance to shape a whole world in your own image. I need you, and your people, to realize my own vision."

The Prophet leaned back, considering. "It's tempting, of course, but temptation is what the Serpent does best. God is using you to test me, and I won't falter. It is against His will for mankind to violate the Heavens."

"Wherever heaven is, it isn't in space. Consider the value of what I'm giving you here, it's an opportunity that no man has had since Moses led his people to the Promised Land. We don't have to be enemies."

"Thank you for your offer." The True Prophet stood up. "Unfortunately I have other business to attend to now. I'll pray for your soul, Dr. Crewe." He offered his hand.

Crewe shook it, nodded formally and went out. Outside the door he breathed out slowly to release the tension. *I've failed. Everything is up to Abrahim now.* The woman who'd shown him in showed him out again. Outside it was starting to rain.

✡✡✡

The New York City police said there were a million people in Central Park, and the tumultuous babble of their voices was a steady backdrop to the steady buzz of conversation in Norman Bissell's control tent. The True Prophet didn't know how they came up with their crowd size estimate, but there was no question it was a big rally. He smiled at that thought. It had been a struggle to get approval for it, given what had happened at the last one, but there were differences. This one was in daylight, for starters. *And this time Markham Plant is under control.* The True Prophet was unconvinced of the sincerity of Plant's devotion to the Believer creed; the man was too opportunistic a politician, too willing to let the end justify the means to be fully trusted. *And yet the end does justify the means when the cause is the glorification of God.* He glanced out the half-open door of the control tent, at the crowd. The white and red and green robes of his followers formed solid wedges of color in the sea of faces. Inside the tent there was a steady buzz of activity as his inquisitors and bishops coordinated the myriad details required to make the event run while he went over the notes for his sermon. The point of today's rally was not to challenge the government but to solidify political support for the Believer faction in the General Assembly. *And Markham Plant remains a tool in my plan, for all his opportunism.* God's will would not be denied, and the assemblyist would come into office knowing to whom he owed his position.

He looked over to where Plant was going over his own notes. There had been a NorAm-wide blackout just three days previously, and public frustration was at an all-time high, anger that would be put to good use in the imminent election. *God has ordained it for our victory.*

Outside, the crowd was starting to chant. "Believe! Believe! Believe!" He stood up. It was time, and there was now nothing that could stand in their way.

As the only passenger on the shuttle, Abrahim rode on the flight deck, in the observer's seat behind and between the pilot and the navigator. Launch was exhilarating, a roller-coaster ride that ended in orbit. Orbital maneuvering was not, though it got more interesting once the spin platform came into view. From a distance it was unremarkable, a fat disk against the star-spattered blackness, looking like a bad imitation of a flying saucer. Abrahim was impressed anyway; he knew what had gone into making it fly. As the shuttle drew closer details began to resolve themselves. Antennas and solar panels protruded from the top, and the gossamer strands of nanofilament conductor extruded themselves from the bottom, visible at this distance only when the sunlight caught the separators that linked the two wires together. They had managed to successfully deorbit the assembly, now connected to a header station hastily constructed atop the Mount Kenya space tower. *We are so close to making this happen.* The reduced cable was a fragile thing; doped for conductivity at the expense of strength, it was barely capable of supporting its own weight, incapable of being repaired. It would not long survive the ravages of the upper atmosphere. It would carry power, not cargo, and not even a great deal of power, when measured against the insatiable demand of an over-crowded world. *But it will be a symbol, and right now a symbol is what we need.* If they were successful the real Cable would soon take the place of this one. If they weren't—then the shuttle he was on would be one of the last shuttles to fly, ever. Abrahim frowned. *I mustn't allow myself to consider failure.*

Beyond the spin platform, showing just a brilliant crescent but still dwarfing the platform, was the main mirror of the orbital smelter, a project currently suspended so that all available resources could be concentrated on making some kind of orbital power station a functional reality. It was five hundred meters across, a film of aluminized plastic just a few molecules thick, bent into a faceted parabolic dish by inflatable struts hardly more substantial than the mirror surface itself. At its focus half a gigawatt of sunlight was concentrated into a space just a meter square, power enough to flash-boil aluminum. It was the largest human-crafted object ever to fly in space, but it was going to be far eclipsed by the solar array they were about to deploy.

The pilot fired the thrusters to position them for docking, and the view rotated until he could see only stars. He kept quiet while the pilot and navigator chattered back and forth, guiding them in on instruments. Eventually there was a gentle thunk and they were docked. Abrahim waited impatiently for the lock to cycle, more anxious to see Daf Brady than he cared to admit. *It's been so long.* Devoting one's life to a mission had its costs, and one was that personal relationships tended to go by the wayside. It was perhaps too much to ask to expect a woman as intelligent and attractive as Daf Brady to stay unattached for any length of time. *We had an attraction, a kiss, another kiss, that's all.* He had hoped to see her—the original plan had slated her to come back to Earth once the cable was spun—but the reality of the compressed development schedule had meant that she had simply stayed in orbit.

She was there, but there was time only for the briefest meeting as he came aboard, a handshake when he was introduced to the whole spin-platform crew. Was it longer, was it warmer than it should have been? If it was it wasn't by much. The tall Khordovsky stood beside her, his hand casually on her shoulder. *Is there something there?*

*Push the thought aside, Abrahim, you have work to do.* After his gear had been brought aboard and the pilots had gone back to the shuttle to begin off-loading the solar-array package, he held a briefing, using finger and sketchscreen to brief the EVA crew on the next day's operation. It would be tricky. The solar array used the same inflated-strut technology that the smelting mirror did, but it was a hundred times bigger, large enough to generate ten gigawatts of electrical power, enough to power the transport cars on the cable's boost track, enough to power *Ark*'s construction, enough, most importantly, to supply a surplus to Earth's power-starved billions and provide some immediate justification for the continuation of the project.

*Which won't placate those who claim we're violating God's heaven.* It amazed Abrahim that in this day and age there were still those who believed such things. He pulled his mind back to the briefing and carried on with his key points. The solar array was cobweb-fragile, and the most delicate automated assembly task that Abrahim had ever designed. Because of its fragility, as every fold opened up it had to be checked for snags, and they had to be cleared with the utmost care before the deployment could continue. That meant four people in suits with maneuvering backpacks had to go outside for the deployment, checking each blossoming section as it opened, ready to tease apart stuck sections with special compressed-gas cylinders.

"Be careful," Abrahim emphasized. "Even these can exert enough force to tear the film. And be very careful when you're maneuvering close to the film. The reaction gas from your backpacks is strong enough to blow holes in it if you get too close. Take your time. Remember, haste is not speed. We've only got one chance to do this right."

The briefing ended, and he'd hoped to find time to talk to Daffodil then, but there was too much to be done first, preparing equipment, testing procedures, getting the power connections ready, and then exhaustion overcame him. With the preparations for launch in Baikonur he hadn't slept in thirty hours. His body clock and the spin-platform clock both agreed that it was noon, but he went to sleep anyway, so he would at least have some rest before deployment started at sunset. Four hours later the harsh bleating of his alarm dragged him from a pleasant dream, its fragments dissolving as he woke, leaving only a memory of Daf's face as he had dreamed it.

Supper was served in tubes, augmented by fresh fruit brought aboard the shuttle. Again there was no chance to talk to Daf. Immediately after eating they began preparations for the deployment. The election was in less than a week. *If this symbol is to have any influence, it must come into play immediately. We can afford no more delays.* If the Cable was complete and sending power down to the grid before the election, it would be deemed a success. Josh Crewe might then hold on to his position, and then the *Ark* project could begin in earnest. If it wasn't complete, the whole effort would be for nothing. And that isn't the only consequence. *If the Believer faction wins, science will suffer everywhere, and humanity will begin its long slide back to the stone age.*

They had another short briefing before the EVA, just to confirm everybody's role. Khordovsky led the outside team; the shuttle crew would use the shuttle's manipulators to position the packed array, and the shuttle's inertial mass would serve to stabilize it and, hopefully, keep it from getting folded over on itself and tangling as it expanded. Abrahim would supervise the deployment from inside the spin platform, using a series of cameras that were integral to the solar array's frame, as well as a free-floating camera bot with its own attitude jets. The original plan had Daf inside to assist, but the outside team was shorthanded as it was, and she was not only suit-qualified but good at it. He was disappointed by that, but tried not to let it show. *I'm letting my personal feelings get in the way of my work.* That could be a problem.

They timed the start of the deployment for sunset. That gave them slightly under twelve hours to get the array deployed, the time when the sun would be hidden behind the Earth. Taking longer than that would expose the gossamer web of photoplastic to full sunlight, and the full ten gigawatts of power would begin to flow. If any of the array was still folded when that happened, the sandwiched fine web of carbon-fiber conductors that both held the structure together and carried its electrical output would short out, and the array would destroy itself. It was all or nothing. In simulation on the ground it took eight hours to get the whole job done, and in simulation a fifty-percent safety margin had seemed ample. Doing the job for real, with so much riding on it, made the risk suddenly seem much higher.

The central conductors were no thicker than heavy twine, not true superconductors, but still carrying more current than a copper wire a thousand times thicker. Farther from the center the conductors' diameter decreased until they were delicate threads barely visible under close inspection with the naked eye. The riggers suited up and went outside while Abrahim watched them through the external cameras, orchestrating their movements over the radio as the operation began. The EVA crew had to be supremely careful, because even without direct sunlight, the glow of the crescent moon was enough to put thousands of volts through the system. Accidental contact with a main conductor would be fatal. His part of the work was delicate and painstaking, monitoring the deployment system that itself monitored the gas pressure in the inflatable strutwork.

Initially the deployment went well. The shuttle off-loaded the bulky deployment packages with its onboard manipulator and then, its mission complete, disengaged from the spin platform, backed slowly away, and then deorbited. The initial assembly of the packages also went quickly, but inevitably they fell behind getting the framework erected; once opened, the huge array sections were unwieldy and their considerable inertia made them difficult to handle and difficult to lock into position. Working in the sharp darkness of the Earth's shadow only made the task harder, and Abrahim began to worry that they might not finish in time. Each section had to be erected individually, its separate segments teased into opening by the riggers, working delicately with their gas jets to overcome the film's natural tendancy to stick to itself. The power leads fed into the huge control rectifiers mounted on top of the spin platform, and from there Abrahim's instruments monitored the power output. As the first section of array opened, the voltage readings slowly rose, and the immense array blossomed like some cybernetic flower under the ministrations of its human keepers.

They were in the last phases when they ran into trouble. The first sign was fluctuating voltage readings from one of the deploying sections. He ordered Daffodil over to check it out, and she quickly found the problem. There was a tear in one of the inflatable tubes that provided rigidity to the structure. Gas leaking from the rip had set the section into a semirhythmic undulating motion, which in turn had wrapped the superfine foil around itself. The voltage fluctuations were coming from microscopic short circuits where the collector wires were touching each other. The potential across the shorts wasn't high enough to do serious damage, not yet, but when the sun rose and hit the array, they would arc and burn out.

Khordovsky jetted over to join her. "It looks bad," he radioed. "We may have to cut this section out."

"Stand by." Abrahim called up the elaborate mesh of the solar array's wiring diagram. Some sections could be removed with little impact on the array. Some sections were primary current carriers that were necessary to collect power from other sections. He quickly traced the problem, only to realize that cutting out the damaged section would be a hazard to the power production capability of the entire array. He keyed his microphone. "Negative, we have to fix it."

"What are the voltage readings?"

Abrahim checked his instruments. "Three hundred kilovolts, approximately. Be careful."

There was silence for a time, then, "I don't think we can do this. The foil is moving too much. It's too risky."

*Too risky.* Abrahim balled his fists in frustration. *Doesn't he know what's at stake here?* "Daffodil, what's your assessment?"

Her transmitter clicked on, but for a long moment there was only the hiss of empty air. "I have to agree, getting that close is asking for trouble. I could tape the leak easily enough if the foil wasn't moving. As it is . . ." She left the sentence unfinished.

Abrahim ground his teeth and glanced at the mission clock. They had just under two hours left before the sun came up and fully energized the array. *I should suit up myself and go fix it . . .* He knew that idea wasn't going anywhere. Khordovsky was an experienced space rigger, Daf had six months on-station, and while Abrahim was trained in a suit, he wasn't skilled in it. Just getting himself ready would take most of those two hours, and he'd probably fry himself on the array as soon as he got out there. *But I can't just abandon this, I owe it to Josh to get this running. He's the one who believed in me.*

He keyed his transmitter again. "Confirmed. Stand by." He drummed his fingers on his console. If the shuttle hadn't departed he might have used its manipulators to correct the problem, though the strength of its attitude jets would put the fragile solar film at some risk. *No use considering that, Abrahim, the shuttle is gone.* The first thing to do was stop the problem from getting worse. He keyed his console, shutting off the gas flow to that section of the array, then swung his external cameras around to give him the best view, and ordered the camera bot to move up behind Khordovsky and Daffodil to get a better view of the damaged section.

What he saw was not encouraging. The tear was only as big as his thumb, but the tangled section was fifty meters long, and included a six-meter section of the main power bus. He glanced around the control cabin; a broom handle would give enough insulation and distance, if they put the tape on the end of the handle and then gently slid it onto the damaged section . . . A second later he was laughing at himself for looking for such a thing as a broom on a space station in zero gravity.

*But there must be something.* He slid himself into the main cabin and found Ruiz, the station chief. "I need an insulated pole, about so long." He held his arms apart to indicate the length, and shortly the entire onboard crew was ripping open storage lockers and tool chests looking for anything that might help in solving the problem. *And really, we should have brought something like this, we should have anticipated the problem and planned for it.* Of course, they hadn't, because the accelerated schedule necessary to meet the artificial deadline of the unexpected election had completely short-circuited the normal check-out and test process. *We threw this together at the last minute for purely political reasons, and now we're paying the price for it.* Like Cayambe.

And of course there was nothing on the station they could use as an insulated pole—nothing they could afford to rip out, at any rate. Abrahim went back to his station and called Khordovsky. "I'm looking at getting you something insulated so you can get close enough to tape the leak. Any bright idea you have, now is the time to bring it out."

"We need at least two meters of length," he radioed back. "And we need it fast."

"*Da,* acknowledged." Abrahim glanced at the mission clock again. They'd lost half an hour already and were no closer to a solution. He maneuvered his camera bot closer to the damaged area to get a better look. *Such a tiny tear to change the course of history.* He zoomed in, the better to document his downfall.

*Zoomed in. What if we used the camera bot?* "Daffodil, can you put a length of sealing tape across the camera lens on the camera bot? I'm going to try to fly it into position."

"I can. Are you sure you're going to have fine enough control?"

"I don't know. I'm the automated assembly expert. If I can't make a robot do it, nobody can. I'm going to try."

"I'll do it." There was a pause, and then her hand obscured the screen as she positioned the tape. "Okay, go for it."

The tape blurred the camera's view, but not too badly. Abrahim held his breath, and nudged the bot's translation joystick, just a fraction, to start it toward the torn tube. Very slowly the solar array began to get closer in the image. The trick was to do everything very gently. He glanced at the mission clock again. *Not too slowly.* They were running out of time. He rotated the bot slightly, nudged the controller again to speed up its approach rate slightly. The tape on the lens obscured the rip, but that was exactly what he needed. As long as he kept bringing the bot closer and kept the rip invisible, the tape would line up over it perfectly on contact.

Except that when the rip was invisible, it was impossible to tell if he was lined up properly. In practice he had to wait until he saw a corner of it peeking out from beyond the edge of the tape, and then make an ever-so-gentle correction to the bot's trajectory. He also had to watch out for the overhanging folds of solar foil. Allowing one of the embedded conductors to touch the bot would destroy it as surely as it would kill a person. Almost as an afterthought he ordered Khordovsky and Daffodil to back away from the operation. *No need for them to be close if something goes wrong.* As the image of the support tube grew steadily closer the corrections became more and more frequent. The scene became blurry as the camera lens got closer to the target than its autofocus mechanism allowed it to adjust for, making the job even harder. Finally, inches away, he made one final correction, and let the bot drift into the support tube while he watched to see if he'd found his target.

The screen went black, and he nearly screamed in sudden frustration. He must've lost track of where the overhanging foil was, or a random ripple had somehow brought it into contact with the bot's metal casing. He hit the joystick controller by reflex to bring the bot back out of the area, but even as he did so he knew it was too late. The bot was destroyed, and with it any chance he had of salvaging the deployment operation. It would be possible to get a replacement module for that array section sent up, but that wouldn't happen until after the election, which really meant it wouldn't happen at all.

He became aware of voices in his head set. Daffodil. "Abrahim, you did it, you did it. It's in position! The tape is right where it needs to be."

"I lost the screen, what happened to the bot?"

"It looks like the top bracket hit a conductor. It's fried, Abrahim, but it doesn't matter. The support tube is fixed. Give it some gas pressure, and we'll see if it holds."

Abrahim hit keys, restarting the gas flow to the damaged array section, and soon he could see the support tube stiffening, and in the process unfolding the tangled foil. Daffodil and Khordovsky moved in, using their gas jets to separate stuck sections. The deployment continued, and there were seven minutes left on the mission clock when the airlock door finally closed behind the EVA team. There was champagne then, four bottles of it that Abrahim had smuggled up on the shuttle. Nobody was supposed to drink in space, but . . . *I am the chief engineer, and who's going to tell me not to today?*

The party went on for some hours, inviting all the usual horseplay that zero gravity invited, and Abrahim went to bed in his tiny bunk when he could no longer hold his eyes open. He was awakened some timeless time later by a hand on his chest. He opened his eyes, struggling to focus in the darkness, and saw Daffodil. She held a finger to her lips, then whispered, "We have to be very quiet. There's no privacy here." She slid herself into the narrow confines of his bed, her body warm and soft against his. He started to say something, but she kissed him first, and really that seemed like a more important thing to do.

"We're ready when you are, Josh." Thom Pelino was relaxed and confident, in his element orchestrating the press, the cameras, the myriad details that went into a major address by the secretary-general on the eve of a critical election.

Josh Crewe nodded. He was tired from three months of nonstop campaigning, tired of interviews, tired of speeches, tired of shaking hands and smiling at people, but most of all just tired. *But this is the road I've chosen for myself, and tonight is not the night to falter.* Thom stepped onto the stage to introduce him, and he took that moment to gather himself before following a moment later. He took the podium as photo flashes lit up the briefing room.

"Ladies and gentlemen, I know you all have a lot of questions about the election, about the direction that I have been taking the General Assembly. Before I go into those issues, I'd like to address one in particular. A large number of people have expressed a great deal of concern over the money that we have been investing in UNISE, in particular in the Cable project." *No need to mention the Believers by name.* "They have been quite right to do so. In a democratic world it is the responsibility of the government to ensure the needs of the people are met." He paused to look around the room, to meet every eye in it. *This is the critical moment.* "I can now tell you that we have successfully deployed the largest solar array ever built in orbit, connected to the Cable's spin platform. This solar array is now providing gigawatts of free power to the Central African power grid, and will provide even more as we expand the system. This world faces a great many challenges right now. It faces no challenge so great as the need for energy. Energy to light and heat our homes, energy to fuel the production necessary to raise the standard of living worldwide. It's no secret that as our population has gone up, quality of life has gone down for much of the world. I intend to see that trend reversed. There are those who have preached simplicity as the answer to the challenges we face. Simplicity can be part of the answer, but without cheap and abundant energy resources, simplicity alone will not suffice for the needs of an advanced civilization the size of ours." He let that sink in for a moment, and then stood back from the podium, to let his audience know he was finished. Immediately every hand in the press gallery shot up. He picked a reporter at random.

"Secretary-General, this project is in Africa. Can you tell us how soon NorAm will see similar benefits?"

"Immediately. The power added to the Central African grid will offset power normally imported over the transatlantic power system from NorAm. In addition, we are now in a position to rapidly add more solar arrays to the system, and we are planning one for the NorAm/SouthAm grid right now." Josh picked another reporter. "Next question?"

"Secretary-General, what about the rumors that you intend to use the Cable as boost infrastructure to mine the asteroids. Can you comment on those?"

Josh smiled. "They're true. Of course energy alone is not the entire answer. We also need raw materials. When the Cable project is complete it will provide us with easy access to high orbit, and to the rest of the solar system and the vast and untapped resources within it. With the success of this technology, I think I can safely say that my government is now prepared to lead the world into a new age of prosperity." He paused. "I would also like to take this opportunity to announce a new project, a project only made possible by the capabilities the Cable has brought us. A project to fire the imaginations of not just our generation but generations to come. This will be a tremendous undertaking, one which will ensure the future of human civilization for all time. I have directed the United Nations Institute for Space Exploration to build an interstellar colony ship, to carry the seeds of humanity to the stars and beyond."

There was stunned silence in the room, and then the same reporter continued. "Sir, if I can ask why?"

"Because I believe in the human race, and I believe in our future. I believe that we must ensure our posterity by spreading it far beyond this tiny globe. I believe that humanity needs the inspiration of great projects, and the challenge of reaching out, and as long as I'm secretary-general, I'm going to pursue programs that realize the small dreams of individuals, and the great dreams that are common to us all."

Josh stopped there and looked out at the thunderstruck faces of the press, every one of them now frantically taking notes. The biggest news of the day had lasted under thirty seconds before it was replaced by even bigger news. In a few minutes the story would break, and the political ambitions of Markham Plant and every other Believer assemblyist would end forever with the next newsfeed. The True Prophet was finished as a power broker. The Believer movement itself wouldn't end so quickly, but it would fade now, and by the time it was finally gone its ending wouldn't rate even page-four news. *We needed a symbol. Now we have it, and the people have something better to believe in than self-styled prophets.* The *Ark* had seized the stage, and with another term to entrench its position in the economy he knew it would be built.

One or two of the reporters had stopped jotting notes and looked up to see what bombshell he might drop on them next, perhaps to see if he really meant what he had said. He smiled broadly "Yes, it's true, ladies and gentlemen, we're going to build that ship. That's official, you can publish that. Humanity is going to the stars." He smiled broadly. "You can publish that too."

# Intermezzo

*We are one with God in birth and death.*
                    —Anonymous14

# L–55

The nurse opened the big double doors from the living room, to let in the warm air of a Burgundy country night. The farmstead had been built into the hillside, some twelve hundred years earlier, because the high cliffs offered natural protection from marauders, and because the spring nearby gave an ample supply of clean water. There was nothing left of the original buildings, but the current farmhouse and barn built around the high-walled courtyard were easily seven hundred years old, their basic structure still intact despite the repeated renovation of the interior. This farm had been first, at least so far as the historians could tell, but eventually other farms had arrived, and a town had grown around the spring, with merchants lining narrow, cobblestoned streets, and then an abbey, a cathedral and eventually two, a chateau and finally a canal. All of the town's wealth had come from the vineyards then, and even now most of it still did. It was a peaceful place, and though she had been reluctant to leave the bright lights of Paris, she had come to be glad that she had.

There was a noise behind her, and she turned to see her patient, carefully negotiating the stairs. She turned to him.

"It's late, *M'sieur*. You should be sleeping."

"Probably." He took another step down, his hand trembling on the balustrade, and she went to help him. "But I can't sleep, so I'm here." His few remaining hairs were long and white and straggling, and the effort of coming down from the top floor had made him short of breath.

"And you should call me to help you on the stairs. *Mon Dieu*, imagine if you should fall."

"I can still get myself around."

She pursed her lips disapprovingly but didn't say anything more, and helped him down the last stairs. He had been a great man once, and such men usually adapted poorly to the restrictions of age and infirmity. When he was down she brought over his wheelchair, and he sank into it with evident relief.

"Is it clear out?"

"It's beautiful."

"Take me outside, please."

She smiled and wheeled him through the already open doors and onto the flagstones of the courtyard. It had been a hundred years at least since the barn had seen a cow, the ancient byre long since converted to garage space, but the original timbers still held up the roof, rough-hewn and blackened with age. She could hear the spring burbling in the background, as it had for the long-forgotten farmsteader who'd originally claimed this little piece of France. *Nothing ever changes here.* Even the canal was three hundred years old, and little new had been built since then, though the abbey was now a community center, and the chateau a hospital.

"Can you bring my binoculars?"

"They're right here. I knew you would want them."

"*Merci.*" He took them and held them to his eyes, searching up into the southern sky with trembling hands. There was a star there, brighter than the others, almost big enough to perceive as a distinct shape.

"It gets bigger every time, doesn't it? Brighter?"

"It does, *M'sieur.*" In truth she couldn't see that it did, but it seemed important for him to believe it was true. She wasn't even sure he could see it at all, not really, between the trembling of his hands and the grey fog that obscured his once sharp eyes. *And yet he always knows where to look.* She waited patiently while he lowered the heavy lenses, then raised them to look again, and glanced at her watch. *An hour to go.* One more hour and then the overnight nurse would come and she could go home. Guillame would have Sophie in bed, and they could have a little time together before bed themselves. The evening shifts weren't bad, and . . .

There was a *clunk*, and she looked down to see the binoculars on the flagstones. For a second she thought her charge had fallen asleep, as he often did at such times, but there was something wrong. Quickly she knelt before him, starting a quick first-aid assessment. He was breathing, but one look at his face told her all she needed to know; the left side side was slack, the other normal. She took his hands in hers to confirm her suspicion, found the left side limp. *A stroke, and a big one.* She took out her pad, tapped it once to call the ambulance.

"No . . ." Her patient was speaking. He caught her arm with his right hand, his grip surprisingly strong.

"*Quoi?*"

"No . . . let me go . . ."

"*M'sieur . . .*"

"Let . . . me . . . go . . ."

She looked at her charge. He *did* have a Do Not Resuscitate order in place, but at the moment he wasn't in need of resuscitation, and with prompt medical attention he wouldn't be. Her pad was speaking to her. She couldn't make out the words, but she knew what they were. *Emergency services, asking for an address.* Her charge shook his head, his hand still on her arm. His left eye was closed with the stroke, the right pleading. He knew what was happening, and he didn't want to become what he was becoming, didn't want the life he was about to face, his last shreds of independence taken away. Her pad spoke again. Slowly she raised the pad to her ear. There were rules to follow in such circumstances, but there was also the right thing to do. "*Je m'excuse, c'est une erreur.*" She tapped it again to disconnect the call. "I'll take you inside," she said.

"No . . . Here . . ." The stroke was clearly mostly on the right side, but her charge's language function had been impaired as well. *A bilateral stroke then.* Without help he would die soon, but he knew that, perhaps he even wished it. There was a table in the courtyard, with an umbrella, surrounded by wooden chairs. She went and got one, sat beside him, held his right hand and squeezed it. He leaned back and looked up again, and she leaned down to retrieve his binoculars in case he asked for them. He didn't, and so she just sat quietly. You couldn't be a geriatric nurse without learning how to help the dying through their last hours. His breathing became quicker, and then after a while it slowed again. The pressure of his hand on hers grew weaker, and he slumped slightly, still facing up to the stars but, she was certain, no longer seeing them.

"Suzanne . . ."

"Yes," she said, though her name was Cecile. She leaned closer to hear him better.

"We're safe now . . ." His words were clear again, and he sounded somehow younger. He was speaking with a different part of his brain, as his mind regressed to his youth.

"Yes, of course, we're safe."

"They can't follow us here, Susie. Not ever. Don't you worry."

"I know, I'm not worried." She squeezed his hand. "Don't you worry either."

"No. We're safe." His hand relaxed further, and he didn't speak again. The nurse sat quietly, listening to the burble of the spring. The overnight nurse would be along soon enough, and they could look after everything then.

# Genesis II

*God offers to every mind its choice between truth and repose.*

—Ralph Waldo Emerson

# L–45

"Abrahim Kurtaski was more than a friend, more than a teacher." Wallen Valori was standing behind a small pulpit beside the coffin. He stopped and looked down, his face registering the emotions caught in his throat, then looked back up to the assembly, as if to find the strength there to continue. Sitting in the right front row of the ranked chairs laid out in the vast main hangar of *Ark*'s construction shack, Aurora Brady looked away, out the open hangar doors to the gentle green of the embryonic ecosystem. The hangar was the only space in the ship large enough to hold the complete complement of *Ark*'s crew. Abrahim was her grandfather, but she felt disconnected from the funeral somehow, as though she were watching the proceedings from a great distance, watching someone else go through the motions of mourning and grief. A dozen of the small utility fliers were parked near the hangar door, moved there to make space for the ceremony, along with a trio of the larger cargo aircraft. Behind them the hangar grew taller, clearance for the huge colony landers being produced on a kilometer-long assembly line. The robotic machines there had been paused in their work and stood frozen, as if they too mourned the chief engineer's passing. The sight of the aircraft moved her in a way the service had not. *I remember when Dedka taught me to fly.* Her grandfather had been there, always been there for her, when she'd taken her first step, and her first solo flight. A world without Abrahim seemed impossible. Wallen was still talking, but his words washed over her without registering, the sound divorced of meaning.

The cargo fliers were designed by Antonov, and so were affectionately called aunties by the crew, which made the smaller utility fliers *dadushka*—literally "uncle" in the Slavic-English slang favored by the riggers. When she was very small . . . *Was I three, or four?* . . . she had learned the words but confused the meanings, and so wondered who the mysterious relatives her parents were always taking to this place or that place were. Tears welled up in her eyes as the day came back to her when her Abrahim sat her down to tell her that her parents weren't coming back, and then he had to explain how an auntie could crash. *I met death far too young.* Abrahim had loved to fly as well, and she would have given anything, *anything* to see one of the agile little craft come taxiing in, so he could pop open the canopy to smile at her, as he had so many times before. It seemed almost possible, and she kept her eyes closed, remembering . . .

The flow of Wallen's words stopped and there was silence. She opened her eyes to see him stepping down to find his seat. She watched him, and saw the priest looking

at her. It was her turn to speak, and she didn't want to go.
Speaking would acknowledge that her last living relative
was gone; speaking would make it real. *And I don't want
it to be real.*

But not speaking wouldn't make it not real. She stood
up, walked to the pulpit and took a moment to gather herself, looking out at the assembled crowd. There were
thousands there, virtually *Ark*'s entire crew, there to pay
their last respects to their most respected member. *And
all of them waiting for me.* She took a deep breath. She
had prepared notes, agonized for hours over the right
words to say. They were in her pocket, neatly folded,
ready for just this moment. They were the best expression
of her love for Abrahim that she could articulate. They
were, she now realized, completely inadequate. She left
the folded sheets in her pocket, and began speaking.

"My *dedka* devoted his life to this ship, this *Ark*. When
he started it was a dream, nothing more. Today we are
building the foremost achievement in human history. He
knew he wouldn't live to see it finished, but he knew also that
others would take up his task. We crew, in our community of
purpose, are the ones to do that. Our children's children's
children will live to see the human race break ground on a
new world. That was Dedka's vision, and of all the things
that he did to make this project real, perhaps the most
important was that he shared that vision with the world. I
am spaceborn, one of the first." She looked down, suddenly
overcome with memories, and struggled to fight back the
tears. *I can't cry, not yet.* She looked up. "I never thought
he was special. It was a long time before I understood that
not every little girl's grandfather had to build her a world

to live in. He *was* special, though. I have always been very proud . . ." She paused, trying to overcome the emotion that was choking off her words. ". . . very proud of Abrahim. I know he was very proud of what we've accomplished here, and proud of every one of you, who have put so much of your lives into this project." She tried to go on but found her throat too tight to get the words out. She swallowed hard, and focused on the back wall of the hangar. "He lived a long life, and he filled every day of it. I know he wouldn't want us to put too much time into mourning him. I know he would want us to keep building his dream, our dream. We're going to the stars, we lucky few, and he's coming with us." She forced a brave smile to her lips. "He's coming with us."

She stepped down then, and the priest rose to take her place. "Ashes to ashes and dust to dust . . ." he began, and Aurora looked away and up, not wanting to see him, not wanting to think. His words seemed empty, quoting some verse in the Bible that promised eternal life after death in a place free of earthly wants. It was surreal to hear him talk about reuniting with loved ones in the afterlife. She looked over her shoulder, saw the somber, drawn faces of the assembly, friends and colleagues united in grief. Some were crying, others looked like they were about to. *Nobody here is fooled, nobody thinks he'll be waiting for us in heaven when we die, nobody here is looking forward to paradise after death. The words that count are the ones from those who knew him.*

Certainly Abrahim wouldn't have had much time for such mystical mumblings, her *dedka* had been a confirmed agnostic. *Pokazukha,* he called religion, shadowplay, form with no substance. "What kind of God is it who hides behind event horizons and beneath the quantum foam?" he had asked when the question came up. In life he had no time for priests or gods, so she was surprised that his will had asked for a funeral service, surprised again that he'd specified that it be conducted by a Russian Orthodox priest. Abrahim's mother had been Jewish, and had she expected any religious official at all, it would have been a rabbi.

Aurora returned her attention to the priest. *Perhaps he did it for me.* Her own Catholicism was limited to baptism and confirmation, only because her grandmother had asked that of her mother before she died, and before Aurora was born. She had hunted Easter eggs and unwrapped Christmas presents in happy ignorance of the underlying religious meaning of the celebrations. *Then why this?* Since she'd been a little girl Abrahim had delighted in surprising her, showing her the unexpected. *And you can still surprise me, Dedka.*

The sermon ended, mercifully short. He had specified that in his will as well, and all at once Aurora understood. She looked over to where Secretary-General DiAngelo sat, in the front left row with the other dignitaries. Many of them had wanted to speak at the chief engineer's funeral, but none of them were. If Abrahim had specified no funeral at all the politicians would have overridden his request, on the theory that Great Words must be spoken at the death of a Great Man, but the demands of faith carried more weight than the mere last wishes of a man. By insisting on the Orthodox service he had denied anyone else the chance to grandstand on his grave. The ceremony would be over quickly, and life would move on; it was her *dedka*'s way. He didn't need the words of powerful men spoken over his grave. His legacy was *Ark* itself.

The priest stepped down and silence filled the improvised chapel, until mercifully the choirmaster raised his arms and the choir broke into a mournful hymn. The pallbearers came forward to the coffin and lifted it. It was plain fir, another stipulation of the will, made with wood cut from *Ark*'s fledgling forests. Aurora fell into place behind the pallbearers as they carried her *dedka* out to the small graveyard beyond the hangar. *Small but growing.* When the graveyard was first established there had been only a square kilometer of soil around the construction shack, irrigated with pumps and covered only in special fast-growing grasses. The first to die on the *Ark* project had been returned to Earth for their burials, and most of the Siberskniks who'd been born downwire still were. Aurora's mother, Abrahim's daughter, had been among the first of the spaceborn, and had been buried in space because they had died before *Ark* had any soil at all; her father had been returned to his native Ukraine. Now a grove of young oaks had grown up around the graveyard, and it had become a landmark. The oaks were Abrahim's idea too, slow-growing and so not the best choice for *Ark*'s designed-for-yield ecosystem, but a powerful symbol of enduring strength. She had seen full-grown oaks during her time on Earth and understood what he meant. He had taught her the importance of symbols.

The sun was shining through the foredome and reflecting off the vast mirror cone overhead to distribute its rays over the whole of the ship's interior world. *All life comes from the sun. It shouldn't surprise me that the ancients thought that heaven was above.* It was different when you already lived in space. Religious conviction was so slightly held among the engineers and scientists of *Ark's* construction crew that they'd had to call downwire to find an Orthodox priest to conduct Abrahim's service.

It was just half a kilometer from the hangar to the grave, but the walk seemed interminable, and then the priest had more incantations to say. The dignitaries looked appropriately somber, the secretary-general himself, the president of the assembly, the director of UNISE, and more she had been introduced to but couldn't actually recognize. The coffin was lowered into the grave, and the bagpiper began to play a mournful lament. She nearly cried then, the tears she had fought back in the hangar. Wallen came up and put an arm around her, and she had to swallow hard to keep from breaking down.

"He lived a good life, Aurora, and a long one." His words were true, and they were meant to comfort, but all she could think of was that her *dedka* was gone, was gone, was gone and was never coming back to her. *He's all the family I had left.* The priest began to move away, and the dignitaries to follow him. The ceremony was moving on, carrying Abrahim inexorably farther away from her, and she felt an urge to throw herself into the grave, to hug his coffin as if it were him, to beg the universe to bring him back to her. She did none of those things, because none of them would do any good.

"Come on . . ." Wallen's hand guided her, urged her forward, and she walked because she had to. *Life moves only forward.* There was a reception in back at the construction shack. It became a blur for Aurora, an endless round of people coming up to give her their condolences, most for the second or third time, more people congratulating her on her ascension to her grandfather's post of chief engineer. "So sorry it had to be under these circumstances . . ." but of course there were no other circumstances under which she could have risen to the position. True also, she had been doing the job in all but name for years now, though Abrahim, his mind sharp until the end, had continued to lend his wisdom and experience to guide the immense project forward. She found herself hungry, for the first time in days, and then found herself frustrated, trying to balance a paper plate covered in mango slices while embracing people and shaking hands, trying to talk and eat at the same time. Like all *Ark*'s food the mangoes had been shipped upwire from Earth and were less than fresh, but she found she didn't care. Eventually the function ended and she went back to her rooms to fall asleep, exhausted.

Her desk woke her the next morning at the usual time. There was no such thing as a day off for the chief engineer, and today the secretary-general had asked to see her. She would rather have put that off, but he was going back downwire immediately so there was no way to postpone it. She showered and dressed, the emotional events of the previous day already seeming to belong to a separate life-time. That done she took a deep breath, gathered herself, and went to the chief engineer's conference room. She would rather have met him in her office, but the secretary-general's staff had insisted on the conference room, and further insisted that the secretary-general would enter first, to be seated when she came in. *Such are the protocols of power.* To Aurora it seemed a trivial concern, and their insistence upon it was an annoyance that she would rather have done without. The *Ark*'s construction crew lacked the numbers and the time to put much effort into the recognition of status; who you were meant nothing, it was what you did that counted. Aurora had earned the position of chief engineer entirely on her own merit, aided greatly by Abrahim's help and guidance, but not at all by his status. *Not too much anyway.* Her father had been slated to fill that role, and while Abrahim had never pressured her to follow in his footsteps, he had certainly been very pleased when she chose to.

The construction shack was a multilevel maze, a small city in a single structure, welded to the forewall base in successively rising levels like a vast stainless-steel fortress built against a protecting cliff. It was the construction crew's center of operations, housing everything from living quarters to fabrication plants, and even a few independent shops set up in disused sections by enterprising moon-lighters. Newcomers routinely got lost, but Aurora had grown up in it and navigated it with practiced ease. The secretary-general's chief of staff met her at the entrance to the office wing and escorted her down to the conference room. There were a pair of Interpol police waiting by the door, an unnecessary formality. They saluted smartly as she came by, and the chief of staff opened the door and showed her in. The secretary-general was waiting, sitting in the chair at the head of the table, with Brison Keyls, the director of UNISE, on his left.

"Chief Engineer, good morning." D'Angelo rose to

greet her, and shook her hand. He was a tall man, photo-genically handsome. "I'm sorry your promotion had to come under such circumstances."

Aurora nodded. "*Zdras*. I appreciate your coming upwire. That was very considerate of you."

The secretary-general smiled, sat back down in his chair and motioned for her to do the same. "I couldn't not come. Abrahim Kurtaski was a legend, a great man in history. The *Ark* project is the largest single item in the world budget."

"It is a great undertaking, sir. We're privileged to be a part of it."

"And you have been doing fantastic work. Abrahim, especially, was key."

"It was his life's work."

"Yes of course." The secretary-general smiled broadly. "What I'd like to do today is discuss the direction that work should be going in."

"Of course. We're filling the ocean now, and we've got about four-fifths of that done. We're farther behind on soil distribution, but our base species seem to be doing well. We're doing well with lander production, though of course that's going to take another twenty years to finish."

"Yes, yes." D'Angelo cut her off, the smile gone. "As you may be aware, we are facing a number of challenges in the administration at the moment. I'm afraid we're going to have to look at some cutbacks."

Aurora's eyebrows went up. "Cutbacks? Why?"

"This is a very expensive project, in terms of raw materials, but more importantly in terms of the energy required to ship them up the cable."

"It doesn't cost anything on the ground. We generate all the power required right here on-station, and supply the global grid with a considerable surplus into the bargain."

"I know you're disappointed." DiAngelo wasn't really listening to her. "Unfortunately I have certain realities to deal with." He stood up. "Mr. Keyls here will work out the details with you." He gestured to the director of UNISE. "I'd like to express, one last time, my condolences, and those of the General Assembly and the people of the world, on your loss. Your grandfather was truly a great man, and he won't be forgotten." He shook her hand and went out, to find the boost car to the spin platform, and his shuttle, and the Earth far below.

Aurora sat back down, somewhat surprised at the sudden turn of the interview and the abruptness of the secretary-general's departure. She turned to Director Keyls. "All right then, what are the details?"

"We're going to be closing down some aspects of the project." He tapped on his pad and started going over his notes while Aurora listened in growing disbelief. She expected an in-depth discussion of trade-offs to be made, perhaps changes to construction schedules, changes to the ecological plan, adaptations to a reduced boost schedule for upwire shipments of water and soil. What she got was a set of instructions, brief and to the point. She was to mothball *Ark*'s systems and move the construction crew personnel downwire, permanently. A skeleton crew would remain on the spin platform to maintain the solar arrays and keep power flowing to Earth. The initial plan should be under way in under a week, with the shutdown completed in two months, preferably less.

Aurora sat in shock when he had finished. Eventually she managed to find her voice. "You can't possibly mean this."

"I'm afraid I do." Keyls leaned back in his chair. "You understand, this is nothing personal. There is a great deal of support for this project in the aerospace world, and UNISE certainly intends to see it continue; however, the reality is, and more importantly the perception is, that this is simply costing too much. The secretary-general is having to make cuts everywhere, and we are no exception. Perhaps at a later date we can restart it."

"But the power we supply pays for . . ."

"And we fully intend to keep producing power on orbit. Don't worry, there's demand enough for every kilowatt you can produce."

"The solar farm can run with a maintenance check twice a year. I'm concerned about my people, not the hardware."

"Everyone will be looked after. Part of my job is to make sure there is an effective transition program for those transferred down to Earth. You're all part of UNISE. We're not going to just abandon you."

"Director, I don't think you understand. I'm spaceborn. There's over a thousand people who were born here, some who've never set foot on Earth. Every single one of us is committed to this project, not as a job, not as a career, but as a way of life, as the only life we've known."

"Yes, unfortunately you aren't the only ones involved in this. This project costs a lot of money . . ."

"So let us sell power and buy dirt."

Keyls leaned forward. "Ms. Brady, let me be perfectly

clear. This is a United Nations project, and you and I, and everyone else here, works for UNISE. We are employees, not citizens. The resources up here don't belong to us, they belong to the people of the world. You can't sell power for dirt, because it's not your power to sell. It's true that *Ark* has paid its way, in the sense that it has been a net positive contributor to the global economy. That's not at issue here. What's at issue is the fact that the return on investment for the public's money is not high enough. Ninety percent of the revenue generated here is returned to this project. If we simply run the solar power system, one hundred percent of that revenue will come back to the public. That's the math."

Aurora's jaw clenched. "You wouldn't be doing this if Abrahim were still alive."

"The timing is regrettable, but this has been in the works for a long time."

"And yet nobody bothered to inform anyone up here."

"This is a policy decision, and the secretary-general and myself have done you the courtesy of informing you first. The official announcement will be made in the secretary-general's address to the General Assembly this week."

Keyls's tones were mild, his expression bland, and Aurora found herself suddenly outraged at his casual dismissal of her entire future. "Spare me your courtesy, *yobany sooksin*." Her voice rose with her temper. "You go ahead and make your announcement, and then you see how good your policy looks when we don't come downwire. You think you've got *yajtza* enough to starve us out?"

"Ms. Brady . . ." Keyls tried to stop her, but Aurora was already storming out of the room.

She walked without thinking, navigating the corridors by instinct while her mind raced. *I don't believe this*. It was inconceivable that they could shut down *Ark*. She had been downwire, spent four years there learning to be an engineer at Cambridge, and another four earning her advanced degrees there. She hadn't liked one minute of the experience. There was grit in the air and wind and rain at random intervals. It got hot and it got cold and there were too many people doing too many things, and some of those people were actively dangerous. Abrahim had warned her about that, but she hadn't really understood until she experienced it firsthand herself. *And it could have been much worse* . . . Most of the spaceborn had been downwire for their higher education, and not a single one she knew had enjoyed it. *What will we do?*

She walked out of the construction shack on the eighth level up, and found herself on the ledge that ran all the way around the forewall at that height. Spin simulated gravity, and that made *out* into *down*, and turned *Ark's* nine-kilometer transparent foredome into a vast window of blue sky, with the sun in the middle and the land wrapped around it. Overhead the mirror cone stretched from the end of the spin platform, in the exact center of the foredome window, and stretched the thirty-kilometer axis cover almost all of the aftwall. The blue was light reflected from the ocean and filtered through the air, reflected again from the foredome to her eyes. When the sun went down the dome would fill with stars, a heart-breakingly beautiful sight.

She walked on, trying not to think about what Keyls had said. The cone served to reflect sunlight down to the soil that would become farmland, energy to feed the ship's nascent ecosystem. The area covered in soil was nearly two hundred square kilometers now, and Wallen's ecologists were starting to populate the land with larger animals. They already had plenty of small ones, honeybees to pollinate flowers and squirrels to scatter the seeds they produced, carrion beetles to bury the dead and earthworms to till the soil, robins to eat the invertebrates and keep their populations healthy, and peregrine falcons to prey on robins in their turn. *Two by two the animals came aboard the Ark. We have come so far, Dedka. I'll miss you.* Ahead of her a river outlet poured crystal-clear water out of the forewall and down to a canal a hundred meters below—enough height that you could see the stream noticeably displaced by the Coriolis force of *Ark*'s rotation, first bowing spinward before curving back counterspinward. There were six such outlets in all, equally spaced around *Ark*'s forewall. They existed to feed what would become six rivers that would wind their way down the ship's axis to the blue ocean at the aftwall. *Not salty like Earth's, but it's the biggest body of water we have.* When *Ark* was fully populated its people would use the rivers for water and transportation, but the system's primary purpose was to circulate silt through the ecosystem. Over ten thousand years virtually all the soil in *Ark* would be eroded away, to pass through the ocean and be revitalized before being pumped back up through the huge electromagnetic pump channels in the ship's floor to the spillway outlets.

*But the water is still clear because the ocean has no silt yet.* She looked out over her world, at the widening strip of green that followed the canal's course to the ocean at

the aftwall. In the center of the strip the trees were tall,
almost mature. Toward its edges shorter trees blended
into shrubs and cereal grasses that faded into the dry
brown of unwatered dirt. Machines there worked to
extend the fertile land, looking like toys in the distance. To
either side of the living patch the still uncovered hull
material was shiny dark grey, curving up toward the vertical
to arch overhead and disappear on the other side of the
mirror cone. High up there were big sections that were
pure black, areas where the transparent inner hull layer of
amorphous diamond had yet to be wrapped in its protective
cladding of nanofilament and steel. When the sun was
down you could see the stars through them, and sometimes she liked to just lie out on the new grass and do that,
watching as the u-carriers danced delicately overhead,
nudging prefabricated cladding sections into position,
blotting out another handful of stars, moving *Ark* another
fraction closer to completion.

*And so we fill the void with life.* When *Ark* was full of
soil the stars would show only through the foredome,
green-and-blue would wrap all the way around the interior.
Aurora frowned reflexively. Most of the hull still had no
soil at all, and of the six river outlets only the one she was
looking at was actually pumping water, and then only at a
quarter capacity. *We have done so much, and we have so
much left to do.* It seemed inconceivable that the General
Assembly wouldn't want to see such a project through to
completion, but she knew better than to imagine that they
would change their minds. The world downwire had its
own priorities. When she had first gone to Earth she had
been amazed that people were largely indifferent to the

great adventure coming to life literally right over their heads. *Ark* was just a bright spot in the sky to them, and most of them couldn't even pick it out from among the stars.

*Dedka, where are you when I need you most?* Abrahim was a wise and experienced man, and he would have had some good ideas on how to change the mind of the secretary-general. He had always had good advice for her, for as long as she could remember. The thought renewed the still fresh pain of losing him, and she sat down on the steel ledge and wept. It seemed wrong, somehow, to be crying like that at her age, and she realized that she hadn't cried, not once, since her parents had died. The realization only fueled her anguish, and she wept harder, curled around a tight knot of grief that seemed to gnaw at her belly like a wild thing in a cage. It was not right that she should be left alone in the world to deal with this, not right that Abrahim should be gone at all. It was not right, but it was true, and so she cried until she could cry no more, until the hurt had burned itself out, and then she stopped. She felt no catharsis after that, she simply felt empty, dazed. *They did it on purpose. Abrahim was too well connected, too powerful, even downwire. He was too clever to let them get away with this, so they had to wait until he died.*

*And I can't let them just force us down.* Anger began to grow in the space the tears had left behind. She was going to have to go downwire herself, to do what might be done, that was inevitable. *It's either go down voluntarily now and stop this, or go down permanently later with everyone else.* That realization came from the cold, rational part of her brain that still thought clearly even in her grief, and so she found herself already resigned to doing what had to be done. Still, she found herself strangely reluctant to stand up, to go back down to her office and begin making a plan. There were so many details to attend to, now that they were almost done filling the ocean. Hull cladding was an ongoing project, and the immense carbon-cycle fusion drive tube needed more tests for its confinement magnets, and the ecosystem, and the fuel system and . . . and . . . and . . .

None of that mattered anymore, not until she could find a way to keep *Ark* going. *Strange how every day seems urgent on a project lifetimes long.* That too was Abrahim's legacy. He had infected the crew with his spirit, driving the work forward with his enthusiasm. Now the mantle of command was settling on her shoulders. *I didn't think it would feel this heavy.*

A soil spreader was working half a kilometer from Wallen Valori's spot by the side of the road, the roar and clatter of its operation muted enough by the distance that he could work undistracted. His attention was focused on a chamomile plant, one of the early colonists of the newly deposited soil. A high-pitched whine rose in the distance, grew louder, and he looked up to watch a fat-wheeled heavy hauler lumber past. Its passage stirred up a pair of monarch butterflies that had been feeding on milkweed growing in the ditch, and they fluttered high in the gentle breeze for a dozen meters before settling again. Wallen watched the huge truck for a minute as it jolted its way to the spreader. It paused at the bottom of the dump ramp between the spreader's broad caterpillar tracks while it changed gears, and then the turbine's whine rose to a scream as it heaved itself up onto the back of the larger machine. The scream faded again, and the truck tilted its bed backward to dump four hundred tons of sterilized topsoil down into the belly of the spreader, there to be sieved, aerated, inoculated with *Ark*'s special concoction of soil bacteria, fungal spores, earthworm larvae, plant seeds and insect eggs, and then cascaded onto one of the multijointed conveyor arms that extended from the spreader like mechanical squid tentacles. The conveyor arms carried the soil out to extend the barren dirt field over the still pristine surface of *Ark*'s inner hull. Most of the life so hopefully seeded into the soil would die, but that which survived would sprout and grow and spread and reproduce, turning brown into green, and preparing the soil to receive the succession of species that would gradually extend their reach into the newly created land.

Once emptied the hauler spun up its turbine again and lurched back down off of the spreader to make the return journey to the loading station at the base of the forewall. Wallen watched it carefully as it turned and wheeled past him again, standing well clear until it had gone by. It wasn't that the truck wasn't smart enough to avoid him, it was that he was smart enough to avoid the truck. Its churning tires were over twice his height, and if it should choose to swerve it wouldn't even slow down in running him over. Once it was gone he returned his attention to the chamomile plant. It was healthy, which was a good sign, its bright yellow and white flowers smiling up at the reflected sunlight streaming down from overhead. The plant was setting seed, and he carefully pulled apart the seed head. Some of the seeds had been eaten, and as he probed a tiny weevil was exposed momentarily. It turned and burrowed deeper into the flower, escaping light and movement and danger.

Wallen smiled to himself. *This is good to see.* The chamomile was a double-edged sword. It was a key transition species in the transformation of barren dirt to grasslands, preferring to germinate on open ground. It thrived on the boundaries between wet and dry and helped to prepare the soil for the genetically enhanced cereal grasses that would follow it. It was valuable in its own right too, as a medicinal species, *Ark*'s variant being genetically engineered to enhance its natural properties as an anti-inflammatory. At the same time it also competed for light and nutrients with food species, and left unchecked it would seriously reduce crop yields, once *Ark*'s ecosystem was established enough to allow full-scale agriculture. The environmental models said the weevils would prevent that, but the real environment was always far more complex than a simulation could ever be. It was Wallen's job to determine if reality matched the prediction. No one had ever constructed an ecosystem even a hundredth the size of what they were attempting to build here.

*And we've already been surprised by the interactions we've found.* Chamomile weevils had become a favored prey of button shrews, which meant that button shrews were flourishing in the sparsely vegetated areas the chamomile colonized first. That in turn had fostered a population boom among pygmy owls, who had moved from their preferred habitat in established woods to the edges of the tree line so they could hunt the shrews. It was a successful strategy in the absence of egg predators like black snakes, but no one knew if the nocturnal owls would be able to continue it once *Ark*'s voyage began and the natural day-night cycle provided in Earth orbit was replaced with the permanent illumination of the fusion tube. Adapting plants to thrive on the voyage was an even bigger challenge, because not only would the fusion tube provide perpetual day, but its light output would peak closer to the red end of the spectrum than natural sunlight. The genomes of the major food crops had been modified with a chlorophyll variant that reached its peak of photo-synthesis under those conditions, but it was impossible to change all of the hundreds of plant species necessary to make the ecosystem thrive. What would happen to those species once the changeover happened, and what would happen to the food webs they supported, couldn't be known in advance.

*We'll lose some species, that's inevitable.* Wallen opened another seed head and found another weevil. They seemed to come one to a flower, and he wondered if they were territorial. The rule of thumb was to provide at least two species for each ecological niche—that way if one went extinct the other would move in to prevent the ecosystem from being disrupted—but species like the chamomile weevils were so specialized that there were no others that had an exactly parallel role. The solution to that was to introduce generalist species that could take over if the specialists failed, but generalists came with their own set of problems, not the least of which was that they were prone to disruptive boom-bust population cycles. Ideally *Ark* would be a veritable paradise, with almost every species in it directly supporting the human population. In practice Wallen would count his job well done if they wound up with a thriving ecosystem of even normal productivity. His nightmare was an introduction that thrived far beyond expectations, outcompeting important balance species and collapsing the food web before it was fairly established.

*But it isn't happening today, thank goodness.* The weevils seem to be keeping the chamomile under control without wiping it out. Wallen carefully clipped off the seed head with the weevil inside and sealed it into a sample bottle, then turned to watch a honeybee busily collecting pollen from a dandelion. The bees had been specially bred on Earth to navigate using a linear source of sunlight, as both the mirror cone and the fusion tube would provide. That job had been done long before Wallen was born. Getting the altered bees introduced had been one of the very first problems he'd faced as an ecological engineer, some twenty years ago now. Bees needed nectar to survive, but flowering plants couldn't reproduce without pollination. That solution had been as simple as plastic flowers full of sugar water. Wallen smiled to himself. *If only all our problems were so easy.* The bee paused to comb pollen off its antennae, turned to orient itself, then flew off clumsily, its pollen pockets laden heavy with the fruits of its labors.

A distant whine rose in the air and he looked up, expecting another heavy hauler full of soil, but it was an Antonov flier, lift fans whirring as it came down toward the spreader. It circled twice around the area as though searching for something, and then came in to settle beside his own. He realized that it was looking for him.

Or rather its pilot was; he had grown too accustomed to machines that directed themselves. He stood up and hiked toward the aircraft, waited while the pilot popped the canopy and climbed out. Aurora Brady.

"*Zdras*, Aurora, how are you?"

"As well as can be expected." She paused, not wanting to say what she had come to say. "I couldn't raise you on your pad."

"I switch it off when I come out here."

She nodded. "That was a beautiful eulogy you said for Abrahim."

"Yours was better, I think. You made people weep, even me."

"Even myself. Wallen, I . . ." She hesitated, still not wanting to tell him.

"You've had a hard week. You should be taking the day off."

She laughed a laugh that almost turned into tears. "What do you think Abrahim would say if he caught me taking a day off just because he died? I'd never hear the end of that lecture." She swept an arm to take in the field. "I don't see you taking a day off."

"If I were to take a day to remember Abrahim, how would I spend it but alone in the fields, watching life and letting it watch me. And then also he wasn't my grandfather, *droogymuy*. It's different, and you drive yourself too hard."

"It runs in the blood I suppose." Aurora shrugged. "I have no choice but to work today anyway." She took a deep breath. *Not saying it won't make it not be true.* "That's why I've come out to see you."

"I don't think there's anything so pressing about weevils that they can't wait until tomorrow."

"It isn't about weevils." Quickly she outlined her conversation with Keyls as Wallen listened with growing amazement.

"Who else knows about this?" he asked when she had finished.

"Only you for now. I want to get my thinking straight on this before I tell everyone else."

"I'm flattered by your trust, Aurora. I am."

"We go back too far, Sibersknik. You're my oldest friend."

"I'm your oldest friend, but I'm no Sibersknik, born downwire or not." He paused. "So the secretary-general wants to stop the project. What is the chief engineer going to do?"

"I'm not going to stop *Ark*, not for a second. The first thing I'm going to do is go downwire and try to negotiate. I don't know how much success I'll have. After that, we need a backup plan. I need you to start thinking of how we can apply pressure."

"Apply pressure, to what end?"

"To keep the project going, of course."

"Why bother doing that? Just stay here. We have enough ecosystem now to support us indefinitely."

"Are you sure?"

"*Da.* Fully developed, and under full-scale agriculture we could support five thousand, at a rough guess."

"It isn't fully developed, and we can't implement full-scale agriculture, not even close."

"No, but neither are we going to have five thousand people."

"How many do you think will stay?"

"Most of the spaceborn, maybe even all of the spaceborn. How many of the Siberskniks will join us . . ." He shrugged. ". . . I couldn't guess."

Aurora shook her head. "Even if we stayed here. It would mean an end to the project. We'd never leave Earth orbit."

"That's our children's problem."

"I don't want to hand them that problem."

"You won't. As long as someone's living up here, *Ark* will be a living project, whether that's official or not. Sooner or later the balance of power will shift in the General Assembly, and some ambitious candidate for secretary-general will start it up again. And that *will* happen in our lifetimes."

She nodded slowly. "I suppose you're right." She looked aft and up, looking at her world reflected around her in the mirror cone. "I just don't like the way they did it, just waiting for Abrahim to die, and then pouncing."

"It was a dirty trick, but politics is full of dirty tricks, and like it or not, the chief engineer has to deal with the politics."

"I'm not going to live downwire, Wallen." Aurora's voice carried emotions choked back through force of will. "I don't care if I'm here alone."

"You won't be alone." Wallen's lips tightened. "I'm not going downwire either." He looked out over his field, from the fresh-spread soil to the dandelions waving in the breeze. Yes, *his* field, his possession of it no less absolute for the fact that he shared it with every other soul on *Ark*. Aurora looked away, her face hard and unreadable.

"I *feel* alone, Wallen." She turned to face him. "I had a plan; now it's gone. I'm not sure what the right thing to do here is." Her hard expression softened to let her worry show through.

Wallen concealed his surprise. Aurora had never shown weakness, not to him, not to anyone, and it surprised him that she was showing it now. Since they were children she had always been fiercely independent, driven by her intellect, her strength worn on her sleeve, as if daring anyone to challenge it. It was a reaction, he had long suspected, to the sudden loss of her parents, a defense against a universe that she had learned all too early might take away that which she most treasured, without any warning at all. *She's still in shock from the loss of Abrahim.* It hurt him that there was nothing he could do to help her when she needed it most.

Almost nothing. He put a hand on her shoulder. "Do what's in your heart, Aurora. Do your best at it, and let whatever happens happen. We can't control the universe, only ourselves."

Aurora sighed. "You're right." She looked back to the mirror in the sky. "I knew you were the right person to talk to." She paused again. "We'll have to call a senior staff meeting and let everyone know."

Wallen nodded. "We will."

That afternoon they gathered all the section heads in the chief engineer's conference room, a utilitarian space with a wide display wall, and two other walls dominated by huge sketchboards, still scrawled with boxes and arrows and bullet lists from the last meeting of the fusion-drive team. Wallen put strapping tape over the display system's camera eyes and disconnected the microphone array himself. In theory there was no way downwire could listen in unless they turned the system on, but there was no point in leaving anything to chance. It was the first time since Aurora and he had been small that he'd felt conspiratorial, and what they were about to discuss would earn them more than a scolding if they got caught. He sat at the far end of the table while she sat at the front, and he just listened as she got up and announced to *Ark*'s leadership what she had told him the previous day. Most of the senior staff people were Siberskniks, and he'd assumed they'd go downwire with regret but little fuss. In fact they were strongly resistant to the prospect of abandoning the project. Petra Krychovik even put forward a motion to cut off power from the solar array to force UNISE to carry on with the project. "We're paying our way here, they're just trying to make short-term political points at our expense."

Bernarde Groot seconded her and went further. "We could take all the solar stations if we wanted. What does *Ark* provide? One percent of total global power, nothing at all. Now we take all orbital power, we have nearly twenty percent. That makes them sit up and listen, *da*. They take us seriously then."

"And how do we get to the other stations?" asked Wallen.

"Put auxiliary tanks on a u-carrier, on a bunch of them. We don't need a lot of delta-v, they're all in orbits coplanar with ours. I can have the flexfab turn out a bunch."

Petra nodded. "We can start that now, have the whole plan ready before they know what's coming."

Gervois Heydahl stood up. "Are you out of your minds? We could get away with dialing back our own power output, we could call that a labor strike. Taking over the other stations would be a criminal act."

Bernarde snorted. "Don't talk to me about criminal action." Bernarde had served ten years in Interpol before a wound received in a gang raid forced him to change careers for engineering. "Talk to me about results."

Gervois sat down as more protestations rose around the table. There was a lot of loud debate after that, and to Wallen's relief the more militant options got scant support. *We aren't ready to go to war with the United Nations.* Nevertheless there was a strong consensus that everything possible should be done to prevent the project from being shut down. *But we'll see how that plays out with the younger crew.* Siberskniks came upwire for the money and complained about the isolation and the endless work, and most Siberskniks wanted nothing more than to finish their contracts and then back to Earth to build a home and family that they couldn't otherwise have afforded, but *Ark* became a way of life for those who stayed, as much as for any of the spaceborn. The scale and scope of the project were seductive. It earned the commitment of those dedicated to a vision larger than themselves. For people like Bernarde or Gervois, who had most of their long careers tied up in the project, simply walking away was unthinkable. It was the riggers and jacks who did the hands-on work who were more likely to accept the end of the project without protest. They scheduled the all-hands meeting for the next day, and for the second time in under a week all work on the project came to a halt as the entire construction crew assembled in the hangar. Again Wallen watched as Aurora stood up to deliver the secretary-general's intention, this time with the senior staff behind her instead of in front of her. The bare details took just five minutes to deliver.

"I do not intend to go downwire," the chief engineer finished as she had the previous day. "I was born here, I intend to die here. It was my intent to spend my life working on this project. If I have to spend the rest of my life simply farming, then that's what I'll do. Those of you who would like to stay with me are welcome."

For a long, silent minute there was nothing but stunned silence, and then an explosion of voices. Aurora called for attention, called for attention again, called for it a third time, and eventually the noise died down enough for her to carry on with the meeting. She invited questions from the audience and a tall rigger stood up. "What severance package is UNISE offering?"

"I have the assurance of Director Keyls that *Ark* project personnel will be looked after. I have no details beyond that at this time."

"You mean to say, you're telling us we're losing our jobs, and you don't even know how that's going to happen?"

"That's exactly correct. I shouldn't be making this announcement at all, but I want you to be fully informed, with all the information we have available as soon as we get it. As the details come out you'll know as soon as I know, and anything you hear that isn't coming straight from me is a rumor with no substance behind it."

It was a good reply to a challenging question, but it earned a rising babble of voices, growing louder, and to Wallen's ear, angrier. Again Aurora called for silence, and again, but the cacophony on the hangar floor only grew, to the point were Wallen feared it might explode into a riot. Aurora gave up asking for quiet and simply waited out the crowd. After a long time the noise settled down again. There were more questions then, and more answers, but Wallen had given up listening, thinking ahead to the challenges that would be facing them. The ecosystem would support agriculture, but it would do so at some cost. Erosion would be a big problem. *Ark*'s biosphere was designed to cycle its soil through the ocean and back, but with eighty percent of the water and just twenty percent of the soil they could wind up with a swamp if they weren't very careful. The species balance would change, and some would go extinct, that was inevitable . . .

The meeting started to wrap up and he returned his attention to what was being said. There was a general understanding on several points. There would be an orderly shutdown of work in progress; nothing would be simply abandoned. The issue of contracts and severance pay would be addressed, and senior staff would negotiate with UNISE to maintain at least a skeleton crew to finish work on the hull and the fusion tube. If that went ahead, personnel to have their contracts extended would be chosen purely on merit. Virtually all of the spaceborn were determined to stay regardless of whether the project was officially extended or not, as well as a decent fraction of Siberskniks, mostly those who were older, with space-born children of their own. With no more support from

Earth there would have to be a concerted effort to get farms going right away to feed the several thousand people who would be staying.

*Farming. It's going to fall on me to lead that effort. It isn't going to be easy.*

"May the Blessings of the Prophet be upon you, brethren." The bishop intoned the words of the ritual.

"May the Blessings of the Prophet be upon us," answered the congregation. Seated in his place of honor behind the pulpit, Norman Bissell stood, and raised his arms in benediction, as the Prophet was expected to. There was a time when he had actually given the blessing verbally in response to the bishop's request. *Or is it an order?* There had been a time before that when he had given the sermon himself, and a time before that when half a billion people had listened when he spoke and obeyed when he commanded. *And now? Now I barely command myself.* There had been a time when the True Prophet believed himself to be more than other men, even as he preached simplicity and humility. There had been a time when he had believed himself immortal, but age had a way of stripping a man of belief and substituting it with equal measures of doubt and painful reality.

The bishop was named Caleb Sully, and he reminded Norman of himself when he was young, ambitious and energetic. He was reading from the Bible. ". . . And God looked upon the earth, and, behold, it was corrupt; for all flesh had corrupted his way upon the Earth . . ." Bissell knew the words so well it was difficult to distinguish Caleb's recitation from the narrative unreeling automatically in his own mind. Genesis 6:12, the story of Noah. He watched with a critical eye as the bishop told the story. *It isn't the words that matter, it's how the story is told.* The young man was telling it well, projecting his voice to the back of the chapel, holding his Bible in one hand but keeping his eyes on his audience, only occasionally referring to the book he so obviously knew by heart.

"Thus did Noah according to all that God commanded him . . ." Bishop Caleb finished the reading with a flourish and paused dramatically before launching into his sermon. His performance was good, his presence was powerful, drawing the congregation into his words as he spoke about the dangers of sin. He knew how to grab their attention, hold it, shape it to his will—but as good as he was, he wasn't half the orator Norman Bissell had been. Bissell could tell that from the audience. They were paying rapt attention to the young preacher, but not quite captivated, not in his sway, willing to take whatever he said and make it their own. Bishop Caleb did not yet have the charisma that would allow him to become truly powerful; whether he had the instincts to create such charisma was another question. Norman looked higher, to the carved wooden beams that held up the church's vaulted ceiling. *I once spoke as God's voice on Earth.* As a young man he had *believed*, not just in his faith, but that he had been chosen by God to carry his faith to the world. *But I wasn't God's servant, God was mine.* The True Prophet had been past sixty when the steady decline of age had finally convinced him that he was not immortal, that prayer would not ease the growing pain in his joints, nor clear his eyes and smooth his wrinkles, nor give him once more a young man's strength, or a young woman's love. For a time after that he had raged against the universe, even turned his back on God for betraying him with mortality. *As though by spurning Him, by withholding my faith I could punish Him for making me flawed and mortal.* Perhaps he had believed that a sufficiently chastised God might have relented and banished death, but God had not relented, and the slow decline had inexorably continued, compromising his abilities, replacing energy with infirmity, forcing him to accept, one by one, younger men in roles he had once reserved only for himself. And as he had come to accept that he could neither buy nor bargain for immortality he had come to fear death.

*And in fearing death I have lost all faith.* How could any Believer fear death, when the Kingdom of Heaven was waiting to embrace the faithful on the other side of the grave? *When I believed I felt secure in the protection of the Holy Spirit.* Age had stolen faith and replaced it with fear, but it had not stopped there. As the bodily pains of age came and slowly spread, as he grew tired more and more easily, as sleep became elusive and rest stopped being restful, the vision of death as a dark and threatening specter had faded, replaced by a softened version, still somber but no longer hostile. Death no longer seemed to reach out with cold and bony fingers to drag his struggling soul into the grave's cold embrace. Now it simply waited for him, with care and patience, like an old friend at the end of a long journey, there to offer respite from travel-worn cares. Oblivion offered relief, from physical pain and from the deeper pains that time could never heal. Death, now familiar, offered comfort and final forgetfulness. *But it doesn't offer a renewal of faith, nor reunification with those you have have lost.*

The sermon ended, the congregation rose, but he remained seated. The bishop looked to him, expectantly, waiting, and finally he stood up, allowing the service to end. *I am a symbol now, little more than that.* With his implicit permission given, the congregation filed out, and he followed them. He had made himself the True Prophet of the Holy Spirit Everlasting, and though his faith had failed him, the mantle he had assumed had turned out to be everlasting nonetheless. *Symbols are still important, I must remember that.* The church was a simple, wood framed structure, built solidly and well in the Believer way. It was large for a Believer church of the last forty years, much smaller than the vast stadiums he had preached in at the height of the Believer wave. *And though I have lost my own faith now, I'm closer to God now than I ever was then.* God, he had come to realize, did not exist separate from humanity, nor did people need to be led into His presence. God was not some being of boundless power, judging, punishing, rewarding. God, to the extent that He existed at all, was manifest in the hearts of every man and woman, expressed in the care they showed each other. God was family and community, and it frequently seemed that the demands of religion interfered with the fundamental message of Christianity. *Love thy neighbor as thyself.*

He was the last through the door. Outside it was sunny and warm, the summer heat baking the humidity out of a countryside still damp from the previous night's storms. A few families were already climbing into horse-drawn buggies, heading back to homes and farms in the rolling hills above the broad and lazy river below. The majority of the congregation were talking on the lawn in small groups, and he moved among them, chatting with old friends, shaking hands with the farmers and craftsmen who were the backbone of Believer society. Despite his loss of faith he still went to church each Sunday, dividing his time between the two dozen congregations of the local Believer enclave. There were still tens of thousands of Believer congregations across the continent and around the world, left behind like stranded pools when the Believer tide had receded, but very few of them lived the true Believer life of simplicity, humility and community.

"Prophet, could you . . . ?" The woman was young and pretty, nearly overcome by shyness in addressing him, and holding a tiny newborn in a pink swaddling cloth.

"Of course, I would be honored." Norman Bissell put his hands on the baby's forehead and looked to the sky. "I call upon the power of the Holy Spirit to bless and protect this child, today and forever, amen." He looked back down at the now beaming young woman. "What's her name?"

"Faith."

Norman smiled and stroked a tiny cheek. "You take good care of young Faith, my dear, and she will bless you more than Heaven ever could."

The young mother blushed and her husband came up beside her. "Thank you, Prophet," he said. "Your blessing means everything."

Norman accepted the man's thanks. *My blessing means nothing, but at this stage in my life I simply can't recant.* The community he had built was all he had left, and the community was built around the Church. And so he continued to appear at services, a living stage prop for those who had taken over from him. *And I do good work here, I give of myself, I guide the young bishops as I wish someone had guided me. This is my redemption for my sins, not in heaven but right here on earth.*

Bishop Caleb was also moving among the congregation, talking and shaking hands. One by one the families said their greetings and left. After the last had gone Caleb went to talk to his two servitors, still in their white robes. Norman waited for him and then they walked together down to the horse paddock by the bishop's residence, where the bishop's buggy and two grey mares waited to take them visiting.

"That was a good sermon today, Caleb," Norman said as the bishop stirred up the horses.

"Thank you, Prophet." Caleb paused as he guided the buggy out onto the road. "I was thinking that perhaps we should reach out to the towns around here. There are so few who know God in this day and age."

Norman Bissell shook his head. "No, Bishop. We have our ways and they have theirs. It isn't for us to draw them into our way of life."

"But there are so few of us. Once we were millions, tens of millions—"

Norman cut him off, more testily than he intended to. "Do you think I don't know that? I built this Church, I led it to its height, and I led it back down again. We have no need of numbers. We have ourselves."

"Prophet, I only—"

Norman held up a hand. "Caleb, no." They rode in

silence for a while before he spoke again. "I'm sorry I snapped. I know exactly what you're thinking. The Bible calls us to spread his Word. We are so few, and there is strength in numbers. We could do so much good in the world, if only we went out into it." He spread his hands. "There are so many other reasons, and you are a good preacher, I'm sure you'd represent us well. Still, we must not do this thing."

"May I ask why, Prophet?"

"It's true our community is small, but that's not important. What matters is, we are a *community*. I made that very mistake when I was young, thinking numbers were what counted, that I had a mission to bring the Church to every man and woman in the world." He shook his head. "I was wrong. Souls aren't like pennies, one just like another, to be collected and saved in a jar. Every person is an individual, every person needs to be ministered to individually."

"We were discussing this at the Elder Council last meeting. We were so much stronger back then, we accomplished so much. *You* accomplished so much, Prophet. We could be that great again. . . ."

Norman looked at the younger man. *He is ambitious, like I was. He craves power, though he hasn't even tasted the drug yet.* "Caleb, our Church lost its soul during that time. A hundred million, half a billion, people listened to my sermons, and one in a thousand followed what I taught. People sent money, but they heard only that part of the message they wanted to hear. The world out there . . ." He swept an arm to encompass the valley and the globe beyond it. ". . . the world out there is full of people with hollow lives, looking to fill them with faith but unwilling to embrace simplicity, unwilling to be part of a community. That nearly destroyed us. I won't let it happen again."

Bishop Caleb nodded and stayed silent, but Bissell could tell from his expression that he was unconvinced. Bissell nodded to himself. *He will bide his time and try again.* That didn't matter so much. A man couldn't control everything, or even most things, even when he was alive. The best he could hope to do was live what life he had left well, in the service of the people he still believed in.

They called on several families, the momentary breach of the natural alliance of bishop and Prophet passing without further remark. It was a pleasant time, and they were plied with more meadowmint tea and home-baked delicacies than he could finish, though he politely accepted some at each home. Breaking bread with happy families was a bittersweet experience, the proud husbands and warm wives reminded him of his own now empty house. *I was truly blessed, to have such love in my life.*

There had been other women; that was a reality he regretted now. The man he had been didn't lack for female companionship any time he wanted it. He had been tempted, and yes, he had sinned, but never once had his heart been turned from his home. *Beth and Marta should have been enough, more than enough. I didn't know how lucky I was.* Beth and Marta were both gone now, and their children had all inherited their father's ambition and so were gone as well. How many years had it been since he'd seen any? None of them had stayed in the Church; Gabriel still visited at Christmas, that was all. *Ambition.* Easier to accept that reason than to listen to what his inner heart told him. *You were gone too often when they were growing up, and now their love can't overcome their anger.* The things that had seemed important then seemed unimportant now, and vice versa. *We grow old too soon and wise too late.* He had embraced the tools of the Devil's Playground to spread God's word, and that had cost him what was most valuable.

The last stop of the day was Arad Wegner's house, and it was there that he first heard the news. Arad had been up to Granby Crossing to shop for some tools, and had picked it up over conversation with a Mennonite man from farther north. The United Nations had canceled the *Ark* project. Arad mentioned it purely in passing and the conversation moved on to the topic of placement candidates for Arad's youngest daughter, approaching sixteen and marriageable age. It wasn't done in Believer circles to linger on news from the wider world, certainly not with the bishop and the Prophet himself visiting, but the news stuck in Norman's mind. *Not one person here remembers when the Church fought this creation. Even their parents hadn't been born.* He had been young then, ready to change the world, confident enough to face down the secretary-general himself. *Ambition and arrogance.* He had really expected to win, had been convinced of his rightness in the fulfillment of God's mission. Joshua Crewe had beaten him, and the hundred million voices who had stood behind his Church had abandoned him as quickly as they had picked him up. The politicians who had sworn allegiance to his cause had melted away as well, their espoused conversions revealed as nothing more than shallow political ploys. He had spent the next forty years preaching, praying, fighting to somehow reclaim what he had lost, and losing everything else in the process. *I was such a fool.* He looked up and saw Arad's daughter peeking around the corner of the stairs, determined to discover who she was to be wed to. She ducked back when she saw him.

Arad and Caleb hadn't noticed her eavesdropping, deep in their discussion over the pros and cons of the various families that she might join. It was improper for her to show such interest, but the Prophet let the moment pass without comment. *Her whole life is in front of her, of course she wants to know.* What was her name? *Elesheva.* He should have been listening to the discussion, but . . . but *Ark* had been canceled, the final victory was his in that battle that only he remembered. *And how do I feel? I feel hollow.*

Wallen Valori put down his hoe and wiped the sweat from his brow, and then leaned back to stretch his aching shoulders. Overhead the sun was beating down from the mirror cone in a way he'd never before experienced. He had known farming would be difficult to make functional in the half-developed ecosystem. He was learning it was also just plain hard work. It had fallen to him, as head of ecoscience, to devise the agriculture plan for those who'd chosen to remain aboard after the UNISE shutdown date. In taking that on he'd found that agriculture bore only a passing resemblance to the work of a field biologist. The digital library in the construction shack had every work ever published on farming, but reading about optimizing soil conditions for tomatoes and putting that knowledge into practice was a very different matter.

Wallen looked at his hoe, the proximate cause of the now nearly constant pain in his muscles. *How did civilization ever function with only tools like this?* Bernarde's flexfab was capable of producing almost anything, given the right inputs, but it was geared toward the production of one-off replacement parts for existing systems rather than for the mass production of complex machines. That made sense in an environment where major pieces of equipment would be shipped upwire from Earth. Except now there were no shipments coming up, and so the flexflab was working overtime to produce the tools needed to set up an agrarian economy from scratch. It took the facility four days to produce all the parts for a single hydrogen turbine, and there was suddenly a lot of demand for turbines, to run pumps for irrigation and tractors for cultivation and for a myriad of other uses that suddenly had become important. It took nearly another week to make the parts for a small tractor. A more serious problem was the lack of feed materials. Some, like steel and carbon, were available in almost limitless quantities. Others, like the polyresins needed to make feed lines and fuel tanks, were sourced from Earth and had suddenly become precious resources in need of rationing. *And in the meantime we need to eat.* For the time being the twenty percent of the crew who'd chosen to stay aboard were able to feed themselves with the onboard supplies meant for those who'd gone downwire. There had also been some success in gathering wild berries and fruit, and some trapping pigeons, but that wasn't sustainable for more than a few months at most. *Agriculture was supposed to be a problem for my grandchildren.*

All of which meant that most of the crew were out every day, working little plots of land with hand tools, and so far having little success. Work on actually building the ship had ground to a halt. Wallen looked down at the line of scrawny tomato seedlings he was trying to raise. They were dying, and he didn't know why. Was it too much water? Too little? Was the soil just fundamentally wrong for them? His books had a lot to say about hydroponics, greenhouse humidity, soil conditioning and other topics related to high-technology food production. They didn't say anything about the fact that new-laid soil's porosity made it soak up more water than he would have believed possible, or that, once saturated under forced irrigation, the soil would slump and collapse and in the process destroy an entire field. They didn't say that it was important to keep all your furrows aligned, or your improvised tractor would destroy half your crop as you worked the other half.

As a biologist he was used to watching nature take its course; now he was trying to coax nature into taking the course he wanted it to take. A big part of the problem was that not enough sunlight made it through the meter of amorphous diamond in the foredome. That made the crops grow much more slowly than they should have, and there was nothing he could do about that. Another problem was his dwindling workforce; fully a third of the crew who'd elected to stay had already changed their minds and gone downwire, disenchanted with the backbreaking labor they were suddenly called upon to do. Newsfeeds on Earth were framing their descent as a defection, and victory for UNISE in what they were presenting as a battle of wills between the spaceborn and the secretary-general over the abandonment of *Ark*. *And having them make this a political issue is all we need.*

He sighed, picked up his hoe and went back to work on the furrow he was digging, soon to be home to another batch of seedlings, these ones to be watered slightly more. They were fortunate in having ample food-crop seed stocks in the biolabs. *Though what this will do to the biosphere I can only guess.* He was too busy trying to grow things to run any ecological models. Trying to avoid too much bending, he worked his way down the furrow, carefully breaking up the soil and mounding it. He was almost done when his pad rang, and he dropped the hoe again, more relieved at the interruption than he cared to admit, even to himself.

"Wallen, it's Aurora."

"What's up?"

"Can you come up to the shack, we've got a problem."

He looked up at the mirror cone, where the sun was already starting to fade, then down to his furrow, which seemed a pathetic result for all the effort he'd put in. "I'll be up right away."

When he got there she pointed her wall live. A newsfeed appeared, the camera focused on Director Keyls. "There is no confrontation in this situation," he said. "The holdouts aboard the colony ship don't pose any threat to the ship, or to the public. We are continuing to monitor the situation, and that is all there is."

The feed broke away to the anchor. "Meanwhile, rebel elements of the *Ark* ship construction crew continue to refuse to obey a UNISE order to return to Earth, in day thirty-nine of the siege."

Aurora pointed the display off again. "Now they're calling us rebels under siege."

Wallen snorted. "That's ridiculous."

"No, it's serious. I just got a call from Keyls himself. He's given me what he calls notice to vacate, and he wants me to go downwire again, to discuss a resolution to the situation."

"What's to resolve? It's just some feeder making news out of nothing. We're here, we aren't bothering anyone. They've abandoned the project, what do they care if we live or die?"

"Evidently they care. The feeds are counting the days we're up here, and it's making Keyls look like he's losing. He doesn't like that. The question is, what do we do about it? My instinct is to ignore him, but I'd like your advice."

"I'd say ignore him too." Wallen paused, considering. "Although this does give us a certain amount of leverage. Maybe we should use it."

"Meaning?"

"We're on the brink here, we really aren't ready for agriculture. I'm struggling to get vegetable crops growing and it isn't working well."

"Wallen . . ." Aurora paused, knowing what she needed to say, and trying to find a tactful way to say it. "I know that you know the importance of this. If we can't grow our own food, we're all going to wind up downwire. People have been farming since the dawn of time. What's the problem?"

"The problem is, I'm a biologist, not a farmer, and farming is a technical specialty all its own. Would you expect a downwire dirt farmer to be able to do your job?"

Of course not. *Ark* is its own unique environment, and we need to find the right crops to grow here. I could pamper a little patch of plants to grow quite nicely. I can't do that with a hectare or more."

Aurora swept her hand at the steel wall, taking in the rest of *Ark*'s interior by extension. "Wheat is growing wild out there."

"Wheat finds its own way."

"So why aren't we growing wheat then?"

"Because we've got no way to thresh it or mill it, and we can't afford the labor to do those things by hand. We need time and equipment to put a mill together, and even if we had one we've got no yeast. That's a trivial detail, but the other ones aren't. In the meantime we need to eat, so row vegetables are what I'm working on because they'll give us the full range of necessary nutrients and they're easiest for us to process. I'm working on legumes too, because we're going to need the protein, since we got no domestic stock at all."

Aurora nodded slowly. "I didn't know our situation was so precarious."

"Neither did I. This has been an education . . ." Wallen absently rubbed the new calluses on his hands. ". . . in a lot of ways. I knew raising crops would be a challenge before we had the ecosystem finished. I had no idea it was going to be this difficult. I was going to lay out the situation at the next senior staff meeting."

"What do we need to do to make it work?"

"We need time, most of all." Wallen pointed a finger at the display. "That's what we can buy with all this feed frenzy about us."

"Meaning?"

"I'm sure the secretary-general doesn't really care what we do, he only shut us down to please his voters. Keyls wouldn't be calling now except the feeds are making him look like he's losing a confrontation. No politician can afford to look weak in public. Give him something to fend off the feeds, and we can get something back. Food shipments at least, maybe proper farming equipment."

Aurora nodded. "Not a bad plan." She pursed her lips. "Except it means I'll have to go downwire again."

"So go downwire. What, did you think you'd like being chief engineer?"

Aurora smirked. "I didn't think I'd hate it this much."

*Ark* was beautiful and, for all her immense size and strength, fragile in the vast empty blackness of space. Aurora Brady forgot everything to just enjoy the sight as her boost car fell away and downwire from the spin platform. The platform was set in the middle of the *Ark*'s foredome, anchoring the orbital end of the Cable on one side, connected to *Ark* with a rotating transfer tube on the other. Beyond the platform the vast foundry mirrors glinted sun-bright, and still farther out huge monofilament nets held floating mountains of iron and carbon waiting to be smelted into steel and diamond and nanofiber. Through the still transparent sections of *Ark*'s hull she could see the blue of the ocean, and the stripe of green that was their sliver of functioning biosphere. Here and there lights flickered in the darkness around the great ship, the attitude jets of u-carriers, each bearing hundred-meter sections of carefully curved steel and carbon-fiber hall cladding to complete the hull's triple-layered structure. It was ample armor against micrometeors and even a far-descended generation of colonists who might forget they lived in a ship and try to dig through the hull. *Multilayered defense. If only that could protect us from what threatens us now.*

She kept watching. *It's beautiful, and it's ours. I'm not going to let them take it from us.* The boost car accelerated down, and *Ark* slid out of Aurora's view, to be replaced with velvet black and brilliant stars. She reached out her hand as though she could touch one, felt the slick smoothness of the intervening silica pane. Somewhere out there, invisible in the night, was Iota Horologii. *I'm coming.* She smiled at the thought. *Don't worry, I'm coming.* She watched the view for a while. Sometime later there was a noise, and Petra Krychovik came up from the boost car's main level, and quietly floated over to watch the view as well. She was along on the journey to handle the news-feeds and to publicize the crew's case if UNISE and the secretary-general remained obdurate. In service of that goal she had prepared info packets detailing the myriad technologies developed for *Ark* and now commonplace on Earth.

The rungs on the Cable slid past faster and faster until they blurred into invisibility, but the Cable nevertheless made its presence felt in the pervasive humming vibration that filled the car as it guided them downwire. The day passed uneventfully, and the next was interrupted only by the gentle deceleration as the car slowed to be transferred to the base tower's tracks. They continued down, into the atmosphere, still decelerating gently. They arrived on Mount Kenya in the middle of the night, to be met by a

UNISE driver and hotel reservations. *We're being well treated at least.* There were a pair of Interpol officers there to guard their door, for their own safety they said.

"That's *pizzdets*," said Petra, once the door was shut. "They're there to make sure nobody knows we're here. This is all to keep the secretary-general from being embarrassed. He's come out and said he won't negotiate with us. He doesn't want to be caught with his fingers in the cookie jar." She patted her stack of press releases. "That's another lever we can use."

"Let's hope we don't need it." Aurora pursed her lips. She didn't have much hope they'd be able to alter the secretary-general's position. The feeds had him backed into a corner. That gave her power, but the sword of publicity was very much a double-edged one. *So we need to keep these negotiations low key, offer to solve his problem if he'll solve ours, work within the sphere of shared interests.*

She found that the discomforts of the homeworld hadn't changed. Mount Kenya was cold and windy, and she didn't want to think of the number of bodies who'd been in the bed in their hotel. The next day the newsfeed on the aircraft to New York told her of an epidemic, *another* epidemic, this one called type C hemorrhagic fever, caused by some unknown virus liberated from some newly violated tropical sanctuary, and it seemed to Aurora she could smell the taint of disease in the cabin air. New York was worse, steaming hot and stinking, of raw sewage in the rivers and pollutants in the air, and most of all of the compressed mass of forty million people crammed into too little space. The government volanter that carried them from the airport to the UN Secretariat building thankfully isolated her from the thronging crowds below, but she could *feel* them there as they flew overhead, and the thought made her skin crawl. Every single street was filled with more people than there were in all of *Ark*, jostling, struggling, competing for room, for power, for food, for survival. In New York those who could afford to wore filter masks and those who could not took their chances. Earth's population had doubled since she'd been born, and that actually represented a slowing of the birthrate. There was no credit to the mess that was UN family policy, it was the epidemics that were making the difference, both the mysterious new ones that could flash up, spread around the world in a week and vanish and humanity's old, old enemies like malaria, once more spreading north, and cholera, inexorably invading the crumbling water systems of the overloaded cities. *Is it any wonder their life expectancy has fallen so far?*

The volanter pilot offered them filter masks, and they both accepted. Aurora's chafed uncomfortably against her nose and cheeks. She took it off when she talked to people, which was a necessary politeness, but if she'd had her choice she would have worn a spacesuit. Every gram of soil that came aboard *Ark* was thoroughly sterilized before being shipped upwire and she hadn't realized until now how glad she was of that. *Was it this bad when I was studying down here?* She didn't remember it so. Petra, a Sibersknik and an urban native, seemed quite at home, spending most of the time on the flight making calls. She had set up a meeting with CERN for them after the meeting with the secretary-general. Centre European pour Researche Nucleaire was building the prototypes for *Ark*'s immense

fusion tube and had lost billions of euros in funding with
the cancelation. The scientists and engineers put out of
work would be *Ark*'s natural allies. Presenting a solid front
that included downwires could only help their cause.

They debarked and were ushered down into the building
by another pair of Interpol operatives. Their first meeting
was not with the secretary-general or even with Keyls but
with his executive assistant, a somewhat pudgy, somewhat
balding middle-aged man named Royer, who wore a
harassed smile that never left his face. He smiled when
he shook Aurora's hand, smiled when he beckoned her
into his office, smiled when he offered her a chair and
refreshments, and absolutely refused to be any help
whatsoever.

"Now, Ms. Brady, I'm sure you're aware that you're in
violation of government policy and the secretary-general's
directive in remaining on board the Interstellar Colonization
Project," he said, giving *Ark* its never-used formal title.

"I am, but that's really not the issue we're facing. We're
here to do what we can to help the secretary-general
manage the public's impression of what's happening. In
return we'd like—"

"I'm glad to see we're all looking for a cooperative resolution to this," Royer smiled again. "I'm sure Director
Keyls will ensure that all of your people's concerns are
well looked after when they get down here."

Petra answered before Aurora could, a hint of acid in
her voice. "Our people don't have any concerns you can
look after, and they aren't coming downwire, that's all
there is to that."

Royer looked nonplussed. "They have to return to

Earth. The secretary-general has ordered it. Now, I'm prepared to assure you . . ."

Aurora and Petra exchanged a look, and Aurora tried again. "Mr. Royer, we aren't here to talk about returning to Earth. We're here to negotiate a resumption of some level of support for the *Ark* project. In return we can guarantee that there will be no disruption in electric power shipped downwire from our solar array and, in addition, offer the secretary-general a public statement to the effect that there is no rebellion against UN authority, which I'm sure he'll find helpful in dealing with the news-feeds and public opinion."

Royer kept smiling, apparently not noticing Aurora's veiled mention of the possibility that *Ark*'s crew might stop shipping power. "But Ms. Brady, there *is* a rebellion against UN authority, and really, it can't be allowed to continue. I'm sure you understand that, though perhaps you don't fully realize the position you've put the secretary-general in. Now we're willing to be perfectly reasonable—"

Aurora cut him off. "Mr. Royer, *I* haven't put the secretary-general anywhere. If he's finding his current position difficult it's entirely due to his own actions. Now, to avoid wasting more time here, do you have any authority to negotiate with us, or is your job here simply to parrot the lines Brison Keyls has given you?"

Royer's smiled vanished. "I hardly think it's appropriate to describe my role here in those terms."

"Appropriate or not, I'm here to negotiate for certain things, at a minimum for a continuation of food shipments, and for spares and equipment. Do you have the power to agree to those things?"

"Of course not, those are completely out of the question," Royer spluttered. "The director has stated—"

"I'm well aware of what Keyls has said. If you can only repeat what he's said, then perhaps it's better that I speak to him myself."

"I can assure you—"

"I'd rather that he assured me in person." Aurora stood up. "Thank you for your time, Mr. Royer." She offered her hand and he shook it coldly. The smile was back on his face, but there was no warmth there either. "You know where to reach us when Keyls is ready to talk."

They went out. The entire meeting had taken no more than twenty minutes. Their escort took them to their hotel. Their room was on a high floor, and Aurora looked out the window at the teeming city with something close to despair. *You knew this would happen, Aurora. You had to do it anyway.* She went to the desk and thumbed it to place a call upwire to Wallen Valori. When he came on she gave him a brief outline of her brief meeting.

He nodded. "And you're going to call the feed conference next?"

"Absolutely. We'll let them know that we can either work with them or against them. Petra is setting that up now. How are things on your end?"

"The same. Bernarde Groot has some progress on Plan B."

"How much?" Plan B was what they had taken to calling the more aggressive options, shutting down power shipments, possibly even taking over other orbital power stations, and using that as leverage to keep the project going. It would turn the newsfeeders' fantasies of an

orbital rebellion into a reality, with unpredictable consequences. It might also turn out to be the only workable
option, if Director Keyls and the secretary-general didn't
prove to be more flexible than their underling Royer had
been.

"Enough to make it work." Wallen paused. "We've also
developed an option for direct action."

"Direct?" Aurora's eyebrows went up. *This is something we didn't discuss.*

"We're working on it. I'll brief you when you're back up
here."

Aurora pursed her lips, tempted to ask him for more
details. *Not smart.* She didn't know if UNISE would be
bothering to listen to her calls or not. She had to assume
they were. "We're flying to CERN tomorrow. I'll let you
know how the conference goes."

They disconnected, and then she and Petra rehearsed
what they'd be presenting to the feeds, going over the
questions she might get asked. The key points they wanted
to get across were simple. The foundation facts were that
the *Ark* project paid for the resources it used with electrical
power, and that the technical advances gained through
*Ark* research were of benefit everywhere. Petra grilled
her until they were too exhausted to continue, and then
they belatedly realized they'd have to coordinate the
arrival of all the feed reporters with the hotel. *I'm not
trained as a diplomat, and a real ambassador would have
a staff to think of such things.* Aurora had never had much
respect for people whose work was primarily social; it
seemed like an easy dodge compared to the rigorous study
required to master a scientific discipline. She was quickly

learning that not only could social interaction qualify as work, it could be hard work, demanding of considerable skill if you wanted to get a specific result. They ate dinner late, drained and not feeling that they had accomplished much for all the flurry of effort they had put in.

Fortunately the hotel concierge stepped in when they told him what they needed, and arranged a meeting room, public-address system and refreshments and organized the signage and the printing of agendas. The question of how to present themselves was a delicate one, because the goal was to show the secretary-general that they *could* make things difficult for him, but not to actually go so far as to do so. They decided that the best approach would be to have Petra introduce Aurora as the chief engineer of the *Ark* project, and use the project logo as a backdrop without any further reference to UNISE or the UN. Any questions on the question of rebellion would be avoided, they would focus purely on the benefits the project brought to the world at large. After that there was a scramble to get the backdrop made up, and then another one to get a frame to hang it on in the hotel's meeting room. Once it was up it was the only distinguishing feature in a space that was expensively furnished and yet somehow devoid of any particular character.

The next day they went down to make their presentation to find the small meeting room jammed to overflowing. Aurora had to fight her way to the front of the room. *I hadn't thought we would draw this much interest.* The efficient concierge had arranged a video feed to an overflow room and supplied two security guards to direct traffic. Petra handed out her information packets, running out almost immediately, and then made her way to the podium. She made a few opening remarks that covered the highlights of what the *Ark* project had accomplished, and then introduced Aurora. Aurora went through her presentation methodically, sticking to the facts, and when she was done she opened the floor to questions. There was an immediate flurry of hands, and she picked one at random. The feeder looked to be in his early twenties, a cartoon version of an eager cub reporter. "Are you telling us you intend to continue the standoff between your rebels and the United Nations?"

Aurora shook her head. "There is no standoff. We're working with the Institute and Director Keyls to find ways to continue the project."

"But you have ignored the secretary-general's order to vacate the *Ark*."

"We have, but I have to emphasize, this is because this project represents sixty years of investment by all the people of Earth. To cancel it now would be to break faith with the commitment our parents made," Aurora relaxed as she warmed to her subject. "We have to see this through to the end."

The reported nodded, tapping on his datapad, and Aurora called on another one, an older woman. "And tell me, why should the average person support this project, when the world is facing serious food and energy shortages?"

Aurora took a deep breath. "Because this is bigger than any one person, and more important than any one problem. This is about realizing a dream for all of humanity." *This is the play line, the one that's going to be on the push tonight.* "This is about unchaining ourselves from this planet."

There were more questions, some even more direct on the question of an orbital rebellion, some outright hostile. She fielded them as best she could, feeling somewhat besieged. *And I should have remembered downwires have no manners.* Before she knew it an hour had gone by. She closed the session, at which point the feeders simply started to yell questions at her, and the security guards had to step forward to prevent them from chasing her out of the room. *The concierge knew what he was doing there. I have to keep in mind that I don't really understand this world.* Back in their room she made a call to Royer, to tell him that they'd held the conference, but she had to leave a message with his reception because he was in a meeting. She smiled to herself. *This should at least get DiAngelo's attention.* The concierge called to warn that reporters were waiting to ambush them in the lobby, and arranged for lunch to be sent up for them. Before it arrived the call chime rang again. Petra answered to find an earnest feed reporter already asking questions. Before she'd managed to brush him off the Call Waiting indicator flashed. She finally got the reporter off the line, and the call chime sounded again. Petra switched it off. There would be time to grant follow-on interviews later.

"Let's see what the feeds are saying with what they've got now," Aurora suggested.

Petra nodded, and called up the newsfeeds on the display. The biggest item was about the northern-hemisphere drought. Western North America was getting rain for the first time in almost a year, but Eastern Europe and Central Asia were now facing crop failure. The next biggest were about type C hemorrhagic fever, which was now raging through Australia, with new cases showing up around the Pacific rim, from Tokyo to Los Angeles. She scanned for mention of *Ark*, and to see what the coverage was like. The first item they saw wasn't good. The focus was entirely on the supposed standoff, and the crew were described as "desperate holdouts." None of what she had said about the project's benefits had been picked up. Instead there was a single clip of her saying "We have to see this through to the end," presented not as a statement of resolve toward finishing *Ark* but as a blatant show of defiance directed at the secretary-general. After her statement there was a brief clip of a harried-looking Royer saying, "UNISE has no comment on the chief engineer's words at this time. The director will be making a statement tomorrow."

Aurora threw her hands up in the air. "They're taking me totally out of context,"

Petra pursed her lips. "Well, we were looking to make an impact. We achieved that mission, at least. Let's see what other coverage we got." She set up the display to show the *Ark* news items in sequence. They scanned through the feeds, and found a hundred variations on the same theme.

Aurora paced angrily for most of the casts. "I can't believe they did that to us."

"Believe it."

"Hmmm . . ." Aurora gestured the display off. "Let's see who's been calling us, maybe we can get a correction out there." They ran through the list of calls that had queued up while they watched the feeds. Most of the call tags were from feed reporters, or anonymous tags that could be assumed to be feed reporters. One was from UNISE, and she pointed that one live. It was from Royer, and his permanent smile had vanished. "Call my office immediately," his image said, "Director Keyls wants to speak to you as soon as possible."

Petra smirked. "At least we got their attention."

"He didn't sound pleased."

"That can only be a good thing from our perspective. What are they going to do? Shut down our world? We should probably call him."

Aurora shook her head. "We'll make him wait. We have their attention now." As she spoke the desk chimed and the hotel's logo appeared above the display. "That's probably him now."

"Make him wait?"

"If it's him calling us, we'll talk to him, but it's not him, it's the hotel's tag. It's probably the concierge." She pointed the call live.

It wasn't the concierge. "Aurora Brady?" The reception system's synthesized voice gave itself away only in its perfection.

"Yes?"

"I have a secured priority call for you."

"Who from?"

"The caller identity is private."

*Who could that be?* Maybe a feeder trying to trick them into answering, but a feeder willing to pay for a secure call might be worth talking to. *We do need to get our message out, now more than ever.* "I'll accept it." A green square flashed on the desk and she thumbed it to verify her identity.

A face replaced the logo, an old man, hair grey and wispy, face wrinkled, but with eyes still sharp. She pointed her own video on so he could see her too. "May I help you?"

"Ms. Brady, I'm Norman Bissell. I'd like to meet with you, if I could."

"Concerning?"

"An area of mutual interest. I'd rather wait until we can speak in person, at your convenience, of course."

Aurora pursed her lips, considering. *We'll have to talk to Royer tomorrow, and probably Keyls, and go to CERN.* "How much time do you need?"

He smiled. "An hour, no more. I'll send a car for you. Tomorrow morning, nine o'clock at your hotel lobby, if that works."

She nodded. "I'll look forward to it." She pointed the call off and turned to Petra. "It seems we've got the attention of more than UNISE."

Petra nodded. "I suppose we should see what he wants."

The next morning the car Norman Bissell was sending turned out to be a volanter, and when Aurora asked the pilot how long the flight was he told her three hours each way, far more time than she'd budgeted for. *The man wants to talk for an hour, but this will take all day.* On the spot Aurora decided to go to see Bissell by herself. Petra would stay behind to deal with Royer and Keyls, and would fly ahead to CERN that afternoon. The pilot took the little craft up and out of the city, heading west and south at seven thousand meters, threading a path through towering storm clouds that shook them with such violence that Aurora felt physically ill. *Who can live in a world where the sky can do what it wants to you?* She started to wonder if the effort to see Bissell was worth the discomfort and decided, reluctantly, that it probably was. *The important thing is to gather support, wherever I might find it. I can't afford to turn anyone away, not at this point.* She tried asking the pilot about exactly who Bissell was, but he was a private contractor and knew only the coordinates he was to take her to. *And if I'd been smart I would have looked that up last night.* The volanter was net-connected but the datalink wasn't working. The pilot told her it was because of the lightning in the storms, and pulled up the weather overlay on his navigation screen to show her all the strikes within range. That did nothing at all for her sense of well-being.

The flight seemed endless, but eventually they came through the line of storms, and the turbulence smoothed enough to allow her to wonder anew at the sheer size of the planet. She had to admit that it had a kind of wild beauty, a primitive power to it that the world inside *Ark* was missing. *Not the kind of beauty I'd want to live in every day, but still impressive.* Eventually they came down again, seemingly in the middle of nowhere, on a back-country road that ran through rolling fields and orchards, at the end of a tree-lined lane.

"Is this it?" she asked the pilot.

"This is it."

She looked around and saw a horse-drawn buggy parked in the lane, the horses placidly cropping grass from the verge, undisturbed by the arrival of the volanter. A man in plain working clothes and a long beard came over from the buggy.

"Aurora Brady?"

"Yes."

"Blessings." He touched his hat in a strangely quaint greeting. "I'm Joseph, I'm to take you to see the Prophet." The beard made him seem older than he was, but up close she could see he was not long out of adolescence. His rough hands and solid muscles spoke of a life of hard physical work, and he moved with a placid confidence.

"The Prophet? Is that Norman Bissell?"

Joseph nodded. "The Prophet."

She accepted that, thanked the pilot, and boarded the buggy. After the violent volanter flight the ride up the lane to the steady clip-clop of the horse's hooves was pleasantly relaxing. It had rained recently, probably from the very clouds that had tossed them around at altitude, and the air was full of the warm, fertile scent of wet apple blossoms from the surrounding orchards, the stench of the city entirely washed away. It was an aspect of Earth she had never seen before. *But the planet is so large nobody could ever see all of it.*

The ride to the main house was short, and her host was waiting for her on the front porch. He was taller than she'd imagined him, and his handshake was firmer than she would have expected from a man of his years.

"Good day, Ms. Brady. Please come in."

"Thank you."

He led her inside. The house was wood-framed with hardwood floors and, surprisingly, it was lit with what seemed to be fuel-burning lamps.

"You don't have electricity here?"

"I do, but only in my study. It's a compromise."

"Compromising what?"

"Practicality with idealism. Do you know who I am?" He led her through the kitchen and out into a spartan study. The windows were open to let in the breeze, and there was an ancient vidscreen on one wall. "Please," he gestured. "Do sit down."

She sat. "I'm afraid I didn't have a chance to look you up before I came. The man who brought me up your lane called you a prophet."

He smiled. "Not *a* prophet, *the* Prophet. I'm the spiritual head of the Church of Believers." He paused and looked. "I fought against the *Ark*, did you know that?"

"I didn't."

"Long ago, it's a footnote in history now. Still, I did. Joshua Crewe was determined to build it. I was convinced he was a heretic." Bissell laughed without humor. "I tried to destroy his ambitions, and destroyed my own instead." He looked past her to a picture on a wall, and she followed his gaze, saw a picture of a young man in white robes with flashing eyes, giving a sermon to a stadium jammed with cheering worshippers. "That was me, when I was young. A different time, a different man. I don't look much like him anymore, do I?"

"You still have the same eyes."

"You're kind to say so." The True Prophet gave her a small smile. "I was the heretic, not Josh Crewe, you have to know that. I abandoned everything I stood for to rally people to my cause. It was a mistake. What good are people when the cause itself is bankrupt? I was so sure I was right at the time, so sure I couldn't be anything but right."

He paused. "I met Dr. Crewe several times back then. He was a close friend of your grandparents."

"Abrahim often spoke of him. He was an inspiration, he used to say."

"He was a unique man, a man driven by a vision. He sacrificed everything to see your project come to life."

"I know the story."

"He died as alone as he lived, I think. He was missing something inside. In his own way he had the same disease I had. My failure cured me, too late perhaps. His success . . . I don't think he ever truly understood himself." The old man paused. "*Ark* has been back in the headlines. I saw you on the feeds, and was motivated enough to look into the status of your project. What I read motivated me to find you."

"I'm surprised you were able to. The feeds didn't mention where I'm staying."

Norman Bissell laughed. "Once I was a man of great power. Now I am just a man who knows others with great power. Some of them will still do me small favors, if I ask nicely."

Aurora leaned forward. "What can I do for you, now that you've found me."

"Dr. Crewe made me an offer once. You might be interested to know the details."

"I would be."

"He thought he was going to lose, not just the *Ark* but everything. He thought that I was going to defeat him." Bissell looked away again, remembering. "I thought so too. I thought God would ensure my victory. He was truly committed to that project. It was more than a goal, more than a dream. He *needed* it, somehow. He was driven, maybe driven insane by it, but willing to sacrifice everything to see this happen, even though he knew full well he'd never live to see it finished. He came here, to this house, sat right where you're sitting now, to bargain with me."

"Why was that?"

"He thought he was going to lose—well, that was part of it. I thought it was all of it. He offered to take my people on the voyage, *Ark*'s voyage, as though that were an offer I couldn't refuse. I did refuse it, of course I did. What he was suggesting was blasphemy. The first *Ark* was built on God's orders, who was he to build another? He was planning to violate Heaven. But there was more to his offer. He knew he had no one to farm, you see, no one who could farm with horse and plow, work with wood and leather and hand tools. No machine made will last ten thousand years, he told me, and there would be no way to bring enough technology to repair and replace what broke. Everything would have to be made with natural materials." The True Prophet laughed. "He had no ship then, it was just an idea. Even his first Cable had been destroyed, he had nothing, and he was thinking ahead sixty years, eighty, a hundred years, to a time when *Ark* was leaving, and the civilization in it would have to be completely self-sufficient."

"He was a visionary. Truly a great man. *Dedka* told me that too."

"No, your grandfather was a visionary and a great man. Joshua Crewe was something higher, maybe a prophet, a real prophet, unlike me." Norman Bissell shook his head.

"I thought I was a prophet, but I saw only what someone else had shown me. Joshua Crewe foresaw things. He told me then what the world would look like today, and he was right. He told me then of the need to build this *Ark*, and he was right." Bissell's eyes narrowed, ever so slightly. "And he knew you would need farmers who could work with horse and plow. Now I hear that you do."

*He knows our problems. How?* "You say you're not a prophet now?" Aurora avoided the question.

"I'm still *called* a prophet, by those who still believe in God. I don't believe in God, not anymore." He smirked at her surprised expression. "And I'm certainly not His prophet. All I am is a man, an old and tired man who came too late to an understanding of what's important in life. I won't bore you with the story of how I lost my faith, it doesn't matter here. Still, I understand the role God plays in my community. We are close, Believers are. We shun the cities, we shun the temptations of the modern world, and we work with our hands, and our backs, and our hearts. Faith is the glue that binds us together, and so I continue in my role, for the good it does others and not myself." As he spoke Aurora could hear a trace of the formidable orator he must have once been, a man who could challenge the secretary-general and expect to win. Bissell smiled wanly, as if recognizing his momentary transformation himself. "You can think of it as penance, if you like . . ." he continued, his voice lower, the flash of his eyes fading again, ". . . for the mistakes I made when I was young."

"And what can I do for you?"

"Do you need farmers?"

"Perhaps," Aurora hedged. "I'd like to know how you formed that idea."

Bissell laughed. "All the knowledge in the world is out there, for anyone who cares to look for it, though wisdom is still hard to come by. I looked into your story, and found that so many of your people had tried to stay but had abandoned the effort. I wondered why they might do that, and so I had some of them asked and learned of the difficulty they had with farmwork. It was then that Dr. Crewe's offer came back to me. It's been in the feeds that your supply shipments aren't coming anymore. I have enough wisdom left to put the rest together."

"Sophisticated wisdom." Aurora paused. *To trust this man, or not.* She searched his eyes, saw the openness there. *But he's an experienced shaman, he can lie with his eyes as easily as his tongue.* Still, he seemed to be an ally, and *Ark* certainly needed all the help it could get. "And yes, we do need farmers."

Bissell nodded. "I'd like to offer you my people, if you'll take them, as farmers, toolmakers, citizens, for your voyage."

Aurora put a finger to her lips while she thought about what he'd just put on the table. Finally she spoke. "It's a generous offer. Can I ask why you're making it?"

"It's simple really. I'm an old man. There are younger men ready to step into my shoes when I die, younger men who I'm afraid will repeat my mistakes, at a terrible cost to my community. The wider world is full of temptations for a young man, an ambitious man. While I'm alive I can stop that. After I'm gone . . ." He shrugged. "Aboard your ship there will be no wider world, nothing to tempt a man away from simplicity and hard work. There will just be us, our community, our way of life, for the whole time of the voyage. I would have that for my people, if you will give it to me."

Aurora raised an eyebrow. "Forgive my doubts, but if you avoid technology, I can't see how you can reconcile that with life on a starship."

"We don't avoid technology, not exactly. What we shun is disruption of the way we live. I use a steel plow, fabricated in a factory of great sophistication, so why not a powered tractor?" He raised an eyebrow, inviting her to consider the question before he gave her the answer. "Because it takes you one step away from working the soil with your hands. What harm is electric light? It separates you from the rhythm of night and day. What harm a store-bought quilt? Easy luxuries are something for other men to envy, divisive things that harm the community. We turn away from things that lead to pride, or to sloth, or envy or any other sin."

"And how will your people view those of us who live our lives in such a sinful way?"

"As we view the wider world today, with tolerance, though separate from us."

"You speak about men a lot. What about women? Are they immune from temptation?"

"Some might say they are temptation." The True Prophet held up a hand before she could argue. "I know you're an accomplished woman, I respect that your ways are different from ours. In our world men have their role and women have theirs. Men provide for families, women raise them, men lead and women follow. I won't say that's right, but it's what works for us."

Aurora considered that. "I'm afraid I'm not comfortable with bringing a religious movement on board, whatever other advantages there may be. Most especially not when you would outnumber us by a wide margin."

"I'm sorry to hear that. Still, the offer is there. Perhaps you'll reconsider in time."

"Perhaps." Her pad buzzed. "Excuse me, but I have to get this." The call was from her hotel, and when she tapped Accept the concierge's face appeared in the screen.

"May I help you?"

"I'm sorry to bother you." The concierge looked worried. "I probably shouldn't even be calling you, but I have some bad news."

Wallen Valori looked out over his fields and bit his lip. The agriculture initiative had become the primary, almost the only, priority in *Ark*. *Before we do anything else we have to eat.* As the one in charge of that initiative he had become, de facto and in Aurora's absence, the leader of the remaining spaceborn, though officially her deputy remained Dmitry Levenko, chief pilot. With his u-carriers floating idle in the spin platform's hangar Dmitry had not raised objections to the change in the pecking order. He was quite happy to devote himself to organizing the technical effort required to maintain *Ark*'s systems under their changed circumstances, and leave Wallen to deal with the dirt.

Given a choice, Wallen would have done the same thing. Growing a crop hadn't been easy, but he was finding it was easier than harvesting one. He had ten hectares of potatoes that had grown relatively well, after he had figured out how to irrigate the field to the level they liked and managed to fend off the rabbits. Now a group of technicians turned farm laborers were collecting the harvest, and none of them were liking it. In the absence of any mechanical assistance the amount of manual labor required to get the job done was staggering. The flexfab had turned out poles and panniers to carry the produce, as well as larger versions to allow the handful of wheeled runabouts they had on board to do duty as carriers. They were storing the crop in an array of hastily constructed storage barns welded onto the construction shack, and a crew of Dmitry's riggers were even now rerouting the shack's climate controls in order to keep the potatoes within the required bounds of temperature and humidity for long-term storage. Preserving them was another problem they were ill-equipped to solve, but right now it was also a problem for the future. As the one directing the farming operation he wasn't necessarily expected to pick potatoes, but he felt it was important to do it, because it was dirty, tedious, hard work. Nobody wanted to do it, and there was a grumbling undercurrent among the rank-and-file that the senior staff weren't sharing the burden of their changed situation equally. *And the last thing we need here now is dissension.* If the spaceborn were to survive without Earth's support, they needed to work together.

Even so, he was glad when his pad rang, giving him an excuse to put down his panniers. He took a moment to stretch his aching back before he answered. "Valori."

"Wallen, it's Aurora. We have a problem."

"What is it?

"Petra has been arrested."

"What?"

"On the secretary-general's personal orders. There's an arrest warrant out for me as well."

"Why?"

"Have you seen the newsfeeds?"

"No."

"Let me give you a reference." Aurora's face was replaced by a feed reader Wallen didn't recognize, talking about the standoff between *Ark*'s crew and the UN. The reader gave a brief and highly overdramatized summary of the conflict, and then summed up with "Today, in a press conference in New York, rebel leader Aurora Brady expressed her determination to continue her defiance." The image became Aurora again, speaking to the feed reporter. "We have to see this through to the end."

The display blinked and Aurora's live image replaced her recorded one. "DiAngelo must be howling mad."

"Where are you?"

"Safe, for now. I was lucky enough to be away when it happened, and luckier still to be warned before I went back. I've found some unexpected friends. I don't want to say who or where."

"Probably smart. Do you know what the charges are?"

"No, but the charges don't matter, they're trumped-up. What's really happening is the secretary-general is making a show of force."

"What can I do?"

"I don't know yet. We're going to have to organize some kind of legal defense. In the meantime, I'm stuck down here. How are things upwire?"

"They could be better, but we've got no problems you

don't already know about." Wallen paused. "I think I should handle the legal arrangements from here. You should be staying completely underground right now, and you're taking a risk just making this call."

"A small one, I'm being very cautious. But you're right. I'm going to keep a very low profile until this is resolved. I'll call you when I can."

She disconnected, and Wallen looked at his potato field. *This is escalating, and that's dangerous.* With Aurora unavailable he was the de facto leader of the spaceborn now, and he had to step up to that responsibility. He took a deep breath and went to his auntie flier. Fifteen minutes later he was back at the construction shack. He went up to the flexfab to find Bernarde Groot bent over a partially disassembled manipulator bed. Quickly he filled him in on the situation.

"And what do you want to do now?" Bernarde stood up and went to his tool bench, walking stiffly where his Interpol wound still hobbled him..

"The secretary-general obviously has no intention of negotiating just because we're asking nicely. We're going to have to get our people back, and in order to do that, we're going to need power—not electrical, political. How fast can you get those auxiliary tanks you were talking about made up for the u-carriers?"

"I've had one of my best and brightest do up the design already. It'll take a few hours to reconfigure the line for them, about a day per tank, two tanks per carrier. How many do you need?"

"Six solar power stations, that's six carriers. We're going to take them all over at once."

"So twelve days, say fourteen to account for problems. You need to talk to Captain Levenko about getting them installed." Bernarde raised an eyebrow. "That's if you're serious about this."

"Deadly serious. They're going to play hard, we're going to play hard. We're going to show them we mean business. Are you up for that?"

"Of course I am. If it were up to me we would have done this right away. Still, I think we should put it to a general vote."

"Aurora's gone. I'm in charge. I don't think we need to vote on it."

"Hmmm, you should speak to Captain Levenko about that too."

"I have." Wallen's voice was curter than he meant it to be. "We have an understanding."

Bernarde put up his arms. "You have an understanding, but this is something else. You're about to make a very aggressive move against the UN. Things could get very dicey in the next week. If you want to have people's support then you'd better ask for it now, or you could find yourself suddenly very alone up here."

Wallen nodded slowly. "Perhaps you're right, but let's not wait for that, let's get those tanks started."

Bernarde nodded and pursed his lips. "Shutting down their power is only indirect leverage. I've got a more direct option in mind, if you want it."

"Tell me."

"This." He held up a section of steel bar stock, twice as thick as Wallen's thumb and two meters long. One end tapered sharply to a needle point; the other had three fingernail-size bumps on it. He handed it to Wallen. "This is just a concept model. I didn't waste any fab time on it."

It was heavier than it looked, and balanced perfectly in his hand. Wallen hefted it like a javelin and felt long-sleeping warrior instincts awaken in the back of his brain. *But it's too heavy to be a weapon.* "What's it for?"

"It's a kinetic energy projectile, basically a big steel rod. On a working model the aerospike and the steering tabs would be graphite, and it would have inertially corrected satellite guidance. I can turn out ten of these a day once I'm configured for it, and hit any target on Earth within ten meters."

"Did you say a target on *Earth*?"

"Of course, did you think it was for throwing at people?" Bernarde smiled. "I got the idea when I realized that an up-fueled u-carrier would have enough delta-v to deorbit. We don't want to do that, but we can use one to put a bunch of these on a reentry trajectory to just about any point we want to hit." The fab engineer smiled a predatory smile. "Right into DiAngelo's living room, just for example."

"Do you have the fab layouts for it?"

"Already done. It's a two-day setup, because of the circuits and actuators."

"Directly attacking them is a serious step."

"This is serious business. This isn't *pokazukha*, Wallen, this is war."

Wallen nodded. "You keep saying that."

"And I mean it, hmmm. Have you ever read Machiavelli, or Clausewitz?"

"No."

Bernarde raised an eyebrow. "So? Well, perhaps you'd rather have me be the leader for the next while."

Wallen looked at the fab engineer. *Is he challenging me?* "Aurora left it to me, I think we'd better leave it that way for now."

"We'll see. In the meantime, let everyone know where you're leading us, they might not like it. Did you want me to turn out some of these?"

"Fuel tanks first. We'll take the power stations, and hopefully we won't have to go to war."

Bernarde snorted. "Taking the power stations *will* be war. There will be bloodshed before this is over, mark my words."

The storm hammered rain on the farmhouse roof while the wind tore at the doors and windows. Aurora Brady looked out the window at the rolling green pastureland beyond Norman Bissell's back porch and decided, for the hundredth or thousandth or millionth time, that Earth was never going to be nice to live on. Cambridge had storms sometimes, and she had never liked them, but the thunderstorms here were something else. This one wasn't so bad, with the lightning strikes indistinct in the clouds and the thunder a distant, delayed rumble, but the second day she'd spent on the farm a storm had brought a strike so close the flash had momentarily blinded her and the accompanying *crack* had left her ears ringing. She had jumped and fled blindly, but there was nowhere to flee except the other side of the house, and so she had stood there in the living room, gripping the back of a carved rocking chair so hard her hands hurt, shaking with fear, and wanting, more than anything, to be aboard *Ark*, where there was hardly any weather, and what was there was designed to be mild.

Norman Bissell had come to sit with her then, not saying anything, just letting his own calm acceptance of nature's rage be a steadying influence. The storm had passed and she had recovered, and now she could watch them without panicking, even when the lightning came close. *Though it's never been that close again, thank God.* There was a kind of majesty to the vastness of nature's power on Earth, and with nothing else to occupy her time she had ample opportunity to appreciate it. *No, I'm never going to like life on Earth, but if I have to live it, this farm is the place to be.* It was a different kind of lifestyle from the frenetic pace she had known in university, one governed by the sunrise and sunset and the cycle of the seasons.

"Why are you letting me stay?" she had asked Norman on the first night after Petra's arrest. "You know you're harboring a fugitive."

"Because we have a tradition of sanctuary," he answered. "And because it's the right thing to do."

"I'm putting you at risk just being here, you and your people."

Bissell shook his head. "I've seen no arrest warrant, and it isn't my place to know who they may or may not be looking for. If they find you here they won't bother me. There are still millions who will listen if I decide to stand up and speak. The Believer movement is a sleeping dragon, and the secretary-general won't want to awaken it any more than I do."

And so she had stayed, and found herself with time on her hands. Free time wasn't something she was accustomed to, something she hadn't really had, she realized, since she was a little girl. *Ark* had always been there to fill her life, but *Ark* was out of her hands now. *Just for now, just for a little while.* The UN was looking for her, she was certain, and she had managed just one further call to Wallen in the two weeks since Petra's arrest. Even that required a jouncing, three-hour journey in a horse-drawn buggy to Granby Crossing, the nearest town of any size, so she could call without using her personal pad. The UN hadn't yet tracked the hotel's call to her and with luck they never would, but it was too much to hope that they wouldn't be monitoring all the traffic between *Ark* and the ground. She'd switched her pad off so they couldn't track that either. It was a strange thing to do and she felt somehow incomplete without it, as though someone had reached in and removed a large part of her brain. For the first week she had carried around an overwhelming urge to turn it back on, to plug herself back into her personal information stream.

And yet, disconnected from the ongoing urgency of the construction schedule, separated from the everyday emergencies that were the daily routine of being *Ark*'s chief engineer, and from the larger, looming crisis of the ship's cancelation, she found something else in the empty space where all that had been, something that at first she didn't even recognize, as her mind ceaselessly spun problem scenarios in her head, devising solutions that she had no way of implementing. It crept up on her slowly, as she paced the back porch and fretted and watched the slow-paced Believer farmhands go about their business around the fields and barns. *Peace.* There was nothing she could do, about *Ark*, about Petra, about Keyls or DiAngelo or even about her own situation. Wallen would have it all in hand . . . *I hope he does, I pray he does . . .* and so she had to simply trust that he did, and wait.

*Peace.* Norman Bissell's house was conducive to it. There was no electricity outside of his study, light at night was provided only by oil lamps. The second day she had managed to quiet her concerns with a book on the medieval church, picked at random from his extensive library, but she found the oil lamps hard to read by and so when night fell she had nothing to do but go to sleep. Norman had given her his guest room, more generously furnished than his own, and she slept beneath a hand-stitched quilt on a cotton-ticking mattress. It was hard to fall asleep those first nights; the thoughts she'd managed to keep at bay during the day came back full force, racing through her mind. *What if . . . Maybe if . . .* She would lie awake for hours, staring at the ceiling in the darkness until finally exhaustion overcame her and she fell unconscious. The next day she would be up before dawn, anxious and unrested and afraid that any moment the Interpol would arrive to arrest her. It took a week before her concerns faded and she fell into step with the rest of the farm, sleeping and waking with the sun.

On the third day she tried to make herself useful around the house, feeling the need to somehow repay the True Prophet's generosity, but there wasn't much she could do. Her domestic skills, already limited to begin with, were not compatible with a wood-burning stove and laundry tubs. One of the Prophet's neighbors' wives, a cheerful woman of fifty-something named Deliah, came by every day to cook and clean, sometimes with one or another of her daughters. Deliah was cheerfully welcoming of Aurora's fumbling help, but made it clear that it was really unnecessary. Norman himself was often out with one of his bishops to visit one of the surrounding Believer parishes, or else working in his workshop. He was a carpenter, she learned, and she found it surprising that at his age he still practiced his trade. There was datagrid access on the desk in his study, and he gave her free rein to use it. For the first couple of days she followed the news obsessively, but there was nothing new about *Ark*, just the usual feed sensationalization, made worse by the fact that there was no new information to disseminate. She resolved to check the news just once a day, in the evening. She spent the next twenty-four hours twitching for an update, but when evening came found herself strangely reluctant to tap the desk on. It wasn't that anyone told her not to, it was just that for some reason plugging into the dataflow seemed incompatible with her surroundings. It would disturb the feel of the house, in some subtle way, and she didn't want to do that. She left the room without turning on the desk.

With time on her hands she turned to reading. Norman Bissell's library was focused primarily on religion and secondarily on history, and most of the books were very old. She read Adam Smith on economics, wading through his flowery style to decipher his insights into the underlying rules of trade. She found understandings there that hadn't made it into her well-filtered and incisive textbooks in school, and she marveled at how much he had unraveled at a time when science was really just beginning to take hold. She read about Peter the Great, and about Rodin, and, for a change of pace, she read the thick Bible that stood on its own pedestal in the center of the room. To her eye it was clearly a mismash of fact and legend, distorted through countless retellings, but it was compelling by turns and so she persisted.

At first she read in the library, but soon she took to reading on the comfortably padded swing on the porch, braving the unpredictable weather and the countryside scents that changed every time the wind did. She grew to look forward to the clop-clop of the work horses as they passed, and waved to the long-bearded farmhands as they came and went on their errands.

The storm arrived as she was rereading the story of Noah and his *Ark*, and she closed the heavy book and took it inside, to watch the rain through the window. Hailstones pelted down, hammering on the windows hard enough that they seemed certain to shatter, but she breathed deep and controlled her instinctive fear. *This house has been here almost a hundred years. It's seen this before, and survived it.* She wouldn't run, though her heart hammered in her chest, and she understood perfectly the ancients who saw lightning as the unleashed wrath of an angry God. The clouds overhead were so heavy that early afternoon had become a darkened twilight, and even after the hail passed the rain continued to come down with redoubled intensity, as if it truly intended to drown the world in forty days.

"Are you learning anything?" Her host's voice made her jump, and she turned to face him.

"From the book, or from the storm?"

"I didn't mean to startle you. I meant the book, but perhaps the storm is teaching you more."

"The storm is teaching me that I don't belong down here. As for the book . . ." She hesitated.

Norman smiled. "You don't need to worry about insulting me with your opinion. My faith is truly gone. To me it's history, no more."

"It's . . ." She hestitated again, not quite knowing which words to choose. "It's poetic in places, but even more violent than I imagined."

"Ah yes. Our mighty God was willing to command the death of the enemies of His people, to countenance rape and murder, and genocidal war. He wasn't so different from the other gods of his time."

"Or the rulers who spoke for them."

"Very astute. Who would dare to oppose someone whose commands came straight from God?" He smiled slightly. "Very few indeed, in my experience. You'll find the spirit of the New Testament comes closer to what you expected."

She flipped forward, after the rain stopped, and found Saint Paul preaching faith, hope and charity. *What a contrast. Here in this book is the whole spectrum of humanity, at its darkest and at its best.* It was, she supposed, no more than she should have expected. Religion was a quintessentially human pursuit; could its foundation documents be anything but quintessentially human? Bissell had the central works of other religions there, including the Koran and the Bhagavad Gita, and she dipped into them to see what they might offer. On the

morning starting her second week of exile she prevailed
on the True Prophet to arrange for a volanter and a pilot
so she could place a call to Wallen. She didn't want to call
from Granby Crossing again, to avoid giving Interpol
something to concentrate on. He obliged and that afternoon
she found herself flying to New York, thankfully in better
weather than the day she'd first come to the farm. She called
from a public desk and got Wallen on the first try.

"Aurora! Are you still safe?"

"I'm in the city, with friends." *True as far as it goes,
and still misdirection for the Interpol's ears.* "What's the
situation upwire?"

"We're holding out."

"And Petra? Any word, any negotiations?"

"She's been arraigned and is being held in custody,
we're trying to work on that."

"Have you got a lawyer for her?"

"We can't, they've frozen all our assets." He laughed a
mirthless laugh. "Gervois Heydahl nearly got away with
putting one on retainer on our government account, but
they caught that. She's got a lawyer from her own funds,
and we're in contact. They aren't letting her speak to us
directly."

"I'm not surprised. I *am* surprised they haven't cut off
your uplinks."

"They did. A couple of the trontechs rejigged the . . ."
Wallen caught himself and substituted words. ". . . found
a workaround."

Aurora nodded. "Well done." *We have to remember
they're listening, always listening.* "Any negotiations on
the larger issues?"

"I've been talking to a guy named Royer."

"I know him."

"He's not giving us much to negotiate on. Keyls and the secretary-general want us downwire. They're willing to be lenient if we cooperate, that's as far as he'll go." Wallen paused. "We've got an action plan prepared, if there's no shift in their position."

"An action plan. Good." Aurora nodded. *But I can't ask him what it is.* "I'll follow the news and check in when I can."

There was little to say after that. She came away from the call reassured, but at the same time she was strangely unsatisfied. The few minutes they'd spent talking hardly seemed to justify the hours she'd spent in the air to get there. *And yet it was necessary. I'm still chief engineer. If all I can do is let them know I'm still alive, that's what I'll do.* She took the opportunity to check the feeds, and found there was no new information, although the talking heads were still counting the days since the "crisis" had started. Most of the people on the street were wearing filter masks, and she realized with discomfort that she hadn't brought hers. She hadn't worn it since she'd arrived at the farm. No one else did there, away from the epidemic prone masses in the city. *Millions of downwires are dying, and they blame it all on us, and create a drama to distract the public from the real problems.*

The flight back was uneventful, and she arrived just as the sun was going down. It was clear, and she waited until it was dark, watching low on the southeastern horizon to see if she could see the star that was *Ark*. She couldn't of course, she was too far west, but even the attempt made her feel more connected with those she had left behind. *What is Wallen planning?* They had discussed taking the power stations. Would he do it? And would it work if he did? She felt suddenly very lonely. *Dedka Abrahim, I need you now more than ever.* Norman Bissell was treating her very well, but the Believers were not her people. She went to bed, but sleep didn't come for hours.

She slept late the next day, and when she came down for a late breakfast she found Norman in the kitchen. "I've been lucky in your misfortune, you know," he said.

Aurora looked at him askance "Why is that?"

"You've had time to see what my community is like. Perhaps you've reconsidered your doubts about taking us on your journey."

It was a question she hadn't considered, and she wasn't quite sure how to answer. He sensed her hesitancy and stood up. "I don't mean to pressure you, but come with me, I'd like to show you something." He led her out of the study, back through the kitchen and down a hallway. It was a large house, too large for just one man, and Aurora found herself wondering where his own family was. *And perhaps that's a question that it's better not to ask.* There were no photographs anywhere in the house, but whether that was because photography was too technical for Believer simplicity, or because he simply chose not to have them she couldn't know. He opened a door, to reveal his woodworking shop, the pungent smell of cut wood strong in the air.

"What is it I should see?" she asked.

"Here." He went to a wooden case that lay open on one of the worktables and selected a tool from it, a small, straight, two-sided handle carrying a blade half a handspan wide in the middle. "This is a spoke shave, originally used to cut spokes for wagon wheels." He handed it to her. "Now it's used for any fine planning on a curve."

"It's beautifully made," she said, turning it over in her hands.

"Thank you. I made it myself. Look at the blade."

She did. It was hard, black and heavy, and at first she thought it was metal, but it wasn't. "It's wood."

"Lignum vitae, ironwood. It's very hard to work wood with wood, but I've been a carpenter all my life, and I've learned."

"Why?"

"In the service of simplicity." He took a length of wood from a shelf near the door and mounted it in a clamp with a deft twirl that belied his age. "This is clear white pine, nearly extinct now. We have one of the last stands not far from here." He took the spoke shave from her, put it against the work piece and deftly slid it away from himself. A thin shaving of wood curled up from the blade. He repeated the motion a few times, then stood back to show her how he'd shaped the pine. "Now you try."

She shook her head. "I wouldn't know how."

"It's simple, you can't make a mistake. Try it." He handed her the spoke shave. She took it and put it to the pine, slid it as he had. The blade sliced wood, dug in and nearly stopped, then came free again and continued the cut.

"Twist your wrist as you go forward, and come back smoothly." He demonstrated and she tried again. This time the blade cut evenly and the pine shavings curled up. "Again, just round off the corners."

She did as he asked, and found the simple process oddly satisfying, as she shaped the square stock into a roughly circular section, finishing the two corners on top, then loosening the clamp to do the other side.

"Ironwood makes the best blades," he said as she worked. "Not nearly as good as metal, of course, and a challenge to keep sharp, but it has its advantages too." Aurora's roundings weren't particularly even, but the rhythmic motion was relaxing, almost hypnotic, and she was sorry there wasn't more to do when she was finished.

"How was that?" he asked.

"Nice . . . Pleasant even."

He nodded. "A machine could do that work, better, faster, cheaper, but it would also disconnect you from the things you make and use. All of the furniture in this house I've made right here, myself. That's what our life is about. You've seen some of what it means to work land with your own hands, and put your own food on your own table; that's our life too. I can't show you what it is to have the same neighbors all your life, to know you've helped build their homes and barns and families, but it all starts here . . ." He picked up the spoke shave. ". . . with simplicity. Our ways aren't your ways, but perhaps this is enough to show you what I'm trying to preserve, and what I'm offering you in our community. This is what I want to bring to your *Ark*."

She nodded. "I understand better than I did before, I think. We have a small world too, those of us who are spaceborn."

"I hope you'll reconsider your position about the compatability of your community and mine."

She paused and thought before answering. "I'm willing to be open-minded. Making agriculture work is a concern for us, one that's rapidly coming to the forefront." *And how is Wallen doing with the farming project?* "We have a bigger problem though. Before we can discuss populating *Ark* we have to have an *Ark* to populate. The secretary-general is shutting us down. I don't suppose your sleeping dragon has power enough to change that?"

Bissell laughed. "It might, but dragons are difficult to put to sleep once you wake them up. I have bishops eager to do just that, and that's exactly why I want to remove my community from the wider world, so power and ambition can't destroy what we have here, as my own very nearly did."

"But you *could* do it, if it came right down to it. Mobilize enough people to force the secretary-general to change."

The True Prophet shook his head slowly, his expression suddenly distant. "No, I'm sorry. I can't."

Wallen remembered the thousands that had filled the construction shack's main hangar when Abrahim Kurtaski had died. The few hundred crew assembled now to save Abrahim's life's work were a pitiful sight in comparison. *We've lost all the Siberskniks, and half the spaceborn.* He squared his shoulders and walked out to the podium. "Fellow crew members, as you know we've been struggling to stay afloat here since UNISE pulled the plug. Such success as we have had has been due entirely to you. I know it's been hard, and the future remains uncertain. Nevertheless, I'd like to thank you all for the faith you've put in myself, and in the senior staff, in our quest to keep this project alive, and viable."

There was a smattering of applause and he waited for it to die out before he went on. "As you know, we have been trying to negotiate with the United Nations, and they have presented an increasingly uncooperative front. Not only have they refused to negotiate with us, they have arrested our emissary, Petra Krychovik, and they have stranded Aurora Brady, our chief engineer, on the ground. They have cut off even food shipments upwire, and attempted to cut off our communications." He gave a nod to Dmitry. "Although thanks to the ingenuity of Captain Levenko's techs at hijacking their ground station, they weren't successful."

There was laughter and louder applause from the crowd in reponse to that. *And that's good, because I need them in a positive frame of mind, or this is over.* He moved away from the podium, opening himself up to his audience. "We are at a crossroads now. We can either push back, or we can surrender. The senior staff and I have come up with a plan to take over the orbital solar stations, with the intent of using them as leverage to earn us fair treatment. It might work, a lot of Earth's energy is coming out of orbit these days, but it will also brand us as criminals. Right now we're being offered amnesty on the ground, if we'll only come downwire. If we do this, I am quite sure that offer will vanish. If we don't win we'll face prison, on the ground. If we do win, we'll have freedom in the stars."

Wallen had more to say, but he didn't get a chance to say it. The crew rose as one, cheering and applauding, and someone started chanting "Freedom! Freedom! Freedom!"

The rest of the crowd took it up, pumping their fists in the air, and then suddenly he was being picked up off the stage and carried around the room. It was unexpected but exhilarating, powerful and frightening. He had another ten minutes of speech prepared, to carefully lay out the options. There was supposed to be a vote on that, and then a call for nominees to stand for leader, and another vote. He had been prepared to step down, had expected to in fact. He caught Bernarde Groot's eye as the crowd finished its circuit. There would be no need for a vote now, there was no point, the crowd had spoken. *Ark's* crew would face down their mother planet, and Wallen Valori would lead them in the effort. *The die is cast.*

There was a vote anyway, of course, but it was a mere formality. The vote to defy the United Nations was unanimous, and the vote to confirm Wallen as leader, title to be determined, was equally unanimous, not that it mattered since nobody chose to stand against him. He insisted on stating that he would only take the position until Aurora returned, but even as he said it he knew that it wasn't true. The social forces at play wouldn't allow him to step down. *Her power came from her position, but my position has arisen from my power.* That he had not sought his power, that it had come purely as a matter of circumstance and timing, mattered not at all. How Aurora would react to the change was something he couldn't know in advance. *First I have to get her back.*

Afterward the senior staff held a conference. Wallen found himself presiding over a heated debate over exactly how to go about their chosen course of action.

"The last thing we want to demonstrate here is

weakness," said Bernarde Groot. "I say we take over every power station and shut them all down at once. The only hope we have is to show them that it will be far too costly to challenge us. We want them to doubt our sanity, and be certain of our ruthlessness. We want them to believe we might just blow the damn things up if we don't get our way, and damn the consequences."

Gervois Heydahl, who had handled logistics, advocated a more graduated approach. "Let's just stop shipping power from our own solar array. That will let them know we're serious, that we can do more, but it won't polarize the situation. If we back them into a corner, they'll have to fight. Leave them room to negotiate."

Bernarde snorted. "That's what we sent Aurora and Petra to do, and look what happened there."

The discussion went around the table, while Wallen kept himself out of it, listening, judging. *I don't have the knowledge to make the right decisions here, but ultimately I'm going to have to decide.* The debate waxed and waned, went back over old ground for a second time, and then a third, while he considered what was being presented. Finally he spoke. "We're going to take them all at once." Bernarde smiled, and Wallen held up a hand. "We're not going to shut them down all at once. We're just going to make sure we're in control before we start giving them ultimatums."

"You realize that there's a maintainance crew aboard Solar Two right now," Gervois säid. With no shipments coming upwire he'd had no logistics to deal with, and so had become the group's de facto intelligence officer. "We don't want to have a confrontation."

"We don't know that for sure," put in Bernarde. "But we send our people armed, just in case."

Gervois gave him a look. "Armed with what?"

"Anything." Bernarde shrugged. "It doesn't matter. They're going to be confronting a pilot and two techs who won't be armed at all."

"And what are you going to do with them? Throw them out the airlock?"

"They can go back down in their own shuttle."

"And what if they fight us anyway? We won't be able to negotiate with blood on our hands."

Bernarde smiled a nasty smile. "We'll be able to negotiate better, *da*? Don't let yourself think this will be clean."

His words echoed in Wallen's brain a week later, as he rode a boost car up from the construction shack to the spin platform. The boost track the car rode was a scaled-down version of the Cable that linked *Ark* to Earth, built to carry the same cars but running at much slower speeds. Because the foredome curved inward, the track dangled in a gentle curve that grew closer to the dome as it went higher, which made the car's floor tilt at an odd angle. It was night and as they climbed past the top of the forewall it felt like they were falling into a sea of stars. As the car rose toward the ship's center of rotation his weight fell away, until he could push himself up to the ceiling with a nudge of his toes and then drift gently back down. For the duration of the short journey he forgot all about tactics and negotiations and simply enjoyed the view.

Reality returned when the car reached the spin platform's landing deck. The spin platform was at the very center of the foredome. Automated handling took their gear off the boost track and cycled them through the transfer tube that linked rotating *Ark* to the non-rotating spin platform. The platform anchored the upwire end of the Cable, and served as the control center for *Ark*'s immense solar array. It had housing for the riggers who worked the foundries and melt mirrors that floated in space all around it, and the utility carriers nested there, either floating at the end of their docking arms or in the big hangar module. In the years before *Ark* had pressure it had been a virtual city in space, with schools and shops and even a park in its spun-for-gravity cylinder, tiny by *Ark* standards, but immense for the time it was built. The gravity cylinder was long gone now, dismantled and smelted down to become part of *Ark*'s hull.

He went to the docking level, where six utility carriers had been fitted with Bernarde's extended-range fuel tanks. Six volunteer carrier crews, four each, had been hastily trained on the mission and were preparing to launch to the solar power stations. In truth there was no reason for him to be there to see them off. He didn't know any of them personally, but they were carrying the hopes and dreams of all the crew with them, and so he thanked them for stepping forward, shook their hands, wished them good luck. *Leadership is about presence, and so I am present.* They didn't look like soldiers but they were all armed with shockrods, newly produced by the flexfab. Bernarde had offered heavier weapons, but the rods were nonlethal, not a threat to the pressure integrity of the solar stations and usable in zero gravity. Dmitry Levenko had insisted that all the crews be armed with them, even though it was only at Solar Two that there was any chance they'd have to use them. "You never know what might happen," he'd said. *And he was right, we are launching into the unknown here.* Wallen didn't let his uncertainty show, though the pilots especially worried him. They were orbit-rated, but there was a wide gulf between the delicate, up-close maneuvers needed to nudge a hull plate into position and the long-range transfer orbits they were being asked to fly now.

He didn't linger afterward, leaving them to suit up and do their preflight checks. He went up from the docking level to the control dome. The controllers greeted him as he came in, then returned their attention to their displays and the jargon in their headsets. He found a place out of the way and waited, watching while the world inside *Ark* rotated majestically beneath him, like a display model under glass. From five kilometers up most of *Ark*'s interior was the shiny grey of exposed hull material; the strip of green and brown that represented the established ecosystem seemed all too small. *We need so much more dirt to make this possible.* The tiny patches they actually had under cultivation were completely invisible.

One of the controllers tapped on his console. "Carrier twelve, you are go for lock release."

There was a brief flare from below, and one of the fat, delta-winged utility carriers drifted backward from its docking arm. A second flare, and it started to rotate gracefully. The utility carriers were obviously meant to fly, but their streamlining was totally ruined by the heavy manipulator arms grafted onto their front sections. They were aerodynamic because they were too big to be sent up the Cable and, at the time they were built, too complex to be put together on-orbit. Accordingly they were built on the ground and launched to *Ark*, where their arms were added as a separate package. Originally they had a backup role as reentry lifeboats in case something went badly wrong on-station, but that function had faded once *Ark* was pressurized. Still, the wings remained, vestiges of the craft's earthbound genesis.

"Charlie twelve, flight director, throttles up, you are in the groove."

As Wallen watched the craft's main engines fired, and it began to fall away from the spin platform.

"Flight, this is charlie twelve. Confirmed, we have a good track." The pilot's voice was clipped flat on the repeater. The carrier dropped Earthward. UC-12's ungainly manipulators had been made even less streamlined by the big auxiliary fuel bubbles attached to them, and to Wallen's eye it seemed like they should make it tumble out of control. *Our carriers have wings they don't need to fly, so my brain expects an atmosphere that isn't there.* All of *Ark* was like that, to one degree or another, conceived on Earth for a voyage no Earthly mind could comprehend. *What else have we brought from Earth that we no longer need?*

The carrier fell away, gaining speed. Space was crowded near the foredome, and UC-12 was heading straight for an ungainly construction of pressure-sealed cylinders, *Ark's* hull-plate foundry. Wallen held his breath, sensing disaster, but the controllers seemed unconcerned, and as he watched the carrier's path took it below and past the foundry. He breathed out in relief. The impending collision had just been a trick of his point of view, the foundry looked closer than it was because there was nothing in space to give it perspective. *I've lived in space most of my life, but I have no real experience with orbit.* It was a reminder that he had no experience leading a revolution either. *And what we have now is a revolution, whatever it was before.* With the departure of UC-12 the *Ark*'s crew had moved from passive resistance of the UN's dictates to active rebellion. When the day was over, they would have declared their independence from Earth. Whether they would get to keep it was another question.

The carrier's engines flared again, brighter this time, driving it straight down toward the planet below to trade orbital height for angular velocity. It would fly an inverted parabola that would have let it catch up to Solar Five in just under twelve hours. Dmitry Levenko had calculated the orbits so all six carriers would arrive at their targets at the same time. Such precision coordination wasn't strictly necessary, since only Solar Two had even the possibility of resistance, but Bernarde and Dmitry had come up with the plan, and Wallen had gone along with it, if only because it allowed them to practice planning for an eventuality where they might well be an active enemy.

The controller keyed his microphone. "Charlie four, flight director, you are clear for lock release."

Wallen watched as another delta-winged shape drifted backward from the spin platform. *Twelve hours to go.*

The prairie sun was brilliant in a cloudless sky, beating down remorselessly, and Norman Bissell, the True Prophet of the Church of Believers, found it uncomfortably hot in the back of the buggy, though the breeze through the windows did provide some relief. The car from the airport had been air-conditioned, and in the transition from one to the other he'd wished, temporarily, that he'd simply let the car take him all the way into town. It would have been an excusable luxury; horse-drawn vehicles weren't allowed on the highway to the airport, and so the car was unavoidable anyway. The driver had even offered to waive the fare for the rest of the journey when he realized Norman intended to get out by the side of the road in the middle of nowhere. Believers weren't as common here as they were in the East, and he'd been surprised when Norman had explained that the problem wasn't money.

*And now the problem is heat.* Actually the problem was much larger than heat. *The heat is just uncomfortable, not dangerous.* The brother who'd brought the buggy to meet him had been thoughtful enough to bring a jug of cool mint tea, and Norman swigged from it gratefully as the horse clopped steadily along past endless fields of golden wheat stretching to an infinite horizon. *Big sky country.* Zooming along in an air-conditioned car would have robbed him of some fraction of that beauty, disconnected him to that degree from the world around him. *And so even as I hurry, I have to remember why it is that I am hurrying, and not sacrifice it in my haste.* To arrive in a car at the Elder Council would send entirely the wrong message, and today was a day when every message would carry weight.

He made idle conversation with the driver as they traveled, a man of middle years named Silas Born. Silas was a second-generation Believer, a wheat farmer himself, with three wives and nine children. As they talked

Norman learned their names and their accomplishments. His oldest son was a servitor at the local church now, his oldest daughter had just been placed with a fine family two counties north, his youngest was just cutting her first tooth. Silas himself was eager to hear the opinions of the Prophet on any subject at all but Norman mostly just listened. *Would we have connected so well in a car? Not quite.* Driving a car demanded more attention, and a shorter journey gave less time to talk. *Technology erodes community, this is the lesson it took me so long to learn, though it was there in my heart all the time.* The problem was, the lesson wasn't clear-cut. Without the car to collect him from the airport, without the plane itself, without all the intermeshed machinery of the modern world that made the plane and the airport and the car possible, then he and Silas Born would never have met at all. *Even this road we're traveling was built by machines.* He learned that Silas's parents had become Believers at a stadium rally that Norman himself had held, back in the time when he'd staged such events like rock concerts. *If I hadn't done that then, he wouldn't be a Believer today.*

No, it wasn't simple to decide when to use technology and when to reject it, nor were machines the only threat to community. They came into the town of Drover, a cluster of buildings that stood out from the prairie so starkly they seemed almost alien in the endless golden landscape. A pair of tall, angular grain elevators dominated the center of town, and the next largest building was the church. There were more buggies on the streets; Brother Silas raised a hand and called "Blessings" to every one as they passed, and to most of the cars too. The Prophet nodded approvingly. *This is what is threatened here, and this is what I have to preserve.* It would solve so many problems to take his people to *Ark*. Aurora Brady's sudden presence seemed to be an omen. *Or maybe I'm just looking for the easy way out, using technology to solve the problems of technology.*

Silas turned the horses into the church drive. A man was waiting by the door for them. Bishop Caleb Sully. *Of course he would be waiting.*

"Blessings, Prophet." Bishop Sully smiled broadly. "I wasn't expecting you to come."

"At my age every day comes as a new surprise." Norman Bissell pulled himself out of the buggy.

"You must be tired after the journey," said Caleb. "I'm sure Brother Born would be happy to give you a meal and a room to rest in."

"Yes, we'd be honored, Prophet." Silas Born sounded almost eager.

Norman shook his head. "Thank you both, but when the Elder Council meets, the leader of the Church should be there."

"Of course, let me help you down." Did Sully's warm expression crack just the tiniest bit? The bishop reached up to offer a hand to Bissell, who took it and climbed down from the buggy rather unsteadily. "I'm glad you were able to make it."

"I'm glad to hear it." Bissell smiled back, enjoying the younger man's not-quite-concealed discomfiture. *He's caught, and he knows it, and now he's going to try to limit the damage.* They walked up the stairs, and though Norman's joints ached after the hours of enforced sitting the journey had required, he accepted the pain and stood straight and walked briskly. *I won't have him see me as a broken old man.* Still the effort told, and he was glad it was a short walk to the meeting room at the back of the church. It was a plain room, large and airy, with hardwood floors and big windows, open now to let the prairie breeze take some of the heat away. Simple wooden chairs were set around a simple wooden table. His bishops were there, and they rose to greet him.

"Blessings, Prophet . . . Blessings, Prophet . . . Blessings, Prophet . . ." They filed by to shake his hand. He might have waved them all back to their seats, but he didn't. *Let them acknowledge my power here, and it will be that much harder for them to take it away.* He looked each of them in the eye as he greeted them, looking for signs of loyalty, of uncertainty, of deception. What he saw was not encouraging. *It's worse than I thought.* But of course it would be. Caleb Sully wouldn't have made a move this overt if he wasn't sure of his support. There was a display projector on the shelf at the far end of the room, and a fuel cell to power it. They were switched off now, but still tangible evidence of the council's intent.

He went to the head of the table, chose the chair that he thought was Sully's and sat in it. "Please, Brothers, sit down. There's no need to stand for me." He smiled when Sully had to go out of the room for another chair, and then squeeze it in between two other bishops at the foot of the table. Sully was a force to be reckoned with on the Elder Council, but the council was too small and well mannered a body for him to have learned how the game of power was truly played. He looked around the room, meeting the gaze of his erstwhile followers. "A moment of prayer, please, Brothers."

They all stood, having just sat down, but he remained seated, a privilege of both his age and his position. "Blessed and Holy Father above," he began, "guide us, Your humble servants, that we may follow close upon Your path. Give us loyalty and humility and allow us to daily rejoice in the glory which is Your presence . . ." He went on at some length, one part of his brain measuring the passage of time while another assembled the familiar invocations into phrases almost automatically. *The words mean nothing, but the time spent is something else.* He kept speaking, keeping his head lowered and his eyes bowed, until he could hear his audience start to shift their weight on the hardwood floor. *Let them wait, and let them know their discomfort is delivered at my whim.* There were a thousand techniques for one man to establish dominance over another, and the True Prophet of the Church of Believers had mastered them all before most of his bishops had even been born. Eventually he judged they had suffered enough, and finished his imprecation to the holy spirit. "Amen."

"Amen." His bishops answered as one, and the relief was evident in their voices. There was a scuffling of chairs as they sat down.

"I apologize for being late, Brothers," Bissell said. "Unfortunately Bishop Sully's message didn't reach me until this morning." He nodded to Sully, who nodded back but didn't manage to keep the sour expression off his face. He had no doubt calculated that a man in his upper eighties wouldn't choose to embark on an eight-hour journey to attend a meeting with last minute notice. "Please." Bissell waved a hand. "Go on with what you were doing. I'll listen and catch up."

Caleb Sully stood up. "Actually, Prophet, we were about to adjourn for the day." There were murmurs of assent around the table.

"No, Brothers. I know Caleb, and all of you, are just thinking of providing an old man with some rest after his long journey. I do appreciate your concern, but I'm not quite so old as you think I am. Bishop Hatley, if you'd be so kind as to switch on the projector?" He pointed to the bishop nearest the shelf. "Bishop Sully, please finish your presentation."

"Yes, of course." Sully smiled again, but the smile didn't reach his eyes. Hatley turned on the projector, and a slide entitled "Outreach Initiative" appeared, with an animated graph showing Church membership numbers over time. The graph slanted steeply upward into the future. Sully explained it, clearly uncomfortable at being caught going behind the True Prophet's back with an already rejected plan to expand the Church, but he was forced to go through with the charade. He could have refused, of course, but he hadn't yet consolidated his power, and to defy the True Prophet in front of the Elder Council would cost him his hard-won position as first-among-equals. Norman Bissell felt sorry for him. *He only wants what I had, when I was his age. Ambition isn't a deadly sin, but it should be.*

He paid little attention to the presentation as it unfolded, concentrating instead on his bishops. They were uncomfortable too, but as Sully went through slide after slide, detailing a media plan, a public-relations plan, a missionary plan and all the other machinery required to activate a populist evangelical movement their discomfort faded, and their interest grew. They were with Sully, every one of them. *Some will share his ambition, some only owe him allegiance.* Sully himself probably didn't realize the depth of his support, or he might have risked challenging Norman right then and there. Indeed, had he not put them all in their place the moment he walked in he could well have. *This is rebellion, nothing less. They won't dethrone me today, but I can't hold this off forever.* He would need to make a drastic change.

Sully finished his presentation and asked for questions. He had overcome his discomfort and, emboldened by the True Prophet's silence during the presentation, was coming across with easy confidence by the end of it. The other bishops weren't quite so brave, and nobody put a hand up.

"Nobody has a question for Caleb?" Norman asked, challenging them directly. "Well, I have a few words I'd like to say. Thank you, Caleb, you can sit down now."

Bishop Sully nodded, trying hard not to let his sudden anger show. His presentation was over, and with the Prophet taking the floor he had no choice but to sit down as commanded, put thoroughly in his place in front of the council, his status now considerably reduced.

Norman stood up. "Brothers," he said, in a tone calculated to make them expect a dressing-down. "Simplicity is the watchword of our Church. A simple life is a life open to God. A simple life is a life free of the temptations so prevalent in our world today. We must always bear this in mind, and use modern tools only so long as they do not come between us and our families, us and our community, us and our God." He paused for effect, saw the bishops looking chastened. "We who lead the Church are bound even more strongly by this requirement. I came to this meeting late, but I came in a horse-drawn buggy for as much of the way as I could, because that is our way." *And I will not add that I also took a charter jet to save time.* "I have to admit I was surprised to find Brother Caleb giving his presentation with a display projector." He looked directly at Caleb Sully, who couldn't meet his eye. *He thinks I'm about to strip him of his bishopric. Let him.* He paused and let the silence drag out, allowing his audience to squirm. They were all complicit in the sin of the projector, and they all knew his feelings on evangelizing. *Time now to reclaim my position.* "Nevertheless, I am pleased to see his thoughts so closely echo my own."

Nobody said a word, but there was shock written on every face. It was not what they'd expected him to say. "Bishops, and fellow ministers, I'm glad to have been able to come to this question, because it's an important one for our Church, and our people. We embrace simplicity; the question has always been, how much simplicity? We live in a time of machines and science, and we can't simply ignore that. Instead we have to pick and choose what we will bring from the wider world into our homes, our families, our lives, and what we will leave outside." He paused to let them absorb that. "Caleb is right. We have become too inward-looking. We need to bring the word of God to every soul on Earth. We need to sing His praises from every rooftop, put missionaries on every street corner. This Church once led a flock of millions upon millions."

Bissell's eyes flashed, his posture straightening automatically, his voice growing deeper, louder and more commanding. *It has been so long since I've allowed this side of myself to come forward, but it is necessary now, to save everything else.* "I stand here today to tell you I am going to lead it forward to that pinnacle again, and to peaks higher still. May God bless us in our quest to serve him." He bowed his head. "Let us stand, and pray for his guidance."

And dutifully the bishops stood and prayed with him, though half of them still looked stunned. Caleb Sully in particular looked like he'd been kicked in the stomach. *And little wonder. I have given him everything he asked for, and taken away everything he desired.*

He ended the prayer, and raised his hands, signalling his bishops that they could leave. As they turned to go he said, "Caleb, wait a minute, will you please."

Caleb Sully did as he was asked, trying not to look uncomfortable.

"I understand you've appointed an inquisitor."

"I know you've spoken against them, Prophet, but—"

"But nothing." Norman Bissell cut him off. "We guide people to our way of life. We don't enforce it with fear. This man will be removed from his position, am I understood?"

"But you yourself—"

"When I was young, I was stupid. Now I'm old and I know better, and you're young. Are you also stupid?"

"No, Prophet."

"We'll see. *I will not have an inquisitor in my Church.*" He put venom into the words. "You are dismissed."

Sully turned and left without another word, thoroughly

chastened, and Norman watched him go. *He will behave for a while now, but he will not give up. He knows I'm old, and he thinks he need only bide his time until I die, and then he can seize control of what I'm about to build for him. Which only shows he still doesn't understand power.*

"I'd like to talk to Brison Keyls, please." Wallen Valori smiled politely.

From the other end of the chief engineer's conference room the image of the man called Royer smiled back. "As I've said, *Director* Keyls is not available. Please, Mr. Valori, we've already been over this ground several times. You are illegally occupying United Nations property. We're prepared to be reasonable. In fact, we've *already* been reasonable, more than reasonable, but this has to stop. You can't defy the secretary-general's decision like this. You simply can't." A note of something between pleading and exasperation had crept into Royer's tone by the end of his last sentence, and Wallen was sure that, in his small and bureaucratic mind, it was literally unthinkable for someone to defy the edicts of the secretary-general the way the spaceborn were.

*Does he even have a first name?* Royer always opened the conversation by saying "It's Royer, of UNISE," as if Wallen might have forgotten since the last time they'd talked. He took a deep breath. "You might be interested to know, Mr. Royer, that we've gone ahead and occupied some more United Nations property. Specifically, we now have people on board all six orbital power stations. We're also prepared to be more than reasonable, but I think you need to do a little more negotiating than you have been."

Royer looked shocked. "Are you *threatening* me?" Across the room and out of the camera's view Dmitry Levenko looked pleased at Royer's discomfiture. He had also dealt with the UNISE underling, and found him exasperating beyond words.

"No, I'm asking, nicely, to speak to *Director* Keyls." Wallen put the same stress on *Director* that Royer had, to emphasize that perhaps the bureaucrat was operating out of his depth.

Royers face stiffened. "I'll relay the information. In the meantime, I have to continue to insist—"

"Thank you, Mr. Royer." Wallen cut him off. "I'll wait for Brison's call." He disconnected without waiting for a reply. He had already spent far too long speaking to Royer.

The return call came in under a minute. "It looks like you got their attention," said Gervois, who was sitting opposite Dmitry.

"Let's hope the rest of this goes as easily." Wallen tapped the desk to connect, and the display filled with the image of a florid-faced, balding man. "Brison Keyls."

"Thank you for getting in touch so promptly." Wallen smiled, putting on his best diplomatic face.

"Let's not waste time with pleasantries." Unlike Royer, Director Keyls was a man with power, and it showed in his demeanor. "You claim you've taken the solar power satellites. I presume you intend to blackmail us into granting your demands."

Wallen shook his head. "We don't intend to cut power shipments downwire, if that's what you mean. We haven't even done that with our own solar array. We just want to call attention to how serious we are about achieving a negotiated solution to this."

"Hmmph. Blackmail is blackmail, however you choose to describe it. What is it you're looking for?"

"First of all, the release and safe return of Petra Krychovik, with all charges against her and Aurora Brady dropped. Second of all, the return of any of our people who've gone downwire, should they want to come back. Third, normalized relations between *Ark* and the United Nations, allowing us to sell power, from our own array, in return for water and dirt and whatever other supplies we need to complete the project."

"You're aware that Aurora Brady has vanished. We don't know where she is ourselves."

"I'm sure she'll turn up when it's apparent she can come back upwire without being arrested first."

"I'm sure she will." Keyls looked down, considering something. When he looked back up his hard expression had softened somewhat. "Are you speaking for everyone up there, or just yourself?"

"I'm speaking for everyone."

Keyls nodded. "There are some things you need to understand, before you take this any further, while all this can still end well for everyone concerned. We don't really care if you stay up there or come down. It's unfortunate that the feeds have made it into more of an issue than it really is, but they have and so we have to deal with it. That forces the secretary-general into a position where he has to be seen to win the standoff."

"We've already offered—"

"Yes, I know that you have." Keyls cut him off brusquely.

"The thing is, you've upped the ante now, and the game is going to get hard. The United Nations is built around the single, fundamental proposition that no single person, no group, no nation or continent is more important or has more rights than any other. The underlying reality is that some people, some groups, some nations are very much better off than the vast majority of everyone else. That's a fundamental inequality that goes all the way back to the dawn of civilization, and it's been the cause of war and death and suffering for all that time. The job of the United Nations since its inception has been to reduce those inequalities, and we have been doing so. We do it slowly, over years and decades, so those who enjoy wealth do not experience too much loss, while those who do not can hang on to hope. It happens to be the right thing to do, the fair thing to do, but that's not why we do it. We do it because if we didn't do it, the entire system would fall apart."

"That's very eloquent, Director, but I really don't see what that has to do with us."

"It's simple. You want to be given what belongs to the people of the world, for your own use. What you're asking for is independent status, in effect to become a nation unto yourselves."

"That's not quite true. That's simply one arrangement we're offering, if the United Nations doesn't want to be seen supporting the project out of taxpayer euros. All we really want is to keep on living the way we have been, and keep working on the project we've devoted our lives to."

"Very noble, but what you're overlooking is that it is

simply not your decision. You are *not* a nation, you are employees of the United Nations. And you cannot be allowed to become a nation, regardless of the cost. The secretary-general has decided that we need the power you're shipping downwire right here on the ground. Now, I happen to know that he didn't make that decision lightly. He made it because we are in serious trouble. Population growth hasn't stopped, and the world can no longer afford the resources that are poured into your project. That's a dangerous situation. Disease and hunger are spreading again, as they haven't in five hundred years. If we give you what you want, every group on the planet with a grievance or a desire will rise up and demand what they think is theirs. War will rejoin plague and famine, and that will be the end of our world."

"All the more reason to finish *Ark* and see it launched, to ensure something of civilization endures."

"A very convienient point of view, Mr. Valori, but not relevant. I've given you the reasons for the secretary-general's decision, but really the reasons don't matter. What matters is that Secretary-General DiAngelo is the senior elected representative of everyone on Earth. He is charged with making decisions on their behalf and this is the decision he has made. I understand your frustration with it, and as I told Chief Engineer Brady we are prepared to do everything we can to mitigate the impacts on those of you who are affected by it, but we do expect you to abide by it."

Wallen nodded slowly. "You're overlooking one thing."

"Which is?"

"We have control of the solar power stations."

"I see." Keyls nodded slowly. "So it's come down to blackmail after all."

"I'd call it negotiation from a position of strength."

"Call it what you like." The UNISE director shrugged. "You have power here, I hope it doesn't cost you too much in the long run. I'll take this to the secretary-general. You'll hear from us shortly."

The display blanked. Wallen looked across to Gervois and Dmitry. "Well, that's that."

Dmitry looked pensive. "We'll see what they do."

After that there was nothing more to say. Wallen went down to the hangar and took an auntie out to look at the fields, but he couldn't concentrate on the problems of farming. *This situation is getting out of control.* He hiked into the scrubland, trying to lose himself in biology, but where once he could spend fascinated hours watching the subtle interactions of the ecosystem he now found the details beneath notice, his mind occupied with speculation on what DiAngelo's response would be. *Ark* was built tough, but nothing was indestructible. If UNISE decided to crash a shuttle into the foredome it would shatter, the ship would depressurize, and they would all die. Would the secretary-general go that far? And if not, what other tactics might he employ? There was no way to know.

Eventually he gave up and went back to the flier, back to the hangar, back up to the chief engineer's office. His intent was to call a senior staff meeting to hash out possible UN reactions, but as he came in a call from downwire came through. He pointed it live and Royer appeared.

"Mr. Valori, the secretary-general has agreed to your terms. Shipments of dirt and water will be resuming immediately, and all charges against your people will be dropped as soon as we can process the paperwork. Our staff will be working out details for a power sales contract. The proposal we're looking at is that *Ark* be incorporated as a private limited company, with UN assets transferred under terms to be negotiated."

Wallen breathed out. *That was far easier than I feared it might be.* "Please tell Director Keyls and the secretary-general that I appreciate their cooperation."

"I certainly will." Royer seemed pleased, but then he always did.

Wallen called the staff meeting anyway, to let everyone know what was going on.

"It's a trick," Bernarde said. "Even money says the first boost car up is full of Interpol in riot gear."

Gervois shook his head. "They wouldn't risk it. They know we'll shut them down. They gave in because they had to."

"And even if they keep their word, how do we know they'll keep on keeping it?"

"At some point we're going to have to trust them."

"Trust has nothing to do with it. Power flows from the muzzle of a gun. We just proved that ourselves."

"And we still have our people on board the solar stations, that's power enough."

"Gentlemen." Dmitry raised and hand to interject. "I think the wise thing to do is meet the first boost car with enough force that we can deal with any treachery."

Wallen nodded. "We'll do that." He turned to face Bernarde. "Can you make us some of those kinetic reentry missiles you showed me, just in case?"

"I already have, and some adaptor racks so a u-carrier can launch them."

"Let's get those up to the spin platform and mounted."

Gervois raised an eyebrow. "That's a dangerous game you're playing, Wallen. We're a lot more vulnerable than they are."

"I know. I'm hoping things won't go so far."

Bernarde snorted. "Hope is not a course of action."

It took three days to get the first boost car upwire, and while it was climbing the Cable Wallen was kept busy dealing with the reams of legalese Royer started sending up to establish the corporate structure *Ark* would need to deal with the United Nations as a private entity. After he'd spent six hours trying to navigate the dense tangle of boilerplate, Gervois suggested they hire a downwire lawyer. That immediately became a problem because their bank accounts were still frozen. Wallen addressed that with Royer, who promised to get them unfrozen, but first they had to indemnify the UN from any damages that might arise from the freeze. He sent up the relevant paperwork, but because the money was in individual bank accounts every single person aboard *Ark* had to sign off on their own individual copy, made up in their name with the correct account numbers. Organizing that was an administrative nightmare, which Wallen was happy to leave to Gervois. Once that was done, UNISE had to have certified original copies of the indemnity agreements. Wallen argued with Royer that digital signatures should suffice, but the bureaucrat refused to budge on the issue, and finally Wallen capitulated and had the paperwork loaded in a boost car and sent downwire. That meant a three-day delay for them to reach the ground. In the meantime he had another argument with Royer over notifying the spaceborn and Siberskniks who'd gone downwire that they could come back up. "Not until the legal structure is in place," the bureaucrat said, and nothing Wallen could say would change his mind. He began to have fantasies of targeting one of Bernarde's kinetic missiles on Royer's office, and then calling him just to watch the impact. He was more successful in getting to talk to Petra, who called on the second day to say she was on a plane to Kenya, and again on the third day to say she was getting on a boost car.

That was the day the first of the cargo cars was due at the spin platform, and Bernarde organized thirty riggers armed with shockrods at the Cablehead transfer lock, ready to take on Interpol should his original suspicion of a trick come true. Wallen waited with them, one hand on a handhold, a shockrod in his other hand. He didn't expect a fight—he was doing it to show leadership—but he still practiced swinging the rod. It was more awkward than he expected in zero gravity. *But we'll be better practiced than they are.* The car arrived at last, and as it came through the transfer lock he realized that it was a cargo car, as expected, and full of topsoil as promised. He breathed a sigh of relief at that. *Finally things are getting back to normal.* They kept a reduced team of ten riggers ready at the lock just in case, but all the subsequent cars were full of dirt or water or, most wonderfully, fresh food supplies. The news of food they didn't have to grow themselves went through the crew like wildfire, and the general mood, which had remained tense, suddenly became euphoric. There was a feast that night in the construction shack, and someone produced a tub of vodka, freshly distilled from *Ark*-grown potatoes.

The next day the mood was much more subdued, with a significant number of people nursing hangovers, Wallen included. Dmitry, who seemed completely unaffected, organized six relatively sober crews to fly to the solar power stations to relieve those who had gone the first time. The team from Solar Two came back with the news that the maintenance crew had shown no resistance, and had actually helped the u-carrier crew familiarize themselves with the power station's systems, simply because they sympathized with *Ark*'s cause. Wallen reported that to Royer, who mostly seemed pleased that the newsfeeds hadn't learned that anyone had been captured, if that was even the word for it. Slowly the tension that had crept into Wallen's shoulder blades began to relax.

Petra's boost car was due at the spin platform that evening, and he spent the rest of the day organizing the restart of the soil spreaders, hampered only slightly by the lack of techs. With food supplies assured they could start getting back to building the ecosystem. He took an auntie out to see how his succession species were faring, and was able to spend two relaxing hours immersed once more in his specialty. He was tempted to leave his pad behind and take more time, but he was hoping for a check-in call from Aurora so he could fill her in on the changed situation and arrange to get her back upwire as well. She didn't call, which worried him slightly, and when the sun started to fade from the mirror cone overhead he went back to the construction shack and took a boost car up to the spin platform to meet Petra.

He arrived just as her car was arriving on the Cable. There was a few minutes' delay while it was decoupled from the boost tracks and cycled through the transfer lock, and then the pressure door swung open. Wallen pushed off his handhold and drifted forward to greet her. He saw two men in blue riot gear, anonymous behind body armor and visored helmets, weapons in the shoulder. *Interpol!* In the instant he recognized them they launched themselves down the center of the receiving bay toward the open door at the opposite end. He started to shout a warning, and there was a series of sharp reports. Something hit him square in the chest and his world exploded into blinding pain. He collapsed into a ball, twitching and gasping for air as the riot cops sailed past, firing as they went. The riggers with their shockrods went down as quickly as Wallen had. More Interpol followed behind the first pair, weapons upraised, spreading out through the spin platform. The squad behind them had zapstraps, and they grabbed him out of the air and trussed him to a handhold. One of them tugged at something on his chest and he felt a sharp pain, though nothing like what had felled him. The cop discarded whatever it was he had pulled free and it floated away. *A stundart.* The Interpol were awkward in their movements, clearly unused to zero gravity, but the superiority of their weapons more than outweighed that. Shouts rose in the background, but he couldn't see what was happening, he was happy enough to be able to breathe. The last two cops closed the lock and cycled the boost car back out onto the downwire track. A second boost car was already arriving at the dock, and someone was yelling something about search teams. He remembered Royer's friendly smile as they had hammered out the legal and logistic details he thought they'd agreed to. *I came to trust him, and that was a mistake.* The realization was crushing. He'd be lucky to escape prison now, but what happened next seemed of little consequence. *I've lost it all, not just for myself but for everyone.*

It was a sunny day, and Aurora Brady sat on the back porch swing of the Bissell farm, watching the wind blow through the trees and not even pretending to read. There was a rhythm to farm life, she was learning. Joseph, the young man who'd first greeted her at the head of Norman Bissell's drive, was Norman's senior farmhand, in charge of arranging the work. His younger brother Michael looked after the barns and stables. Both of them lived in a smaller house a kilometer up the road from the Bissell home, still on the farm property, but with its own separate driveway. The brothers would be at work by first light, milking the cows and feeding the horses before going out to the fields. Sometimes neighbors would come over, to help take off a field of hay, or to lend a wagon or plow. Sometimes they came to ask for help with their own farms. At meal times Deliah would call Aurora to help her set the table, which had become her token domestic task, and then ring a big bell hanging by the kitchen door. Norman would come out of his woodshop and not long after the brothers would arrive from the fields for the meal. Prayers were brief, and the food was always tasty and plentiful. Lunch was a short meal, meant mostly to provide sustenance to fuel the afternoon's work, but dinner was more relaxed, and the household would take time to talk. Conversation would open with some piece of news from what the Believers called the wider world, but Aurora quickly learned that this was almost a formality. The topic would quickly shift to family and community, and once shifted it would stay there. She found that frustrating at first, when a subject she found intriguing vanished to be replaced with local gossip she knew nothing about. Eventually she came to accept that this was simply the way the social rules worked. It was the Believer way of including the wider world in their lives without allowing it to interfere with the important business of the community.

A gust set the windmill spinning, pumping water up out of the well to the cistern. Aurora watched the blades turning, counting the revolutions almost reflexively. *Another hour until lunch*. The meals were the day's anchor points, and so she had been surprised to find Norman gone at lunch hour two days previously. He had gone to the Elder Council, Deliah told her. He was still gone, and she found she missed his calm presence. Her pain over Abrahim's death, which had begun to fade, returned as well. *Have I replaced Dedka with Norman as a grandfather figure?* She laughed at the thought, but there was an underlying truth to it. She had never wanted a family of her own, perhaps in reaction to her early loss of her parents. Instead she had channeled her energy into *Ark*, partly out of loyalty to her grandfather's vision, but also because in devoting herself to something that would endure far longer than she would, she was insulating herself from another loss.

*And when did I decide to do that?* She remembered

making up her mind that she was going to become chief engineer, that was the day she had declined to play with Jenika Donnaz because she had to study for a math test. She'd been eleven years old, and finally coming to terms with the fact that her parents were really never coming back. Somehow that awoke in her a fierce desire to excel, to become the best at everything she did. She began to compete ruthlessly, with her classmates, with her friends, most especially with herself. Getting the highest mark on a test wasn't acceptable if the mark wasn't at least an A. Coming first in a race wasn't good enough unless she also beat her own personal best time. *But what was I running from?* The truth, only visible in retrospect, was that she was running from herself, from the reality that the universe was much bigger than she was, and could devastate her life on a whim. *And I have been running ever since, to the top of my class, to the top of my profession, to my grandfather's rank of chief engineer.*

She got up from the porch swing and paced, uncomfortable with that thought. The backyard was edged with tall trees, and beyond them were wide fields of young corn. She felt the urge to run again, to physically run, and though she didn't like open spaces on Earth she went down off the porch into the yard. The grass was cool under her bare feet and she realized that she had never gone farther than the porch since she'd come into Norman Bissell's home. *And how long have I been here?* She'd lost track of the days, but long enough that the corn had grown up considerably since she'd arrived. She walked quickly, driven by something she couldn't identify, to the lane that ran past the barn to the fields. It was muddy in places but she didn't care, responding only to the need to *move*. Farther down the lane became sandy and drier, and she started running, feeling her muscles stretch and flex, ignoring the pebbles that dug into the soles of her feet. She ran until her heart was pounding, and ran farther still, up a hill and along a line of rusted wire fence, until the lane ended at a tree-lined country road, where she turned to jog down the centerline. The rough pavement hurt her feet too much to ignore, so she simply endured it, letting the pain cleanse her as she ran on, out into the tremendous, unknown vastness that was planet Earth. It was frightening and exhilarating at the same time. When she'd gone to Cambridge she'd carefully limited her world, moved on a fixed track between her rooms and her classes, and declined invitations that might have taken her out of her accustomed orbit. It was as if she was trying to preserve in her mind the enclosed universe of *Ark*, a world where nothing could get in to hurt her, where no one could take away what she loved.

*And yet they are taking it away.* She felt anger then, at Brison Keyls for the way he'd canceled *Ark*, at the secretary-general for finding it expedient to order the cancelation, at Norman Bissell because he wouldn't sacrifice his world to save hers. She came to an intersection and kept on running, channeling her anger into her muscles, running harder, letting the pain in her abused feet feed her fury. *They took away everything I ever worked for, everything I ever cared about, and now I'm trapped here and I can't do anything, not one single damn thing.* She screamed in rage, and found herself even more infuriated when the trees didn't splinter in response. *And I'm never*

*getting Abrahim back, or my parents, and I've worked so*
*damn hard for so long and it's wrong, wrong, wrong!* And
she didn't want the thoughts that she knew were coming,
so she screamed again, louder this time. The trees still
didn't shatter and she ran off the road to the closest one,
a medium-size oak, and started tearing branches from it,
still screaming, but the larger branches were too big for
her to break so she hit the trunk instead, beat it with her
fists as though with sufficient ferocity she could destroy its
very existence. The effort hurt her hands but she didn't
care, taking the pain as a welcome substitute for the loss
and fear she could no longer keep at bay. She kept on until
she was too exhausted to continue and then collapsed at
the tree's base, putting her hands to her face to weep
uncontrollably, not even conscious of the sting where her
tears trickled down to mix with the blood seeping from
the torn skin on her knuckles.

The Interpols left Wallen and the other prisoners
hanging on the wall by the spin platform's transfer lock,
like so many sausages in a butcher's shop. He found it a
thoroughly humiliating experience. As time wore on the
prisoners had to ask for water, for food, and to use the
washroom. Just two officers had been left in charge of
them while the remainder of the cops took boost cars down
to secure the construction shack. Because the prisoners
badly outnumbered the guards they refused to remove the
zapstraps that secured their hands behind their backs.
That meant that one of the guards had to serve as escort
on every trip to urinate, to help the prisoner on and off
with their clothes. Inwardly, Wallen seethed.

*Not that there's any point in showing resistance.* The guards had the upper hand. Instead, Wallen concentrated on listening to what they were saying, trying to learn what he could about the operation. Over time he gathered a handful of facts. There were two platoons of police, which he figured amounted to about sixty all told. Their orders were to round up all the spaceborn, and then transfer them downwire as soon as possible. He had hoped to overhear what was coming over their radios to learn how the operation at the construction shack was proceeding, but their radios were silent. *That's because they aren't set up to use our systems.* Almost everything in *Ark* was built with stainless steel, which very effectively shielded radio frequencies. To get around that problem the ship had an internal transponder network to relay signals by wire where they couldn't go over the air. There was nothing special about it, but you had to be using the right frequencies and the police didn't have them. *That tells me two things. First, they put this together too fast to get all the intelligence they needed. Second, they can't communicate well.* Both facts might become important later.

Eventually someone came up from the shack to tell the guards to bring their prisoners down. They were unstrapped from the walls and herded into boost cars. When they arrived at the shack the Interpols had everything under tight control, and Wallen gathered that they'd encountered little resistance. They'd established their command post on the administrative level, and Wallen had to stand in a line outside his own office with a bunch of other late-arriving prisoners, still zapstrapped, waiting for whatever Interpol would do with him next.

"Have you heard?" asked the woman in line next to him.

"What?"

"Two of us have died."

Wallen's eyebrows went up. "Do you know who?" *Anyone I know?*

"One was Gervois Heydahl. He had a heart attack when they hit him. I don't know the other one. I heard he fell from the spin platform."

"No talking," interrupted a guard, his hand on his shockrod.

Wallen's muscles twitched with the desire to hit the guard. *Gervois is dead.* He felt numb. *He was always the one trying to calm things down.* He was summoned to the next room, where they photographed and retina-printed him, a completely unnecessary step since all his biometrics were on his personnel file, as they were for all UN employees. From there he was taken to the gymnasium, which the Interpols were using as their main prisoner-holding area. *Gervois is dead.* Wallen felt a cold anger build within him. *It should have been me, Bernarde, even Dmitry. He was innocent, completely innocent.* The entrance to the gymnasium was guarded by cops carrying stundart-loaded shotguns, but conditions were better than they had been in the spin platform's boost-car dock. Inside were plastic folding chairs set up in widely separated rows, full of silent crew members, sitting and waiting. More cops watched from the spectator galleries on the second level on either side of the gym floor. Once he was inside, his zapstraps were removed and replaced with a single band on the left wrist with a number on it corresponding to the number on his chair. Food and drink were provided, in the form of a bottle of water and a sealed package of UN disaster rations waiting under their chairs. He found himself sitting next to Bernarde Groot and wanted to ask him about Gervois, but guards were patrolling the rows of chairs, strictly enforcing the no-talking rule with their shockrods. Wallen opened his food package and found his appetite gone. He forced himself to eat anyway. *Because who knows when I'll get another chance.*

The cops were calling people by their numbers, taking them away and then returning them. The process took hours, and as one of the last brought in Wallen was one of the last ones called. *The punishment of captivity is endless tedium.* He was zapstrapped again and escorted down to the chief engineer's conference room. The Interpols were using it as an interview room and he smirked a little at the irony. His escorts sat him down across from a fit-looking female officer with iron-grey hair.

"Your name?" she asked, sounding bored.

"Wallen Valori."

She wrote that down, and recited without looking up. "Wallen Valori, you are under arrest for criminal trespass and conspiracy to commit theft of United Nations property. Please be advised that anything you say can and will be recorded and used against you in a court of law. You are entitled to legal representation of your choice. If you cannot afford legal representation the government will appoint a representative on your behalf at no charge to yourself. Do you wish to speak to a lawyer?"

"I'd like to know about Gervois Heydahl."

She looked up. "Who?"

"Gervois Heydahl, he's one of my . . . one of *our* people. I heard he died."

"I'm afraid I can't discuss that. Do you wish to speak to a lawyer?"

"What do you mean you can't discuss it?" Wallen's voice rose in anger. "He was my friend, a peaceful man. He was innocent. What happened to him?"

She sighed, as though she had expected better from him. "Sir, I can't discuss that. Do you wish to speak to a lawyer?"

He looked at her and felt the urge to hit her. *So maybe it's just as well I'm cuffed this time.* "Yes," he said through clenched teeth. "I'd like to speak to a lawyer."

She looked to his escort. "You can carry on with him."

"Yes, ma'am."

He was returned to the gymnasium as unceremoniously as he'd been summoned, unstrapped and sent to his chair for more waiting. When he sat down Bernarde met his gaze, and held it. Wallen raised an eyebrow, a silent question mark. Very deliberately Bernarde lowered his gaze to look under Wallen's chair, then raised it again and gave a small nod.

*And what does he mean by that?* Wallen nodded back, and reached under his chair to pick up his half-eaten ration pack. As he did something caught his eye, a small pair of diagonal pliers that had been hidden beneath the package. Casually he picked them up and slipped them into his back pocket. They would serve to cut open a set of zapstraps, if it ever became expedient to do so. He looked back to Bernarde. *And where did he get them?* He remembered the cops shouting about search teams as the second boost car came through the transfer lock, but he'd never been searched himself; he even still had his pad on his belt. Maybe the follow-on group thought he was being searched by the cop who'd plucked the stundart from his chest. *It doesn't matter why; they overlooked me.* Bernarde would likely have been captured while working in the flexfab, he might well have had the pliers in his hand at the time. *If anyone could beat a search, Bernarde could.* With his bad leg escape wasn't an option for him, but he'd just made it a possibility for Wallen. *Where to escape to is another question entirely.* If he could make it to the hangar he could get an auntie and fly it up to the spin platform. From there he could shut down the boost track, and the Interpols would be caught on the ground, suddenly prisoners themselves, unless they could persuade one of the spaceborn to pilot a *dadushka* up there. *Not likely.* He had to assume that the UN had taken back the orbital power stations when they launched their raid on *Ark*, but having sixty Interpol cops as prisoners . . . *Not hostages, not hostages* . . . would give him considerable leverage, especially if he went public with Royer's bad-faith bargaining. *But is the platform guarded?* He had to assume it was. *It's still worth trying, if I get the chance.* Rationally it seemed unlikely to work, but he found that rationality didn't matter. He was angry at his treatment, angrier over Gervois, and the Interpols had become the enemy, it was as simple as that.

Time dragged past, and then the guards called a bunch of prisoners, who came back a while later to distribute blankets. People were stretching out on the patch of floor in front of their chairs. *How long are we going to be kept like this?* Wallen wanted to talk to Bernarde to tell him he'd been right in predicting bloodshed, to ask him about Gervois, but it simply wasn't possible to do it without attracting the guards. Prisoners caught talking were hauled away zapstrapped, no doubt to await their fate in some much less comfortable way, so he stayed silent. Some prisoners dozed, and he lay down on his blanket and closed his eyes, but he found himself too wound up to actually sleep. Eventually he dozed, and then some time after that one of the cops came in and announced they were going to be moved in groups of twenty, back up the boost track to the spin platform, and then downwire to Earth. For some reason they started with the highest numbers instead of the lowest, which meant that Wallen was in the first group. They were zapstrapped one more time and herded in single file down to the administrative level. With some shock Wallen realized that if he was going to escape it was now or never.

He checked front and back, and saw the cops at either end of the line were too far away to see what he was doing. It was easy to slip the pliers from his pocket into his right hand, but he quickly discovered it was absolutely impossible to maneuver them to cut the zapstraps. *Now what?* At the Interpol command post there was more paperwork to be finished, and the prisoners waited in a silent single file while it was done. He saw Dmitry Levenko at the other end of the line and a plan occurred to him.

"Excuse me." He pitched his voice so the nearest cop could hear him.

"Yes?"

"I need to use the facilities."

The cop rolled his eyes. "Fine." He called over another Interpol, who escorted Wallen to the washroom. Wallen endured once more the indignity of having someone else lower his pants so he could urinate, but it was worth it. When they got back he simply fell in at the end of the line, beside Dmitry, as if he belonged there, and the cop didn't question it. He traded glances with the senior pilot, turned around and waved the pliers so Dmitry could see them. Dmitry nodded in understanding, and turned so he was back-to-back with Wallen, took the pliers and, surprisingly quickly for a man working with his hands cuffed behind his back, got them around the zapstraps. The pliers dug into Wallen's wrists as Dmitry worked, chewing his way through the tough plastic. He ignored the pain, and suddenly the pliers' jaws met with a *clack*, gunshot-loud to his ears. He held his breath, but the cops didn't appear to notice. They both turned again, backs to the wall, and Dmitry gave him a tight smile. Wallen nodded, visualizing the route he'd take to the hangar, going over the Antonov startup checklist in his mind.

They kept waiting and Wallen, now impatient, had to restrain himself from simply making a run for it. A cop came down the line to verify their just-taken retina prints, and then, finally, they were told to line up to be taken down to the boost car. They filed out to the corridor with an Interpol at the front and back of the line. *This is it.* He separated his wrists, just to confirm in his own mind that they really were free, and as they passed the cross corridor down to the senior-quarters section he turned left and dashed down the hall. Shouts rose behind him, but the guards would have to fight their way past the line of prisoners to catch up and that gave him a running start. He ran with a plan, turning left at the first intersection. The administration level was a newer part of the construction shack, the senior quarters were older, built before *Ark* got her atmosphere. At the boundary between them the pressure doors were still in place. He came to the first door, dived through and slapped the seal release. Nothing happened, and he realized with consternation that the system had been long disconnected. He slammed the door shut by hand and spun the handwheel to engage the locking dogs. It seemed to take forever but they finally slid into place, just as a dull *thunk* announced that someone had put their shoulder to the other side of the steel. Almost immediately the handwheel began to unspin. He grabbed it and used his weight to hold it down. The wheel jerked in his grasp several times and then stopped. *Have they given up so easily?* It seemed unlikely. There were a dozen more Interpol on the administration floor, and while he was holding the door shut they could send someone around and behind him, delayed only by the length of time it took them to figure out the layout of the shack's corridors. That might take them as long as ten minutes, certainly not much longer than that. He could do nothing to stop them. Voices came faintly through the metal, too faint to understand, but they had the flavor of shouted commands. The Interpols were taking action. The wheel jerked again against his hand.

*And I need to move. Now.* Before he could do that he needed something to wedge the wheel. He looked around, but there was nothing remotely suitable within reach. *Come on, Wallen, think.* He had nothing in his pockets, only his pad on his belt, nothing on him but the clothes he was wearing. *Shirt, pants, socks, shoes.* With sudden inspiration he tore off a shoe and shoved it into the handwheel's spokes. It came heartbreakingly close to working, but the shoe wasn't quite large enough to jam it shut. Cursing, he tried again and got the same result. The wheel moved again. The cop on the other side wasn't making a serious effort to open the door, he was just making sure Wallen had to stay where he was until his teammates could get around him in the parallel corridors. Wallen grabbed the wheel and yanked it back. *Nine minutes, maybe eight. Think!* With the other hand he started to put his shoe back on, then stopped. *Maybe, just maybe.* He held the wheel with one hand and started unlacing the shoe with the other. *Seven minutes.* He got the lace free and started tying one of the spokes to the door's locking bar. *Five minutes.* Done! He kicked off the other shoe and started to run, down the corridor past the senior quarters. He could hear shouted voices ahead of him, coming down the ladderwell from the section ahead, and he turned back the way he had come. A long-closed hatchway led down a level, and he spent a precious minute struggling with its locking lever while praying it hadn't seized shut. Boots thumped in the corridor.

He wrenched at the lever with desperate force and it came free, sending him over backward. The hatch popped open, and he dived down it, heedless of the pain of the thin metal rungs on his sock-clad feet. The next corridor led to the flexfab and he ran down it, his socks slipping on the smooth industrial carpeting on the floor. In the flexfab nobody had told the machines to stop, and the ranks of mechanical arms were still bending, picking, placing, working, passing, in an intricate and strangely beautiful choreography. He didn't stop to admire it, he just ran down the central aisle full-tilt, sliding under the central conveyor in his socks. The sounds of pursuit were close behind him. Interpol had found the open hatchway and followed him down. On the other side of the flexfab was an automated warehouse and the machines there were equally busy, fetching, loading and sorting, the quiet whir of their operation undisturbed by the day's drama. On the other side of the warehouse was another pressure door, but with no way to secure it he didn't bother to shut it. *And I should have kept that other shoelace.* He had no time to regret the decision. Beyond the pressure door was a staircase, and he ran down it past the fuel cells and support equipment to the hangar.

There was another pressure door at the entrance to the hangar and he stopped here and caught his breath. *I made it!* He stepped through and started to shut the door, then froze. On the opposite side of the huge space the massive hangar doors were open, but a pair of figures in Interpol riot gear were guarding the entrance that led up to the control tower. They looked alert, but they didn't seem to be actively searching for him. That didn't matter, because he'd never be able to get an auntie out of the hangar while they were there. There were footsteps above him. *I can't stay here either.*

He went into the hangar and dropped to a crouch behind a wheeled cargo trolley, then made a quick dash to hide behind the landing gear of one of the *dadushka* carriers. He stole a glance around the wheel strut, then risked another dash to the closest auntie, and was momentarily tempted to get in. *But there's no way you could get airborne in time, Wallen, so just stop thinking about that.* He looked back to the pressure door he'd come through. His pursuers would be on him any second now, he was rapidly running out of time. There was an open space ahead of him, and then the skeletal bulk of a partially assembled colony lander, sitting at the bottom of the silent lander-fabrication line. Marching down the kilometer-long gallery were six more of the towering craft, each progressively more complete, waiting patiently for the robots to begin working on them again. At the far end of the line the finished landers were moved into *Ark*'s departure gallery, there to endure through the long, dark millennia until the ship arrived at Iota Horologii and the colonists needed them to descend to their new home.

There was nowhere else to go, and no time for second guessing. Wallen sprinted for the assembly line. Once there he moved to the yellow-painted center line. Doing that slowed him down because he had to dodge around fabrication machines and equipment, but it gave him more cover than he would have had running down the clear aisleways by the walls. The far end of the facility was an eternity away, and for the entire distance he expected the explosive pain of a stundart slamming into his back. Nothing happened, and when he reached the nose of the last lander he stopped, panting hard and trembling. He crept forward to a tool cabinet and peered around it, back down the aisleway in the direction he had come. The Interpols were there, at the far end of the line. They hadn't seen him, but they had to know he was there, because they were searching diligently, coming toward him. There was a length of titanium bar stock on top of the cabinet and he grabbed it. It wasn't much of a weapon in the face of stundarts, but it was better than nothing.

*And of course they know I'm here, because they knew I couldn't have gotten out of the hangar.* On the other side of the aisle was the open entrance to the departure gallery, thirty meters high and a hundred meters wide, big enough to roll a lander through. The gallery doors were stainless-steel and a solid meter thick, to prevent intermediate generations of colonists from disturbing the landers before they were needed. He had twenty-five meters to cover to get inside the gallery, all of it in full view of the cops. They were still too far away to catch him, but if they saw him and gave chase they'd be through before the ponderous doors could close.

*And there's no point in waiting.* Wallen took a deep breath and sprinted. He was through and into the gallery in seconds, and then it took him a precious minute to search through the control panels on the other side to find the door release. He pulled down the heavy switch, a hydraulic motor whined, and the massive steel slabs started to slide shut. Directly over his head the warning klaxon sounded and he jumped back in sudden panic. Red lights were flashing on either side of the doors, and any hope he had of maintaining stealth evaporated. Heart pounding, he turned and ran down the gallery, paralleling the heavy-duty trackway set in the floor. Overhead lightpanels blinked on as they sensed his approach, casting oversized shadows on the walls and floor. The departure gallery ran around the entire circumference of *Ark*'s forward rim, and even with its thirty-meter height the curve of the hull made the ceiling seem to press down on him. The launch racks in this section were empty, so even in socks his footsteps echoed endlessly in the cavernous space. Somewhere, he knew, there was an accessway to the computer station that controlled the whole gallery complex, but he didn't know where. Logic dictated that it would be somewhere near the construction shack, but on a project the size of *Ark* the most logical design didn't always make it into the final plans. *And maybe it's in the other direction.* It was too late to go back now, all he could do was run until he found it, or was caught.

He ran until his legs burned and had to slow his pace. *Still no sign of it.* Footfalls echoed behind him and so he forced himself forward. A loaded launch rack appeared, with three of the massive landers lined up nose-to-tail in front of the huge launch-bay doors. The racks behind it were full too, and he ran with renewed hope. The Interpols would have to slow down to search between the big birds, and that would buy him time. He was halfway to the closest one when he saw a thick conduit running across the ceiling, and then branching out into tributaries that ran to the launch racks. He followed it with his eyes, across to the inner wall of the gallery and down almost to floor level, to a point where it penetrated the wall and disappeared. Beneath the end of the conduit, flush against the inner wall of the gallery and hardly distinguishable from it, was a pressure door. He ran to it with a last, desperate burst of speed, hauled it open and staggered through. The titanium bar he'd taken as a weapon served to jam the handwheel. *Safe, for now at least.* He bent over, hands on knees, breathing deeply to recover, then looked up to see where he'd found himself.

The space behind the pressure door was twenty meters on a side and four or five high, jammed full of electronic gear racked in glass-fronted cabinets taller than he was. There was no question of using modern processors to run *Ark*'s systems; they could not be guaranteed to last the journey. In the racks were banks of core memory, tiny ferrite toroids strung on hair-fine wires, immune to stray cosmic rays and the erosive force of electric current. The processing elements were hand-size diamond-substrate slabs with etched-on transistors big enough to see with the naked eye. The interconnects were corrosion-proof gold, thickly plated onto silica-glass circuit boards. The room was eerily silent after the echoing emptiness of the departure gallery. He moved deeper inside, hoping for another door. There was none. *I'm safe, but trapped.* The only way out of the departure gallery was back through the hangar complex, and Interpol wouldn't leave it unguarded.

*And yet power has to get in here somewhere.* The ceiling was covered with a maze of cabling channels spreading from the big conduit over the door. They dropped thick tentacles down to the equipment racks, but the cables all looked like data carriers; none were heavy enough to provide power for all that equipment. *So where does it come from?* He examined the racks more closely and found that each rank of cabinets was mounted on a heavy metal base a handspan above floor level, just enough room for cables to be run. He went back to the far end of the room and found the bases all connected there to a square metal trunk running along the base of the wall. In the far right corner the trunk ran up the wall and vanished into the ceiling, and there beside it was a recessed pressure hatch. *Jackpot.*

*The question now is how to get up there.* He tried jumping for it, and felt foolish when he didn't come near it. He studied the problem for a moment, decided that he could reach it by standing on the closest equipment rack. There was nothing to climb on, so he just jumped up and grabbed the top edge of the cabinet, but the slick metal didn't give him enough grip to pull himself up. He tried again, and again, and came frustratingly close, but it became obvious that he wasn't going to get up that way. *Think, Wallen, think.* If he broke open the cabinet and used the circuit boards inside as footholds, he could get up easily, except he doubted they'd take his weight. *Think.* He tried bracing his back against the cabinet and his feet against the adjacent one and levering himself up like a mountaineer climbing a chimney formation, but again the metal was too slick to give him enough purchase.

The solution, when he finally found it, was painfully simple. The thick conduit over the door to the gallery was at the same height as the cabinet tops, but much easier to get a grip on. Wallen jumped, grabbed it and pulled himself up, and with some precarious maneuvering was able to jump to the nearest cabinet rack. From there it was a series of easy hops from cabinet to cabinet to the one nearest the hatch. He leaned over carefully, got his hands on the locking lever and found it stuck. *Of course it's stuck, they're always stuck.* He cursed under his breath and yanked harder, but he lacked leverage and it refused to budge. He clambered down, went back to the pressure door and retrieved his length of titanium bar, scrambled back up and over to the hatch, praying that the Interpol cops wouldn't try the pressure door before he got up and away. With the bar for leverage the hatch opened easily, and he breathed a sigh of relief. He considered rejamming the pressure door, decided not to bother, and stuck the length of titanium in his belt. The hatch revealed a set of rungs leading up into darkness, and getting through it was a matter of jumping for the bottom rung. He made it, barely, and dangled, then pulled himself up, rung by rung. It wasn't easy and he bashed his face against the steel when his grip slipped on the fourth rung, barely avoiding a nasty fall.

He cursed and gritted his teeth, pulling himself up again through sheer force of will, until he was able to get a foot on the bottom rung. He nose and cheek throbbed painfully. *But you're through, Wallen.* He'd planned to close the hatch behind him, but there was simply no way he could in his current position. *If they find it, they find it.* He wasn't going to climb down and rejam the pressure door at this point. The titanium bar had nearly fallen from his belt in his struggle, and he took a moment to readjust it before he started climbing.

The access shaft was unlit and the light from below faded almost immediately. The steel rungs were painful on his sock-clad feet, and his breathing echoed strangely in the confined space. He climbed until his arms burned and he had to stop to rest. Fortunately the shaft was narrow enough that he could lean back against the wall behind him with no risk of falling. That helped his arms, but there was nothing he could do but endure the abuse his feet were getting. He climbed again and rested, climbed again and rested, and began to wonder just where he was climbing to. He had expected the shaft to connect to the forewall ledge. That would allow him to get on top of the construction shack and make another try for an Antonov, this time from an unexpected direction. *Only I should have climbed that high by now.* The ledge was only a hundred meters up. He looked up, straining his eyes to see even a glimmer of light, but there was none. *And nothing to do but keep climbing.* He started counting rungs, resting after every hundred, but then he lost track of how many times he'd stopped and started again. *Four, or six, or eight?* The darkness started playing tricks on his eyes, and every step became agony. He started stopping every fifty rungs, and then every thirty, and he began to fear he would climb in darkness until he died. *And what if there's a hatch at the top that I can't get open?* That didn't bear thinking about. He gritted his teeth and climbed onward, and when the light came on it nearly blinded him.

*Interpol!* But no barked commands followed the light and he slowly opened his eyes again, squinting against its intensity. Level with his head, on the right hand side there was a landing with a closed pressure door, with the power trunk leading through the wall beside it. The access light had sensed his presence and turned itself on. Above him the ladder continued on into the darkness. He climbed onto the landing and unsealed the door, went through and found himself in a room full of arcane equipment. Daylight streamed through three large openings in the opposite wall. He went to the nearest, looked outside and was immediately struck with vertigo. He was halfway up the forewall, five hundred sheer meters above the ground and several kilometers around the forewall base from the construction shack. Far below he could just make out the ribbon of the forewall ledge. *No way down.* He sank back from the opening and sat on the floor, letting his feet recover. *How long have I been climbing?* He thought to check his pad for the time, but he couldn't remember when he'd started.

The largest single feature in the room was a huge mechanical rack system, loaded down with what looked like stainless-steel ingots. It was attached to a simple conveyor that looked like it was meant to carry the ingots straight out the middle opening and drop them down the forewall. *How strange.* The third opening was easier to understand. There was a large bronze bell hanging in it, and a striker attached to what had to be an electromagnetic driver. The bell was to help the colonists keep time under the perpetual daylight the fusion tube would provide. The first opening, the one he'd looked through, had only brackets on the floor, space for equipment not yet mounted. Farther back in the room was a computer rack, but it was empty, with the power-trunk umbilicals dangling unconnected. *They haven't finished this yet . . .*

He realized he was thirsty but there was no water supply, and nothing to do but go back to the ladder and climb onward into the darkness. The pain in his feet spread up his calves to his knees, and the shaft became a grueling test of will. He kept on only because he had no other option, wincing on every rung, until he found the overhead hatch by slamming his head against it. He saw stars and fell backward, grabbed in panic for a rung and hung on, shaking his head to clear it. *Get a grip, Wallen, you've got a long way to go yet.* He got the hatch open and climbed out onto a wide ledge, directly beneath one of the four massive support pillars that had cradled the fore-dome in the proper position while the forewall was being assembled. The support soared up above his head in a graceful convex curve, and on the other side of the crystal clear foredome the sun was brilliant in a jet-black sky, unfiltered by any atmosphere. The power trunk continued up the support pillar, and so did the ladder. Wallen looked up at it with shock. *I should have seen this coming. Ark's* power came from its solar array, connected to the ship through the spin platform, The power trunk could have lead nowhere else. He was going to have to climb all the way up.

For a long time he stood, looking up at the overhanging curve of the pillar with something close to shock. *I can't do this.* He had just climbed a thousand meters and the effort had exhausted him. The spin platform was four kilometers higher. Worse, the foredome's inward curve meant that he would be climbing partially inverted almost the whole distance. The ladder, when he looked closer, wasn't even a proper ladder. It was a series of handholds, meant for use in zero g and no doubt last used when the foredome was still being assembled, long before *Ark* was spun for gravity. The handholds were smaller than ladder rungs and spaced farther apart. They would be difficult to climb in the best of circumstances, which these most definitely were not. He looked down at the hatch he had just come through. *I could go back . . .* Interpol would be waiting for him down there, it would mean surrendering, but even prison would be better than the long, slow fall that awaited him if—no *when*—he slipped and fell off the pillar. He looked back at the handholds. *There's no way, Wallen.* He had planned to fly to the spin platform, not climb.

And still, something made him walk over to it, grab a handhold and lift himself up. He climbed a step, then another, and held himself there, judging. There was definitely more strain on his arms, but not much as he'd expected. *Why? Because this far up gravity is down to four-fifths what it is on the ground.* Taking that into consideration, maybe the overhang wasn't impossibly steep. He could climb it, perhaps, if he could figure out a way to rest now and then. He contemplated the chain of handholds for a long minute, then stripped off his shirt. It was long-sleeved, heavy denim, and it just might do . . . He wrapped it around his waist, arms to the front, and tied the left sleeve around the right with a double hitch. The right sleeve dangled free from the point where the knot was. He went back to the handholds, climbed up and looped the free end around a waist-level rung. He found he didn't even need to tie it off, the handholds were textured to give a good grip, and he could keep the shirt from slipping just by hanging on to the free end. He leaned back, bracing his feet against the lower handhold and letting the shirt take his full weight. It held. *I can do this.*

A sudden clacking sound startled him, and he looked up to see a bird swoop low past his head, snapping its beak. It pulled up, pivoted on a wingtip and swooped back down at him, close enough that he ducked instinctively. It was a peregrine falcon. He hopped off the ladder, went to the opposite side of the support pillar. The pillar cradled the foredome with spring steel flanges, and built on the lowest one, right at eye level, he found a messy-looking nest with three fluffy chicks in it. The falcon screamed and swooped again, and he jumped to the other side of the pillar, laughing.

"Well, ma'am," he said to the bird. "It's good to have some company."

In answer the falcon dived again. Wallen waited until she was safely past, and then began to climb with a smile on his face. She came back at him, this time so close that he felt the beat of her wings on the back of his neck when she braked to pull up. Her beak and claws could do a lot of damage, but as long as he was moving away from the nest she was unlikely to use them. He climbed quickly, and found that the extra load on his arms made it easier on his feet. Thirty meters up he paused and wrapped the shirt arm around a handhold. He turned to look back over his shoulder and saw the landscape below reflected in the mirror cone, a spectacular sight. The peregrine had been joined by her partner and they were both circling, occasionally sliding in to take a closer look at him, but seemingly satisfied that they had chased him off. He started climbing again, putting effort into it and only resting when he absolutely had to. It took him two hours to climb what he estimated to be the next thousand meters, and by then he was parched thirsty and hungry too. His shoulders were on fire and his feet were in agony, but at the same time the climb was getting noticeably easier. The curve of the support pillar was less steeply inverted, and his weight had decreased by nearly half.

*Keep at it, Wallen.* The next thousand meters took him only an hour and a half. The sun had gone by then, but the moon was full and it provided enough light to climb by. Overhead the lights of the spin platform's landing deck appeared around the curve of the pillar. *I'm doing this, I'm getting away with it.* He was climbing easily now, with his weight just a fraction of what it was on ground level. As the spin platform grew closer and the g-level fell toward zero he found he could almost run up the handholds. Some time after that it became unnecessary to use his feet at all, and he just pulled himself along with his hands, using a steady, alternating rhythm that felt closer to swimming than climbing. As he came to the last few hundred meters it was more like flying, and he had only to grab every second handhold to guide himself. He was nearly to the platform when he missed a handhold.

It was a trivial mistake, easily corrected. His momentum was still carrying him up, and he had only to grab the next one. He did grab it too, but because of the first miss his timing was off, and so he didn't come off it squarely. He missed the third handhold entirely and then he was slowly falling. Even that wouldn't have been a problem if he had been in a true gravity field, but *Ark* used centrifugal force to substitute for gravity, which meant the Coriolis effect came into play. It appeared as a gentle spinward offset to his motion as he slid past the handholds, just enough to make him miss the fourth handhold as he drifted down past it, and then suddenly all the handholds were out of reach. The support pillar was drifting sideways away from him as he fell, and he knew he had just killed himself.

It took a long time to fall the first fifty meters, long enough that he had time to curse, and then to compose himself and think. In that distance he had drifted perhaps ten meters from the pillar, and seemed to have stopped moving away. A few seconds later he was clearly getting closer again, and understanding dawned. *I've passed the inflection point on the Coriolis curve.* He would get one more chance to save himself. He positioned himself carefully and waited for his moment as the pillar accelerated back toward him, picked out the handhold he would grab, and lunged for it as it came past. He came painfully close, actually touched the handhold with a single finger, but he was falling perpendicular to the rotation axis, and the foredome curved out and away from him as he got lower. After that he was falling free, with an accelerating counterspinward drift. He began to feel a gentle breeze on his face as his relative motion increased, and when he looked up he could see the spin platform start slowly rotating. Soon he would have more relative motion counterspinward than he did downward. It would take a long, long time for him to reach the ground, spiraling steadily around *Ark*'s axis of rotation the whole way down. When he finally hit he'd be going sideways so fast he'd leave nothing but a long red streak on the ground.

*Unless!* He looked up and counterspinward, searching in the darkness for what he knew had to be there. The foredome had four support pillars, each certain to have handholds like the one he'd just climbed. In less than thirty seconds the next one would be sweeping past. He'd be farther down the foredome's curve and so even farther away from it, but if he could contrive to bring himself closer he might be able to grab it. The foredome was still only a couple of meters away, tantalizingly close. *I just need to change my velocity vector.* Before he'd even finished the thought he was grabbing the titanium bar from his belt, praying that it had enough mass to do the job. He did a zero-g twist to face counterspinward, and then threw the bar away from the foredome with as much force as he could. Ahead of him he could see the oncoming support pillar looming out of the darkness. At first the bar didn't seem to have given him any appreciable velocity toward the dome, but then he saw that it had. He drifted slowly closer as the support pillar came around, and he saw that he was going to make it. He twisted again as he came toward the dome to make contact. *Gently, gently.* The last thing he needed to do was push off as he was touching down. He extended his hands toward the surface and let his fingertips graze it ever so softly, trying to finesse his touchdown, but the pillar came up too fast. The impact was hard and he grunted in pain. His horizontal velocity was gone, and then he was sliding slowly down the corner formed between the dome and the pillar. He pressed his palms flat, one on each surface, hoping there would be enough friction to stop himself, but there wasn't and he kept going down. *And you're going to die for certain now, Wallen.*

And then suddenly his hands hit something solid, and he grabbed on with the long-dormant instincts of his tree-dwelling ancestors. It was so reflexive an action that it took him a second to realize that he was no longer falling, and when he did he just clung there, trembling with reaction, his hands clamped so hard his fingers hurt. Only slowly did he realize what had happened. He had slid past one of the pillar's spring flanges, like the one the peregrines had nested on, and it had saved his life. On the other side of the foredome there was an infinite sea of stars and he let himself hang there until the shaking subsided. *All I have to do now is get back on the handholds.* The gravity was still low enough that it was no trouble to hold on, even with just one hand, but he found it psychologically impossible to relax his grip with the vision of the long drop death so fresh in his mind. Instead he reached around the pillar with his right leg, and slid it up and down the inboard face until he got his foot secure on a handhold. Only then was he able to let go with one hand to reach around and grab a rung. He was almost on the ladder when the dangling sleeve of his shirt snagged on the very flange that had saved him. Very carefully, with his free hand, he untied the knot that held it to his waist. When it came free he didn't bother trying to recover it, he just left it where it was and got back on the ladder. After that he climbed cautiously, one hand, one foot after the other. The time for easy grace in microgravity was over.

He was feeling somewhat better by the time he reached the bottom of the landing deck, but when he finally climbed up onto a maintenance platform he found himself suddenly, violently nauseated. It was only the fact that his stomach was totally empty that prevented him from throwing up. He took a moment to gather himself, looking down to the dimly moonlit ground far, far below. *I climbed, all that way.* It hardly seemed possible, but the throbbing pain in his feet and the burn in his shoulders told him otherwise. He caught a glimpse of himself, faintly reflected in the foredome, his hair plastered flat with sweat, a huge bruise on the side of his face, shirtless and shoeless. He laughed, quietly at first, and then louder, heedless of who might hear him.

A distant whine rose to a loud whir, and he looked down to see an auntie rising toward him, riding lights flashing. He could tell from the turbine note that the pilot had his fans tilted backward, braking his upward flight. His stomach felt suddenly heavy. *Dear God, please don't let it be the Interpols, I've come so far . . .* He climbed up into the lower level of the landing deck, then launched himself up the central access tube, at home again in zero gravity with walls on every side. He grabbed a handhold at the main-deck level, and moved down to the cargo area. He found a good place there, in the shadow of a *dadushka* cargo module. It gave him cover and a clear view of the deck, with the accessway immediately behind him so he could vanish if he had to. There were a lot of places to hide in the spin platform, but first he had to see what he was dealing with. *And I'm not going to give up that easily.*

The auntie pilot was good, bringing his craft up and over in a smooth arc and sliding smoothly between the safety nets before killing his forward motion with one quick surge of the fans. The craft settled gently until the landing-deck magnets grabbed the skids, hauling it down the last quarter-meter to land with a solid *thunk*. The turbine shut down with a falling whine, and the canopy popped open. A dark figure floated out, with a weapon held to his shoulder. *Interpol!* Wallen turned to kick himself back inside, already mapping out where he was going to run to, when something made him pause. The figure had a weapon, but no helmet, or riot gear, and there was something familiar about the way it moved . . .

"Dmitry! *Zdras, muydroog!*" Wallen let himself float up into view, but not too quickly. He had no desire to get hit by another stundart, no matter who fired it.

"Wallen! Is that you?" Dmitry lowered the weapon and kicked off gently, to float in a shallow parabola into the cargo area. "*Ezoomlyet!* But how did you get here? And where's your shirt? And your socks?"

Wallen laughed. "You wouldn't believe me if I told you." His expression grew serious. "We should see if there's any Interpols up here. They would have been foolish to not leave a guard."

Aurora Brady picked herself up from beneath the oak tree, looking dazedly at her damaged hands. *What's happening to me?* Never in her life had she had an episode like the one she had just experienced. She looked up at the oak, reminded that oaks were Abrahim's favorite trees. *And why did I come here?* She had no answer to that. She got up and winced in pain, looked down and saw that the soles of her feet resembled raw hamburger, caked with blood and dirt. Carefully picking her way through the ditch she hobbled out to the road, looked left and right, and realized that she didn't even know which direction she had come from. *I think I'm losing my mind. I need to get back to* Ark. Even as she thought it she knew there was something wrong with her reasoning. *Ark* had not kept her from losing Abrahim. Sacrificing her life to its construction had not saved her from the pain of living, and the ship couldn't save her from insanity, if that what was really happening to her.

*So why do I want to go back?* The answer came unbidden. *Because I've used* Ark *to hide behind.* Ever since she had decided to become chief engineer she had let nothing stand in her way, and in doing so she had very effectively avoided having to deal with . . . *with anything.* She had confined her love life to brief and shallow liaisons, rejected the spiritual world as a complete waste of time, kept even friends at a distance. In devoting herself entirely to her career she had systematically cut herself off from any emotional ties at all.

It was no wonder she'd finally run down the road, screaming in nameless fury when she'd lost *Ark.* All those long-buried emotions hadn't gone away, and it had been the one thing that kept them at bay. They were bound to erupt. *And why did I run from the True Prophet's porch?* The answer was stunningly obvious the moment she asked the question. *Because I found peace there.* To think she had enjoyed her quiet days reading and contemplating! *I didn't guess where that would end!* She laughed an unsteady laugh and then looked at the road again to figure out which way to go. A trail in the long grass showed her the way she'd first run up to the oak tree, and with that as a clue she turned back the way she had come, walking with slow, mincing steps. *I need help, but first I need to get home.*

She had gone a tedious distance when the rhythmic clip-clop of hooves came from behind her. She stopped and turned around, to watch a Believer buggy draw close. Joseph was driving it, with Norman beside him. They pulled over and stopped, and Norman leaned out. "Aurora, what are you doing out here?"

"I went for a run," she answered, because she wasn't ready to explain it all yet.

"Well, climb in and we'll give you a ride home." Norman offered his arm to help her up. She hesitated, not wanting to show him her hands, but then took it and climbed into the buggy. She saw his eyes take in her bloody knuckles, and then move to her feet, but he said nothing. They rode in silence back to the farm, and only then did she realize how far she'd run. *Miles and miles, fast and hard.* Joseph dropped them in front of the house and then took the buggy up to the barn to put the horses away. Norman helped her inside and through to the back porch, to sit her down on the same swing she'd started her mad flight from. She saw him look at her feet again, but still he said nothing. *He's a very good minister. He knows when not to ask questions.*

"So, would you like my news?" he asked finally.

"I would."

"The sleeping dragon has awakened. The Church of the Believers is going to rise again."

She raised an eyebrow. "I thought you were dead set against that."

"I am, but life didn't offer me the option I wanted. I had to take the best of a bad set of choices."

"Which are?"

"Lead my Church or see someone else lead it." Norman smiled without humor. "I've decided to lead it, much to the chagrin of my striving younger bishops. How would you like my help in recovering your ship?"

"In return for a place aboard it?"

Norman shook his head. "No. I'm going to do this because I have to do this. Any populist movement needs to oppose the government on something, and the issue of *Ark* will work as well as any. I still hope you'll change your mind, but I'm offering this without condition."

Aurora considered that. "Ironically, I'm not sure I want to go back to *Ark* now."

"Oh?" Norman leaned forward. "Why is that?"

Aurora hesitated. *Should I tell him?* She wasn't sure she wanted to tell *anyone* about her . . . *What was it? Not a breakdown* . . . about her episode.

And yet she also recognized the genuine concern in the old man's eyes. He wasn't there to judge her, he had been nothing but kind to her for the duration of her stay. She took a deep breath and told him, of her run and the tree, and her tears, and of her sudden understanding of the not entirely positive role her career had played in her life.

Norman listened and nodded, asking gentle questions now and again to uncover points she hadn't considered herself. When she had finished he sat back, stroking his chin thoughtfully. Finally he spoke.

"Would you like an opinion?"

"Certainly."

He looked away for a moment, looked back. "You've learned something through this. You've had time and space, for maybe the first time in your life, and some underlying truths came to the surface." He smiled gently. "Maybe more dramatically than you have liked."

She nodded. "Yes, I think you're right."

"You've changed today, and because you've changed, everything in your world has changed. *Ark* served a purpose in your life, but if you go back to it tomorrow it won't serve that purpose any longer, because you've moved beyond that."

"So what should I do? I had *Ark*, now I have nothing."

"Do what's in your heart."

*But my heart is empty.* Aurora didn't say it, but even the thought hurt. "That's what Wallen always tells me," she said instead. They sat in silence for a while, and then Norman got up. He came back with Deliah and a bowl of water. They used it to soak the crusted blood and dirt from her feet. It hurt but she bit her lip and didn't cry out, while the water ran black and red. The bowl was emptied and refilled and the process was repeated until her self-inflicted wounds were clean. Deliah wrapped bandages on her feet, and then the process was repeated on her hands. They were in better shape, really just badly skinned knuckles, but it was nice to have someone fuss over her a little and so she didn't protest. When it was all done Deliah went to prepare supper, and Norman excused himself to look after suddenly urgent Church business. She sat alone on the porch with a pitcher of cool mint tea and watched the sun edge down toward the horizon. Her footprints were still in the mud by the lane, and it seemed as if she were watching herself set out on her mad run. *Not watching me, watching another woman, with another life.* It seemed surreal that that woman had been herself, just a few hours ago; she felt so different. *Do what's in your heart, Aurora.*

The bowl of water that her injuries had been washed in was still sitting on the porch beside her, tinged red with her blood. She leaned over and scooped some out, contemplating it in the palm of her hand as it slowly drained through her fingers and back into the bowl. *Life is like water, always flowing, always changing. You can never hold on to it.* It was a surprisingly simple observation, made more surprising because it had never occurred to her before. She scooped more water out of the bowl, and on an impulse poured it over her head. It dripped down her bangs and onto her shoulders and she whispered words she thought she had long forgotten: "In the name of the Father, the Son and the Holy Ghost I baptize thee Aurora Bethany Brady, Chief Engineer of the starship *Ark*."

She smiled to herself at the private ritual and stood up, feeling reborn. She walked gingerly into Norman's study, and was surprised to find him with his desk switched on, talking to a tall man in a business suit. He held up a finger to ask for her patience, still talking.

"Yes, that would be good. Thanks, Mark. I'll talk to you soon." He made a gesture to end the call, and turned to Aurora. "You're looking better."

She nodded. "I've decided I'd like your help, it it's still available. And I've decided I'd like your people on my ship, if you still want to come."

Norman smiled. "Of course, and of course. Let's get busy."

The peace in the True Prophet's home vanished in that instant. The next several days were frantically busy, and she spent them almost entirely at Norman's desk being introduced to people. The first call was to a lawyer named

Allison Skell. Norman had Aurora outline her legal situation, then assigned Allison to get the charges against herself and Petra stayed, an option Aurora hadn't even realized was available. The next call was to a high-powered businessman whose company built experimental installations for CERN. He had a considerable amount to gain from a reinstatement of *Ark*'s fusion-drive research program, and arranged to fly out to the farm to speak to Aurora the next day. After that was a prominent personal-rights champion, who rearranged his schedule to come in to help frame the debate over the rights of the crew in their dispute with the UN. The introductions continued until Deliah rang the bell for dinner, but in a sharp break with Believer etiquette Norman kept on talking about the campaign they were about to embark on. That effectively excluded Deliah and the brothers from the conversation, but Norman made no apology for the discourtesy, and after dinner he took Aurora back to his study, where they worked late into the night by the incongruous combination of oil lamp and the light from his desk display. There were more calls, incoming and outgoing, and Aurora was astounded that Norman was able to command the time of so many movers and shakers so quickly.

"I thought you'd given up all your power," she said, after he'd finished getting a commitment of support from a five term assemblyist.

"Power isn't something you have, it's something you make, or you take. The favors people will grant me are limited, based on old loyalties and debts. What people will do for me in return for my service in their own cause is something else entirely."

She nodded, slightly in awe. The True Prophet was reemerging in Norman Bissell, the humble carpenter crumbling away to reveal him as he had been in his prime. Despite his years he still possessed tremendous energy, and the flash in his eyes had become a *presence* that demanded attention when he spoke. *The dragon has awakened, and his name is Norman Bissell.* She went to bed exhausted and woke up at dawn, to find him already working when she came downstairs. There were more introductions. "You are going to have to handle these people," he told her. "You have to know them, know what they can do for you, and what they cost."

"You do that so much better than I ever could."

"So learn. I'm an old man, you won't have me around forever."

"I'm lucky to have you now," she answered, and she meant it.

He taught her some basics of human interaction and psychology, how to use eye contact to establish dominance, how to stand, how to enter a room as if she owned it. After that they launched into another round of calls. Many of the highly placed people they talked to called him Prophet, and she was surprised to learn they considered themselves Believers. Their lifestyles obviously had nothing to do with simplicity or humility before God. She asked Norman how that could be so.

"These are the people I left behind," he answered, and left it at that, which was explanation enough for Aurora.

Allison Skell called before noon to report that she'd succeeded in getting all charges stayed against both Aurora and Petra. Petra had been released and a volanter was on its way to pick her up. She would be at the farm in four hours or less. In the meantime Aurora could consider herself no longer under an arrest warrant. The news was a tremendous weight off her shoulders.

Allison had more to say. "You should know that beyond these two cases Interpol is heavily involved in something to do with the *Ark* situation."

"What are they doing?" Aurora asked.

"I haven't been able to find out yet. Baikonur launched a bunch of shuttles with Interpol personnel aboard, and the Mount Kenya site has been closed to public access, that's all I know right now. I've got some inquiries out there, I should know more soon. I'll call when I do."

"Thank you," Aurora said, and Allison disconnected.

Aurora turned to Norman. "That's worrisome." She put her hand to her lips while she considered the news. "I'd like to know what they're doing up there."

"Allison will know soon," Norman reassured her. "Her firm is one of the best."

"I can do better than that. Now that it doesn't matter if they track me, I can call Wallen from here." She went to get her pad, more pleased than she would have imagined at the opportunity to hear his voice. *In all the years we've been friends we've never even kissed.* She found herself surprised at that thought, and wondered where it had come from. *Was he one of those things I've been hiding from?*

Wallen closed and tied shut the pressure doors that led up from the four support pillars, just in case the Interpols below tried to follow his suicidal climb. While he was doing it Dmitry did the same with the doors to the spin platform's landing deck. With their backs secure Wallen led Dmitry forward, searching for any Interpols who might be guarding the platform. He wasn't eager to get hit by another stundart, but he had no weapon and Dmitry did. If he took the first hit Dmitry would have a chance to get off a shot, and that was more important. *And I hope there's simply no one here.* They went through the *Ark* side first, stopping in the control room long enough to depower the boost track down to the construction shack, then cautiously checked through the cargo areas and service bays. It was strange to see the spin platform without the usual bustle of jacks and riggers. He felt tremendously vulnerable with neither shirt nor shoes, and kept his eyes open for something, anything that would serve as a weapon. He found nothing, but fortunately they didn't find any police either. *But I didn't think we would, not on this side, because they would have come to the landing deck when Dmitry flew in.* Once they had the *Ark* side secure they went through to the space side, drifting cautiously from handhold to handhold through the rotating transfer tube. *If there's any police, they'll be here.* The big pressure doors on the tube irised open loudly, and Wallen cringed at the noise, but there was nothing they could do about it. Again they found nothing, and kept moving forward.

They went straight to the control dome; if there were any Interpols on watch that was the logical place for them to be. The only way to enter the dome was straight up the access tunnel in the middle of the floor. He came up to the intersection with the tunnel and looked cautiously around the corner. The pressure door at the top of the tunnel was open, a flagrant violation of procedures. *But the cops won't know the procedures.* He traded a glance with Dmitry, who moved into position to cover him. When Dmitry was set Wallen launched himself up the tunnel and into the dome, gritting his teeth against anticipated pain. The pain arrived in due course, not through an Interpol dart but because he was so intent on the impossible task of scanning all three hundred and sixty degrees as he came through the floor hatch that he neglected to grab the handrail on his way past. He wound up cracking his head on the top of the dome. Dmitry was right behind him, but there was no one there. *Don't relax yet, Wallen.* Dmitry searched through the command screens and put the Cable's boost-car receiving lock on manual. With that done no one arriving from downwire would be able to get into the spin platform. They went back down, sealing the pressure door behind them, and kept searching. It was eerie to see the platform so deserted, but he gradually began to believe there really was no one there. They slowly worked their way down to the hangar level and went down the access tunnel to the hangar itself. He was completely unready when the shot went past his ear.

It was Dmitry who fired, at the closer of two Interpols who appeared from inside the hangar, just ten meters away. His shot caught the cop on the arm and the Interpol went down, twitching. The second cop raised her weapon and fired. Had she targeted Wallen, who was closer, Dmitry could have gotten another shot off and with the range so short the fight would have been over. Her training was better than that, and she went for the most dangerous threat. Her dart went past Wallen's head, and Dmitry

screamed and gurgled behind him. Without thinking
Wallen launched himself at the Interpol. She had already
pumped another cartridge into the chamber and she fired
again, but she wasn't used to zero gravity and the recoil of
her first shot had started her slowly spinning. Her dart
went wide and she pumped the shotgun again, but before
she could fire Wallen was on her. His momentum
slammed them both into the wall, to rebound and drift
into the middle of the tunnel. He swung a punch and hurt
his knuckles against her helmet, while she kicked at him
and tried to bring the shotgun to bear. He flailed upward
and forced the muzzle out of line just as she fired again.
Pain burned in his forearm, but it wasn't the paralyzing
pain of a stundart. *Powder burn*, some distant part of his
mind told him and he grabbed the barrel. They struggled
for control of the gun, but in zero gravity neither had any
leverage, and they tumbled, bouncing off the walls in
random directions. She broke the stalemate by driving a
knee into his groin, spiking pain as bad as a stundart
through his testicles. She wrenched the weapon free at
the same time. Wallen doubled over, moaning while she
pumped the gun and raised it to her shoulder. With
strength born of desperation he kicked her away, and she
careered toward the hangar, spinning too fast to aim. At
the hangar door she collided with her still paralyzed
colleague, bounced down and had to let go of the shotgun
to grab a handhold and stabilize herself.

Wallen had recovered from his own spin by then, and
saw the shotgun floating free in the middle of the tunnel.
He overrode the pain in his groin and launched himself
for it at the same instant she did. They wound up colliding

with the gun in the middle. She got a hand on it but he knocked it clear. It spun away, smacked hard against a hatch cover and went off, sending another dart richochetting around the tunnel. He held onto her, intending to beat her with sheer size and mass, but she was trained and strong and wearing body armor. He needed a weapon, but before he could relocate the shotgun she head butted him with her helmet, hard enough to make him see stars. While he was recovering from that she drove an elbow into his face, hitting his jaw where it was already bruised. Dazed he kicked at her, but his bare foot wasn't going to inflict damage through her armor. It *did* send her spinning away again, which gave him enough respite to clear his head.

Pain jolted through his arm and he jerked back reflexively. One of the stundarts had drifted past and its charged prongs had grazed him. That gave him an idea, and he took two long seconds to carefully grab it by its tailfins, clenching it in his fist, prongs forward. He looked up to see her launching for the shotgun, which had drifted to the far corner of the tunnel. In desperation he kicked off, but there was no way he could catch her before she got the gun. She grabbed it, and managed to twist herself around to bring it to bear. He was in midleap and unable to change course when she pulled the trigger at point-blank range. The firing pin fell with a dry click. Her face registered surprise and then panic and she racked another cartridge into the chamber with desperate speed, but it was too late, he was on her. He jabbed the stundart into her thigh, and she screamed and convulsed. He grabbed her weapon and spun to train it on the other cop, who had recovered enough to move and was trying to get to his own gun. The cop stopped moving, meeting Wallen's gaze. Wallen nodded approvingly. "As long as we understand each other." The words came out through clenched teeth.

Dmitry had started to recover as well, and he pushed himself over to the cop, took a set of zapstraps off of his equipment belt and cuffed his hands behind back, then used a second set to attach him to a handhold. He then went to do the same to the woman, who was still curled up and moaning. Finally he fished the other two shotguns out of the air.

"Are you okay?" Wallen asked.

"*Pizzdets, muydroog,* It hurt more last time." Dmitry was still moving cautiously. "Let's see what they were doing in the hangar."

"You aren't going to get away with this," warned the male cop.

Wallen looked at him in disbelief. He pushed his shotgun over to Dmitry and kicked himself over to the cop. "Look," he said, locking eyes with the man. "I've had a really long day, and this platform has a lot of airlocks, so let's just be friends, *da*?" The cop's eyes widened in fear, but Wallen didn't wait for a response. "Come on, Dmitry."

Dmitry passed him back his shotgun and slung the extra one on his back, and they went into the hangar, weapons ready. There was no one there, which only made sense. Had there been more Interpols they would have responded to the fight.

The hangar was the last space they had to search, and when they were done Wallen lowered his shotgun. "Whew."

"*Da.*" Dmitry floated over to a racked u-carrier and straddled its nose as if he were riding it. "Now what?"

*Good question.* "We take stock. We can do a few things. Do you think they took the power stations back too?"

"They must have. They couldn't leave them with our people on board."

Wallen nodded. "Maybe taking them wasn't such a good idea."

Dmitry shrugged. "Maybe none of this was. Who knows? Did you want to go and live downwire?"

Wallen shook his head. "No."

"So we had to do something. We haven't lost yet."

"No." Wallen looked up at the ceiling, thinking. "We're secure in here, for now. We have food and power. What options do we have?"

"Lots. We can dial down their power. We have Bernarde's kinetic penetrators." He pointed to one of the other u-carriers. "Already mounted."

"I don't want to escalate this any further. We've already lost Gervois."

"Gervois was a grown man. He knew the risks."

"Did he?" Wallen cocked his head at Dmitry. "I'm not sure I did."

"*Pizzdets*, you were a fool if you didn't."

Wallen shrugged. "Maybe I was. Maybe DiAngelo was making the right decision." He looked up to meet Dmitry's gaze. "Ever think about that?"

Dmitry laughed. "You're a fool now for sure. You're thinking of what that fat parasite Keyls said. Twice *pizzdets*! Do you think this is really about the poor and hungry on Earth? This is about the secretary-general's power, nothing more. All those billions of euros he's saving in canceling us aren't going to feed starving children, they can't eat money." He spat on the floor in disgust. "They're going to line the pockets of the wealthy, as they always do. Our problem is we have no constituency downwire anymore, all us little spaceborn believing in the importance of our dreams." He swept his arm. "They think they can shut us down easy. Surprise, we shake up their cozy little world a bit. So what, they need it." He tilted himself forward on his perch. "Just imagine. The secretary-general is wetting himself right now, waiting to hear back from his cops and getting nothing. How many people can say they made the secretary-general wet his pants."

Wallen laughed. "At least we're standing up for who we are."

"That's the spirit, *muydroog*," Dmitry came over and clapped Wallen on the back. "They're lucky we don't deorbit a thousand tons of steel, that would wake them." He pushed himself off, heading back to the accessway. "Come on. We're going to be here a long time, let's go find some food, and see if our guests in blue know how to drink."

Wallen pushed off after him. He was halfway there when his pad rang. It was a voice-only call.

"Wallen, it's Aurora."

"Aurora! *Zdras!* What's happening?" He put out a hand to grab the launch rack next to him so he wouldn't float out of the hangar. *No need for the Interpols to overhear this. Or Dmitry.*

"A lot. What's the situation up there?"

"Not good. Interpol raided us. Gervois is dead."

"Oh my God! Gervois?"

"*Da*, I'm afraid so. Dmitry and I have gotten away to the spin platform, barely. Everyone else is a prisoner in the construction shack."

"Everyone else?"

"So far as we know. The police are all down there too. We've shut down the boost track, and the Cable too."

"So they can't leave?"

"Not unless we let them. What's happening down-wire?"

"We've got Petra released, and we're putting together a campaign. It's early yet, but promising."

"What do you need us to do?"

"It sounds like you're doing the best you can already. You've bought us time, just don't let them ship people downwire."

"Not going to happen."

"Good. I have to go, Wallen. Your news is going to change things, bolshoi, but my pad is on full-time now, keep in touch." She paused. "Wallen, I miss you."

"You too," he answered, but she was already gone.

The power and sophistication of the True Prophet's organization astounded Aurora, especially considering the speed with which he had put it together. It made the naïve attempt at a news conference she'd attempted with Petra seem exactly as amateurish as it was. There were two magic ingredients. The first was money, which seemed to flow in unlimited streams from the Church's coffers.

"Where does this all come from?" she asked him, after she

happened to see an astronomic bill for the transportation and housing of two thousand people for a demonstration.

"From tithing," he told her. "All Believers give generously to the Church, and the Church spends little." He chuckled.

"And you can spend the Church's money like this?"

"Why not? I own the Church." He saw her shocked expression. "It isn't quite that simple, but the short answer is, I can do what I like with the money. I live simply by choice, not necessity."

*And I'm looking at the proof of it.* The second ingredient in Norman Bissell's power recipe was people, getting two thousand bodies to fly somewhere in the first place. There were, she learned, thousands of churches around the world who owed their allegiance to the True Prophet. He had only to stand up to claim their loyalty, and when he did their members thronged to his cause. In the first week five thousand Believers marched on the Secretariat building, protesting the cancelation of what they called God's *Ark*. In the second week the demonstrations were tens of thousands strong. These were a third class of Believer, Norman told her, neither the core group of rural-dwelling, simplicity-embracing, polygamous farmers who truly lived the faith, nor the power players who embraced the religion as a necessary accessory to their position in life, not materially different from a golf-club membership. These were largely middle-class, living lives indistinguishable from those of their neighbors of any other faith, but watching their lifestyle erode in the face of ever-widening shortages. For them the simplicity inherent in the Believer creed was a touchstone, a reassurance that no matter how bad things got they and their families would be able to survive.

"Of course, that's not true," Norman added. "If they want that kind of security they can't have the life they're used to. They have no idea what it really means."

"So why don't you show them."

He laughed at that. "Peace comes to the peaceful. I learned that, a long time ago. They think they can buy what can only be earned"

Her own role was to be the face of *Ark*, and it was a demanding one. Allison Skell's firm set her up with a public-relations team and she was on three feed shows the first week, but it was the Interpol debacle of having two police platoons trapped aboard the ship that really threw fuel on the fire. In the second week she was on twelve feed shows. The feeds had already been playing up the confrontation and they became relentless in trying to pry inflammatory statements from her, as they had with her first disastrous press conference. This time, wiser and well coached, she dodged them every time, staying focused on her message, which was to continually present the myriad benefits the *Ark* project had yielded humanity. On *Ark*, Wallen and Dmitry started sending the Interpol cops downwire two at a time, and the feed frenzy grew wilder still. Petra was also fully occupied on the feed circuit, and every evening they met with Norman and the public-relations team to plot out how they would handle the next twenty-four-hour feed cycle, incorporating the day's events and the government's response to their message. Royer was on the feeds at least as much as she was and looked a lot more harried, his permanent smile seemingly frozen on his face. Director Keyls appeared twice, expressing his hope for a positive resolution to the situation.

"They're ready to deal," Norman told her when he saw that. "It's just a matter of time now."

At the start of the third week he showed Aurora a feed of the now constant Believer protests in front of the Secretariat building. A young man in bishop's robes was addressing the crowd, relating their experience to that of Noah in the Bible.

"What do you think of him?" Norman asked.

"He speaks well," she answered, not sure what he was looking for with the question.

"I was thinking I'd put him aboard *Ark* as your Prophet."

She gave him a look. "But *you're* the Prophet."

"Yes, but I'm not going aboard your ship."

"But . . ." Aurora gave him a puzzled look. "I thought you wanted to come aboard *Ark*."

"No, not me. I'm going to ride my dragon until it goes back to sleep. After that I'm going to stay on my farm, and work wood and grow corn, for whatever years I have left. All this is for my people." He pointed at the display. "Young Caleb there is a good man, hardworking and smart, but he needs to be delivered from temptation. This will do that. He can be the link between the crew and the Believers. They will farm, and their tithing will go to him, and he'll make sure you get fed for keeping the ship running. Make sense?"

Aurora nodded. "I suppose it does."

That Sunday the True Prophet stood in his robes before a cheering crowd of a quarter million to deliver a sermon on *Ark*. On Monday the government capitulated, exactly as he had predicted it would. Of course, it was not called that. What Aurora presented to the public, in a press conference, sitting beside Brison Keyls, was a negotiated deal that saw the incorporation of an independent public corporation to administer the *Ark* project, with the Church of the Believers as a major participant. Economically the corporation would be self-supporting, with revenue generated through existing on-orbit solar-power facilities. The buyout of government-owned assets would be amortized over the lifetime of the project. It felt strange to be sitting beside men who had made themselves her enemies, working towards a common purpose. *But I have not beaten them so much as overcome myself.* She had won *Ark*, but more importantly freed herself.

There was a final flurry of paperwork, of meetings, of arrangements to be made, and then suddenly it was over. She flew back to the Bissell farm one last time, to collect the meager few belongings she had there and to say good-bye. She hugged Deliah, and Joseph and Mark, and Norman himself took her out to the main road in his buggy.

"I'm sorry you're not coming upwire," she said. "You've taught me a lot."

"I'm sorry you're leaving," he said. "You've been a delight to have in the house."

"I'll be back downwire, I'm sure. It's going to take years to finish loading the soil aboard. We'll need to talk about which families to take."

"I'll be here."

She blinked back a tear when he said it. *He won't always be here. He said himself he's only got a few years left.* For a moment she didn't want to leave. *But life is like water, you can't hold on to it for long.* She hugged him, hard, and then climbed down from the buggy and crossed to the waiting volanter. The ride to the airport was storm-free, the jet flight to Nairobi was interminably boring, and then there was another volanter flight to the Cable base tower. As they came down she could see trains of hopper cars dumping good African topsoil onto conveyors, to be processed and sterilized, loaded into boost cars and sent upwire to *Ark*. And the sight made all her efforts seem worthwhile. Petra was already down there, waiting for her at the passenger terminal, company for the three-day ride into orbit. *Three days of peace.* She was looking forward to it.

*But there's something I have to do first.* She took out her pad, placed a call.

"Wallen Valori."

"Wallen," she said, smiling. *Do what's in your heart, Aurora.* "It's Aurora. I'm coming home."

# *Intermezzo*

*Oh! I have slipped the surly bonds of earth*
*And danced the skies on laughter-silvered wings;*
*Sunward I've climbed, and joined the*
    *tumbling mirth*
*Of sun-split clouds—and done a hundred things*
*You have not dreamed of—wheeled and soared*
    *and swung*
*High in the sunlit silence. Hov'ring there*
*I've chased the shouting wind along, and flung*
*My eager craft through footless halls of air.*
*Up, up the long delirious, burning blue,*
*I've topped the windswept heights with easy grace*
*Where never lark, or even eagle flew—*
*And, while with silent lifting mind I've trod*
*The high untrespassed sanctity of space,*
*Put out my hand and touched the face of God*
                    —John Gillespie Magee

# LAUNCH DAY

The chief engineer pushed himself up the accessway and floated into the fusion tube's control room, tacked on to the bottom of the spin platform's landing deck. Gravity at that level was just a dozen centimeters per second squared, enough to give a sense of down and not much more. You could sit, but you couldn't really walk. He launched himself on a long, graceful parabola to the main console, where the squeeze-field controller was monitoring the startup of the drive.

"How are we looking?" The chief engineer leaned over the controller's shoulder to see the readouts himself.

"The field is stable at fifty percent and we've held it there for an hour. We're ready to ramp it up whenever you like."

"Good." The chief engineer turned to look out the panoramic windows. The mirror cone had been taken down for the fusion tube startup and the vast cylinder of *Ark*'s interior world surrounded him, the land far below sharply divided into sections of light and shadow by sunlight no longer softened by reflecting off the cone. The land around the construction shack was carved into a neat patchwork of farm fields; farther away the fields merged into the uniform green of forest and grassland that stretched back to the distant blue ring of the ocean. Overhead he could see the entire length of fusion tube, a fat, silver cylinder that stretched the great ship's central axis to a vanishing point against the distant aftwall. In the other direction the foredome curved down to join the forewall, visible only where the sunlight glinted against its transparency. A sliver crescent of Earth was visible where they met, and he could just make out the gossamer rails of the Cable, dropping away from the spin platform to the planet far below.

He took a deep breath and turned his gaze back to the instrument panels. The view was hypnotically beautiful, but it delivered three kinds of vertigo at once and there was work to be done. *Today I need to concentrate. Today is success or failure, there will be no in-between.*

"Start the boundary vortex," he ordered. "Bring the field up a little more."

"Field now at fifty-five percent," the field controller reported.

The chief engineer nodded. "Fuel control, start the methane feed, just give me a few grams."

"*Da*, starting now." A second later the fuel technician added, "Fuel line pressure is ramping. Accelerator voltages are good, we're feeding."

"Chamber pressure coming up," added the squeeze-field technician. "Plasma temperature is spiking."

"Boundary vortex flow is good," put in the cooling-system tech.

"Field instabilities?" asked the chief engineer.

The field controller shook his head. "Everything's flat, it looks good."

"Let's just take our time, bring everything online slowly." The techs tapped their consoles and the readouts responded, bearing silent witness to the titanic forces now at play in the core of the fusion tube. Reflexively the chief engineer looked up at the long, silver cylinder again, but it showed no outward change. *Which is a good thing.* The only change he might see would be the explosive rupture of the superconducting nanotube magnet windings if they failed to contain the thousand-tesla magnetic field that confined the fusion reaction. That would end the startup, his career and possibly humanity's entire dream of interstellar flight. *And perhaps my life too.* They were only two hundred meters from the tube, and a bad rupture could easily destroy the control room. *Somehow that seems the least of my concerns.*

"Plasma loading is complete." The fuel tech paused, checking his readouts. "It looks like we have fusion."

"That's confirmed," added the field controller.

The chief engineer nodded and breathed out. "Good, let's throttle up." *We've passed the first test.* In the fuel injector, methane molecules were being broken and stripped of their electrons so the naked carbon and hydrogen nuclei could be accelerated into the center of the field, where the inexorable magnetic pressure there compressed them to twice the density of the sun's core.

"Field strength is seventy percent. Reaction temperature is twenty million kelvins and rising."

"Good, let's have some throttle."

The field controller tapped his console again, dialing down the field strength on the magnetic nozzle at the far end of the thirty-kilometer drive tube. The most energetic nuclei began to leak through the weakened barrier, moving at a significant fraction of the speed of light.

"Tube fields are good at seventy percent. Bringing them up to eighty percent."

The chief engineer put a finger to his lips, watching the process, his mind jumping ahead to anticipate what might yet go wrong. "More throttle, and more fuel."

Slowly, inexorably the readouts inched higher. The chief engineer watched in silence now, as his acolytes progressively awakened the furies that would drive *Ark* to another star. The magnetic-field strength peaked at its full rated maximum, and slowly they brought the fuel flow up to match it. At the far end of the drive tube the particle exhaust reached ten percent of lightspeed, and a camera link showed it as a faint blue-violet line, reaching out laser-straight until it faded into the inky blackness surrounding it.

"We are running stable," the fuel technician reported. "Reactor flow is constant at eight kilograms per second."

The chief engineer smiled. *And so, we are under way.* There was no sensation of acceleration, the tremendous thrust the drive provided served to accelerate *Ark's* massive bulk at only a millionth of a gravity. It would be seventeen years before they even broke free of Earth orbit but the thrust would continue, decade by decade, century after century, until *Ark* was moving a significant fraction of lightspeed herself. He looked up to the fusion tube again and saw the first tangible hint of their success. It had begun to glow a faint, dull red. The tremendous energy produced in the tube was trapped in a thin layer of xenon gas, spun in a high-speed vortex to protect the inner surface of the fusion tube while leaving its center in vacuum to keep the fusion plasma from quenching. The xenon circulated over and through a graphite sponge and before being siphoned off through microchannels cut into the hydrogen-cooled tungsten inner heat sink that formed the inner wall of the fusion tube before being recirculated into the vortex. A second system cooled the inner heat sink, channeling its heat past the field coils in their liquid-nitrogen bath and radiating it through the silica-clad tungsten of the fusion tube's outer sheath. As he watched, the tube's color rose slowly up the spectrum, cherry red to hot orange to brilliant yellow-white. The tube section immediately above the control room was different, thicker and with cooling sufficient to allow water vapor to condense against it, but even so the rest of the tube was hot enough that he could feel its heat. The readouts were stable. He breathed out, recognizing the tension he'd been carrying only when it was released. *We are under way*.

"Disconnect the Cable," he ordered, and was surprised by the sudden applause that rose in the control room. *And I should have seen that coming.* They had cut their link to Earth, and from that instant forward the long dream was realized. Their fate was their own. He went on with the startup checklist, verifying that every system in the drive was running smoothly. There were no moving parts in it anywhere, just magnetic pumps and thermosiphons. No other approach would serve for a system that would have to run, hands-off and undisturbed, for ten thousand years or more. On the ground below, the sharp sun shadows softened and faded under the fusion tube's light. *We don't need the sun any longer. We have our own now, to light us through the long, dark night of our journey.* On the other side of the foredome the stars were waiting patiently.

# Genesis III

Mathematics is the language with which God has written the universe.

—Galileo Galilei

# SHIPYEAR 177

Nikol Valori climbed the stairs past the spillway, where silt-heavy water spewed in rhythmic, dark brown pulses from the huge river outlet a hundred meters up the forewall. From there it fell in a thunderous, rushing torrent to crash and churn at the forewall base. The steel behind the cascade was green with two hundred years of luxuriant moss, and around it a vast fan of wild vines inched their way toward the suntube. Their fruit was a free cornucopia for anyone who cared to come and harvest it, but only deer and nesting birds did. The land next to the forewall was Crew territory, a rule as ironclad as it was unofficial, and harvesting food was something the Believers did. The roiling water collected in a broad, clear pool at the base of the waterfall, sending spray up to join the perpetual gentle mist that hugged the base of the forewall. The water stilled in the pool momentarily, rippling gently against its sides, before slipping away and aftward to become the Silver River. A pipe diverted some small fraction of the flow to a settling tank that separated out the silt and provided the University with running water. It was a simple system, set up by some long-dead builder of the original crew, when the decision was made to turn the hodgepodge of welded-steel buildings that made up what they called the construction shack into the University. Ever since, most of the Crew had lived and worked there. *If you can call what we do work.* Nikol held an advanced degree in physics, another in history, and he still wasn't sure he'd ever done anything truly useful for his world. *I have spent my life learning and teaching things that won't be useful for ten thousand years, if ever.* The "*if ever*" qualification was almost blasphemous. It was the received wisdom among the Crew that science, history, mathematics and all the other disciplines of the University would be absolutely essential when *Ark* reached Heaven. Of course they could hardly believe otherwise, because keeping that wisdom alive was the entire purpose of the Crew. *Without that purpose, we might as well be singing to the stars.*

He pushed the thoughts aside as he climbed the stairs up from the University, established in the warren of rooms that had once housed who-knew-what arcana during the ship's construction. They weren't in the official diagrams of the ship, but they had obviously been of some significance. There were long-abandoned conduits in the walls, marks on the floors were equipment had once been mounted. Some of the equipment was still there, halls full of intricate mechanisms that nobody knew how to use anymore. Once the construction shack had been the nerve center of the greatest engineering project in history, its residents almost casual about the tremendous power to create that they commanded. It was built of the same stainless steel that made up *Ark*'s hull, huge plates that had been joined to the forewall by actually *melting* the steel in place. It was a technique far more durable than they had needed to use. They'd done it just because it was easiest for them. Nikol stood in awe of that. The construction crew had *built* things; there was nothing in *Ark* they hadn't built, which was a slightly amazing thought. They had built them to last, even these supposedly temporary construction buildings, where two hundred years later only a handful of the overhead lightpanels had gone dark. The Crew who were their descendants merely learned things, and there was something sad about that. *We can't even fix the lightpanels.*

He went through the library and past the classrooms to the communications room, where a constant watch was kept on the broadcasts from the home world. It had been the construction crew's operations center, and bronze bas-reliefs of Joshua Crewe and all of the prelaunch chief engineers were set into the back wall, underlined with their names etched deep into the steel. Below them were the names of everyone who had participated in the building of *Ark*, ranks and ranks of them. His own ancestors were up there, and he himself was a descendant of those first chief engineers, a fact he regarded as of little importance, though the University hierarchy seemed to make much of it. *The deification of ancestors, another sign that we have lost our way.* More than half the names were in Cyrillic, but no one spoke Russian anymore.

Nikol quickened his steps. He had an appointment with the current chief engineer. Her office was in the senior administration hallway, beyond the communications room, but he went past it. Melany Waseau had asked him to walk on the ledge, the wide walkway that ran along the top of the University complex, one hundred meters up the forewall and right the way around *Ark*. It was a custom they had had, some twenty years ago, when they were both eager students, absorbing all their world could teach them. He went out a set of well-worn double doors and climbed another flight of stainless-steel stairs, feeling the strain on his knees. *When I was young I used to run up these stairs.* Age came to all men. When he was young he used to run the annual Ledge Race, thirty-one kilometers, all the way around the vast ship's circumference. *When I was young . . .*

The chief engineer was waiting for him, leaning on the railing and looking out over the countryside toward the aftwall.

"Nikol, *zdras*." She smiled.

"*Zdras, m'droog*. Melany, it's good to see you." He embraced her. *When I was young, I loved Melany and never told her. I wonder if she knew?*

"You should see me more often then."

Nikol nodded. "I haven't had the time, since Lynne . . ." He didn't finish.

"I'm sorry, Nikol. I know how hard it must be."

"Everyone gets one life—birth, death and the time in between. She lived hers well."

The two were silent for a moment; then Melany spoke. "I brought tea if you'd like some."

"Dandelion?"

"Of course. I remember what you like."

Melany picked up a well-worn daypack, made of some tough prelaunch synthetic, and took a thermos flask out of it. Nikol looked out over his world. The mist was lighter than usual, and he could see over the roof of the University and the Prophet's Tower, over the tops of the arrow-straight Douglas firs that grew fast and tall in the moist and well-nourished soil near the forewall and on to the point where the forest thinned and the trees grew shorter where Believer logging had made itself felt. After that there was a broad belt of domesticated land, broken into a patchwork of farmers' fields and orchards, dotted with houses and barns, bisected by the rivers that the silt pipes fed. Farther aft the patchwork frayed into smaller farms, separated by stands of still virgin forest, where the younger sons of the Believers were clearing land to establish their own dynasties. A third of the way to the aftwall the forest had restablished itself in thick green luxury, no longer formed of the tall, mist-loving firs but of bushy ironwood and oak, until it met the distant ocean shore, an indistinct blue in the hazy distance. *Most of our artificial world is still uncolonized. The crew built our ocean, but how long has it been since anyone has stood on its shores?* On either side the world arched up in both directions until the sides met at the suntube, and the ocean glinted silver where the suntube's light hit it at just the right angle. The view from the ledge was one of the best in *Ark*. *Except it's an enclosed one. I have no horizon here.* He looked up at the foredome, but it was impossible to see any stars. *And that is something else we have lost.*

The chief engineer had unscrewed the lid of the flask. There was a cup nestled inside it; the lid itself formed a second cup. "I hope you know I would've come, had I known . . ."

"She didn't linger, that was a blessing." Nikol Valori paused, started to say more, then stopped. Some things were better left unsaid, and for others there were no words. After a moment he said something else. "She didn't want a service."

"And . . ." Melany paused, searching memory for a name. ". . . Kylie, how is she?"

"She's as well as can be expected. No child should lose her mother, but she's young, she'll adapt." He studied the view for a long time, fighting down emotions he didn't need to have brought to the surface. "You didn't ask me here to ask about my family."

"No, I didn't. That doesn't mean I don't want to hear about them. You've always been hard to talk to, Nikol."

"Touché. I don't make it easy to be my friend. Why did you ask me here?"

She poured the tea, still steaming, and handed the lid cup to him. "To talk you out of resigning. I want you here, Nikol. I want you to run the simulation center."

"You know I don't want it. There's hundreds who'd jump at the chance." He drank his tea, almost too hot to swallow. She'd laced it with honey and spice, just the way he liked it, and he felt its bittersweet warmth flood through him. *She does know me, she does care.*

"None who know the systems as well as you."

"You're flattering me now." He swallowed the cup down, wincing at the burning heat in his throat.

"The truth isn't flattery." She sipped her tea. "Another truth is you always did drink too fast."

"Sipping isn't my style, and I'm complimented by your *truth*." Nikol put an ironic stress on the last word. "Still, I'm happy with my decision. The University will manage without me, and my students are in good hands."

Melany sipped her tea again. "I can't believe teaching kolkoz children is a challenge for your mind."

"It's a challenge to my spirit, and I'd appreciate it if you didn't call them 'kolkoz.'"

"I'm sorry. It's common slang, I don't intend it to be derogatory."

"Of course you don't, you are too educated for that, it's only what everyone calls them—every Crew, that is." Despite himself Nikol heard the passion come into his voice. "The fact is, it's derogatory by nature. It implies the Believers are only peasants, cargo, something that we, the educated, enlightened crew, are carrying from point A to point B, with no contribution to make on the voyage."

"Some might argue that the cargo is the entire point of the voyage."

"Some might, but no one does, until someone like me points out their use of an insulting term for an entire class of people. However, you're correct. The *cargo* . . ." He stressed the word to emphasize his point. ". . . the cargo *are* the entire point of the voyage. *They* are the ones with the skills we're going to need, the skills necessary to pioneer a new world. They till the soil, grow crops and raise stock, not us. They build and sew and carve and mill. There's going to be no requirement to demonstrate Euler's theorem when we get to Iota Horologii. Nobody is going to care about the factors leading to the rise of the UN as a world government."

"You used to say the same things when we were young. You still chose to go into academia."

"When I was young I thought I had no choice. Crew schools don't teach us the skills we need to do anything else."

"Crew skills are still necessary, even if we don't use them every day. There's going to be a need to be able to operate *Ark*'s survey instruments in order to select a landing site. Somebody's going to have to pilot the shuttles into the atmosphere." Melany sipped her tea again, then, satisfied with its temperature, she drank more deeply.

"*Ark*'s computers can do the planetary survey by themselves, and the autopilots in the landing shuttles are certainly going to be more reliable than some far-distant Crew descendant whose learned skills are four hundred generations removed from anyone who's actually flown anything."

"We have the simulators, that's why I need you—"

"Do you really believe the simulators are going to be working in a thousand years?"

"They were built—"

"Of course, of course, everything's been built to endure. Look at this flask." Nikol picked it up from where it rested on Melany's backpack. "The finest flask ever built on Earth, with an iridium-alloy double shell, vacuum-sealed for insulation, an integral heating element, inductive of course so the connection can't fail, no moving parts. I can't imagine what it must have cost the Earth economy to make, but it'll be holding hot tea long after you and I are dust. Still, do you really think it's going to stand up to a thousand years of use?"

"It was engineered to last ten thousand."

"Of course it wasn't." Nikol gave her a disgusted look. "It couldn't be, nobody had any experience engineering something to last so long, not once in all of Earth's history. It was engineered to last a long time, because the construction crew wanted their children and their children's children to live as they did, but how long? Sooner or later someone will break the element trying to clean lime scale out of it with a stick, or drop something heavy on it and crack the shell, or find another use for it and ruin it as a kettle, and if none of those things happen the metal will just slowly wear until the vacuum fails. It's just a flask. What chance have complicated simulators got? What chance have computers got? We've lost half of them already."

"We'd better hope computers can last that long, because we've got one flying the ship."

"*Ark*'s computer has to *operate* for ten thousand years, it isn't going to be *used*, and that's the difference. That's why it's carefully sealed away from prying human hands. All the ship's systems are. *We* are the weak link in the system, and the construction crew knew we would be."

"That's not true. We have maintenance access if necessary."

"*If* the computer decides it needs our help. It hasn't once, in two centuries. I pray it never will, because who among us could actually fix it?"

"You could, or I."

Nikol raised an eyebrow. "Could you really, Melany? Fix for real when you've only practiced on models, in a pressure suit you've never really worn, on a system you've never touched?"

"I don't claim it would be easy."

Nikol snorted. "The fact is, neither of us could even fix this flask. The builders didn't build it to be fixable, they built it to last. We can't fix it because we lack the tools to work the alloys. The builders left us halls full of machines, and not one of us can actually *use* them."

"We use the simulators, and the teaching stations."

"Not the flexfab."

"Only because we lack the raw materials."

"Only because we're too lazy to go out and collect the raw materials the builders saw fit to give us."

Melany threw up her hands in exasperation. "Why create a University to pass on knowledge that will never be used?"

"Because our ancestors were human, that's why. Because once the builders finished building their jobs were done, and the important work passed to the Believers—simply farming and raising families and living their lives and waiting for the day we arrive at Heaven. The construction crew became the cargo at that point, but they didn't want to be cargo, and they didn't want to be farmers either, and most especially they didn't want the balance of power on the ship to pass to the Believers, where it naturally would because they produced the food and did the work and they outnumbered our ancestors. So the crew became the Crew, the sacred holders of the flame of knowledge, and they created this playpen of learning for us that we call the University, and the myth that somehow these vast systems they'd built, designed and redesigned to run hands-off for lifetime after lifetime, somehow they needed us to look after them. We look down on the Believers because of the quaint superstition they call their faith, but look at us, we've turned learning into sacred ritual, sanctified our exalted position with tradition and ceremony because we do nothing of substance to justify it. We have become a new priesthood, only our mythology is built of empty facts instead of empty belief, so much so that we even live on their tithings." He held up his left hand, where his little finger bore the iron ring that marked an engineer. "Look at this. I call myself an engineer, but I've never built anything. I call myself a researcher, but I've never discovered anything no one has ever known. What have I done? I've studied what *other* people have built and discovered, people long dead on a world I'll never see. I lack scope for discovery and resources for construction. What's left to me? I can't farm, so I'll teach, and each young Believer who learns to ask questions will be a victory. I'm making a difference in their lives, because it's the only difference I can make. Do you see?"

"You've said all this before. Nikol, I, *we*, still need you." She moved a little way down the ledge. "Walk with me."

Nikol fell into step beside her. "You need me to renounce my heresy before I contaminate others, you mean. Will you put me to the Inquisition if I don't recant, shun me if I don't conform?"

Melany shook her head. "That's their barbarity, not ours, and a perfect illustration of why we shouldn't associate with them. They are superstitious savages, and that's not derogatory, that's simply true."

"I'm not blind to their faults. I work to uplift them, not exalt them."

"Uplift them to what? If our own way of life is so bankrupt, where are you leading them?"

"To science, of course, to knowledge. Education truly is priceless, just not empty education, rote facts learned for the sake of learning. Facts don't matter except as they aid *understanding*, that's something we've lost track of in the Crew. The Believers have never really had that, but it's something I can give them."

"You'll fly full in the face of their dogma, and I'll have to make explanations to the Elder Council. You'll be lucky if you don't wind up in front of the inquisitor yourself."

"Perhaps, but I'm careful in what I say. I don't intend to blind them with enlightenment."

"Nikol, come back to us." Melany's voiced was imploring. "Teach here, if you won't run the simulators. We have students too, young and curious minds that need inspiration."

"I can't, Melany. It isn't the students, it's the University. It's Burkins and Stroink and all those old fossils who care more about their status than their subjects."

"Stroink is ready to retire. You could be the next chancellor. With my backing, you *will* be the next chancellor."

"I don't want to be chancellor." The stainless steel beneath their feet had been given a rough texture to aid traction, but there was a path in the middle worn shiny by two hundred years of Crew, walking and running and simply enjoying the view. *How many have come before me here? How many more will come after?*

"Nikol, you're making my position difficult."

"It's not my intention, but neither is it my responsibility

to make things easy for you. You're chief engineer. It's up to you to deal with the problems that come with your office." Nikol walked to the edge of the shiny strip.

"That's what I'm trying to do. You aren't cooperating."

"Tell me, just who is it who finds it so uncomfortable that I'm doing what I'm doing. You aren't so small-minded that you care personally. I'm sure Stroink is happy to see an end to my agitation and Burkins is glad to be rid of a rival."

Melany didn't answer at first, and they walked on in silence for a while. Farther away from the University the ledge was less worn, and the shiny path in the middle was flanked on either side by metal that carried a whitish patina left by the minerals carried in the mists. Lichen and moss crusted the steel, and in places sucker vines had climbed all the way up from ground level, their main branches thick enough to hold a man's weight, if the man was careful. Here and there even bushes had found enough nutrients to grow on the inhospitable surface.

"It's the Prophet," she said at last. "He isn't comfortable with you teaching Believer children."

"The Prophet? The Crew have been teachers since *Ark* was launched, it's what we do. What does that stripling care that I'm one of them?"

"I say the Prophet, but it's really the Elder Council objecting through him. There's never been a senior professor of the University who stepped down to teach a parish grade school. His—I should say *their* concern is that might be interpreted as a push to expand the Crew's influence at the expense of the Church's."

"Surely they've got more common sense than that."

"Surely you have more common sense than that," Melany shot back. "The rank-and-file Believers have always been suspicious that we'll lead their children away from the Bible. That isn't the council's concern, their concern is that others will choose to see it that way. There's some power struggle going on with them, I don't have all the details, but the Prophet isn't doing anything useful to control them for me. Just your presence will give them an excuse to challenge his rule."

"Control them yourself. There's no need to use him as a mouthpiece."

"There is, actually. It's tradition, and we alter it at our peril. We might find it ridiculous that they give such authority to a boy, but to them, he *is* God on Earth, literally. He's supposed to be our advocate, but I think the bishops, or a faction of them, are trying to get him under their thumb."

"If that's true then the both of you have larger problems than me to deal with."

"We do. We aren't popular with the Believers, Nikol, and we rely on them completely for virtually every necessity of life. As long as the Prophet stands with us we are safe, but if the Prophet isn't with us . . . I don't have to tell you how bad that could be."

"All the more reason for us to climb down from our ivory tower and learn how to look after ourselves."

"Nikol, that's . . ." Melany stopped. "I can see I won't convince you, I know I can't stop you. I'll even grant that you might be right that we've lost direction in some ways." She paused, and turned to look out over the countryside again. "I have to work with what we have, and that includes Stroink and Burkins and everyone like them. It takes time to make changes." She looked back to him, studied his face with an intensity that he found slightly uncomfortable. "Just be careful what you say to those children. We don't need to see you up in front of an inquisitor. Seriously."

"The Prophet's got no authority to do that."

"The Prophet isn't my concern, and the council has whatever authority they can make stick."

"Not among the Crew."

"Perhaps among the Crew."

Nikol stopped, and turned to face his friend. "Melany, you're not saying you'd hand me over if it came right down to it."

The chief engineer met his gaze, then looked back out over the vista, staying quiet for a moment that stretched out and out until Nikol began to think she simply was not going to answer. Finally she spoke. "I'm saying that things are sensitive right now. I'll do what I have to do to keep our people safe. Our people and our way of life." She turned to face him again. "Don't give me any hard decisions, Nikol. Neither of us will like the way they turn out."

Charity Parish school was a prelaunch building, metal-framed and with glass windows. To Jedediah Fougere it smelled of wood and chalk and homework. For fifth grade they had a new teacher, and at first Jed, who had had the kindly Mrs. Dolorson since kindergarten, had been unsure about him. However, as the first morning's lesson progressed, he began to grow more comfortable with Dr. Valori.

"Night." The new teacher drew a big circle on the wooden chalkboard. "The Earth is a ball, and the sun is another ball, so light from the sun can only hit one half of it at a time." He drew a much smaller circle, and drew lines from it to the larger circle to show the effect.

"Excuse me, sir." Jed put up his hand. "I thought you said the sun was larger than the Earth."

Dr. Valori smiled. "Indeed it is, Jedediah. If the Earth were the size of a cherry, the sun would be a ball almost as big as I am. I drew it this way because the sun is so far from the Earth that it *looks* much smaller—but it doesn't matter too much. Imagine it the other way, so this big circle is the sun and the small one is Earth. See, still only about half of it gets sunlight—just a tiny fraction more than the other way." He looked to see if Jedediah was following. "The Earth spins like this . . ." He illustrated with his hands. "So all of it gets sunlight every day, but only half of it at a time. The other half of the time it's dark, they call it night, and the only light is from the stars. We don't get night in the *Ark* because we live on the inside of a tube instead of the outside of a ball, so the suntube lights up everywhere all the time. You can't see the stars through the foredome, because of the reflected light from the sun tube, but they're out there."

"Doesn't *Ark* spin too?" asked Jed.

"It does. Every ninety seconds. That's what gives us gravity, or rather centrifugal force, which feels like gravity to us, standing on the ground inside *Ark*. *Ark* isn't big enough to have real gravity like Earth. If *Ark* were the size of this piece of chalk . . ." He held up his chalk to illustrate. ". . . then Earth would be as big as the school."

Jed nodded slowly, absorbing that. Dr. Valori was the first male teacher he'd had, but he seemed nice, and if all of fifth grade was as interesting as the first day he would have a good year.

The lesson went on, describing other ways life on Earth was different from life in *Ark*. The biggest difference was that everything in *Ark* was built by people; even the plants and most of the animals had been designed carefully. Certain berries were made so they produced medicines to help sick people. Ironwood trees—*lignum vitae*, Dr. Valori called them—were made to grow much faster than they did on Earth, and much harder too so they could be used for tools. People had already changed cows and pigs and horses so much there was no need to change them more, but sheep had been made so their wool would just come off at shearing time, rather than needing to be cut off, unlike Earth sheep.

"And people will change too," said Dr. Valori. "Only much more slowly, and we can only guess in what ways. People on Earth look different from place to place because each place has a unique environment, different amounts of sunlight, different ranges of temperature and different foods that were available. Today we look pretty much like Earth people look, but as time goes on we'll adapt to *Ark*'s environment, we'll be different from Earth people."

Matthew, Jed's best friend from their very first day of school, put up his hand. "Sir, people look different from each other in *Ark*."

"That's true, Matthew. What I mean is—" Dr. Valori's answer was interrupted by the tolling of the noon bell from the Charity church tower. "What I mean is, it's time for lunch. We'll continue this in the next lesson."

The class got their lunches from the shelf at the back in the room, and ate them around the craft tables. Jed ate his with Matthew and his other friend Abel, while Abel went into detail about the size and quality of the new hog barn his father was building. When they were done they ran outside to the playground. Jed paused to get his leather toss ball from his desk and ran after them, planning on a game of catch or tagball, but on his way out the door he found himself face-to-face with a girl he didn't recognize, her hair pulled back into pigtails, dressed in a simple ruffed frock.

"*Zdras*," she said "I'm Kylie. I'm from the Town."

"Blessings. I'm Jed."

She smiled. "Come on, I'll show you where there's a whole bunch of frogs."

Jed hesitated. The Town was where the Crew mostly lived, a kilometer foreward of the little village of Charity where the schoolhouse was, itself three long kilometers of trudging back and forth from Riverview, the Fougere family farm. He wasn't allowed to play with Crew children, *unchurched* Crew children his father called them, because as unbelievers they were all going to Hell. He looked over to where Matthew and Abel were already playing tag with some of the other boys. He didn't want to commit a sin.

"They're really interesting." Kylie pronounced it int-ter-rest-ing, carefully separating each syllable. Without waiting for an answer, she turned and headed for the path leading toward the creek, and away from the playground.

He hesitated again. Mrs. Dolorson, his fourth-grade teacher, had made it clear that the path was strictly out of bounds. Did the same rules apply in fifth grade? Dr. Valori hadn't said so explicitly, and he didn't know for sure that Kylie was a Crew just because she lived in the Town. It was Abel's mother's day to watch the schoolyard at luncheon recess, and she was sitting on the fence by the road talking to another mother. If he got in trouble he could claim he didn't know. For a moment the lure of the forbidden fought against the rules imposed by adults. Twenty paces down the path Kylie turned around. "Come on," she said insistently, impatient as only a nine-year-old girl could be.

Matthew and Abel were running and yelling with the other boys. Jed glanced at them, then ran off to follow Kylie. The frogs were there as advertised, leopard frogs, big and fat and green. They caught one each and tried to race them, but the frogs just hopped into the long grass beside the stream and had to be chased down and caught again. They grew bored of that game when it became clear the frogs weren't going to cooperate, and instead watched a bumblebee gathering pollen. Eventually the church bell rang again, followed quickly by the clanging of the school bell. They ran back to the schoolyard, arriving out of breath and with muddy shoes, but unnoticed by any adult. Kylie, Jed decided, was not only pretty but clever, and a worthy new friend even if she was a girl.

He walked partway home with her that afternoon, to the end of the Charity road, where the crossroad led forward to the Town and aftward to Riverview. On the way he learned that her father was Dr. Valori, which made her Crew for sure, since her father was. When he discovered that, he tried to warn her that she had to become a Believer to avoid going to Hell, but she just laughed and said there was no such thing as Hell, there was only Heaven, and it was a planet like Earth. He didn't know quite what to make of that confident assertion. He did know it would be better not to raise it with his father. John Fougere was a man of temper, and he brooked no disagreement when it came to matters of faith. Fortunately, his father showed little interest in what happened at school. To him education was simply a way of keeping Jed from underfoot until he was old enough to start doing serious work around the farm. Jed decided he wouldn't mention Kylie either, and then the question of playing with a Crew wouldn't come up.

At the crossroads he said good-bye to his new friend and walked the rest of the way home, past green pasture-land, tilled fields full of corn and oats and the rolling orchards of apples and cherries that hid the river from view. Riverview was one of the most prosperous farms in *Ark*, and as the oldest son Jed was going to inherit it. It was supposed to be a tremendous privilege, but it didn't seem that way. He spent his waking hours that weren't in school either doing his chores or making himself scarce to avoid having more chores assigned. His father felt children should be seen and not heard, but Jed had learned that he got in the least trouble when he wasn't even seen. After school he would stay out of sight until suppertime, often hiking down the orchard lane to the river to explore the trails there, watching squirrels or swallows or just throwing sticks in the water to see them swirl downstream in the eddies. He only had to be back in time for supper. Suppertime was a ritual in the Fougere household, with everyone's presence expected and a certain formality. After supper his usual routine was to carry the slops out to the pigs, feed the chickens and clean out the henhouse, and then climb up into the hayloft of the horse barn to whittle or play in the warm and quiet semidarkness. He would go back just before bedtime, for a slice of buttered bread with peach jam laid out by Ruth, his father's second wife, before being tucked in by his mother.

He played with Kylie again the next day, and over the next weeks they became fast friends, though he was careful to spend time with Matt and Abel as well. The weeks slowly turned into months, the passage of time marked only by the tolling of the church bells and the alternation of school days and church days. At home the crops came in, were harvested, milled and sold, and the fields were replanted. At school he learned math and spelling, history and science and the story of *Ark*. Saturdays were especially difficult, the day he couldn't avoid chores by avoiding people, his day to do heavy farmwork, plowing and planting and harvesting, so that when he grew to inherit Riverview he would have the skills to run it. Sundays and Wednesday evenings were given over to going to church in Charity to listen to the bishop deliver his usual sermon, and Sunday afternoons there was Sunday school, taught by the bishop or sometimes by his wife. As befitted one of the leading families in Charity Parish, the Fougeres sat in the front pew, his father closest to the aisle, then his mother and Mary, his older sister, and Jed himself, then Ruth, holding baby Magda, then his uncle Thomas and finally his grandparents, who had lived at home with them but had now moved to a new house in Charity. It was a small family by Believer standards, and Matthew and Abel had both expressed their envy that Jed didn't have to share his elders' attention with a half-a-dozen siblings. Jed himself was unsure that having less of his father's attention would be a bad thing. The hard work was made no easier by his father's constant criticism. John Fougere was a demanding man, and he frequently found fault with Jed's worthiness to succeed him. Over time Kylie became his best friend, and since he never officially asked her whether she was Crew or not, and his father never asked him about it either, it was as if the reason for his initial hesitation in allowing her into his life didn't really count. Fields he'd helped plant he now had to help harvest. Dr. Valori introduced fractions into their math class, and told them interesting tales of Earth history. Christmas came, was solemnly celebrated, and went again, and his life moved steadily through its normal orbit of home and church and school. It seemed to Jed as constant and unchanging as the suntube overhead. It never occurred to him that it might ever change.

Nikol Valori looked up through the mist, trying to get a glimpse of the foredome through the forest canopy, but it was pointless. Tall pines and firs thrived in the constant mist that fell from the edges of the foredome's ice cap, as well as the abundant groundwater from the headwaters of the rivers. They made it very difficult to see anything overhead at all, but at least he could see enough of the suntube to keep a steady course forward. He returned his attention to choosing his path. The thick canopy combined with the carpet of pine needles on the forest floor to keep the undergrowth down, which made the going easy. Still,

Nikol took his time. His backpack held a leather water-skin, some cured sausage and a few other supplies; Kylie was spending the day with a neighbor and there was no reason not to enjoy his surroundings. There was more in the forest than the chance to see the foredome. If he found what he was looking for, so much the better. If not, he still needed the exercise.

An hour forward he was getting exercise. The mist got heavier closer to the forewall, the tall conifers had given way to smaller trees and tangled blackberry bushes grew in thickets beneath them. Their thorns tore at his clothing, and the dew on them quickly soaked him through and through. He had to hack his way forward with his ironwood bush knife, sweating hard and making slow progress. *A good steel blade is what I need here.* Metalworking had become a lost art aboard *Ark*, but Nikol was about to reinvent it, and despite the hard going he found himself enjoying the exploration. *The crew has been too frightened of honest work for too long.* He pushed ahead, forded a small stream and finally came up against the vertical grey steel of the forewall. It loomed overhead, seeming to go up forever to the point where the foredome bulged out and over. Kiwi vines as thick as his wrist clung to it, and a colony of thrushes chirped and warbled in among their leaves, occasionally peeking out only to dart back into cover. Overhead a pair of peregrines circled, which explained why the smaller birds were hiding. He plucked a couple of kiwis, but they were hard and sour, unripe. He got his waterskin and took a long, deep drink, both to wash away the taste and to hydrate himself. He had long way to go before he would be done.

*And now the hard work begins.* He retightened the straps of his backpack and set off counterspinward, away from the University, trying to keep as close to the forewall as he could. Midway between the river outlets there were shipsteel drops, where a mechanism high up the forewall metered out ingots of high-chromium steel. It had been the intent of the builders to provide *Ark's* inhabitants with a steady supply of the material to help support their civilization over time. It had been the discovery of this fact that had finally convinced Nikol that the Crew's role was purely symbolic. *Not only did the builders not trust us to maintain the ship systems, they didn't even trust us to ration steel.* At first he had been insulted by the implication, that the builders had not had enough faith in their own descendants to work and make sacrifices for the success of the mission, but he had gradually come to terms with it. The builders were showing only a shrewd understanding of human nature. Given unlimited access to a resource, it was inevitable that someone, somewhere down the line would choose to exploit it immediately for short-term gain, at the expense of the long-term picture.

It was hard going right next to the forewall; the underbrush was thick and wild. A couple of times he startled deer, and once he saw a tawny flash that might, or might not, have been a clouded leopard. He tensed when he saw it, and gripped his bush knife tighter. The leopards were *Ark's* keystone predator, one of the only species in the artificial world that might pose a threat to a man. *I don't know enough about moving in the forest, my life has been too sheltered.* There was only one way to change that, and that was through experience, and there was only one way to get experience, and that was by getting out and trying things and making mistakes. With luck he would make no lethal ones. *I have to remember our environment was engineered to be benign.* The builders must have come to the realization at some point that it was impossible to build an absolutely safe environment and accepted a certain amount of risk on behalf of their descendants. Little comfort for Nikol if he wound up eaten by a leopard.

The evening bell sounded, telling him he'd hiked past dinner, and that meant it was time to turn back. He looked back along his trail, the sweat and moisture chill on his skin when he stopped moving, and then looked forward again, unwilling to admit defeat quite so easily. The way ahead of him was more open. *I'll just go through to the other side of the clearing.* He did so, and on the other side of the clearing there was a game trail that led him forward again, and then, not even expecting to, he found what he been looking for. He nearly missed it, so dense was the undergrowth beside the trail. He nearly chose to detour around the thicket that hid his treasure, but a glint of shiny steel grey caught his eye, and he hacked his way through the shrubbery to find a comical pile of steel ingots. He nearly cackled with joy at the sight, picked one up and hefted it. It was heavy, easily twenty-five kilos, and there had to be a hundred tons of steel in the pile. The builders had rationed *Ark's* population to a kilo of steel per year per person, based on an average population of twenty thousand people, and the documents he'd read detailed long discussions over how much was enough, and how much was too much. They had failed to anticipate the social dynamics that would govern the use of the resource.

The Believers were still using and repairing prelaunch tools and building new ones using ironwood, which fit well with their strong tradition of woodworking. The Crew had started out with advanced metalworking tools, but as they moved more and more toward pure academia the machines in the workshops had fallen still, and now sat unused. Nikol wiped moisture from his brow with his sodden sleeve, a reflexive and futile gesture. It was going to be a lot of effort to get even one ingot back home; there was no way he was going to be able to carry two. *I can understand more why they gave up on metalworking.* It was going to be a backbreaking job to transport enough steel to do anything useful.

*And yet I will do it.* In truth, he *had* to do it. It was one thing to teach, and it was far better to teach unfettered by the University's stultifying emphasis on regurgitation of knowledge, but it was another thing entirely to *do*, to create with his own hands, to discover with his own mind. It was a fundamental drive within him, long buried and long unsatisfied. The Believers were master woodworkers, there was nothing he could discover there, perforce, he would rediscover what it was to work metal. For too long Nikol had dealt with abstract knowledge, first as a student and then as a teacher. It was time to do something concrete. He took off his pack and put the steel ingot into it, using the waterskin to cushion the hard metal against his back. The pack was uncomfortably heavy when he shouldered it again, and the straps dug into his skin. He would be sore when he got home, sore the next day, as underused muscles protested this abuse. He didn't care about that. The burden he was carrying was freedom.

✲✲✲

It was getting close to Easter when the bishop died, and there was a funeral where Jed had to dress in black. His uncle Thomas harnessed the two black mares to the buggy and the women of the family wore black veils. The service was on a Saturday, and the Prophet himself was there to lead the congregation in prayers of thanks for the years of devotion the old bishop had given to the church, and to the district of Charity. The whole experience was somewhat surreal to Jed, with many of the adults crying and hugging each other as the plain pine coffin was lowered into the new-dug hole in the small graveyard by the church. He understood what death was; nine years living on a farm had made that very clear to him. He understood the old bishop wouldn't be coming back, and he had liked the old bishop and knew he would miss him, but he didn't feel particularly sad, or indeed particularly much of anything. He had been sadder when Simon the barn cat had died, because Simon used to come up and sit with him in the hayloft while he whittled with an ironwood knife, alternately hunting for mice and coming over to purr and be patted.

The Prophet also introduced the new bishop during the ceremony, and anointed him to lead the Church in the district. The Prophet was a young man, even Jed could see he was really barely more than a boy, and he seemed uncertain in his role. By contrast the new bishop, Bishop Nemmer, exuded confidence and physical strength, with a deep and impressive voice and flashing eyes. He had led the congregation in Joseah Parish, so far spinward that it was on the other side of the suntube and a considerable distance aftward, and now had come to Charity. By the time the service had ended Jed thought he was an huge improvement on the old bishop. At the next Sunday's service that theory seemed to be borne out. He delivered a sermon on the ten plagues of Egypt so vivid that Jed, normally bored to tears at the old bishop's rambling speeches, found himself sitting on the edge of seat as the story unfolded. After chapel came Sunday school, also taught by the bishop, and Jed expected great things of Bishop Nemmer here as well. The old bishop had taught them simple and moralistic lessons about what was right and wrong, what God expected of every Believer, and Josh had found them, like his sermons, utterly boring. The new bishop said they would begin with what they had covered in the sermon, and began to elaborate on the lessons to be drawn from the ten plagues of Egypt, drawing quick sketches on the blackboard to illustrate key points in the story. It was much more like one of Dr. Valori's history lessons, and when it was done Jed put up his hand, for the first time interested rather than simply dutiful. The bishop pointed to him and Jed stood up and spoke as he had been taught.

"Blessings, sir. My name is Jedediah Fougere."

"And what is your question, Jedediah?"

"Why did God kill all the firstborn of Egypt, when he eighth commandment says 'Thou shalt not kill'?"

The bishop shook his head. "God made the Commandments, he can't break them because he is above them. It was a terrible thing he had to do, but Pharaoh forced him to, by disobeying his commands."

"Couldn't he have just killed Pharaoh, or even made him do what he wanted?"

"He could have, but Pharaoh's people needed to be punished too. They went against God, and were evil."

"But sir, even so, it wasn't the children who did anything wrong. God killed them for no reason."

The bishop's face grew suddenly angry. "Jedediah Fougere, that is blasphemy."

"But sir . . ." Fear surged in Jed as he realized he had transgressed one of those indefinable adult boundaries and landed himself in trouble.

"Do you think you know better than I do? Do you think you know better than God?" The bishop's intense eyes were suddenly focused hard on Jed.

"No sir, I just don't—"

"We will have no more from you today, young man." The bishop strode forward and grabbed Jed by the ear, hauling him away from his desk. "You'll spend the rest of the lesson with your nose in the corner."

Ears burning, Jed stood in the corner, somewhere between angry and humiliated, and resolved never to put his hand up in Sunday school again. He had liked the new bishop for his narrative skill, but try as he might to find the forgiveness of Jesus in his heart, it just wasn't there. He hadn't meant to commit blasphemy, and it seemed to him that his question was fair while the bishop's answers had not actually answered anything. At the end of the day the bishop had sent him home with a note to his father. He walked home slowly, dreading the reaction he knew he would get. He wasn't disappointed. His father read the note before dinner, his face growing increasingly hard.

"Jedediah, it is not your place to question the bishop."

"But Father—"

"Do you think you know better than him?" his father interrupted.

"No, Father, I just—"

"You just chose to defy him in his own church, is that it?"

"No, Father—"

The flat of his father's hand came down across Jed's face, knocking him to the floor. "Don't lie." His voice was loud and angry. "No son of mine will be a liar and a sinner." He shook the note at Jed. "I have it right here in the bishop's own hand."

Tears started from the corners of Jed's eyes, but he was determined not to cry. He stood up again, struggling to speak around the tight lump in his throat. "Father, I only asked because I didn't understand—"

"The first book of Timothy, chapter five, first verse. Rebuke not an elder, but entreat him as a father." Jed's father grabbed Jed by the scruff of his shirt and hauled him out of the house toward the horse barn. At the barn he grabbed a length of bridle leather, pushed Jed up against the wall of the birthing stall. "I will not have you bring disgrace upon this family, you stupid little boy. I will not have a sinner living under my own roof." He raised the leather high. Jed gritted his teeth. The leather came down, but Jed bit his lip and refused to cry. The whipping went on for a long time, driving pain into his body with every stroke, as his father held him there against his struggles, until finally his resolve cracked and the tears came.

Afterward his father left him, tossing aside his improvised lash with a gesture of disgust, as though anything touched by Jed's flesh was ever after too impure to again be used by the hand of a Believer. For a long time Jed just stood there, no longer sobbing aloud but helpless to control the tears welling from his eyes. Eventually he reached around behind him to touch the interlaced welts on his back, wincing as he did so. His father had been too angry to even make him remove his shirt, but the cotton was too thin to have offered much protection. Eventually the evening bell rang, time for dinner. The evening meal was sacrosanct in the Fougere house, but he found he had little appetite and no desire at all to see his family. Missing dinner might earn him another whipping, but he was beyond caring at that point. He climbed up into the hayloft and found a warm corner to sit and nurse his wounds. The loft was comforting in its familiarity, the smells of hay and horses blending in familiar ways. It was lit with only the light that managed to filter through cracks between the boards. He would have preferred night, as Dr. Valori had described it, a darkness so complete that he could be invisible within it. He wished Simon would come and comfort him, but Simon was no longer there, and the new barn cat didn't care much for human company. *And it isn't fair to be punished twice, and isn't fair to be punished just for asking.* Eventually he got on his knees and prayed, asking God to forgive him for his blasphemy, most of all to get his father to forgive him. For good measure he added a prayer for God to resurrect the old bishop as he had resurrected Jesus. Frequently Jed had wished, *not prayed, not prayed because it would be a sin to pray for such a thing,* for the old bishop to go away just because he was so boring and Sunday sermons seemed so interminable. It occurred to him that even such a wish might make him responsible for the old bishop's death, which would certainly be a sin. Could the new bishop be God's punishment for that sin?

The problem with both prayer and sin was that results took so long, if they came at all. How many times had he prayed for an end to his father's anger? Time passed, and he imagined running away, perhaps to live with the Crew, maybe with Kylie's family. Eventually he began to feel better, and hunger started to make itself felt. He considered going in but did not yet feel like facing his family so he just sat where he was. A long time later, the barn door opened and closed, and footsteps on the loft ladder made him tense. His father might be as outraged at his missing dinner as he was at his questioning of the bishop.

He relaxed when a familiar face appeared. It was his uncle Thomas.

"No supper for you, young man?"

Jed shook his head.

Thomas held up an apple. "Well, I was going to give this to one of the horses, but I guess you might as well have it." Thomas tossed the fruit to Jed, who caught it reflexively. "No appetite?"

Jed shook his head again. Thomas nodded. "Well, that which does not destroy you can only make you stronger." He came over and ruffled Jed's hair. "Why don't you come inside, your mother will be getting worried."

Jed nodded and stood up. His uncle led the way back down the ladder and out of the horse barn toward the house. Thomas was the younger brother, uninherited and so far unmarried. He helped with the management of the farm, supervised the hands at whatever needed doing, and as the best bow shot on Riverview farm, kept the rabbits under some degree of control. Jed envied him in his relaxed and easy manner, and the effortless way he seemed to move through his day. Rabbit hunting was a necessary chore, but was nevertheless a lot more fun than fieldwork, and he was the only one among all the family and farmhands who didn't back down from John Fougere. Josh followed him down the ladder, feeling better, and by the time they reached the front door of the house he'd finished the apple. The Fougere home was a rambling wood frame structure, built by Jed's thrice great-grandfather before *Ark* boosted and extended by every son of the family since. It was well built and well appointed, as befitted the main house of one of the most successful farms in *Ark*. The windows were glass, even in the newer sections. Glass was a pre-boost luxury, a cultural holdover from Earth houses that were built to be fortresses against wind and weather, and there were some in the church that said it amounted to vanity to install it, because every new pane had to be bought from someone else. Most new-built houses had open windows, with curtains and wooden shutters for privacy and to shut out the light for sleeping. The Bible spoke against pride of property, but Jed had heard the old bishop say more than once that the Fougere family had a lot to be proud of, always while admiring the house and buildings. To Jed, all the house conveyed was oppression and he found he wanted to go anywhere but back inside.

Thankfully, his father had already gone to sleep. His mother was sitting in the kitchen, looking worried. Wordlessly she took him up to bed and tucked him in, her eyes pained when she saw his bruises, and she fussed over him as though that would somehow make it all better. After she left it took him a long time fall asleep, looking at the thin streaks of light from the suntube filtering through the shutters. Breakfast in the morning was as it always was, as if nothing had happened the night before. His father left the table early to organize the hands in the orchards, and Jed went in to school as he always did.

At school it occurred to him that Dr. Valori might answer the questions the bishop would not. All morning he considered whether he should raise the question of the ten plagues with his teacher. He didn't want to earn another punishment, but Dr. Valori was always encouraging his students to ask questions, and it didn't seem in his nature to consider a mere question to be blasphemy. Then, too, there was the issue of vindication. He had first asked his question of the bishop because he couldn't understand how God could kill innocent newborns. When he had asked it, he had been sure that the bishop would have an explanation. Having had time to consider it it now seemed that there could be no explanation. Babies were born innocent, the old bishop had taught. Whatever their parents had done couldn't be their fault. If that were true then it meant his question wasn't blasphemy, because the Bible itself contained a contradiction. He had asked his first question looking for an answer. Now that he had discovered his own answer, he wanted to know that he was right. He waited until lunchtime and then rather than running out to play with either Kylie or Matthew and Abel, he paused in the classroom to ask his teacher why God hadn't just stopped Pharaoh from doing bad things, instead of killing all the firstborn.

Dr. Valori looked at him sideways. "That's a good question, Jed, but it's one you should ask your bishop."

Jed made a face, annoyed at the evasiveness of the answer. "I have asked him, sir, but I didn't really understand what he said." He left out the story of his subsequent punishments. "I mean if it was wrong for Pharaoh to enslave Israelites, why wasn't it wrong for God to kill the Egyptians' children? He said it was because the Egyptians needed to be punished, but two wrongs don't make a right. And it was Pharaoh who did wrong, not the children."

Dr. Valori nodded slowly. "I understand your confusion, but I'm afraid I don't have an answer for you."

"Why not?" Jed blurted the question in sudden frustration, then clapped his hands over his mouth, certain he'd gone too far.

Dr. Valori didn't seem to notice his sudden apprehension. "Well, Jed, not every question has an answer. I'm a scientist, so I can only answer questions about science and nature, and perhaps some history. Questions of religion belong to the Church."

"But it's a question about people, and you're a person too."

His teacher looked at Jed for a long moment, considering him. "What did the bishop say?"

Jed hesitated. "I got in trouble. I shouldn't have asked."

Dr. Valori nodded. "I'm not surprised." He came around his desk to sit on the bench beside Jed. "You're a smart boy, Jed, so I'll try to explain without getting us both in trouble. It's good to ask questions, that's what leads to understanding, but it's important to be careful what you ask, and who you ask. Religious questions are specially tricky."

"But what about the plagues?"

"I'm afraid I can't tell you, I'm not a Believer."

Jed looked up. "My father says that the Crew are all going to Hell because you don't believe."

"I don't think he's right, at least I hope he's wrong, but I can't talk to you about it. On Earth people could afford to fight about such things, but *Ark* isn't big enough for fighting, we need to get along. Before *Ark* was launched the builders came to some agreements about how they could work together, how we could work together. One rule is that Crew and Believers should keep themselves separate, except the Prophet himself would always live with Crew. That's so the Believers would always have a reason to tithe so the Crew could concentrate on learning. I wanted to teach in a parish school, but because I'm from the Crew I had to get special permission from the bishop, the old bishop, to do that. One of the things I agreed to is that I wouldn't talk about religious questions."

"And that's why you can't tell me why God did what he did to the Egyptians?"

"Exactly right." Dr. Valori smiled. "And I think that's enough theology and politics for now, Jedidiah *m'droog*. Kylie's having her birthday next week. Why don't you ask your mother if you can come?"

"I will. Thank you, sir."

He spent the rest of the lunch hour adventuring around the schoolyard with Matthew and Abel, and when he got home that night asked his mother if he could go to Kylie's party after church the following Sunday. She gave her permission without asking if Kylie's family was Crew, and he didn't volunteer the information. *It isn't bearing false witness if she didn't ask*. Somehow he wasn't quite sure that was true, but he still couldn't see that there would be any sin in a having a friend who was Crew. The next Sunday the Sunday school lesson was on the battle of Jericho, which again raised questions in Jed's mind, but this time he knew better than to ask them of the bishop. He kept his doubts to himself, and when his mother asked him how the lessons had gone he just smiled and said "Fine." He saw the concern in her eyes, the worry and the desire to do something for him, but there was fear there too. "I have to go and see to the chickens," he said, and slipped away before she could ask more.

Jed's mother never contradicted her husband, never stepped in to spare Jed his anger. Her time came afterward, to comfort him, to let him cry his tears against her breast, but as Jed grew older and his relationship with his father became more polarized her comforts seemed to matter less and less, until finally he simply found them annoying. It was as if, in trying to find in himself the strength to stand up to John Fougere, he found her support lent him only her weakness. After he'd fed the chickens, he went down to the river beyond the orchards, coming back only when it was time for dinner. After dinner he did his chores dutifully, and then climbed up to the hayloft to whittle and be alone with his thoughts. His back was still sore from the previous week's punishment, and it hurt somewhat as he leaned against the rough boards of the barn wall. He ignored the discomfort. There was really nothing else he could do about it. He'd been whittling a duck out of a hunk of good clear pine, and he wanted to get it finished in time to give it to Kylie for her birthday present. Uncle Thomas had offered to help and paint it once it was done.

His welts were mostly healed by the following Sunday, and the duck was finished. He could hardly contain himself through the bishop's sermon, and Sunday school seemed to drag interminably while he waited impatiently for the noon bell to release him. After the bells sounded he hiked up to Kylie's house for the party with a neatly folded note with directions to the Valori household in his pocket, the duck in a decorative red cloth bag that Mary made for him, and a bottle of preserves from his mother for good measure. It took a good two hours for him to get to the Town, and he was somewhat trepidatious when he reached it. It was far bigger than Charity, with wood-framed houses that even he could see were prelaunch-built, all with glass windows and metal door handles. Most of them had small gardens, but it was obvious the Crew didn't have to feed themselves, with more space given to flowers than food. A slight mist hung in the air, swept down from the permanent clouds that surrounded the top end of the sun tube. Dr. Valori had explained how the suntube evaporated water from the ocean at the aftwall and how it moved up the thin air at *Ark's* axis to condense against the cold foredome. The huge white circle in the center of the foredome was actually solid water—it was called *ice* in that state. Around the edges, where the air was thicker and warmer, it melted and ran down the forewall. The cold made some of the water condense before it even got to the ice layer, like warm breath on a windowpane, and that made the clouds that then got pushed down by the air circulation to cause mist and rain in direct proportion to how close you were to the forewall.

There were few people on the roads, and in the distance

Jed could see the squarish grey outlines of what could only be the University, built right into fore-wall when the Builders made *Ark*. Most of the Crew would be there during the day, he supposed, learning science and getting ready for the far distant day when *Ark* would arrive at Heaven. He carefully followed the directions on his now-crumpled note carefully, until he found himself standing in front of a well-kept Crew house, nowhere near as large as the Fougere home, but still somehow intimidating. Sounds of laughter came from inside, and he gathered his courage and went to knock on the door.

Kylie answered it, with her father behind her, and he was led into the living room, where the other children had already started with the presents. She hugged him when he gave her the duck. He found her enthusiastic affection was slightly embarrassing, but at least Matthew and Abel weren't there to witness it; he was the only Believer guest, all Kylie's other friends were children of Crew families. It made him feel somewhat awkward that he didn't know any of them, and he felt strange when they didn't say grace before the meal. The adults had organized some good games for after the cake, bobbing for apples and a treasure hunt that required solving puzzles to get clues. He teamed up with Kylie and they got the highest score, although the prize went to the next-best team because Dr. Valori said it wasn't right for her to win at her own party. Eventually the other parents came to collect their children, and one by one the other partygoers went home, until it was just the two of them. Kylie led him through a field to a row of tall pines. One in particular had branches arranged almost like a ladder, and they climbed up. Some thirty feet up Jed was surprised to find a broad platform of cut lumber hidden in the boughs.

"This is my secret place," Kylie told him.

"Did you build it yourself?" asked Jed.

Kiley shook her head. "No, my cousins did, a long time ago. They don't use it anymore, and nobody else knows it's here."

"You can see all the way to the ocean."

"And to the forewall, but those other trees grew and they're in the way now." She hesitated. "You mustn't tell anyone about it. It's secret."

"I won't."

"Promise?"

"I promise."

The sat silently for a while, enjoying the view, and then she said, "You're my best friend, Jed."

Jed nodded, not sure what to say. Abel and Matthew had been his best friends, but all they wanted to do was play games. Kylie was more serious, like her father, and like Jed himself. They were together, and alone, at the top reading level in their class, and they vied for first place on math tests. Abel and Matthew would collect chestnuts in huge numbers, just because they were fun to collect, and occasionally fun to throw at each other, but it was Kylie who noticed the teeth marks on one, and then used chestnut bait to draw out and then tame the squirrel who was eating them. For two weeks she and Jed had stopped at the crossroads after school, to lie motionless in the grass and watch the small creature scurry back and forth in nervous haste, caching the wealth of food they had provided for it. Their reward came when they found its nest, high in a hollow in an old gnarled oak tree. They climbed carefully up while the squirrel chattered angrily below them, and used a prelaunch stainless-steel dinner plate as a mirror to reflect light inside to see the cluster of tiny pups huddled there.

And it was true that Kylie was his best friend; did it matter that she was Crew and a girl? He decided it didn't. "You're my best friend too, Kylie." They sat in silence for a moment, and then she asked, "Do you have your whittling knife?"

He nodded and offered it to her. She took it and said, "Give me your thumb."

"What are you going to do?" he asked, looking at the knife apprehensively.

"On Earth, when people are best friends they mix their blood to prove it. I read it in a story about pirates."

"What are pirates?"

"They're thieves who sail the oceans, but they're noble thieves, with an honor code." She looked aftward and up the curve of the world to the blue ring of water at the aftwall. "I want to live on the ocean one day, like they do." She took a deep breath, in and out, and then returned her attention to Jed. "Give me your thumb.

Jed looked dubious. "I don't want you to cut me."

"You can do it yourself." Kylie put out her own thumb. "Here, I'll go first."

She looked at it for long moment and then with one sudden motion stabbed the sharp, black blade in. She shook the injured digit and red blood welled in the small wound. "Now you." She handed him the knife.

It was harder to cut himself than he thought it would

be, he kept reflexively jerking his hand away whenever he went to make a slice. Finally he put his hand flat on the platform so it had nowhere to go, closed his eyes, counted to three and jabbed. There was a sharp pain in his thumb and he opened his eyes to find a small wound oozing blood. It was bigger than he'd meant it to be and it stung, but he wasn't going to admit that to Kylie. He went to rub the digit on his pants to staunch the bleeding.

"Don't do that, we need the blood," she said. Solemnly they mashed the cuts together, mixing their blood. "Best friends forever."

"Best friends forever," he answered. Their thumbs were still touching, and the ceremony seemed to demand something more. After a moment Jed leaned over and kissed her on the cheek. Kylie giggled. "Let's go down to the stream."

Jed wiped the blood off the wooden blade, and they climbed down, but before they got to the stream there were some rabbits to watch, and then they got hungry and went back to Kylie's house.

"When are your parents coming, Jed?" Dr. Valori looked up from plucking a chicken in the kitchen. "Or will you be staying with us for dinner?" As he asked the University bells pealed seventeen o'clock and Jed realized how far he had to go to make it home in time for dinner.

"They aren't coming, sir. I walked here." In the distance the Charity church bells began echoing the University, carrying news of the changing hour out into the wider world.

"All the way from the other side of Charity? That's too far for a boy your age. Wait there and I'll get the buggy and take you home."

Jed had a sudden vision of arriving home sitting beside Dr. Valori in the buggy. There would be no concealing the fact that Kylie was Crew in that case, and his father would not be pleased.

"No, thank you, sir. I'll go myself. I'm used to walking places."

To his relief Dr. Valori didn't insist. He said his goodbyes as quickly as politeness would allow, and then started running. He had just an hour to cover the distance it had taken him two hours to travel on the way up. With no way to gauge the time it was taking him he had no choice but to run as hard and fast as he could the whole way. He arrived exhausted and sweaty, but in time to run up to his room and change before sliding into his seat at the supper table. His nearly late arrival went unremarked by his father, and his mother asked only once how the party was before the conversation moved on. His father and his uncle were discussing the growing size of families and the effect that would have on *Ark*'s population and their demand for fruit and corn and cattle and pigs. There was some tension in the discussion that Jed couldn't quite put his finger on, but as long as he wasn't in the focus of it he saw no cause for concern.

One of the benefits of teaching grade school was that there was no pomp or ceremony attached to graduation. Schoolchildren simply cheered and ran outside to play when the school year ended. Unfortunately Nikol Valori hadn't quite managed to sever all his ties to the University, and so when convocation arrived he found himself taking a seat on the institution's auditorium stage, uncomfortable in his tasseled mortarboard and his academic robes, resplendent with the golden trim that symbolized the scientific disciplines and the scarlet collar of a full professor.

The space now called the auditorium was the largest room in the University by far. Once it had been a hangar for the *dadushka* fliers the construction crew had used to move around inside the ship when they were building the ecosystem. Most of the *dadushka* had been moved into storage behind the meter-thick stainless-steel seals that separated the departure gallery from the ecocylinder, to remain there until *Ark*'s computer decided there was an emergency that required human intervention and opened them. A handful of fliers were still in the hangar as training hulks, and a couple of those could probably still fly, if there were hydrogen to charge their tanks. There was no hydrogen, and the airframes were used to train pilots and mechanics who would never practice their skills on a real aircraft. Nikol found that strangely sad. *What a thing it would be, to live in a world where I could build such a machine and fly for real.* He found his seat and, reluctantly, sat down to wait out the ceremony. His robes seemed heavy and constrictive, but he knew his distress didn't stem from any failing of the clothing itself. It was made of heavy cotton, beaten soft by the Believer seamstress who'd made it for him and she had made it to his measure and it fit him well and comfortably—what made him uncomfortable was what it stood for. Convocation was a ceremony, and the University had far too many ceremonies now, and far too little substance.

But there were students he'd taught out there on the floor, students who had worked hard and long for their degrees, and their effort and accomplishment was real, even if the system that supported it was increasingly divorced from reality. *And so here I am, participating in what I thought I'd abandoned.* The students, dressed in their own robes at the back at the auditorium hall, were sitting in silence, while the auditorium filled with chattering parents and well wishers. The rule was that if you spoke during the ceremony you would be failed from your program, and nobody wanted to fail at this late stage of the game. Nikol pursed his lips. It was an overly authoritarian rule, made purely to serve the University administration's desire to make the ceremony easier to manage, and he didn't approve of it. Bellingham came in and sat beside him, his robes bearing the green trim of the medical profession. *One of the few professions we have that still does real work.* Still, even doctors had their scope of responsibility severely curtailed in *Ark*'s sealed environment. Every last one of her original complement had been put through a pathogen-cleansing protocol so extreme it had nearly killed them. *And yet even mice got aboard.* It was likely that somewhere in the ship there lurked a pathogen that needed only to awaken, a small mutation perhaps, or a jump from an animal host, to become a killer. The thought was not reassuring. A sudden, deadly plague run amok in *Ark*'s small population could turn their world into a ghost ship. *Not quite a ghost ship; the ecosystem will keep running without us, until the hydrogen is gone and the suntube fades. Small comfort to us.*

Bellingham made himself comfortable. "The chief tells me she's asked you to come back to the University."

"She has."

"I've never understood why you left in the first place." Bellingham held up a hand to forestall Nikol's reply. "Don't get me wrong, I'm not one of those who say the kolkoz are unclean and unworthy. They're my patients, good people, hardworking people."

"I'd appreciate it if you didn't call them kolkoz."

"Believers then, whatever you like. Working among them is a noble thing, I'm proud to do it. At the same time, you're a full professor. You've got more in you than teaching grade school."

"I'm doing more than teaching, I'm blacksmithing now. Working with steel."

Bellingham's eyebrows went up. "That's supposed to be an improvement?"

Nikol considered his colleague for a long minute. "Did the chief engineer ask you to talk to me?"

Bellingham harrumphed. "Nothing of the sort. I'm just saying, you can do better. You've got a rare mind, Valori. Don't waste it."

"You think I'm wasting my talent?" Nikol paused, considering how far he wanted to go in making his point. *As far as I have to. I've spent too long being silent.* "I'll show you wasted talent. Watch this." He stood up and looked into the assembled graduates, found a young man with the same golden trim that his own robes bore. He beckoned the student forward, watched his eyes grow wide. To be called out of the assembly by a full professor, just minutes before graduation, could only be bad news in his world. He climbed up on the stage, looking nervous.

"Don't worry, young man, you're not in trouble," Nikol

reassured him. "I just want to ask you a few questions." He turned to Bellingham. "Observe."

"Of course, Professor." The student's voice still carried worry.

"What did you study?"

"Physics, Professor."

Nikol smiled. "You don't have to call me Professor every sentence either. Can you tell me Planck's constant?"

"It's six point six two six oh six times ten to the negative thirty-four joule-seconds, Professor . . . sir . . ." The student stumbled, unsure of how he should act now that the rules had changed.

"And the speed of light?"

"Two hundred ninety-nine thousand seven hundred ninety-two kilometers per second."

"Now tell me, how can you prove those values are correct?"

"They're all listed in *Physical Constants and Formulae*, Seventeenth Edition, sir."

"Yes, but how do know *Physical Constants and Formulae* has them right?"

The student looked confused. "I'm not sure what you mean, sir."

"What if I told you the speed of light was two hundred thousand kilometers per second, not three. How can you demonstrate that I'm wrong?"

"Sir, with all respect, the numbers in *Physical Constants and Formulae* were derived by the best scientists on Earth with the best possible equipment. They can't be wrong."

"And if I don't accept what's written in the book?"

The student's expression moved from confused to

nervous. "But sir, the book *is* right. It's the fundamental reference work of physics."

"Imagine you didn't have the book. How could you prove me wrong then?"

"Well, I don't need the book itself, sir, I've memorized all the relevant constants and formulae." The student couldn't quite repress the pride in his voice as he said it.

"I see. Well, I'll ask you a different question. Give me Newton's second law."

The student nodded, more at ease now that he was once again on familiar ground, answering direct questions in his chosen field. "The acceleration of a free body as produced by a net force is directly proportional to the magnitude of the net force, in the same direction as the net force, and inversely proportional to the inertial mass of the body."

Nikol nodded. "And how does inertia work on a free body moving in a rotating reference frame?"

"The body appears to experience a force pushing it to the outer diameter of the frame, centrifugal force."

"Very good. State the law of gravity."

"Objects are attracted to each other in direct proportion to their masses and in inverse proportion to the distance between them, squared."

"And which is more important here in *Ark*, gravity or inertia?"

The student looked puzzled again. "I don't understand what you mean, sir. All laws of physics apply everywhere in the universe."

"That's true." Nikol paused. "Ever play catch when you were young?"

"Yes sir."

"Can you throw a ball farther spinward or counterspinward?"

The student laughed. "Counterspinward."

"What if you throw it straight foreward or aftward?"

"It curves spinward, but with all due respect, sir, these aren't science questions."

"Why isn't it science?"

"Well, every child knows that."

Nikol nodded. "You're right, every child does." He considered the youth for a minute. "Why do things fall when you drop them?"

"Well . . . sir, I mean . . ." The student stammered, suddenly frightened, knowing he was expected to know the answer, and knowing that he simply didn't. "Well, they just do. They fall—"

Nikol cut him short. "That's all right, young man, I've bothered you enough. Enjoy your graduation." The student's face showed relief and he turned to go back to his seat. Nikol turned to Bellingham. "You see."

"See what? He seemed to know his stuff to me."

"Yes, he knew his stuff, but what is his stuff? Some empty incantations about physical law, nothing more. He's memorized his physical constants to six decimal places, but has to accept the book's word that they are correct. He knows the formulae for inertial movement in a rotating reference frame, but he doesn't understand that we *live* in a rotating reference frame, and that's why things fall when you drop them. He knows the difference between gravity and inertia, but he doesn't realize that things here don't fall quite the same way they will on a planet. He's memorized the rules but he understands nothing. He's not a scientist, he's a mystic, and *Physical Constants and Formulae, Seventeenth Edition,* is his tome of magical lore."

Bellingham harrumphed. "Physicists and philosophers, they live with their heads in the clouds. You won't get argument from me on that point. Still, I think you're making too much of this. The boy knows his facts, he isn't making them up."

"No, but he might as well be. What good are facts with no understanding? It's an exercise in futility. Look at how he acted, terrified that I'd deny him graduation. It isn't as if I could take the knowledge out of his brain, but in our delightful little world the knowledge in his head counts for nothing. It would count for nothing even if it weren't just a collection of empty, useless facts, which it is. What we value isn't education, it's the official recognition that a person has gone through an appropriately approved process to enter the educated class. That's functionally identical to the priesthood of the Believers. Look at his attitude! See how he defers to his seniors, like any acolyte. He was terrified I might find something he hadn't already memorized, and it didn't even occur to him that he might know something I didn't. He came right out and said that something can't be science if everyone knows it. That's because science has become a collection of esoteric secrets, dispensed and sanctified by the high priests of this very institution, which is to say, you and I. He might as well be memorizing the Book of Job, for all the relevance his knowledge has to the world he lives in. My daughter playing at the pond is more a scientist than he is, any child is. Watch how they observe the world, soak up its lessons, experiment with it. Young children haven't had their curiosity extinguished by what we pass off as education."

Bellingham laughed. "You're lucky we have no inquisitors or the chief engineer would have you put to the question. There's a difference between us and the Church."

Nikol snorted sardonically. "Give it time. We'll have them yet."

Bellingham pointed. "I think they're starting."

They were starting. A proctor came out to center stage and held up his arms, standing there as a symbol of silence until the crowd of parents and well-wishers below noticed him and became as quiet as the students. Nikol watched as the ceremony began. *And if they could they'd suck the facts out of my brain for my heresy, they'd certainly do it. Or maybe not. Where rote learning replaces research and recitation counts for understanding, facts are no longer truth anyway.*

Once the crowd was silent the proctor lowered his arms and turned to face the arch at the back of the stage where the University executive waited. A steady drumbeat started, and then the Board of Governors came out, looking somber and serious in their gowns and caps. As they approached the front of the stage the proctor turned back to the waiting assembly and swung his arms in a gesture that told them all to stand. They did, and as the executive passed the ranks of seated faculty they stood as well. Nikol stood with them when his turn came. *I find this protocol noxious, and yet I still sanctify it with my own participation.* It was expected that as a professor he would be there to see his students graduate, and he had two more of these heavy pageants to get through before the last of his protégés earned their own gold-trimmed robes. *And then I won't have to come anymore.* He nearly laughed at his own thought and suppressed it. *And I should take responsibility for myself and admit that I don't have to come now. I'm here because I'm expected to be here, and simple expectation is enough to make me abandon my principles and waste my time.*

Except he'd hurt some feelings if he didn't come, and respecting other people's emotions was a perfectly valid principle. He abandoned his self-flagellation and resigned himself to enduring the ceremony. Melany was last in the line of University dignitaries, and as her subordinates took their places on the benches placed at the front of the stage, she moved to stand in front of them at the podium, resplendent in the formal robes of the chief engineer. The Prophet was waiting for her there, and he raised his arms, symbolically blessing her. Most of the Crew actively rejected the Believers' religion, but the link between the Church's tithings and their own survival demanded the symbolism of his presence. *Thus the merger of study and religion is complete.* The Prophet was a callow youth, younger than most of the graduates, and without even the benefit of the crippled education they had received. On one level it astounded Nikol that ultimate authority for graduation rested with such a boy. *But it shouldn't. This is all* pokazkhua, *all of it, and he is only playing the role he's been given in the play.*

The ceremony was long and laborious and time dragged heavily by. Nikol found himself tuning out the droning words of Melany, the Prophet, the various heads of the various faculties, the student valedictorian, the parentis-elect and all the rest who'd come to inflict their words upon the newly qualified disciples. Instead he found himself studying the weave of his robe and the repeating patterns formed by the ranked students in their ranked portable chairs. There was an underlying symmetry there, and in more than the geometric sense. The fabric was Believer-grown cotton, because only the toughest and heaviest of the prelaunch synthetics had survived the time since departure, and over half the chairs were of native wood for the same reason. *Earth's memories inexorably fade, replaced by that we create here.*

Eventually the ceremony ended, the students all threw their hats in the air and cheered, as tradition demanded. The solemn assembly became a noisy gathering, filling the vast hall with the sounds of celebration. Nikol moved into the crowd, congratulating those he had taught the previous year, welcoming proud parents, greeting his erstwhile colleagues, or at least those who would acknowledge his existence. The crowd thickened toward the back of the hall where long tables waited, laden down with food and drink. *All of it grown by Believers, delivered by Believers, prepared and served by Believers.* He looked around at the smiling faces surrounding him, eating, drinking, talking, celebrating the achievements of the graduating class. *We have lost so much, and nobody here even realizes that.*

A hand on his arm. Melany.

"Chief Engineer." He smiled his first genuine smile since the ceremony had ended. "A pleasure as always."

"I was hoping you'd come, I need to talk to you." She kept her hand on his arm, urging him toward the parked *dadushka*, where the crowd thinned away to nothing.

"Not to convince me I need to come back, I hope."

"Exactly that."

Nikol's eyebrows went up. "I'm flattered, of course . . ."

"Nikol, I know there are problems with the system. I want to fix them, and I need your help." She sensed his coming rejection and interrupted him to forestall it. "We've been gifted with a tremendous treasure in our knowledge base, we have to keep that alive."

"Most of it is already dead. No matter how hard you try you can't reanimate a corpse. It isn't that the effort isn't noble, but what we have in our databanks is the working knowledge of a planet of twenty billion people. There's no way a few thousand of us could possibly make that live. The Crew is just maintaining the forms of study because it doesn't know what else to do."

"Don't make it sound so trivial. What we do is important. You're right that we need to do more than simply study what other people have discovered. I'm bringing in some changes." She put a hand against the flier they were standing beside. "We're looking at getting these airborne again. We want to do a study of shipsteel and see if we can re-create it. These things are going to have an impact on the way people live their lives."

"No, Melany." Nikol paused, trying to suppress the sudden anger he felt. There was no point in turning Melany into another burned bridge. Nevertheless when he spoke his passion was clear. "What you do—you, not me—what you do is *not* important. What you do is make the exaltation of form over function into high art." He smacked the side of the *dadushka* with his open palm. "You can't make this thing fly, we don't have the fuel, and we can't make it. You can't re-create shipsteel, because we don't have any raw materials. The builders *supply* us with shipsteel."

Melany was silent for a moment. "You worry me, Nikol. The builders are long, long gone."

Nikol rolled his eyes. "I don't mean the builders themselves, I haven't lost my sanity. *Ark* meters it out. There's piles of it at the foot of the forewall. I'm learning to work it."

"I didn't know that."

"Of course not. I only know because I specialized in studying *Ark*'s construction, but everyone *should* know. Why else do we have machine tools to work shipsteel?"

"Leftovers from the builders, I thought." She gestured to the flier. "Like this and everything else."

Nikol shook his head. "Everything we have comes from the builders, but they wanted us to be able to do things for ourselves. We haven't and that's the tragedy. I tried to puzzle out the flexfab. Too much knowledge has been lost."

"Everything is in the databanks."

"Only the theory. The practical working knowledge is gone, and the theory can only take you so far."

"I don't agree with you."

"You can't agree with me, your position won't allow it. Believe me anyway, I tried. Answer me this, why are you so eager to bring me back into the fold?"

"Because you're one of the best professors we've got."

"And because if one of your best professors lowers— no, *desanctifies*—himself so much as to teach children in grade school it throws the whole system into question."

Nikol was angry now, and though he realized that he was taking out his own frustrations on Melany he was unable to stop himself. "Just one heretic can destroy the whole system, and so heresy cannot be allowed. Our ancestors were scientists, but we're a priesthood." He held up a hand before she could interrupt him. "No, hear me out. We have a sacred body of knowledge, just like a priesthood, we have a hierarchy and rituals, just like a priesthood. We have the required rigidity of thought, the required disdain for the uninitiated, the required rigorous exclusion of those deemed unworthy."

Melany stiffened. "Unlike a priesthood, our body of knowledge is based on truth."

"Based on truth, but divorced from reality. You don't have to agree with me, just realize this. There's already one priesthood in *Ark*. There isn't room for two. Sooner or later there's going to be a clash."

There was hurt in her eyes, no less genuine because he might be right. "We were friends, Nikol. Close friends."

"We still are, Melany." He meant it too, but they stood on opposite sides of a widening gulf, and he no longer knew how to bridge it. He shook her hand and went out of the auditorium, leaving his robe hanging from the outboard winglet of one of the fliers. He wouldn't be back for any more convocations. His last students would just have to graduate without him.

In time fifth grade became sixth grade, and to Jed it just seemed natural that he would spend more time with Kylie and less with Abel and Matthew. He found school more interesting now, and was starting to regret that seventh grade would be his last year. All Believers left school after seventh grade, while the Crew went on to at least thirteenth grade, and many took advanced studies after that, as Dr. Valori had. He chose to work with Kylie whenever he got the chance, and it became their habit to meet in the mornings under the chestnut tree at the crossroads, and then walk in together to school. After the day they would reverse their steps to the tree, and frequently they would linger there, feeding their squirrel, discussing their lessons or the plans for their next adventure. There was some teasing from the other children, who seemed to think there was something inherently strange about boy-girl friendships, but they ignored it and eventually it went away. Sometimes, when their mood was more serious, they'd talk about their respective futures. Kylie was going to study biology and become a doctor, Jed would inherit Riverview and raise crops and stock. Inwardly Jed felt his future was more of a burden than an opportunity, but Kylie thought it was exciting. "I can come over all the time and ride horses and swim in the streams. It'll be fun."

His eleventh birthday came and went, and with it an expansion in his chores. It was time for him to start learning how to run a farm, his father said, and put action to words by putting Jed to work in the fields. On a Saturday morning before Christmas Jed found himself behind the knife plow, guiding a team up and down, plowing the furrows in one of the aftward fields. A light drizzle had cooled the air and softened the ground, but it was still hard and heavy work and his furrows left a lot to be desired. His father made it clear that he expected better, but Jed had no idea how he could improve. The knife plow was so big he could barely hang on to it, let alone guide it. The horses just dragged him along, and it was only through their familiarity with the routine of plowing that he accomplished anything at all. He was exhausted by the time the bell rang for the noon meal, and he took the horses back to the barn and handed them over to Josiah, the stablehand, with a sense of relief. Lunch was on by the time he got up to the house, and he was more than ready to eat. Saturday lunches usually involved his father questioning him on the details of what he'd done that morning, but this time his father didn't even look at him through the whole meal. He seemed tense and distracted, and though tension in him usually translated into short, sharp words for Jed, this time he barely spoke a word. Jed ate in silence himself, listening to Mary natter on to his mother about Matthew Dermit, her current fancy. Mary was of age to be declared marriageable, and normally such open campaigning on her placement would have provoked a reaction from their father, but he ignored that too. His brooding preoccupation made itself felt around the table and the atmosphere grew uncomfortable, but finally his mother took up her plate, signaling the end of the meal. Jed was about to excuse himself to go and finish the plowing when his father pushed back his plate.

"I think we shall go to afternoon services, Mother," he said. There was a tightness in his expression that overcame his attempt at a relaxed pose.

"Of course, John." Jed's mother smiled her barely perceptible smile.

"Jedediah, harness a team and hitch the buggy."

"But Father, I have to finish the plowing . . ." Plowing

was work, but since the incident with the new bishop Jed had taken a strong dislike to church services.

"The plowing will wait." John Fougere's voice was stern. "Do as I say, boy. The bishop is expecting us."

Jed opened his mouth to protest, closed it again as he saw the tension lines tighten in his mother's face. There was nothing to do but obey; protest would only create a fight without changing anything. "At once, Father."

He went out to the barn and got Josiah to help him get the buggy, then drove it carefully up to the house. He was a confident rider, and getting better with a team pulling a plow, but still a little uncertain with a buggy and wagon. He'd been there the day Jack Pullman's father's team had run away, spooked by God only knew what. The cart had rolled on a corner and pulled the team into the ditch, and Jed could still hear the screaming, broken horses struggling to get up, and see the shattered remnants of the cart with the crumpled body lying so still beneath it. There had been a funeral then too, as there was for the old bishop, and Jed was well aware that a team hitched to a harness bar was less controllable than a horse you were astride yourself.

"Remember your manners, Jedediah." Jed's father waved a hand as he pulled the buggy to a halt in front of the house. "Be a gentleman, help your mother up."

He did so, and helped Ruth and his sister up as well for good measure, then clambered back up himself to sit on the first bench between his father and his uncle. *But why are we going to church today?* His father stirred up the horses, and Jed's curiosity had to wait.

The churchyard was full of buggies and horses. The

bishop held services every day, but most families attended only on Sunday and their chosen family day, unless it was a special holiday. Jed traded a glance with his uncle. Wednesday was the Fougere family day, and this was Monday. Something was up. Inside, the pews were crowded close with Believers in their worship clothes, the Maddas, the Fludds and the Rossnens. The crowd was buzzing with chatter. After what seemed to be a long time Bishop Nemmer came up to the pulpit in his ceremonial white robe. He held up his arms for silence, perhaps unconsciously mimicking the shape of the cross on the wall behind him. The crowd stilled.

"Blessings, Brothers and Sisters," he began.

"Blessings from God," answered the congregation, as they were expected to.

The bishop pulled back his hood, seeming even taller looking down on the congregation from the pulpit, his eyes alive with the light of God. "I would like to thank you all for coming today, on such short notice. Today is a great day for our parish, a great day for Believers, a great day for God." He went on with his sermon, which emphasized duty and obedience more than usually, and warned against the dangerous secularism represented by the Crew. "They call themselves a Crew, but do they tend this vessel that's carrying us to Heaven? No, the builders wisely put us in God's hands when they launched our *Ark*. Do they till the soil or log the forest? No, the builders gave that job to us." Bishop Nemmer was in fine form, and there was a great deal more like that. Diatribes against the Crew had become a frequent component of his sermons, and while most of the adults still seemed to find him a captivating speaker, Jed had come to find him as boring as the old bishop.

He had drifted off into a daydream about building a treehouse like Kylie's when a sudden change in the congregation yanked him back to the here-and-now. His eyes focused on a red-robed figure, fully hooded, who now stood at the front of the assembly. An inquisitor! The bishop had just introduced him, and was standing aside. Jed looked over his shoulder to see two white-robed servitors standing at the church entrance, waiting to be called on, and in the meantime effectively blocking the only exit. A thrill of fear shot through him. This explained his father's tension and the unexpected call to church. He had seen an inquisitor only once before, and then from a distance, but there was no mistaking the red robe, nor the fear it engendered in all who saw it.

The inquisitor made the sign of the cross. "Any who have a sin to confess should come forward now to know God's forgiveness."

The congregation sat in silence. Even the virtuous feared the inquisitor, but nobody moved, even though early confession might ease the sentence. Jed sweated through a long, painful wait until finally the inquisitor spoke again.

"Aeron Neufeldt, stand, please."

Aeron stood. He was a middle-weight man of middle age; his farm wasn't quite as prosperous as Riverview, but solidly in the second rank of producers.

"What have you to say, Aeron?" asked the inquisitor.

"I saw my wife with a Crew, Jake Toller—" Neufeldt was cut off by his wife's voice.

"Aeron, what are you doing?" There was fear and panic in Shealah Neufeldt's face.

Neufeldt ignored her. "I want to know the truth of this, Inquisitor."

The hooded figure nodded. "Shealah Neufeldt, you stand accused of adultery," it intoned. He made a gesture and the servitors came forward.

"I didn't, I never . . . Aeron, please . . ." Shealah grabbed her husband's arm, but he looked icily at the front of the church while the servitors came and dragged her off him. They hauled her, protesting, up to the end of the chapel. The bishop undid the rope that held the cross from its place of honor behind the dias and lowered it to the ground. Shealah was unceremoniously bound to it with tight ropes, cinched around her wrists to hold her in place for the Inquisition to come. "Aeron! Aeron, please, I've always been faithful . . ."

A thrill of fear shot through Jed as he realized what was happening. Shealah Neufeldt hadn't kept herself separate from the Crew. She had broken the rules, and was about to be punished for it. He looked suddenly to his father, whose face set like stone as he watched the spectacle. Had John Fougere somehow found out about his bloodbond with Kylie? Was he about to be put to the question over sharing blood with a Crew? *I only kissed her on the cheek. Father couldn't give me to the inquisitor for that, he wouldn't have* . . . But Jed couldn't shake the feeling that perhaps his father had.

The inquisitor came toward Shealah, his whip coiled at his waist. To Jed it seemed like a blacksnake, coiled and ready to strike a hapless rabbit. "Shealah Neufeldt," he intoned. "Did you commit the sin of adultery with Jake Toller, of the Crew?"

"No! I did not." Her voice quavered, but it was clear and her face was defiant. She raised her chin. She was a proud woman, she wouldn't be brought low easily.

The inquisitor brought his whip down, and Jed jumped at the sharp crack as it bit into her plain chapel-going dress. Shealah grimaced, but did not cry out, and the question was repeated. "Shealah Neufeldt, did you commit the sin of adultery with Jake Toller of the Crew."

"No!" She shouted the word angrily.

Again the whip came down, harder this time, and again the question was asked. This time she didn't answer, only shook her head with her lips pressed tight together against the pain. The question was repeated, and Shealah answered with her eyes, burning with an anger that answered for her where her voice would not. Undeterred, the inquisitor continued. The question, the refusal and the burning lash were repeated again, and then again, and Jed found himself unable to tear his eyes from the horrific spectacle. On the sixth stroke a strangled cry escaped Shealah's mouth. By the twelfth stroke she was crying, her head hanging down, no longer bothering to deny the accusation even in her expression, though she still refused to answer. The lash had torn her clothing in places, and her hands and feet were starting to turn blue where the ropes had cut off the circulation. Jed found himself wishing he could shrink into the pew and vanish, if only to spare himself having to watch. Time seemed to inch past as the whip stroke rose and fell and Shealah's cries turned into screams that rose and fell with it, as she begged and pleaded with the inquisitor, with her husband, with the bishop to let her go, until finally she fell silent once more, barely even responding to the lash, though the front of her dress had been reduced to shreds, and bright red lines laced angrily over her breasts and belly. Jed became vaguely aware of the tolling of the church bell in Hope, the next village over. Their own bell wouldn't ring until the Inquisition was done. Most of an hour had passed without his being aware of it. The inquisitor had grown frustrated and was putting real muscle into the strokes, grunting as he laid them in, and his voice was short of breath when he demanded her confession. Jed looked over to see Mary twisting her handkerchief as though the lashes were landing on her, her eyes wide and her face pale. His father's face was set grimly, his mother was looking out the window, her expression far, far away, Ruth's hand clutched tightly in hers.

Finally, after a particularly hard lash, Shealah stirred and said something, though it was too low to be audible.

The inquisitor paused, his whip upraised. "What was that?"

"I did it." Shealah spoke louder.

"Did what?"

"I slept with that man, whoever he is. I slept with a Crew. Is that what you want to hear?" She raised her head, ignoring the inquisitor to lock eyes with her husband. "I laid down with him, Aeron. I did it a lot." Her voice grew angry and her eyes flashed. "Every day, Aeron, because you're not good enough. Every day, because you're too small a man to satisfy a woman. I laid down with him every day while you tilled the fields, you miserable little man, because he was so much better than you. My father told me you weren't good enough for me." She struggled against the ropes that held her to the cross, as if her anger would be enough to break them, and her expression made it clear that Aeron Neufeldt was fortunate that she couldn't. She spat at him instead, then slumped down, crying bitterly.

For a long, long minute there was silence in the church, broken only by Shealah's sobs. The congregation sat there, the bishop stood with his mouth hanging open, even the inquisitor seemed taken aback by the sudden power of her rage, his whip hanging slack. Jed realized he was holding his breath, and it took a considerable effort of will for him to breathe again.

It was Aeron Neufeldt who finally broke the spell, his jaw working, his own face so red it seemed to Jed about to explode. He stood slowly, his eyes at first locked on the gob of spittle on the chapel floor, halfway between his wife and himself. He started to speak, and only a harsh croak came out. He swallowed hard, and then in a voice that cut like an ironwood knife he said, "I divorce you, I divorce you, I divorce you." Then he turned on his heel and stalked out of the church.

Again the congregation sat in stunned silence at the spectacle. The bishop stepped forward and took the pulpit. "Look at this poor woman, see how she suffers for her sin." He turned to gesture to Shealah. "Take pity on her. How can we blame her when we ourselves allow Satan's workers to thrive in our midst, when we feed them and clothe them, when we send our impressionable children to school to learn from them who knows what lies, to be turned against the Bible, to have their eyes closed to God."

The bishop looked around the congregation, meeting every eye one by one. His gaze crossed Jed's, sending a thrill of panic through his spine, seemed as though he were suddenly naked, as though the bishop could see right into his soul and root out the guilty secret of his friendship with Kylie hidden there.

"Look at her," continued the bishop. "She committed the sin of adultery, she suffers for it. And yet that sin cannot be committed alone. So where is the man who tempted her into betraying her husband? Why isn't he up there beside her, being purified on the cross?" He held up his arms as if imploring God for the answer, then brought them down to point accusingly at the congregation. "Because he's Crew, that's why. Because he thinks he's above our laws, because he thinks he's above God."

The sermon went on for some time while Shealah hung there, and afterward the congregation filed out quietly, the normal cheerful post-service babble reduced to a subdued murmur. Jed rehitched the buggy, and the family rode in silence back toward home, Jed watched the fields slide past without really seeing them, the steady clip-clop of the horses' hooves providing a counterpoint to his thoughts. *It could have been me up there, it could have been Kylie.* The thought of the inquisitor's whip coming down on him filled him with fear, the thought of it coming down on Kylie filled him with anger. Even his father had nothing to say until they were home. He finally spoke when they were dismounting the buggy.

"Jed, you put the horses away and finish your chores." There was a hardness to his father's voice that stifled protest before it might be voiced. *But I haven't eaten.* Jed didn't say it, avoiding the inevitable rebuke. He saw his mother open her mouth, then close it. Her eyes met his. The penalty for missing dinner was to go hungry, but his mother would see that there was a snack waiting for him when he went to bed. Jed didn't argue, grateful for the chance to be alone with his thoughts. Something had changed in his father. Normally he spent the entire ride home from the chapel expanding on the bishop's sermon, stressing the requirement to live the life that God had demanded of his subjects. Jed hated the lectures, but he found his father's withdrawn silence even more disturbing.

He put away the buggy team, and went out to feed the chickens. He couldn't get the image of Shealah bound to the cross out of his mind. He knew it was forbidden for Believers to marry Crew, and adultery was against a Commandment, though he was a little unsure of exactly what adultery was. It was the harshness of her treatment that was shocking. Inquisitions were rare, and he'd never before seen one in which the inquisitor actually used his whip. Usually transgressors simply hugged the cross, knelt and begged forgiveness. The whip would be touched to their back in a completely symbolic way. Once he'd come into church to see a young man actually tied to the cross, for what transgression he didn't know. The man's expression was vacant, his eyes focused on something far beyond the physical, and the entire service had gone on as if he wasn't there. Jed hadn't dared to ask anyone who he was or what he'd done, but his father had lectured them on disobedient sons on the way home. The point was clear enough.

He finished with the chickens and headed for the horse barn, only to meet his uncle coming the other way.

"Blessings, Uncle Thomas."

"Blessings, Jed. Are you done with your chores?"

Jed hesitated. A question like that was usually a preview to more work, but he couldn't lie to his uncle.

"Yes, Uncle. I have schoolwork though." The work in question was to study for a math test still a week off. He hadn't planned to do it so early, but it might serve now to avert more chores.

"Well, that will wait a bit. I'm going to plow the west field. It's high time you learned how to run a team properly; your furrows would stagger a saint. Come give me a hand."

"Yes, Uncle." Jed trailed his uncle to the horse barn, and helped him harness the team, two new drays they were breaking in. They drove the team out to the west field and began. After the first three furrows his uncle rested the horses and leaned against the wooden fence rail that marked the edge of the field.

He wiped sweat from his brow and drank deep from his water flask before offering it to Jed. "What did you think of today's performance?"

"The Inquisition? I was scared, Uncle. I didn't like it."

"I saw your face, that's why I thought I'd ask you."

"I know sinners deserve punishment, and adultery is against a Commandment."

"Do you know what adultery is?"

"Sort of. It's not keeping yourself separate from the Crew."

Uncle Thomas shook his head. "No, not exactly, though I can see where you got the idea. You're young yet for the full explanation. Let me just say in very broad terms that it happens when a man loves a woman who is not his wife."

Jed's eyebrows went up, his original fears returned. *Do I love Kylie? I kissed her, does that make me an adulterer?* The change in rules left him even more guilty than before, and the fear he had felt while watching Shealah being whipped on the cross returned full force.

"What's wrong, Jed?" Uncle Thomas's face was suddenly full of concern. "You look like you just saw the devil."

"I . . . I . . ." Jed looked down, suddenly ashamed. "Nothing, Uncle."

"Something, obviously." His uncle reached down and raised Jed's chin. "Don't tell me you've been sinning in the bushes yourself."

Jed shook his head violently. "I didn't mean to, Uncle, I didn't know. I don't want to be whipped." He looked up, scared. "Please don't tell Father."

His uncle laughed. "Well, aren't you the precocious one. Don't worry, I'm not going to tell anyone. Who's the lucky girl of your affections?"

"Promise you won't tell?"

"My lips are sealed."

"Kylie Valori."

"I don't think I know her."

"She's in my class, my teacher's daughter."

Uncle Thomas nodded. "A Crew girl."

"I didn't . . . I mean . . . she never said she was Crew . . ."

"No, it wouldn't have occurred to her that it might matter, I expect. And I don't suppose it occurred to you to tell your parents either, once you figured it out."

"They never asked," said Jed, defensively.

"I'm sure they didn't. And exactly what did you and Kylie do to commit adultery?"

"I . . . I kissed her."

"Anything else?"

"Only once, Uncle, and only on the cheek."

Jed's uncle laughed gently. "Well, I wouldn't worry. I don't think there's enough there to support an Inquisition."

"We . . . we also mixed our blood," said Jed, motivated by his uncle's easy manner to unburden himself completely.

Thomas's eyebrows went up. "What does that mean?"

"That we're best friends." Jed explained what Kylie had told him about pirates, suddenly worried anew. "Was that a wrong thing to do? It was her birthday, and she wanted to."

"Yes." Uncle Thomas pursed his lips, thinking. "Well, I'm quite sure there's neither adultery nor sin in what you've done, Jed. Nevertheless, I think you've been wise in keeping your friendship with her away from your father, and away from the bishop too, while you're at it."

Jed heaved a sigh of relief. "But if there's nothing wrong, why does it have to be secret?"

"You're a smarter boy than that. Just because there's no sin doesn't mean it won't get you in trouble. Shealah Neufeldt was blameless, I feel morally certain. That didn't keep her off the cross."

"She said she did it, while she was on the cross. The cross compels truth."

"I think it's the whip that does most of the compelling," Thomas said, pressing his lips together. "And it only compels what the sinner thinks the inquisitor wants to hear."

"Why would her husband accuse her if she was innocent?"

"Well, that's a bit of a mystery. I can imagine a couple of reasons, but they're nothing more than theories."

"Tell me, Uncle"

His uncle leaned back. "One part of the puzzle is that their farm is really Shealah's, or it was. She inherited because her father had no sons. Aeron is a second son himself, so he'd have no land if he hadn't married her. The Prophet—the previous Prophet, of course—was going to place her with the bishop, the old bishop, back when he was a young man, or younger anyway." Uncle Thomas laughed. "She wanted Aeron, but of course that didn't matter. Still, she was smart enough to know how to get him in the end."

"How did she do that? I thought the Prophet placed wives on God's command."

"Indeed he does, Jed. But sometimes, just sometimes, people's desires get in the way of that. Shealah saw what was happening, and moved in with the old bishop before the marriage. She would have been his third wife, but she made his household such a living hell that soon he was begging the Prophet to call off the wedding. That gave her power, you see. She let them know that she would show the world a vision of the bishop that the Church would rather not have them see. Everyone would believe her because she had lived there, and everyone would be talking about it because the cancelation of a placement is very big news indeed. The price of her silence was placement with Aeron. It isn't often that a woman beats the Church, but she did."

"That still doesn't tell me why Aeron would accuse her like that, especially if they loved each other so much."

"That was twenty years ago, Jed, I wasn't much older

than you when it happened. People change in that much time, what the change was, I can't tell you. I can tell you that, now that Shealah is a fallen woman, that farm is going to belong to Aeron. He's only ever had one wife. Maybe the Prophet will see fit to place another with him. We'll see how generous his tithing gets over the next year or so." Uncle Thomas stood up. "Come on, these furrows aren't going to plow themselves."

They went back to work, Jed straining his muscles to control the heavy plow as the horses plodded up and down the field. The world of adults didn't make a lot of sense, but he was relieved to know that he wouldn't be going to Hell for adultery, or worse yet, to the cross.

Melany Waseau heard the clanging before she rounded the corner of the Valori house, metal on metal, rhythmic and ringing. The smell of hot steel mingled with the smell of wood smoke. When she came into the backyard she found the source of both. Nikol Valori had transformed his yard into a forge, and was hammering a piece of red-hot steel into shape. The forge was a simple enough affair, a raised hearth of clay brick supported a bed of coals, their flames blown hot by air forced through channels beneath them. The air was supplied by a wooden blower fan, cranked enthusiastically by Nikol's daughter. Overhead a chimney carried away the smoke and sparks. The flower bed that had been the centerpiece of the garden had been replaced by stacks and stacks of cordwood, shiny blocks of ship steel piled beside wooden racks that held tongs and hammer and various other implements she didn't recognize.

"Nikol," she called. "What are you doing?"

"I'm blacksmithing." He looked up from his work and smiled at her. "Or at least I'm trying to." He was wearing heavy leather gloves, and picked up the half-shaped bar of steel and thrust it into the coals, making sparks fly.

"You're filthy," she said, and he was, his bare forearms and face streaked in soot, his hair matted with sweat.

"I know," he replied. "I'm healthy too."

And, now that he mentioned it, he did look fitter, the muscles in his arms and shoulders corded tight, his body leaner than she'd seen it since they'd both been students.

"Can I ask why?"

"I'm building myself a role in the community. Teacher, blacksmith, neighbor, that's me."

"Can you spare a few minutes?"

Nikol removed the now red-hot bar from the heart of the forge. "I can." He put the steel down on the hearth. "Kylie, *devuchka*, why don't you see if you can find us some lunch?" Kylie stopped turning the blower and went inside. Nikol dusted off his hands and perched on a pile of bricks. Melany looked around and sat, by default, in one of the old garden chairs that had been pushed to one side to make room for the forge.

"Not bad, is it?" He gestured to take in his handiwork. "The Believers' original steel tools are starting to wear out. I get half a cord of wood for just a good kitchen cleaver."

"It's impressive," she said, and leaned forward. "Nikol, I've come to ask your advice."

He laughed. "I can't help but feel I've been very disappointing to you, in both help and advice. I'm flattered that you keep coming back in hopes that I'll improve."

"I can trust you to keep secrets. I can trust you to tell

me the truth." On the hearth of the forge the workpiece was slowly cooling, orange fading to cherry red fading to black.

"Even though I've abandoned all you hold dear."

"Maybe because you abandoned all I hold dear. I tried to speak to Stroink. He won't listen."

Nikol hesitated, unsure what to say next. "I was short with you the last time we spoke. I'm sorry for that, I hope you can forgive me."

"You've never been easy company." She smiled. "It's part of your charm."

"You know I'm not coming back, don't you."

"I know. I'm having a different problem." She took a deep breath. "The Elder Council isn't listening to the Prophet."

"Why should they? All he does is parrot what you tell him to."

Melany looked annoyed. "He isn't the puppet you think him to be. He lacks experience, but he's an intelligent young man, well trained for his position in life."

"I won't argue the point with you. What's the immediate problem?"

"They've been holding Inquisitions without his approval."

Nikol raised an eyebrow. "And this concerns you?"

"Not the Inquisitions themselves, the Prophet would approve them as a matter of course, it's a formality. But if they aren't following the formalities . . . The Prophet is our only means of influence . . ." She trailed off, unwilling perhaps to make her worries real by voicing them.

"You're worried about the tithing. If grain doesn't come to the Prophet, it won't come to you either."

"Exactly."

Nikol nodded, pursing his lips while he mulled that development over. "Well, if you want my assessment, your concern is quite legitimate. The Prophet is not the most intelligent man in *Ark*, nor the most ambitious. He's a spoiled child, content to collect wives and wave his staff around at high holidays. I can't see that he's made any great investment in leading the Church, so doesn't surprise me that the Church has little interest in following him. Still, I don't think the congregations will be going along with their bishops against the Prophet. He is the literal embodiment of God in *Ark*, and if the bishops desanctify him, who will they call on for their own authority?"

"I don't know, I've never seen him like this. He came to me after the last meeting of their Elder Council, and he was literally shaking, he was so scared. He wouldn't tell me what they'd said to him, only that I had to protect him."

"It would take strong threats to get a reaction from that man. How old is his eldest?"

"Three, something close to that . . ."

"You might be better off to install him as Prophet, appoint yourself as his caretaker and deal with the elders directly in his name."

"A three-year-old? And what about the Prophet? We can't just bypass him."

"So do something with him."

"What do you mean?"

"Need I be blunt? He needs to be removed from his position, permanently. I'll leave it to you to figure out how."

Melany looked shocked. "Are you suggesting I kill him? I can't do that."

Nikol shrugged. "This is about power, and power has its own demands. You're the high priestess of the Crew cult. You can't put yourself above ecclesiastical intrigue or you'll find yourself and your religion displaced by a stronger God."

Melany bristled. "Don't call me a high priestess. Mischaracterization doesn't help."

"It isn't a mischaracterization. I'm not being difficult, Melany, and I'm not downplaying the size of your problem, in fact I think it's more serious than you suspect. It was inevitable that sooner or later the Believers would tire of their extraneous priests. The days of the Crew are numbered."

Melany's voice was plaintive. "We don't oppress them, all we do is teach, and learn."

"You don't have to oppress them, because the Prophets and the Elder Council have done that for you all these years, extracted ten percent of all they produce so we Crew could lead comfortable lives in our ivory towers. It hasn't been brutal oppression, nothing like you might read in an Earth history, but it's oppression all the same. It was inevitable that sooner or later there'd be a Prophet too weak to keep a grip on the church. It's your misfortune to be chief engineer when that happened. Some ambitious bishop, or a group of them, has realized that they can gain power by exploiting the natural resentment of the people toward the Crew to dethrone the Prophet. Do you know who it is?"

"No."

"Find out. The Prophet made the mistake of not making himself popular with his followers—or rather you made the mistake of not ensuring that he did so, since it's obvious he hasn't got any idea of what is necessary. Inevitably his bishops have taken it upon themselves to interpret God's word independently of him. Don't take it personally. This is about power and ambition, nothing more."

"But if they stopped tithing what will we do? What will we eat? We have stores for a month at the University, maybe more if we stretch it. After that . . ."

Nikol shrugged. "This had to come, maybe not in our generation, but it was inevitable. My strong advice to you, and to the rest of the Crew, would be to find ways to make yourself useful. I teach in a parish school, so the community knows me. I'm learning to blacksmith, so I'll have something to trade for food. If the Crew falls, I'm not going to fall with it, because I'm planning now, working now, to make sure that Kylie and I will have enough to eat. I can't do much to help anyone else, but anyone willing to work can be my apprentice. Shipsteel is heavy, and there's tons of it yet to haul back from the forewall. I'll trade knowledge for work, and that's not a bad deal."

"The whole of the Crew can't become blacksmiths."

"No, but I'm offering what I can." Nikol sighed. "The end of the University isn't going to be pretty, but it's coming. You still have some time left. If I were you I'd take the entire Crew aftward to the forest and start clearing land."

"Nikol, you know they won't do that. Could you imagine Stroink behind a plow?"

"Yes, and it would be a disaster. He's going to have to

learn, though, if he doesn't want to face worse. If I were you I'd tell them what's going to happen, and tell them that they're going to have to change the way they live promptly. And then I'd resign my position and get aftward to get the best land I could myself." Nikol hesitated, considering whether he ought to say what he wanted to say. "You could come here, if you wanted." He did his best to keep his voice casual. "I could use the help, and Kylie . . ." He stopped himself before he said too much. *Twenty years later and Melany still has a spell for me.*

"Leave? I can't leave." Melany didn't seem to have caught the significance of what he was suggesting. "I'm chief engineer, I can't just run away and hide. I'm responsible for these people."

"No, they're responsible for themselves. Bellingham will do fine, the Believers will still need doctors. Stroink . . ." Nikol shrugged. "He's made his choices. If the faculty don't want to do what's necessary, they're going to have to deal with what happens." The back door opened, and Kylie appeared, carrying a loaf of bread, some cheese and sausage and a pitcher of water. "Let's not talk more of this," Nikol went on. "I don't want to upset my daughter."

"You'll tell me, won't you Nikol, if you hear anything? You have much better contact with the community than anyone I know."

Nikol sighed. "It's funny how every priesthood needs spies. You'd think with divine guidance they wouldn't." He straightened himself in his chair, and leaned forward. "I'll tell you what I do know, from what I hear in Charity. Bishop Nemmer is building hatred against the Crew, and tithing is his leverage. He's doing it deliberately, and he's doing it successfully. When he chooses to unleash that hatred, tithing will stop. What else will happen . . ." He shrugged. "I don't know. I'm doing my best to be useful. That's the best advice I can give." He took the bread and cheese from Kylie and began cutting it to serve. He paused after he handed Melany her slices and held up the knife. "I made this," he said. "It's the first thing I made that didn't bend or break." He smiled. "It isn't all bad. There is a future to be had here, and a lot to be learned."

It was a month after the Inquisition of Shealah Neufeldt that the bishop came to dinner, and the Fougere household was buzzing with excitement. His mother and Ruth spent the day in the kitchen, cooking and preparing, and when Jed came home from school he was pressed into service scrubbing the dining-room floor while Mary washed the precious prelaunch chinaware, fragile ceramic with inlaid floral designs that simply couldn't be made in *Ark*. Conversation in dinner revolved around the tithing. Usually it was made in pigs and grain, but Bishop Nemmer wanted some of it made in lumber this time. The population was growing, fast, and he wanted to build a larger church to properly hold services. "Why, in a few years you won't be able to get all of Charity into our church," he declaimed expansively over dessert, "and simple Christian charity demands we give something to the aftward parishes, they have such a struggle clearing land."

"You'll get whatever you need from us," replied Jed's father. "The Fougeres have always been generous in tithing. I'm going to be felling a good stand of ironwood for the new barn, I'd be pleased to give some of that in lieu of grain."

"It isn't your generosity that's my trouble, it's keeping enough of the tithe from the Prophet's hands." That last sentence surprised Jed. The bishop had always taught that the Prophet's word was God's Word, but it sounded like they were having a difference of opinion.

"Jed, Mary, you're excused." John Fougere nodded to his children, signaling that it was time for them to leave as the conversation moved to adult topics.

"I think I'll go and survey that stand, now that you mention it, John," said Thomas. "We're going to have to know how we're going to cut it before Sunday."

Ruth excused herself as well to go and nurse the baby, while Jed's mother busied herself with cleaning up. Jed wasted no time escaping in the general exodus, before someone could think of some extra chores that needed doing. He went to feed the chickens and pigs, and then to the hayloft, to whittle and think and enjoy his own company. He hadn't been there long when he heard voices. They rose as the speakers came closer, and then he heard the barn door opening.

"I can handle my own daughter!" His father's voice was clear and hard-edged.

"While she's a girl you can. What about when she's grown to a woman? She's marriageable now—"

John Fougere cut Bishop Nemmer off, a hint of irritation in his voice. "She's not marriageable until I say she is. When you find someone decent to place her with, I'll declare her."

"Someone decent." The bishop sounded exasperated. "Donald Madda—"

"Donald Madda's got three wives already. My daughter will be a first wife." There were footsteps and Jed shrank back into his corner. Would they come up into the hayloft?

"His son Luke—"

"Is a lout and a simpleton. I'll wait for young Colin to come of age first." The footsteps stopped and then receded again.

"Colin is Donald's second son, he won't inherit."

"He'll run that farm when he's old enough, you know it and I know it. If it goes to Luke there'll be nothing left of it in ten years."

"The Prophet won't place Mary with a second son, you know that."

"Luke will prove he isn't sound to inherit eventually. Donald is blind when it comes to him, but the Prophet won't see such a fine farm go wasted."

"You're a hard man to convince, John Fougere." The bishop's voice grew harder. "Just bear in mind, Mary is marriageable now. It isn't seemly to keep her undeclared, and she might not wait that long herself. Shealah Neufeldt was consorting with a Crew. Now she's gone to the Prophet and she's demanding to keep Aeron's farm."

"How dare you, *how dare you* compare my daughter to that harlot." Jed's father's voice was suddenly loud and angry.

"You misunderstand me, John." The bishop's tones were placating. "I'm not questioning your daughter's virtue, I'm pointing out that it's better not to wait. What if she were to go to the Prophet herself, with a suggestion for her placement? He might just give it to her."

"She wouldn't dare."

"Last week, I'd agree with you. What if Shealah gets what she's asking for? She won't be the last woman who suddenly finds it in her heart to go straight to the Prophet."

"She won't get it. The Prophet speaks for God."

"The Prophet speaks for the chief engineer. The Crew want our land as much as they want our tithing. That land should go to Aeron, but the Prophet is going to attach the land to the Temple." The bishop snorted derisively. "He might as well give it to the Crew directly. And who do you think is going to run it for him? Shealah herself. It's an insult."

"Bishop," a note of warning crept into John Fougere's voice. "I won't hear words against the Prophet, no not even from you."

"And why not? The Prophet is still a man, and this Prophet is a feckless youth. He may hear the word of God, but he lives with the Crew and the Crew are a poison in this world. Where do you think the lad got the idea of attaching that farm? From the chief engineer. The Crew are trying to take Believer land, land our fathers cleared and worked, land that belongs by right to Charity Parish. This decision doesn't serve God."

"That's blasphemy." Up in the hayloft Jed heard the anger grow in his father's voice and cringed involuntarily. "Watch your tongue in my house, Bishop. I will not have these words."

"It's reality." The bishop's voice was cold. "We are the chosen people, on a voyage to Heaven with God's eye on us. The church is under threat from within and without. There is no hiding. Someday soon you're going to have to decide whether you stand with the church or with the Crew, and I'll tell you right now that the Prophet stands with the Crew."

"Bishop!"

"I won't intrude further, John Fougere, but think on this. Your son is being taught un-Creation by a Crew professor with the Prophet's sanction. Un-Creation! That's blasephemy too. We're going to be seeing more Inquisitions soon. In the meantime, consider where you want to see your daughter placed."

There were footsteps and the sound of the barn door opening and closing. For a while after that there was silence, and then Jed heard his father moving around. The sound of the pump and running water told him he was watering the horses. At one point he froze as his father came up the ladder to the hayloft, terrified that he was about to be caught eavesdropping, but his father only threw some hay down for feed. It seemed to take an eternity for him to finish, but finally the barn door opened and closed a second time, and he knew he was once again alone. Even so he waited a long time before climbing down from the loft and going back to the house for bed. It took him some time to fall asleep as the bishop's words and his father's echoed in his head. He resolved to ask Dr. Valori about what he'd heard, but the next day was Saturday. On Sunday the bishop delivered a particularly cutting sermon on the dangers of associating with the Crew, how only the Bible contained the wisdom necessary to get *Ark* to Heaven, and how the unchurched crew were doomed to Hell. During the prayer he implored God to give the Believers strength to resist the Crew's temptations. It did not seem particularly different from any of the bishop's other sermons to Jed, long on implication and incantation and short on interest. To him words preached in church were extensions of the Commandments, lists of things that shouldn't be done, or that must be done, for flawed men to remain pure in God's sight. They were about prayer, and ritual, and the admonishment of sin. It never occurred to him that they might have any further impact in the day-to-day world.

He discovered on Monday just how wrong he was. It began as any other, with the breakfast bells sounding from the church and the walk into school, and he went to the chestnut tree to meet Kylie, as he always did. As he came around the corner nearest the crossroads he saw a cluster of children there. Voices rose over the fields, chanting.

"Crew, Crew, we'll get you. Crew, Crew, we'll get you."

One of the figures pushed another, a girl in a frock, and she fell. The other children formed a ring around her and she vanished from view.

Kylie! Instinctively he started running. "Kylie!" He could see the gang throwing things, and time seemed to slow down. He had only two hundred meters to cover to get to her, but it seemed to take forever to cover the distance.

". . . unchurched Crew!"

"You're going to burn in Hell! Burn in Hell!"

". . . cry, Crew girl, cry . . ."

"Stop!" His shout went unheard over the chanting. "Stop! Kylie!"

As he approached the circle he could hear her crying, but there wasn't enough room to get between the shouting children in the circle to get to her. She was lying on the ground in the center, and they were throwing chestnuts at her. Red rage swept over him, but some part of his mind remained calm, almost detached, and it seemed to watch him from a distance as it calculated the best way to handle the situation. *Take the biggest*, it said, and then watched as he went for the largest boy, a husky seventh-grader named Nebiah, nearly twice his size. He grabbed the boy's arm as he made to throw another chestnut, pulling it backward and wrenching him to the ground. His opponent grunted in surprise, and then Jed was on him, driving his fist down and feeling a crunch that could only be Nebiah's nose breaking. Nebiah swore and blood started to stream from his nostrils, but he fought back, and he was stronger than Jed. A chestnut smacked into his head hard enough to make his skull vibrate, spiking pain and making his vision blur, but he ignored it, driving his fist down into Nebiah's face over and over. The calm part of his brain assessed the situation. *If he gets up, it's all over.* Nebiah was struggling, trying to buck him off, one arm crooked to ward off Jed's attack, punching him with the other wherever he could find an opening. More chestnuts rained down, bruisingly hard, as the other children began to chant. "Fight, fight, fight, fight, fight."

Nebiah landed a punch in Jed's face hard enough to stagger him back, then surged upward, rolling Jed off him. He lunged to get on top of Jed, and Jed twisted out of the way and spun to his feet. The two boys stood, facing each other, both bleeding profusely from their noses. The barrage of chestnuts stopped, but the chanting went on. *If I don't beat him now, I'll have to fight them all.* Jed stepped forward, driving his knee up into his adversary's groin.

Nebiah went down screaming, clutching his testicles, and Jed kicked him in the ribs, once, twice, three times, until he saw Nebiah wasn't defending himself, was just lying there crying and bleeding. He had won.

He had won, but only the first battle. He was in the center of a circle of unfriendly eyes, standing beside Kylie. The other children looked stunned, unsure what to do, but their hostility was palpable. He had cheated the pack of their prey.

"Who's next, come on, who's next." He could barely get the words out, his voice was so choked with rage. "You filthy cowards, who's next?" He pivoted, saw their expressions, saw the war between fear and the desire to hurt written there, saw realization dawn that despite what he'd done to Nebiah they still outnumbered him. He couldn't beat them all, not even one at a time, and they wouldn't come one at time. Only surprise had let him fight Nebiah alone.

He locked eyes with one of them. It was Matthew, his best and oldest friend. Shy Matthew, who wanted to be liked so much he would always trade the treats from his lunch, stolid Matthew, who always ran out of imagination in imagination games, loyal Matthew, who had stood by him even in squabbles with Abel. Now Matthew's face was hard, and he had a handful of chestnuts, but in his eyes Jed could see uncertainty. Matthew was part of the group, and he wanted to be part of the group, wanted to be part of the forceful imposition of the group's power, but at the same time Jed was his friend. Matthew's gaze wavered, and Jed lunged at him. Matthew turned and bolted, and Jed switched course for a tall sixth-grade girl, who fled as well. The boys on either side of her turned and ran with her, and that was all it took. The group dissolved into individuals, scattering like swallows from a cat, and leaving Jed alone with Kylie and Nebiah, still crying on the ground. Jed leaned over to help Kylie to her feet.

"Are you all right?"

She was still sniffling, her face red. "Jed, you're bleeding."

It was only then he realized that the front of his shirt was soaked in blood. He pinched the ridge of his nose to stop the flow. "It won't kill me. What happened?"

Kylie made a few fruitless attempts to straighten her crumpled and torn frock. "I was just by the tree, waiting for you. Maggie and Joan came by and we were talking, and I don't know how it came up, Maggie said I only had a nice dress because my father was Crew. I told her I wasn't . . . that it wasn't true . . . and they said it was, and Maggie pushed me, and then the boys joined in and then they started throwing chestnuts . . ." She started crying again.

He put an arm around her and they walked toward the school, leaving Nebiah still lying there. The other children were still in front of them, walking in their own groups now, each keeping a safe distance from the others. When they got to the schoolyard Kylie helped him wash the blood off his face and shirt at the pump. In the classroom everyone took their seats in class as they always did. Except for a few hostile stares the incident might never have occurred—a children's secret kept from the teacher. Dr. Valori began the lesson, on how *Ark*'s ecosystem worked and everyone got out their notebooks. Jed had just begun to take notes when Nebiah came in.

There was no concealing the fact that Nebiah had been in a fight. His face was bruised and cut, one eye blackened and swelling, his nose swollen and lopsided. He was limping, and the class fell silent as Dr. Valori took in the spectacle.

"Nebiah, what happened?"

"Blessings, sir. There was a fight."

"I can see that. Who was it with?"

"Jedediah Fougere, sir."

"I see." Dr. Valori's voice was serious. He got up and went out. "Jedediah, Nebiah, come with me." He turned and went out, and reluctantly Jed followed him, walking ahead of Nebiah. The Charity Parish school had four classrooms. Three were used for teaching for the early, middle, and upper grades, the fourth for storage and for the teachers to do their preparation work. Dr. Valori led the boys to the fourth classroom, and told Jed to wait in one of the two straight-backed wooden chairs there and took Nebiah inside. Jed waited, feeling ill. He liked and respected Dr. Valori, and he didn't want to be in trouble with him. *I was protecting Kylie, it was the right thing to do.* Somehow that reason seemed flimsy with the benefit of hindsight. The incontrovertible fact, as Nebiah was surely relating to their teacher right now, was that Jed had thrown the first punch, and had attacked when Nebiah's back was turned. The incontrovertible fact was that he had beaten Nebiah when he was down, and that Nebiah's injuries looked serious. He'd seen the look the other children had given him as he went out into the hall behind Nebiah and Dr. Valori. It was the self-righteous delight of seeing an adversary caught by authority. *You're going to get it now.*

It seemed to take forever for Dr. Valori to finish with Nebiah, and Jed kicked his heels as he sat there, thinking of what he might say that could mitigate what he had done, his stomach knotted tight. His father would beat him when he found out, that was inevitable, but losing Dr. Valori's respect was a far more painful prospect. *I only did it to protect Kylie.* Jed doubted that line of defense would get him far. Dr. Valori had shown himself to be absolutely evenhanded when it came to his daughter. He could expect no favoritism or special treatment on that front. He strained to hear what Nebiah was saying behind the classroom door, but though he could hear the voices he couldn't make out the words. His eyes traced the grain patterns in the wood on the walls. There was nothing else to do.

It seemed to take an eternity before the door opened. Nebiah came out, looking chastened, but not so chastened that he didn't give Jed a look of hostility on his way past. His nose was straighter now, the nostrils plugged with cotton, and Dr. Valori had fixed some sort of splint to either side of it. Jed went into the room, and his teacher closed the door behind him. He didn't seem angry, he simply asked Jed to describe what happened in his own words. Jed told the story as simply as he could. There wasn't much he could say in his own defense. He had hit Nebiah from behind, and had kept hitting him even after he was down. It was only when he recounted the fight that Jed realized his own knuckles were bruised and swollen. Dr. Valori's lips tightened when he described how the other children had been throwing chestnuts at Kylie, but he made no comment. When Jed had finished, he looked at the window, his expression distant. He looked away long enough that Jed began to fidget uncomfortably. Even a lecture would be better than the silence.

Eventually Dr. Valori looked back. "Thank you, Jed. You can return to class now. Please send Kylie in."

When he got back to class he found that Mrs. Dolorson had taken over and was going over spelling corrections. He relayed Dr. Valori's request to her and took his seat. Mrs. Dolorson told Kylie to go and talk to her father, and quelled the class's sudden whispering by smacking her ruler on the teacher's desk. Nebiah wasn't there, and Jed found it impossible to concentrate on the lesson. Kylie didn't return to class either, though Dr. Valori came back to call other children for interviews, all those who had been involved in the fight. Neither Matthew nor Abel nor anyone else would talk to him at lunch, so he ate his alone, and went back to sit at his desk while everyone else went out to play. Dr. Valori was back for the first lesson at the end of the lunch hour, a stack of papers in his hand.

Jed expected a lecture, followed by a punishment, but Dr. Valori simply gave a very brief summary of the fight, stated his disappointment with those involved, handed each of them a beeswax-sealed letter and sent them home. His manner seemed calm, but there was something different in his tone, something about the way his jaw was set when he paused between sentences, that said he was not. Something had changed there, something deep. It was a relief to be out of the classroom and the oppressive presence of his classmates, but Jed trudged the distance back to Riverview disconsolately. He considered throwing away the letter, or at least unsealing it to find out how much trouble he might be in, but to do either invited a far harsher punishment. Better to get it over with sooner rather than later.

But not too much sooner. He dawdled on the way, in no hurry to meet his fate. It was strange, how normal the world seemed, how unaware it was of the changes within it, how indifferent to the dread that now lurked in his own heart. The road was the same as when he walked in the morning, the familiar landmarks just as he had left them. On either side of him the world still curved up and arched over the suntube, and the fields still ripened beneath its steady warmth. Halfway up to spinward and aftward he could see Hope, the village at the center of the next parish. It always seemed that Hope couldn't help but slide down the steep slope, it was at such a crazy angle, but it never did, and when his father had taken him to Hope one day to look at horses it seemed that Hope was at the bottom of the world's arch, and Charity should be the one to fall. Beyond that was a lake, he didn't know which one, crystal blue and ringed with white sand amid the brown and green patchwork of fields. His eyes followed its river aftward to the ocean, a deeper blue cylinder up against the grey aftwall, hazy in the distance. Most of the distance to the ocean was the uniform green of mature forest, with just a few farms cut out along the waterways. The world was big and most of it was unused. The woods were full of game, and he wasn't a bad shot with a rabbit bow. For a long time he thought maybe he should just head out there, away from school, away from church, away from his father . . .

*Away, just away.* It was a frightening thought. Eventually he ran out of time and had to go home. He gave the note to his father immediately before dinner, on the theory that the meal would allow time for his anger to cool. His father read it dispassionately, his face hard. He nodded slowly, as if considering what to do, while Jed tried not to look scared. Finally he said, "We'll talk about this later," and went to sit down with the rest of the family. Jed found such restraint in his father almost more frightening than the sudden outburst of anger he had anticipated. Discussion over dinner was mostly between his father and his uncle on the good prices pigs had been fetching recently. The two of them went out after dinner, and Jed was in bed and pretending to be asleep before they were back. He remembered, as he lay there, that he had intended to talk to Dr. Valori about the bishop's words to his father in the barn. The excitement and upset over the fight had wiped that concern from his attention, but he resolved to tell his teacher about it in the morning. Eventually he slept, only to be wakened by Ruth at an hour that seemed all too early.

He felt slightly better at breakfast, though very tired. The welts where the chestnuts had struck him were now painful bruises, and his nose was still tender. His father still made no mention of the note, and he hoped against hope that it had been forgotten. That hope ended when he went to pick up his school bag.

"You won't need that, Jedediah," his father said. "You'll be coming with me today."

"But, Father—"

His father's face darkened. "Give me no insolence, I've made my decision."

Jed's guts clenched and fear. "Yes, Father." He waited silently until his father was ready and gestured for him to follow.

At first he was certain he was to be taken to the horse barn for a beating, but there was no anger in his father's face, instead, his father took him out to walk the fields. He still didn't seem angry. "It's time you start learning how to run a farm. Your uncle and I have planned some changes. The world is changing, Jed. You look at all the young families around. John Sackmore just had his eighth child, and not one of his wives is thirty yet. The population is growing fast, and pigs are going to be in high demand."

"But you've been selling pigs." For a moment Jed thought he'd gone too far in implying his father had made a mistake, and he winced, expecting at least a tongue-lashing, but his father took the remark in stride.

"Pigs grow fast too, with eight or twelve in a litter. If you didn't eat them you'd drown in them. Anyone can have a hog barn."

Jed nodded. "Abel's father is building a big one."

"What doesn't grow so fast is good, cleared land to grow corn for pigfeed, and good horses to work it. We're going to turn the pig barn into a second horse barn, Jed, and we're going to build a third barn too, put more land into raising corn to sell to pig breeders, and we'll do just fine."

They walked farther, over the hill toward the orchards on the other side of the stream to check on the breeze pumps that pushed the irrigation water lazily through its channels. The breeze pumps turned slowly in the steady, gentle wind, and John Fougere went over them carefully, making sure all was in working order. "Let the hands build things," he said. "Let the hands fix things, but always check yourself to make sure they do the job right."

He shoveled mud from the bottom of the pump channels so it wouldn't clog the paddles, and Jed helped. It was a pleasant change to have his father speak kindly to him, almost as an equal. They finished with the pump and went back up the hill toward home and lunch. His father stopped at the top of the hill, swept an arm over the landscape.

"This will all be yours one day, Jed. You'll be old enough to marry in a few years, and we want the elders to place some good wives with you. What do you think of Ellen Madda?"

"Father, she's a little girl," Jed blurted, before he could stop himself.

His father stiffened. "Mind your tongue. She'll be a woman soon enough. Tomorrow we'll start you with plowing and seeding the west field."

Tomorrow, that couldn't mean . . . "Father, am I not to go back to school?"

"No. You've enough education to run a farm, what you need now is experience. This fight, over a Crew girl no less . . . The Crew aren't like us, and I never wanted to see you taught by that man in the first place." His father's voice grew harder. "The bishop was right. I won't have your mind turned from God."

Jed opened his mouth to protest, then closed it in silence. There was an air of finality in his father's words, and arguing would be pointless. They walked the rest of the distance in uncomfortable silence while Jed pondered the possibility that he'd have Ellen Madda placed on him as wife. *I could always marry Kylie later.* Except he doubted she would want to be a second wife. *Or perhaps even want life on a farm, if she knew what it was really like.* Everyone seemed to think he should be pleased about the wealth of his much-foretold inheritance, but more and more it seemed to be nothing but a burden. *And why am I thinking of marrying Kylie?* It was a strange thought, but when he considered he realized that it had been there all along. They were best friends, she was a girl, what more natural than that they be married when the time came?

The next day was devoted to plowing and planting, as his father had said, and the next, and the next, and the next. Jed found it exhausting. When he had only worked on Saturdays his body had time to recover from its exertions, but now he found himself facing each day still tired and sore from the previous day's labors. By the time the Sabbath day came he was utterly spent, his hands blistered, every muscle aching, every joint sore. Sunday was the day of rest, but he found it too occupied with the usual Sunday service to be restful. Since Shealah's crucifixion Jed had been unable to look at the bishop as he had before. His services never mentioned her directly, but they went heavily into the Godless nature of the Crew and how their secular ways seduced the faithful away from the true path of God. The Crew were parasites, he said, taking from the community and contributing nothing. They were Satan's agents, working to undermine the Believers' faith in God, working to stop the chosen people from completing their ascent to Heaven. They were a test, said the bishop, included on the *Ark* to see if the Believers might falter before Saint Peter's gates, and the time would soon come to see them cast into endless night. Believers would have to be watchful, of themselves and of each other, because it was impossible to know when a Crew might arrive to tempt them into sin. His sermons had taken on a dark intensity since Jed had overheard him and his father talking in the horse barn. He kept expecting another Inquisition, but there hadn't been one, at least not so far. The cross, hanging as it did at the back of the alcove behind the bishop, seem to loom with hidden menace now, awaiting its next victim with infinite patience. When he saw it he saw Shealah upon it, being whipped without mercy until she confessed. Today was no different, except instead of Shealah he saw Kylie, crying as she had when his classmates had formed a chanting ring around her and pelted her with chestnuts.

He shook his head at that vision and looked down, not wanting to remember either incident. He missed Kylie, and her absence hurt more than the hard physical labor did. He sat through the service in silence, rode home in silence, and when he put the horses out to pasture he forgot to latch a gate. The next day found the horses out of their paddock and into the new-sown oats in the next field. His father cuffed him for it, and made him replant the damaged rows after supper. By the time he'd finished and got the horses put away for the night he was exhausted. Everyone else was long asleep by the time he got to bed. At breakfast he was so tired he could barely keep his eyes open, and the thought of another day of plowing seemed too much to bear.

"Did you finish the oats last night, Jedediah?" his father asked.

"I did, Father."

"I have two sows that need to be taken to market. You'll do that today. Take no less than twenty tokens for them."

"Yes, Father." Jed kept his expression even, but inwardly his heart swelled with elation, his tiredness washed away in an instant. A day at the market in Charity would be a welcome respite from the fields. More importantly it would bring the chance to drop by the school and see Kylie.

"And make sure the buyer makes the first offer." Jed barely heard his father's admonishment. He finished breakfast as fast as he thought he could without showing his eagerness, then ran out to the barn. Josiah was feeding the horses, and he helped Jed get a buckboard hitched with the team, and then load the pigs. Jed had driven a team by himself, but never so far as the Charity market, and he felt rather proud to be entrusted with the task. He had a few anxious moments as they set off, things seemed to happen so much faster when he was by himself, but he had a stolid and reliable team who knew exactly where they were going. The sows settled down in the straw in the back, and soon they were arriving in the market day bustle of the Charity village square. He had slowed down as he passed the school, hoping Kylie might see him in his new position of responsibility, but everyone was in class and he didn't see her.

The market was an informal affair, and farmers and craftsmen and Crew folk from the Town mingled and did business with noisy good humor beneath the suntube's perpetual brightness. He pulled the horses up, climbed down and walked them through the square to an unbusy corner, where he unhitched the wagon. He took the horses out of the square and turned them into the Charity common pasture, then went back to sit with the hogs. It was considered unseemly to call out to potential customers, which suited Jed just fine. Selling hogs might well be a lot of work, but waiting for someone to come and buy them was easy—or so it seemed at first. As the morning wore on a few people stopped to look at his wares, but none were so interested as to ask him the price. A pair of inquisitors came past, anonymous beneath their red hoods, and Jed's breath caught in his throat. He had never seen even one in public like that before; indeed, it seemed few people had. Conversations stilled suddenly as they came close, to bubble up again even more after they passed. For a long, tense moment it seemed they were looking at him and Jed bit his lower lip, trying to look casual. They went by without turning, and he breathed out in relief. They moved on, out of his sight and, he presumed, out of the market; at least, he never saw them again. After a while the excitement they'd caused died down, and time began to drag. He became bored and took to inexpertly weaving hay into straw mats, as he had seen Mary do. The church bell sounded eleven o'clock, and a few of the vendors who'd sold out early began to pack up. Jed began to worry what his father would say if he came home without having accomplished his task. *Perhaps I need a better location.* He had chosen his corner of the market because it was easy to get the wagon in without any tricky maneuvering of the team, but it was not the most trafficked side of the square. He considered moving it to one of the newly vacated spaces in a busier area, but that would require going back down to the pasture, running up the horses, rehitching the wagon, moving it, unhitching it again and returning the horses to the pasture, which wouldn't leave much time at all to sell the pigs. He was glumly considering what to tell his father when he spotted a familiar face in the crowd, Solomon Garcio, Abel's father. He remembered Abel's talk of his family's new and expanded pork herd. He jumped off the wagon and ran over.

"Blessings, sir," he said when he got close, slightly out of breath.

"Blessings, Jedediah." Brother Garcio looked surprised. "Why aren't you in school?"

"My father told me to bring these sows to market and sell them. They're fine animals, would you like to see them?"

"It wouldn't hurt to look." Abel's father followed Jed back to the wagon. Once there, he ran a practiced eye over the pigs, patted a flank, examined their feet and their eyes. "These are well finished, good healthy stock," he said. "They haven't been bred."

The last wasn't quite a question, but Jed answered it anyway. "No, sir." Hope rose in his heart. Solomon Garcio wanted the sows for breeding stock. He'd buy them, and he'd pay a good price.

"Hmmm . . . Tell you what, young man. I'll give you thirty-six for the pair."

"I can't sell them for that, sir. My father told me not to . . ." he had been about to say *take less than twenty*, but brother Garcio had offered eighteen right up front. That was practically twenty, and more than once he'd heard his father talk about the fine art of bargaining. ". . . take less than twenty-five," he heard himself say. His voice didn't waver as he said it, but he suddenly found his heart beating faster. He'd show himself worthy, more than worthy, of his father's respect if he got twenty-five tokens each for the pigs. *But what if he says no . . .* The market would be closing soon and Solomon Garcio was the first serious buyer he'd had all day. If he went home empty-handed he'd be lucky to get off with a cuff. The instant confidence he'd felt when he'd upped the price to twenty-five vanished as quickly as it had come, and he almost blurted out *I meant twenty.* He somehow managed to swallow the words. To back away from his first price like that would only invite Brother Garcio to bargain him down, and he really could go no lower than twenty. It seemed to take forever for Abel's father to answer, and when he did it did nothing to relieve Jed's sudden worry.

"Well, let's have another look at them."

Solomon went over the pigs again, this time more carefully. He stood for a while, considering, and finally said, "Fair enough, young man, twenty-five. Your father breeds good stock."

Jed breathed out, only then realizing how tense he had become. "Thank you, sir. I'm sure you'll be pleased with them."

Brother Garcio counted out the money from his coin bag, and Jed helped him unload the pigs from the wagon. The market crowd was starting to thin out as he went to get the horses back from the pasture. He hitched them to the wagon, and with new confidence climbed up on the seat to take them home. He swung past the school again, hoping to see Kylie, eager to bask in his new adult status. He didn't see her in the playground, but his former classmates saw him, and one by one the groups stopped playing to watch him. Nobody said anything, but the hostility was palpable.

*But I'm not going to let them stop me.* He wasn't a schoolchild any longer, he was a farmer, a marketer, the heir of Riverview, and he was above petty schoolground rivalries. He pulled the wagon to a halt in front of the school building, threw the horses' reins over the rail and went in to talk to Dr. Valori.

He went into his old classroom, and found himself surprised at how strange the room felt after such a short absence.

"Jed!" It was Mrs. Dolorson, sitting at Dr. Valori's desk. "Where have you been? I've been getting concerned." At least she seemed glad to see him.

"I'm sorry to have worried you, ma'am. My father has me working on the farm now." He hesitated. "Is Kylie here?"

"Dear me, no. She's going to the school at the University now, after what happened."

"And Dr. Valori?"

"No, he left as well." Out in the playground the school bell began to clang, calling the students in after lunch. "Jed, you should . . ."

But Jed wasn't listening to what she had to say. A vast black chasm seems to have opened in front of him. *I'm never going to be able to see her again.* "Thank you, ma'am, I have to go now," he said. Scuffling feet in the hallway told him his classmates were coming in. He went out, wordlessly, meeting their gaze as he passed. Not one said hello to him, not even Abel. He had chosen sides, and their side was not his.

Outside he climbed back on the wagon and stirred up the horses. On impulse he turned the team around and headed for Kylie's house. Doing so would make him late getting back and invite his father's wrath, but he found he didn't care. He had fifty tokens in his coin bag, a decent improvement on what his father had thought he could get for the sows, and that success would help to offset any trouble he got into. He was struck, as he had been when he came home the day of the fight, by how unchanged the world seemed, how the suntube shone on relentlessly, the same as it had when he had been a schoolboy and not a farmer, as it had when he was born, as it had for his entire life, giving no hint at the passage of time.

He was halfway there when he saw a figure walking down the road, a girl, blond hair . . .

"Kylie!" He snapped the reins, encouraging the horses into a trot. "Kylie!" She turned around and he waved. Half a minute later he was pulling the wagon to a halt beside her.

"Kylie, what are you doing here?"

"I was coming to see you. I wanted to thank you for standing up for me." She hesitated. "My father said I should come in today and thank you, that Mrs. Dolorson said you had been at home all week."

Jed nodded. "My father has me working on the farm."

Kylie clambered up into the wagon to sit beside him. "I don't know why they were so mean to me, I didn't do anything. I don't even know most of them."

"They don't like it that you're a Crew. I was going to tell your father, the bishop has been speaking against the Crew in church, saying they're a poison, even speaking against the Prophet."

"What's wrong with being a Crew? If we go to Hell for being unbelievers that's our problem, not anyone else's."

"I don't know." Jed hesitated. "I miss you, Kylie, I wish it hadn't happened."

"So do I." They sat in silence for a while. "We can still be friends, can't we?"

Jed nodded. "As long as my father doesn't find out. He didn't even know we're friends in school, at least he didn't know you were Crew, until the other day." He sighed. "He does now. That's why I'm doing farmwork."

"I'm so sorry, Jed."

"It wasn't your fault."

"I'm still sorry." She stopped. "I don't want to talk about it. It's neat that you get to drive the wagon. Can you take me for a ride?"

Jed hesitated. *If Father sees us together it won't be good.* Reflexively he looked behind him to see who might be there. The aftward road from Charity would take them straight past Riverview, but there was a side lane not a hundred meters ahead that would take them up over the orchards and down to the river. It was only early afternoon yet, and his father would be out overseeing the hands in the spinward fields. "Sure," he said. He jogged the reins again and the team started off, the ironwood wheels creaking. It took some hauling to get the horses to turn into the side lane, they knew how close they were to home and food and rest. He persisted, and managed to get the wagon around the curve, and they were off.

For the rest of the afternoon, it was as if the incident at the crossroads hadn't occurred. The lane wound through the orchards, fragrantly bursting with cherry blossoms.

At the end of the fields it curved down to run along the riverside, aftward again to the lake and on to the Danielson farm and beyond. They left the wagon in a small clearing with the horses contentedly grazing, and swam in their underwear in the cold, clear water. Later they followed a game trail through the woods that lined the riverbed, until they came upon a small herd of deer, munching down the fallen fruit from a wild-grown stand of oranges. They crept up on the herd quietly and got within an easy bowshot before the senior doe snorted and looked up to see them. She jumped off and the herd followed her. There was a secret spot there, a protected space in the crook of a fallen log, in a leafy hollow beneath a willow beside the citrus trees, with just enough room for the two of them to squeeze in side by side. They sat there a while, eating oranges and talking. The two-o'clock bells sounded, and then the three-o'clock, and then they had to go. Jed drove the wagon back up the lane, while Kylie ate oranges and talked about what she was learning in Crew school. The horses balked again as they came to the main road, now even more eager to get back to the barn, and Jed had to wrestle them to get them moving in the direction of the Charity road. He had planned to drop her under the same tree they'd always rendezvoused under, but somehow when they got there it didn't seem right to let her walk the rest of the way home. The four-o'clock bells pealed before he had her there, and he realized with a sinking feeling that he would be late for supper, a cardinal sin in the Fougere family. He urged the horses to a trot. When they got to her house, Dr. Valori came out to greet them.

"Will you have supper with us, Jed?"

"I can't, sir, I'm expected at home."

"Well, you're welcome any time. I didn't have a chance to tell you, but I owe you a great deal for standing up for Kylie like that. That was a very brave thing to do."

Jed found himself at a loss for words. He hadn't felt brave doing it, he'd felt scared. "Thank you, sir," he finally managed to say.

Kylie jumped down from the wagon. "I'll see you soon."

"I hope so." Jed wasn't so sure he would see her again, it would certainly be much harder too if he didn't get home in time. He got the team turned around and headed back aftward toward Charity, and home. He tried to urge them to speed, but the heavy drays were built for pulling power, not speed, and while they'd break into a clomping trot for a while, they refused to keep at it for long. The five-o'clock bells were ringing as he was unhitching the horses in the barn. He hurriedly led them into their stalls, then ran up to the main house. He burst in the front door, kicked off his shoes and ran in the dining room in time to be impaled on his father's cold gaze. His mother met his eyes, tension lines clear in her face, and Mary gave him a look that spoke volumes. His mother's parents traded a glance, and Jed saw his father's hands were pressed together for grace. Barely in time, maybe . . . Had he started yet? Only his uncle Thomas gave him a welcoming smile.

Jed sat down and put his own hands together and bowed his head, and the rest of the family did as well. *Not quite late then.* That was a relief, but the frosty reception showed he hadn't got away scot-free either. The silence stretched out to uncomfortable length, and then John

Fougere began his prayer. "Our Father, whose Heaven we voyage to, Hallowed be Thy Name. Thy kingdom come. Thy will be done on Earth, in *Ark* and on Heaven. Give us this day our daily bread, and forgive us our trespasses, as we forgive those who trespass against us. And lead us not into temptation, but deliver us from evil. For Thine is the kingdom, and the power, and the glory, for ever and ever." He paused at the end and looked up at Jed before he finished. "Amen."

"Amen," echoed the family one after the other, Jed answering after his uncle and before Mary, as befitted his place as oldest son.

His mother began serving the vegetables, fresh young potatoes from the lower field and steaming corn-on-the-cob from the ripe crop in the upper. His father carved the meat, a haunch of fresh pork. The Fougeres set a fine table, as befitted their position, but Jed found himself suddenly without appetite.

"So Jed, did you sell the hogs?" His father's gaze was hard on him.

"Yes, Father, twenty-five tokens each." Jed kept any hint of pride out of his voice, but he was pleased with his performance. He'd done well, and that unexpected coup would lessen his father's wrath. It would be poor manners to show money at the table, but the coins were a firm mass in his coin bag, hard against his thigh in the carry-pocket of his pants.

John Fougere nodded. "I see. And did you get that price by telling Solomon Gracio that I would accept nothing less than that for them?"

Fear shot through Jed. When his father asked leading

questions like this it meant he already knew the answer and disapproved of it. *But I got a good price, what could be wrong?*

And there was nothing to be gained by compounding the problem. "Yes, Father."

"I see." His father's expression darkened. "I'll see you at the barn after dinner to discuss this."

"Yes, Father," Jed replied. The tension around the table slowly subsided and the conversation picked up, but Jed found he had lost interest in talking as much as he had in food. He forced himself to eat while dinner dragged on, and when it was over he walked out to the barn to await his father's displeasure.

He didn't have to wait long. His father appeared and wasted no time. "Show me the money."

Silently John handed over his coin bag. His father counted out the money, forty iridium disks from one side of the bag to the other, ten that he held out in his hand. When he was done he looked up. "Well at least you haven't stolen any."

The injustice of the implication stung hard. "However I've displeased you, I'm no thief, Father!" Jed blurted the words even as his better judgment was telling him to stand mute.

His father's fist struck like a bolt launched from Heaven, wrapped tight around the ten heavy coins. It caught Jed on his temple and sent him spinning to the ground. He looked up, his vision momentarily blurred, tears already starting in his eyes though he refused to allow himself to cry openly. *Not this time, not this time, not this time.*

"Yes you're a thief. You stole these ten tokens from Brother Gracio just as if you'd taken them out of his pocket. What was the minimum price I gave you?"

"Twenty tokens, Father." Jed got hesitantly to his feet.

"Twenty tokens. And did you have Brother Gracio offer first, as I told you to?"

"Yes, Father."

"And what did he offer you?"

"Eighteen tokens each, Father."

"A fair offer from a fair man, and yet you lied. You lied and told him that I told you to accept no less than twenty-five."

"Please Father! Solomon Gracio is building a new pig barn. Those were prime young sows. He was happy to pay twenty-five. He would have paid more."

"I don't care if he would have paid a hundred. You lied."

"I bargained!"

"With lies!"

Jed opened his mouth to argue further, closed it when he saw his father's upraised fist. He looked down at the dirt. "Yes, Father."

"So." His father looked at him and the silence stretched uncomfortably. "Tell me where you were this afternoon."

"I went to the market in Charity, Father," Jed said, avoiding the question.

"Don't treat me like a fool, Jedediah Fougere. Where did you go after the market."

"Down to the river." Jed's voice was low with repressed anger of his own.

"Down to the river." His father's lips tightened, his suspicions confirmed. "And who did you go with?"

*So that's what this is really about.* His father wouldn't be asking the question if he didn't already know the answer. Jed raised his eyes to lock them on his father, daring him to strike again. "Kylie Valori."

The fist came down, harder than before. Pain exploded and Jed went sprawling, tasting dirt. He put his hand to his face to feel it already hot and swelling, but the tears that had started with the first blow dried up completely, replaced by a cold rage that constricted his throat past the ability to speak and clenched his own hands into fists.

"Kylie Valori." John Fougere spat the name, his voice shaking with the anger he had previously kept under control. "She is Crew, landless, unchurched Crew. I will not ask you if you sinned with her. I will not ask you that. You will not see her again." He paused, his jaw working, and when he spoke again his voice was cold with fury. "The counterspinward fallow field needs plowing. It will be done before you sleep." Without waiting for a reply Jed's father turned on his heel and stalked off. Only then did Jed cry, the feelings of anger and frustration and hurt welling up, and he pounded his fists in the dirt. After a while he went into the barn to harness up a team to the plow. The fallow field was a full hectare and it would be halfway to breakfast bell before he was done. It was unjust and unfair and . . . He stood up, squeezed the tears from his eyes and took a deep breath. There was no point in bawling like a child; fallow field wouldn't plow itself. He went to the barn, turning his anger to productive use, and hitched a pair of mares to one of the chisel plows. He didn't even consider running away. There was nowhere he could go. He cracked the reins harder than he meant to and the horses started, lurching the plow forward so Jed had to scurry to keep up. He drove the team out to the fallow field and got started. He was already tired and sore, and the field was a full day's work for a grown man. He wrenched hard at the plow, letting his anger overcome the exhaustion. *I won't always be smaller than him, not always . . .*

He'd done twenty furrows and the hard physical work had taken the edge off of his mood when a familiar shape came through the hedge gap.

"Uncle Thomas." Jed pulled the team to a halt and raised a hand.

"Jedediah, my favorite nephew. How goes the work?"

Jed wiped sweat from his brow and smiled at the old joke despite himself. "I'm still your only nephew, Uncle. And the work goes well enough I suppose."

Thomas looked at the swollen bruise on the side of Jed's face. "I see my brother has left an impression."

"It wasn't fair, Uncle." Some of Jed's anger and frustration returned. "I was only trying . . ."

"You were only trying to get the best price you could."

Jed nodded and rubbed his jaw reflexively. "Yes, you think he'd be happy."

"Hmmm. It wasn't the price he was unhappy about."

"I didn't lie, I bargained."

"You did both, but it wasn't the lying he was unhappy about either, not really."

"It isn't as if I lied about the pigs," Jed went on, reluctant to move the conversation to the real reason his father was angry. "They're fine sows of a good line. I've done no harm to Solomon Gracio."

"Hmmm, no." His uncle sat down on a furrow. "Sit down and I'll share a few things, if you like."

"I have to finish this field first."

Thomas waved a hand. "Sit down, sit down. Rest those beasts and let an old man feel he's doing his job as an uncle and then I'll help you with the plowing. Deal?"

Jed nodded and sat down reluctantly, unable to think of another reason not to.

Thomas smiled. "Now I'll talk first about truth, and I'll be brief because I know you don't want to hear it. First of all this has nothing to do with Solomon. He's quite happy with his purchase I'm sure."

Jed sighed. "I know the ninth Commandment as well as you, Uncle."

"No, this has nothing to do with the Commandments either." Thomas noted Jed's expression. "Don't look shocked. What is a Commandment but a rule written down by a man?"

"Uncle . . ." Jed groped for words. "That's heresy!"

"So do me a favor and don't tell the bishop I said it. I don't need an Inquisition." Thomas held up a hand to forestall further argument. "Don't make me explain myself, not yet anyway. I have your soul to save, before I can worry about theology." He paused to let that sink in. "You're a good salesman, Jed. Your father knows livestock better than any man in *Ark*, but you beat his named price by twenty-five percent. How did that come about?"

"I knew from Abel that his father has his new barn built; now he needs sows to start filling it. He doesn't want meat or even just a litter, he's starting a line. I knew he'd pay better than market rate for a pair as good as I had." Jed hesitated. "I mean, I suppose I knew all that, I wasn't really thinking it through, I ran and got him when I saw him, just by chance. I was going to tell him twenty, at the last minute I told him twenty-five. There wasn't much interest in them before I saw him really. It was a risk."

"Good thinking, good plan and good instincts, all three. And how did you feel when you got your price?"

Jed answered slowly "I was pleased that I'd gotten more than Father wanted for them."

Thomas nodded. "And how did you think your father would feel when he heard?"

Jed looked away. "I thought he'd be pleased."

"Anything else."

"I thought . . ." Jed looked up. He hadn't really thought of his motivations before, but his uncle's questioning left no choice. "I thought he'd be forced to acknowledge I'd done a good job."

"Even a better job than he could have done himself?"

"Perhaps . . ." Jed paused. "I know that's prideful, Uncle, it's just that . . ."

"Just that he's always hard on you and sparse with praise, and you wanted to show him you were as good a man as he, perhaps better. Well, you certainly did show him." Thomas ran a hand through the youth's hair. "What did you expect him to do, congratulate you and admit you were smarter than him?"

"He might have done as well. He couldn't have gotten more, I'll swear that on the cross."

"You're right about that, young man, but what did you expect his response to be?"

"I don't know. I suppose I didn't think about it."

"You were too busy feeling smug, imagining him being forced to praise you as you humiliated him ever so subtly in front of the whole family."

"Uncle! I'm not so petty."

"No, you aren't, but your father is. He's a petty, angry, small-minded man who uses his piety as a stick to beat everyone around him. You can't be faulted for playing his game by his rules." Thomas paused, looking away. "However, you can be faulted for not rising above it. You're a man now, Jed, not a boy. What's more, you are a better man than he is, a better man than he'll ever be, so act like it."

Jed looked up at his uncle, not sure whether he should be proud of the implied praise or wounded at the rebuke. Thomas went on without stopping. "Which brings up another question. Why did you lie to Solomon Garcio?"

Jed moved his gaze away, up the curve of the world and aftward to the ocean, hazy in the distance, and wished the question would go away. Thomas waited patiently for an answer, as though he had all the time in the world. Jed knew from the way he'd asked the question that there was a lesson his uncle wanted to drive home, and he knew from experience that neither time nor evasiveness would stop Thomas from getting an answer. Sometimes even patience could be a trial. He sighed, resigned to the inevitable. "To get a better price, I guess."

"Couldn't you have done the same thing without lying?"

"I suppose. Maybe. I don't know." He looked at his uncle. "Does it matter?"

"It matters to you, I don't care what your father thinks, or Solomon Garcio. You told Solomon your father wouldn't accept less than twenty-five tokens as a negotiating tactic. What did that gain you?"

Jed thought about the question for a moment. His uncle's questions often had hidden barbs for the unwary quick answer. He was like Dr. Valori in that. "Well, it meant that if he wanted the sows he had to pay twenty-five, take it or leave it."

"So another way of putting it is, you told him you lacked the power to sell them for less. You told him your father was the one in charge."

"I suppose."

"Well don't just suppose it, think about it long enough to understand that it's true, or find a reason why it's wrong."

"Uncle, what is the point of this?"

"Or you can ask distracting questions in the hopes that I'll give up trying to teach you anything."

Jed threw up his hands. "Fine, I agree, you're right."

"Essentially you saved yourself from having Solomon pressure your price lower by abdicating personal power."

"Yes." Jed said it reluctantly, irritated by the implications in Thomas's argument, though he couldn't put his finger on why.

"Not only did you explicitly say that your father had more power than you did, you also told Solomon that *he* had more power than you did too. You told him you were afraid of him."

"What? Uncle, I said nothing like that. I've got no cause to be afraid of Abel's father, he's always been kind to me."

"No? If you weren't afraid of him, why didn't you just say 'I won't take anything less than twenty-five,' rather than saying your father wouldn't?"

Jed shrugged. "I don't know, it just seemed easier."

"Easier because he couldn't argue with your father, who wasn't there, while he might bargain quite hard against you. He had to take it or leave it, because you didn't have the power to bargain with him."

"I suppose." Jed looked at the dirt.

"You suppose. I won't make you say I'm right this time." Thomas leaned back against the wagon. "Sometimes not having power is a kind of power all its own. That's a lesson your father has yet to learn. All the same, you shouldn't be handing your own power away so freely to people like Solomon and your father."

"I don't understand."

"Consider this. If you hadn't been afraid of Solomon Garcio, if you hadn't worried that he might outbargain you, then you would have told him that *you* wouldn't accept a coin less than twenty-five for those hogs, you, not your father. He would have scoffed and told you they were worth fifteen, he would have told you no other farmer would give you more than twelve, and he would have generously offered eighteen, just out of respect for the Fougere family. And, if you were right about how much he wanted them, he would have given you twenty-five at the end of the day because that's what they were worth to him, because that's how much he paid. The difference is that when my brother later asked you how you came to get that much for them, he wouldn't have had the ninth Commandment to hit you with."

"You make it seem so straightforward."

Thomas laughed. "The truth is too slippery a thing to be straightforward, but it has a lot of power. When you use it, you gain that power. It also means you have to be careful how you use it, careful about when you tell it, how you tell it, who you tell it to. And while I'm mentioning that, let me mention that half the truths you come across are better left locked up in the back of your brain. Silence is just as powerful as truth, if you can use it well."

"I know I shouldn't have sinned like that, Uncle." Jed hung his head, feeling shamed about his action for the first time. "I'll never lie again, Uncle."

"Whoa, boy, let's not go that far. Untruths are a form of power too, but the more you use them the less power they have. Save them for when you really need them."

"Are you telling me to lie, Uncle?" Jed asked, confused.

"I'm telling you to use the brains God gave you to figure out the right thing to do on a case-by-case basis. Ninety-nine times in a hundred that means telling the truth. When it's necessary to lie, as opposed to simply convenient, you'll know it."

"Not when I just want to get a better price on some hogs, you mean. I can see that was wrong." Jed hesitated. "I don't think that's really what Father was angry about."

Uncle Thomas raised his eyebrows. "No? What was it really then?"

"After the market I went and played with Kylie."

"The same Kylie you told me about before?"

"Yes, Uncle."

Jed's uncle laughed. "I can see why your father wouldn't like that."

"I didn't kiss her, Uncle, I promise. I didn't sin."

Thomas took in Jed's glum expression and reached over to ruffle his hair again. "There are bigger sins than sharp bargaining, Jed. Bigger sins than kissing a Crew girl. I've sinned . . ." The big man looked away and stopped speaking.

"What did you do?" asked Jed, suddenly intrigued. His uncle's manner hinted at depths Jed hadn't suspected existed.

"Let's just leave it that I've sinned." He stood up. "Perhaps one day God will forgive me. I doubt your father ever will." He smiled. "Now you go hitch another team, and we'll get these furrows done."

Jed headed up to the barn, thinking over what his uncle had said and wishing that Thomas, with his patience and wisdom, were his father.

Bishop Nemmer's sermon that Sunday was about the people of Earth, whom God had punished with a plague, just as he punished the people of Noah for their rejection of his word. He went into detail about how the Plague of Earth had struck down God's enemies. Only the Believers, safe in the their *Ark* as Moses' family had been in his, would survive the wrath of God. The Believers were the new Chosen People, he said, chosen by God to voyage from the living Hell that had been Earth to the planet of Heaven. All things of Earth were evil, he said, contaminating the purity of *Ark* and all within it. He went on like that for a while, and then he called on the congregation to reject everything of Earth, to embrace all that was of Heaven. They should cast aside everything Earth-made as inspired by Satan, cast it out of their lives to purify themselves. Then he started talking about the Crew. They were not Believers, they were Earth people, carriers of the same plague that had destroyed the world, he said. They were a pestilence within the body of holy *Ark* itself. They were a test of faith, sent by God to determine if the Believers were truly worthy of Heaven. It was not enough to cleanse themselves, God required that all of *Ark* be purified. It was time to return to the ways of poverty and humility before Jesus that were the core of Believer faith.

The bishop spoke with flashing eyes and a voice so passionate and deep that Jed found it frightening, and after he had done speaking he led the congregation outside, where a large pile of firewood and tinder was set alight. He led them all in hymns to the glory of God, and the worshippers started a line past the flames. One by one the whole congregation filed past and threw things into the flames. It took Jed a while to realize that everything being sacrificed was prelaunch—glassware, tools, books, trinkets. When the Fougere family's time came not one of them had anything to throw in, save Thomas, who with an expression Jed couldn't decipher, threw a multibladed pocketknife into the flames. There were looks from the rest of the congregation, and they weren't friendly. It was clear the Fougere family had been expected to sacrifice more. The bishop began preaching again, speaking of the need to purify themselves through fire, the need to prepare themselves for more and deeper sacrifice. God's anger with Earth could not be allowed to spill over to *Ark*. They would have to be strong to do what must be done, and those who were not strong enough would be broken and cast aside, and their souls would fall back to Hell, like all those that had remained behind on Earth. Only the pure in heart would be allowed to proceed to Heaven.

Jed kept expecting the bishop to mention the Crew again, but he didn't, and much of what he said seemed aimed directly at the Fougeres. "From those to whom much is given, much is expected," he said. They endured the rest of the sermon, and though the usual greetings and blessings were exchanged with the rest of the congregation at the end of the service, there was a sudden cold distance in their neighbors' words. The family returned home from church in uncomfortable silence for the second time in a month. His father's face was ashen, his uncle's pensive. Ruth held the baby close, whispering to her as though it were the child who needed comfort and not Ruth herself. Jed's mother held Mary, her expression somewhere between weary and worried. Jed bit his lip. *Something has happened. I need to know what.*

Nothing was said that night, though his father and his uncle went off to talk in the barn, the usual tension between the men seeming to have eased somewhat. His mother and Ruth and Mary busied themselves with housework, and Jed took advantage of the lack of attention to go to bed early. The morning bells woke him some ten hours later, and he got up feeling very refreshed, and at breakfast his uncle announced, "Come on, Jed, you and I are going hunting."

Jed glanced reflexively at his father, who said nothing

and didn't return his look. He hurried through the rest of his bacon and eggs in silence, anxious to finish before some other chore got wished on him to interfere with the day's plan. It was a rare treat for Jed to get away hunting with his uncle. Rabbits were the business of the day, though there were deer around too. Sometimes they would come up through the trees that lined the riverbanks, and make themselves a nuisance among the berries, but there was something almost taboo about hunting deer in Charity Parish. Hunting for meat was for those who couldn't feed their families with farming.

He finished and ran to grab his bow, but his uncle stopped him. "Grab a change of clothes, we're going to be gone overnight. Come down to the barn when you're packed." Jed's eyebrows went up at that, but he knew better than to ask questions, he just went up to his room, threw the essentials into his leather daypack, then ran down to the barn to meet Thomas. His uncle had one horse saddled and was bridling a second.

"Where are we going, Uncle?"

"I thought we'd go down toward the aftward forest and see how far we can go."

"What about the rabbits?"

"The rabbits will wait for us to get back."

His uncle finished with the saddling and Jed helped him load the saddlebags. They set off, away and aftward. Jed had never really gone in that direction, he realized. School and church, Charity and the market and his friends and everything else important seemed to lie forward, though he'd never really realized it before. Before the next hour bell sounded from the church steeples they were well outside of Charity Parish and into Blessed, the next parish aftward. The landscape was beginning to change as well, with more trees and fewer and smaller fields. Jed had known that Riverview was an especially prosperous farm. What he hadn't known was that Charity Parish was an especially prosperous parish. In Blessed, the farms weren't just smaller, they were noticeably less developed. The farmhouses were not so well built, and luxuries like prelaunch window glass and fine new iron-wood barns were nonexistent. Another hour bell later they were aftward of Blessed, and there were no more well-ordered orchards or wide grazing pastures. The people here lived in cabins of hewn wood and their small fields had been laboriously cut from mature forest, with goats and sheep grazing around huge stumps that had yet to be dug out to allow the proper tilling and planting of a crop. There was a different mood among the people too. In Charity Parish neighbors would wave and smile, in Blessed they nodded as you passed. Here toward the edge of the forest they seemed indifferent and the few looks they drew in passing made Jed uneasy.

"You're learning something here now, Jed," his uncle said, noticing his discomfort.

"I am, but I'm not sure what."

"What do you notice?"

"People are poorer, there's not so many horses."

"What else?"

"I'm not sure."

"How many women do you see?"

Jed paused, thinking back. "None, now that I think of it."

Thomas nodded. "A farmholder in Charity might have two wives, or three, even a farmhand is as likely to be married as not. There's about as many boys born as girls, so that means a man here in the aft-lands is much more likely to go unmarried."

"Still, some of them must be. We should see *some* women."

"Some are, but you won't see their wives on the road, certainly not unaccompanied. When something is scarce it's valuable, and when it's valuable you hide it away so someone won't steal it."

"How can you steal a person?"

His uncle laughed without humor. "You'll understand soon enough. Just understand this. Farmers give fealty to the Prophet with dutiful tithing and loyalty, those the Prophet favors he rewards with wives. Those he doesn't favor go without. All these second and third sons have little reason to love the Prophet."

"That's a sin."

"That's a reality, Nephew." Thomas paused. "I was born and bred a Believer, but when I look at how the Church works, it seems entirely too worldly for me. Bishop Nemmer comes from Joseah Parish, which is as poor as this one or poorer, and that's where his power base comes from too. I don't know what the internal politics of the church are, but he wasn't chosen to come to Charity Parish by accident. Everything he's done since he got there has been a direct challenge to the Prophet—and to us and people like us."

"But to challenge the Prophet, that's challenging God."

"That's a risk he appears willing to take. You saw what

happened at chapel, that was a direct warning to us. That's why I thought it best to come down here and see what we might find." His uncle paused. "That and I thought it would be good to get you out of the way for a while."

"But what of Father and Mother and Ruth and Magda . . ."

"Riverview is a strong farm, and my brother is a strong man. He's got the hands to help out, and they're loyal to him. I doubt the bishop will want to confront him quite so directly, not yet anyway, though he's got his eye on us, no question. If he's going to get any leverage it'll be through you."

"Through me? How?"

"By giving you the honor of joining the priesthood."

"But I don't want to join the priesthood." Jed looked puzzled and his uncle laughed.

"You're right, you don't. You'll start as a servitor, which means that your life will not be your own from that day forward, and Riverview will become the property of Charity Parish church when you inherit, which is the real point. So we're making you unavailable for a few days. Maybe this will all settle down." He looked pensive. "I hope so. In the meantime you're going to get some real practice with your bow, just in case you need it."

The crested a small rise and found a small church beyond it. The church was small and not nearly so well built as the church in Charity, but its was well kept up, and its grounds were immaculately groomed, in stark contrast to most of the farms in the area. The parish sign on the gate to the churchyard read Bountiful, which struck Jed as ironic enough to be funny. He smiled to himself, and then his smile froze on his face as they came past the building and saw a cluster of red cloaks on the other side of it. *Inquisitors!* There were twenty there at least.

"Don't stare, boy." His uncle's words came to him, pitched low enough that only he could hear them. "Just give them a wave and keep going."

Jed did as he was told, and after a second's hesitation one of the hooded figures waved back.

"Uncle, why are there so many of them here?" Jed asked when they'd put the church far enough behind them that he could speak normally without fear of being overhead.

"I don't know, Jed." Thomas's expression showed concern. "I don't know, but it's bad news for someone. Those were awfully young men to be inquisitors, if I'm any judge." He looked down and read Jed's worry in his face. "They're no concern of ours right now though, and I pray they won't be later."

Jed nodded, and they rode on in silence for a while, while he absorbed that. *I was right that things are changing. Knowing how to fight and shoot and survive are going to be important, but they aren't going to be enough.* If the social order failed, as his uncle seemed to be implying it might, as his own observations warned was already happening, then he needed to have allies. *But who?* Not the backward and dangerous aftward people, and certainly not his neighbors in Charity, he'd made enemies of them when he'd made enemies of their children, notwithstanding the willingness of Matthew's father to buy his pigs. Not his father, antagonistic as he was toward Jed, and not his mother, subservient as she was to the head of the household. Certainly not the Bishop Nemmer, who disliked Jed personally and would certainly make life under his father seem blissful should he gain Jed as a servitor. Uncle Thomas was on his side, and his support meant much within the walls of the Fougere household, but in the bigger picture he was just one man, without land, more importantly without *power*. The Crew? He missed Kylie, and Dr. Valori seemed like a good man, but the Crew weren't his people.

*And so I am going to have to be able to look after myself.* The realization came to Jed slowly as the horses clopped their way past the last of the small holdings and into the forest proper. The road petered out into a winding trail that curved up and down through towering first-growth oaks and ironwoods. Now and again a startled squirrel scampered through the leaf litter and up a tree, to chatter in annoyance as they passed. Eventually the trail itself faded into the forest floor, and they used the suntube overhead to navigate. The forest smells were rich, and close, and light darkened as the canopy closed overhead. The enclosing gloom seemed appropriate.

Melany Waseau, chief engineer of the Crew, did not often feel nervous in her position, but as she went to the True Prophet's Temple, set in a tower high above the Auditorium, she had to admit to butterflies in her stomach. She had to walk through the big, empty space, her footsteps echoing from the distant walls, the silent *dadushka* fliers seeming to watch her, as though their double-bubble canopies were eyes. There was something very wrong. The young servitor who'd brought her the message was panting and out of breath. The message itself was hastily scribbed on a scrap of pre-launch paper. All it said was "Please come at once."

And so she was coming, hurrying because the Prophet had never sent such a note before, and it could only mean bad news. There was another servitor waiting for her at the entrance to the tower, holding the door open, looking scared. *Not a good sign.* "Blessing, Chief Engineer," he said as she passed, the relief in his voice was palpable.

"Blessings," she answered automatically, and resisted the urge to run up the winding stairs to the Prophet's quarters. *What's going on?* The Temple tower had once been used to control flight operations in *Ark*. The lower two levels had been converted to quarters for the Prophet's attendants, the next two as his private quarters, the two above held his wives, and the top level, glassed on three sides and giving a view aftward as good as the one from the forward ledge, was the Temple proper, where the Elder Council met and the highest Believer rituals were carried out. As she went up she saw one of the women peering out from behind a door, a baby held to her breast, her eyes frightened, and Melany's concern grew. *I should have brought help.* She hadn't, and it was too late now.

At the top floor her way was blocked by four inquisitors, anonymous and menacing in their hooded red cloaks. She advanced on them, trying to project a confidence and authority she didn't feel. "Move aside. This is a Crew area, and I am chief engineer."

The inquisitors didn't move, and she took a deep breath and raised her voice. "I am chief engineer, and I don't know what is going on here, but I *will* speak with the Prophet."

Again the inquisitors didn't move, but then a voice called from inside the Temple. "Let her through."

And then she was inside. She had expected to find the Elder Council in session, but it wasn't. The True Prophet was, however, trussed naked to a wooden cross, the little authority he had ever held stripped away with his robes. He was nothing more than a frightened and frail-looking youth. A fifth inquisitor, menacing and anonymous in his hooded red cloak, stood before the cross, a vicious-looking whip in his hand, and she could see the angry red lines that covered the Prophet's body.

"Chief Engineer." The Prophet's voice shook; he had obviously been crying. "In God's name, make them stop."

"What is—" she started to say, but a voice cut her off.

"Welcome, Chief Engineer." She turned around to face the speaker, saw a man she didn't recognize in bishop's robes, flanked by two more inquisitors. "I am Bishop Nemmer."

"Bishop Nemmer," Melany spoke with ice in her tones. "This is a Crew area, under my authority. Have him cut down immediately."

"No." Nemmer shook his head slowly. "I won't do that. I don't think you understand. Our Prophet has defiled himself." There was a vicious edge to his voice. "Our Prophet has defiled our Church. He has turned away from God, and now God must see him punished him for his sins." Nemmer's eyes were intense, locked on hers. "And the Crew has no authority here. Not anymore."

"They've stopped the tithing." The Prophet sounded desperate, pleading. "Make them stop, I'll tell them not to do it, make them—" His words were cut off in a scream as the inquisitor in front of him brought his lash down, hard.

"He won't you know." Nemmer ignored the Prophet, keeping his eyes locked on Melany. "He won't ever issue another edict on your behalf. Look at him. Did you really think his position would last a second longer than I wanted it to?"

"Where are the rest of the Elder Council?" As she spoke Melany thought furiously. *Is he acting alone? This might yet be reversed.*

Nemmer shrugged. "That's unimportant. I am acting on God's word now, and five hundred men, five hundred new inquisitors of the aftward parishes, act on my word."

Melany looked at Nemmer in stunned amazement. *This is far worse than I might have dreamed. He's created an army.* She remembered Nikol's warnings on the realities of power, and with sudden crystal insight saw how events would unfold. With the Prophet eliminated Nemmer would take control of the Elder Council, by force if necessary, though the mere threat of it would probably be enough. That was easy, his larger problem would be getting the Believers to follow him instead of the Prophet. *He's cut the Prophet out, and he's going to take command as the voice of God in* Ark. The realization was a cold certainty in her heart, and taking that reasoning one more step explained the current drama. Bishop Nemmer had used the tithing as leverage, as a tool to build resentment among the Believers against both the Crew and the Prophet. *And I cannot allow him to succeed.*

"Bishop," she began, but Nemmer cut her off with a wave of his hand.

"I don't speak to unchurched Crew. If you seek conversion, come to Charity Parish church on Sunday, and God will know you then."

"I thought God was always and everywhere in *Ark*."

Nemmer smirked. "Don't play games, Chief Engineer. You'll find the church is generous to the poor, as the Lord commands us to be. It behooves the poor to be humble in return."

"Do you think . . ." Melany's temper flared, and she found herself momentarily lost for words. "Do you think we're going to come groveling to you for charity? You *owe* the tithings to the Prophet. That was the agreement, between your ancestors and mine. That was how you came to be on this ship at all. We won't plead for what's ours."

"What I think, Chief Engineer." Nemmer's eyes were hard and cold as he spoke. "What I think is that the time of the Crew is long past. You contribute nothing useful to justify your existence."

"We contribute *knowledge*. We maintain the living culture of Earth. The University is important, you can't just throw that away."

"Knowledge." The bishop snorted. "You can eat that, if it satisfies you, or see what you can trade it for in the Charity market square if it doesn't. Believers are not going to feed the deniers of God, not now and not ever. You will be punished in your turn, cast down as Jesus cast down the mighty in his time. In the meantime . . . I have business to finish here." He made a gesture and the two inquisitors advanced on Melany. She held up a hand to stop them. "I can leave on my own." And indeed it was all she could do. She heard another crack of the lash, another scream from the hapless Prophet, and she clenched her fists in impotent rage. There was nothing else she could do. *I need to tell the Crew this. First I need a plan.*

Nikol Valori had spent the day hiking up his now well-beaten path to the forewall and the continually shrinking pile of shipsteel ingots there. His first hint of the trouble was as he walked up the Town road toward home, Kylie and supper. The first cheering wagonload of Crew aroused only his interest, but more followed it and he knew what must have happened. The wagons were laden down with sacks of flour, with piles of fruit and vegetables, even with caged chickens and squealing pigs, and the faces of those that rode them were both angry and exultant. Most of the faces were men, Crew men, with a scattering of women. Most of them carried improvised wooden clubs, occasionally a farming implement, and they shook him in the air as weapons. *The Believers have stopped tithing, and the fools have gone to collect what they felt was theirs by right.* Nikol took a deep breath and quickened his pace. *I hadn't thought it would happen so quickly.* He had expected riots, hoarding, and stealing when the tithing stopped, he had feared food raids and murder and possibly civil war. He hadn't expected any of that to happen until hunger set in, and on that basis he had expected at least a week of warning, time to read the signs and make a decision as to how to best protect himself and Kylie. *At least a week, and I hoped for a month, or longer.*

He had not counted on the moral outrage of a newly disenfranchised priestly class, had not thought the restrained, refined sensibility of the University establishment would lend itself quite so easily to mob violence, but he recognized it when he saw it. As he watched a fight broke out on one of the wagons, over what he couldn't tell, and a panicked sheep leapt free, tumbling as it hit the ground, then leaping to its feet and running off, bleating madly. *I didn't expect them to take action, because I thought them incapable of any action to which they were not forced, and I was a fool to be so blind.* He had been gone six hours, just the time to make a round-trip to the forewall on foot. The triumphant shouts of the wagon-mounted raiders had drawn other people from their houses. They were friends, neighbors, acquaintances, people he'd known all his life, and they frightened him as a mob. People on the carts were throwing sacks of flour, cornmeal, vegetables, and who knew what else to the gathering throng. It was market day, and all too obviously the Crew had gone into Charity in force. A woman on one of the carts was heaving watermelons to the crowd, oblivious of the fact that no one was catching them. The melons broke and splattered when they hit the ground, to be trampled under the hooves of the horses pulling the following wagons. Bags split and grain spilled, and several more scuffles broke out as people in the crowd fought for the spoils, but mostly there was just yelling, voices raised in self-righteous anger and the exhultation of victory. He caught a few snatches above the general clamor.

". . . damn kolkoz . . ."

". . . deserved it . . ."

*The fools, the pizzdets fools.* He broke into a run. The University had a month of supplies, Melany had told him. That was a month to negotiate, to plan, to take measured action to adjust to a new reality if everything else failed. That opportunity was lost now, there would be war between the Crew and the Believers, and while neither side had any recent experience with violence he had little doubt that the instinct for organized murder would surface as easily as it always had in the human heart. The most important thing now was to keep Kylie safe.

His rational mind told him that Kylie *was* safe, at home where he'd left her just as she always was. It would take the news of the market raid some time to spread among the Believers, and it would take more time for them to organize their retaliation. He probably had several hours. Beneath the reasoning was naked fear, and it allowed little room for measured introspection. He had to get back *now.* It was all he could do not to drop the twenty five kilos of steel on his back, but he overrode the instinct. He had worked hard to get it, and it would delay him only a minute or two. Blacksmithing, and the regular hikes to collect ingots of ship steel had melted away his middle-aged fat and hardened his muscles, and with the impetus of adrenaline he ran the distance with no difficulty. It seemed to take forever for him to get home, although in total time it was probably only a few minutes.

It was quiet in front of his house, the main commotion being down on the Main Street, although a few faces peered through curtained windows. The door was jammed shut when he got there, and it took him a few minutes of fruitless shoving to realize that Kylie had deliberately locked herself in. *Smart girl*. She had seen what was happening, and taken the best action she could. He went around to the back, but that was jammed shut as well. He knocked loudly, called her name, and after a pause he heard motion behind the door. She opened it, her face worried.

"I'm sorry, I didn't mean to lock you out, it's just—"

"No, you did the right thing."

"What's happening?"

"I don't know exactly everything, but I do know we're in trouble." He saw the sudden concern on her face. "Not us in particular, *devuchka*. I think everyone's in trouble, Crew and Believers alike."

"What are we going to do?"

Nikol hadn't thought that far in advance, but there was really only one answer. "We're going to leave."

"For how long?"

"I don't know. For a while."

"Where?"

"I don't know that either, *devuchka*." He saw the worry in her eyes. "Somewhere safe."

"Are we ever coming back?" She was fighting back tears, fighting to be strong. She didn't want to be a burden to him, he could see the determination not to crumble fighting with the fear in her face, and it stabbed his heart to see her bravery.

"I hope we are, we'll have to see what happens. We're in a better position than a lot of people."

She nodded. "What do I have to do?" She sounded shaken, but there was a new resolution in her voice. She had vanquished her fear.

He took her into his arms and hugged her tight. "You have to be as brave as you're being right now. You have to know in your heart that I will always, always take care of you." He found himself having to fight back his own tears. "I promised your mother, it was the last thing I ever said to her, I promised that I would take care of you, and I will."

She hugged him tight in return, nodding fiercely, unable to answer, and he knew it was because if she did her fragile control would shatter and she would cry like the child she didn't want to be. *I have to take my own advice here, I have to be brave, I have to hold it together for both of us.* He put her down and they went inside. She'd used a chair to wedge the door, and closed and locked the shutters as well. He didn't yet know where they were going to go, but they would need supplies and provisions. Provisions he had, thirty days' worth, although unfortunately a lot of that was in the form of fruit preserves, pickled vegetables and meat that didn't lend themselves to travel. He did a quick inventory, and found he had about a week of dried meat, dried fruit and hard bread, food that was nutrient dense and suitable for carrying. More problematic was the question of how it would be carried. He had his own small backpack that he used for his hikes to the forewall, and Kylie had her book bag for school, but they were lacking anything larger. Also lacking, he realized, were waterskins, tools, anything to make a shelter out of, even a basic map. *I never thought we'd have to abandon our home.* Even as he thought it he realized, in surreal fashion, that once they left they would never be coming back. He picked up the biggest knife he'd made, a heavy, forward-curved multipurpose blade called a *kukri*, based on a Nepalese design he'd found. It was big enough to chop down a decent-size tree, fine enough to shape its wood into another tool. It could butcher a deer should he be so lucky as to catch one, and kill a man, should it ever come to that.

He hefted the blade and swung it, considering how best to use it in a fight and feeling long buried instincts coming to the fore. *It will come down to killing before this is over.* There was a chilling certainty in the realization. *I thought I was ready. How very wrong I was.* Facing the situation, he realized that the deficiencies in his inventory were only the start of his problems. He had little practical experience in the woods, and none at all with long-term survival in the wild. He couldn't hunt, couldn't fish, couldn't find nuts or berries without wandering randomly until he stumbled onto them, couldn't track or trail, didn't know how to avoid the big cats. *I'm lucky that* Ark *was designed to be easy for humans to live in.* If they were to survive, it would be thanks to their benign environment, and not at all due to his own planning and foresight. *I knew this conflict was coming, I deluded myself into believing it would have a peaceful solution.* He had hoped to establish himself within the Believer economy, to become independent of the tithing and separate from the Crew, to establish himself as a productive member of a productive community. That would've worked, if the Crew had accepted their fate calmly, but they hadn't. Anger had won out over the desire to negotiate, even over rational thought. The exultant looters couldn't be unaware that the Believers outnumbered the crew by twenty to one or more, and yet they had chosen their rash act anyway.

*And can I really have anticipated that?* The question

was irrelevant. All that mattered was getting himself and Kylie to safety. They packed a few belongings quickly, tied up in bed sheets, and he quickly cut two poles from a pine tree behind the house. Tying one end of the ungainly packages to either end of each pole created two reasonably balanced loads that can be carried on their shoulders. He put the most essential things in his backpack and Kylie's book bag, starting with a steel prelaunch hatchet, a model he'd been trying unsuccessfully to duplicate in his forge. He also included the *kukri* knife, the water skin, the bulk of the dried meat, a blanket each, some sundry supplies he felt they couldn't do without. The lack of water was the most serious concern, but that could be addressed by staying close to streams and rivers. When it was all assembled it seemed pitifully inadequate when measured against the task of surviving alone in the forest.

He looked out the window. The road outside was quiet, the mob had moved on, or dispersed. There was nothing to suggest that anything had changed at all, and for a moment it seemed like madness to even contemplate leaving the security of their home, leaving all he'd worked for all his life, and taking his young daughter out into an uncertain and dangerous future. *Maybe we should just wait, maybe this will all blow over.* In his heart he knew it wouldn't. The world had changed, and he had to change with it. He helped Kylie lift her now overloaded book bag, and shoulder her small pole with its improvised burden bags. He hefted on his own backpack, shouldered his own load, and they went out into the road. The next decision to make was what direction to take. It would have to be foreward, to the woods he had learned so well in his steel-hunting searches.

He knew the territory in that direction, and it was away from Charity Parish and the Believers, who were very certainly already gathering to retaliate on the raiders. There would be food enough from berries and fruit, and perhaps he could figure out how to snare small game. *A skill I put off learning too long.* It was too late to regret that now. Going foreward could only be a temporary solution. The near constant mist and frequent rain meant they would be more or less permanently wet unless they had better shelter than he could build in the short term. It would be acceptable for a couple of days, survivable for a couple of weeks, perhaps, but it would be miserable, and not sustainable in the long term. Going directly aftward was out of the question, they'd run straight into any angry Believers coming out of Charity.

They set off down the road, and Nikol had to force himself not to turn around and look back. *My forge, and all that shipsteel . . .* It would be nice to think that it wasn't all wasted, that they would be back and then he would once again be blacksmithing. *It was going so well, I was supporting us, learning so much . . .* He pushed the thought aside. There was no time for regrets now. Instead he looked up the curve of the world to find the crossroad through Charity, let his eye follow the thin dark line until it narrowed to a thread, moving up past the cluster of buildings that was Hope and farther, up and counterspinward to the point where the land arched over the vertical and overhead until it was lost in the glare of the suntube. There were other villages there, places he knew only as names on the University's maps. Those places would hear of the Crew raids and the retaliation of Charity's

Believers, but they wouldn't have experienced them first-hand. Once the situation had had time to settle down they might find shelter there, trade work for food, maybe even start blacksmithing again. He looked down at Kylie, gamely trotting beside him, her small frame bent forward under the weight she carried. He remembered her tears the day her schoolmates had attacked her, the bruises from the chestnuts, most of all the hurt of rejection from those she had considered her friends. *I can't expose her to that again.* Two hundred years of tithing had left a deep scar of resentment in the Believer soul, where the Crew was concerned. Released of its religious restraints, it would burn hot. How long it would stay hot he could only guess.

Jed could smell the smoke before he could see it. At first he didn't think anything of it. He and his uncle were riding back, after four days of hunting in the virgin aftward forest, each with a gutted deer carcass awkwardly lashed to their saddle, and several brace of rabbits and squirrels as well. It had been a good trip, and a welcome change from the tensions of home. The smoke smell grew stronger, and gradually it entered his awareness that this wasn't some aftlander's cooking fire, this was something much bigger.

"Look." His uncle pointed, as they came around a corner of the path. They were on a small rise, just breaking out of a treeline that marked the edge of a stump-filled smallholding. A thick dark plume was rising up toward the suntube, black against the silver-white of the foredome's ice layer. "Something's wrong."

"Is it home?"

"It's in that direction. Let's pray it isn't Riverview."

They rode on in silence for a while, contemplating the smoke plume. As their road turned this way and that it seemed sometimes that it came from somewhere beyond Riverview, other times that it could only be their farm itself that was on fire. Tension grew in Jed's belly, but there was no point in expressing it. They would find out the truth soon enough.

They came to the aftward border of Blessed Parish just after the noon-meal bell. There were some figures standing at the crossroads there, men and horses, and as they grew closer Jed could see they were all in the red robes of inquisitors. Their uniforms brought to his mind the merciless interrogation of Shealah Neufeldt and he looked to Thomas for reassurance, but his uncle stayed silent, his expression unreadable, though his eyes narrowed briefly. He finally turned to Jed as they approached the group. "Whatever you do, don't say anything, just follow my lead. Don't show fear, don't ask anything, if they ask you anything, just tell the truth, as briefly as possible."

Jed nodded, and found his heartrate speeding up. *Something has definitely happened. Something is wrong.* The smoke cloud in front of them had grown and spread, reaching almost all the way to the suntube. It wasn't a good omen.

The inquisitors were waiting, watching as they drew nearer to the crossroads, four on the ground, four on horseback. In addition to their normal robes, Jed could see they all carried wooden staves a good two meters long.

"Blessings, Brethren." Thomas smiled widely and waved as they came up to the group. "What's the news?"

One of the mounted inquisitors came forward, his hood uncharacteristically thrown back. His stave, Jed now noticed, was sharpened at one end, and he saw that the others were too. *Those are weapons, this could get dangerous.* In spite of himself, he felt afraid.

"Who are you?" The inquisitor was a big man, broad shouldered and heavy set, with dark hair and hard eyes.

"I am Thomas Fougere, and this is my nephew, Jedediah."

"I see. What's your home parish?"

"Charity."

"Charity Parish . . ." The man considered that, as if he could weigh the words to determine their truth. "Who's your bishop?"

"Bishop Nemmer. If I can ask, Brother, do you know—"

The inquisitor cut Thomas off with a raised hand. "I'll ask the questions." His voice was as hard as his eyes. "What are you doing here, on the far side of Blessed?"

"I took my nephew hunting, as you can see."

"Hunting." The inquisitor traded a glance with one of his fellows on horseback. "Not like the wealthy farmers of Charity to stoop to hunting deer, is it?"

The other shook his head. "Not at all."

Thomas shrugged. "Meat is meat. Deer fills the belly as well as pork."

The inquisitor nodded, his manner softening slightly. "That it does." He seemed to reach a decision. "You can go on. Be careful."

"Brother, what's happened?" asked Thomas.

"We've turned out the Crew, that's what's happened. The Town is burning, you can see it from here, part of

Charity too, but we made them pay the devil for that, I can tell you. There's a lot of them running around loose still, we're hunting them down."

"Hunting them down?" Thomas's eyebrows went up. "Why?"

"To kill them, what else? Parasites, that's all they are." The inquisitor smiled as he said it, and Jed suddenly realized why the sharpened end of his stave was stained darker than the butt. "The men anyway. The women, we keep them for ourselves."

Thomas nodded. "Blessings, Brother." He stirred up his reins and went past. Jed nudged his mount to follow him, breathing out slowly. There was something tugging at the edge of Jed's awareness, but he couldn't quite put his finger on it. They were halfway across Blessed Parish before it came to him.

"Uncle," he asked. "Were those *Riverview* horses they were riding?"

His uncle nodded grimly. "They were, Jed. I don't know what we'll find when we get home."

The inquisitor's last words were burned into his brain, and he couldn't help thinking of his mother and Mary. *The women we keep for ourselves.* He didn't even let himself think of what might have happened to Kylie.

After . . . *How long has it been? Three weeks? Six?* Nikol couldn't count the time he and Kylie had been living in the bush beneath the forewall. Long enough that their skin was sore and sloughing off in places from constant dampness and the clothes were starting to rot from their bodies. Finally he had decided to move himself and Kylie into the University. It was a dangerous decision, because the Believers had an army now, or at least a faction of them did, thugs in red cloaks with spears and bows and an easy readiness to do violence, and they too were moving into the University. They had attacked it, and made prisoners of the Crew. It was their base of operations, and they were busily transforming the place into a fortress. It was a calculated risk, but the University was a very large space, much of it unused even when the Crew had occupied it. It was rambling and much-modified over the century of *Ark's* construction, and Nikol knew its secrets as no Believer ever could. They came and went by way of the forewall ledge, invisible from below if they were careful to stay away from the edge, and lived in an upper level storage room, full of arcane equipment of forgotten purpose left behind by the builders. It also had a pile of heavy fabric pads, also purpose unknown, but they made serviceable bedding. Their first night warm and dry had been heavenly, and they quickly discovered that the red cloaks, busy with imposing their rule on their world, had neither the need nor the inclination to climb the endless stairs to the upper levels of the structure. They had safety for the short term, and more importantly shelter. He needed a long-term plan, but that would have to wait for a while.

They also had water and sanitation from the University's water system, and every few days would make a food gathering expedition, up the stairs to the forewall ledge, along it for three kilometers, to a place where the creeper vines grew thick enough to climb up and down as easily as a ladder. His frame, tautened by blacksmithing, grew lean on the exercise and the steady diet of fruit, roots and nuts, while Kylie, with the agility and lightness of youth, learned to swing herself up and down the forewall face as easily as she could walk. As their damp-ravaged skin began to heal Nikol felt better than he had in years, though he had begun to crave meat in a way he wouldn't have imagined possible. He continued to experiment with snares made with wire salvaged from builder equipment, but had no luck.

The red cloaks, by contrast, were having no trouble getting meat. They were bringing in cured sides by the wagonload, as well as fruit, vegetables, grain, and finished goods to furnish the place to their liking, a standard of living that seemed far higher than what even the Crew had been accustomed to. For a war that had started over tithes, the Believers seemed to have merely traded one yoke for another still heavier one. None of that surprised Nikol. The methods of tyrants were ancient and well proved. *Give the commoners an enemy to revile, then control them through their hate and fear.* At that they were better off than the targets of that hate and fear. Kylie found a spot high on the ledge where a tenacious bush gave cover, and with little else to do he took to watching *Ark*'s new masters, studying their movements, even making notes. In another long-abandoned storage room he found a surveying instrument of some kind. Its fuel cell was long empty, but its optics were in perfect working order, and he used it to observe their comings and goings. Every day saw a steady trickle of captives dragged up the road to the auditorium, increasingly gaunt and bedraggled as the days crept past. Some of them were put to work on fortifying the University, digging a perimeter trench and lining it with sharpened stakes, erecting a rampart of earth and logs, building a prisoner stockade. Others . . . He didn't like to think about that. The red cloaks had erected crosses on the road leading down toward the town, and prisoners who raised the ire of their captors were lashed up to die of starvation and thirst, with their bodies left to rot away as an example to others. He saw Stroink go that way, and Bellingham, his value as a man of medicine not high enough to save him. The female captives were kept separate from the men, and the red cloaks who supervised them had no compunctions about stopping work for a round of casual rape. Nikol's jaw clenched the first time he saw it, and his hand instinctively when to his *kukri* knife—but ultimately there was nothing he could do to stop them. He turned instead to his notebook, writing down every detail he could discern through his lens. *At least these crimes won't be forgotten.*

What began as observation became obsession. He found a dusty parabolic dish antenna in another storage room and he and Kylie dragged it and its mounting up to their observation post. He replaced the feed horn at the antenna's center of curvature with a salvaged funnel and ran some flexible tubing from that. Sound bounced from the dish was focused into the funnel, and by aiming it at a group and holding the tube to his ear he could, usually, make out what was being said. Putting the dish on the forewall ledge was a risk, its sudden appearance might alert the red cloaks to their presence. It was a small risk, he rationalized to himself, but he couldn't escape the fact that it was unnecessary, and as such unnecessarily endangered Kylie. He warred with himself over that, but in the end it was Kylie herself who convinced him to do it. She seemed to share his need to bear silent witness to the unfolding atrocity, her fear overridden by something deeper and stronger in her character. He compromised by taking her to the forest for three days immediately after they installed it. He used the time to try some new trapping techniques, which yielded them a rabbit on the third day. They had left twigs around the dish, where anyone examining their eavesdropping post would have to disturb them. When they came back the twigs were undisturbed. The rabbit became a tasty stew, cooked in old builder glassware over a small and well hidden fire.

Having gotten away with installing the dish, they tried it out. It worked surprisingly well, and when it was aligned on a group he could make out their voices, tinny and distant, but clear enough that he could make out what they were saying. With the ability to listen as well as watch his notes exploded, incidents, times and dates, names and relationships. Kylie came with him, and they took turns watching, listening, recording. They learned that the red-cloaked thugs were inquisitors, and that they were led by a bishop named Nemmer, who had killed the True Prophet for denying God, and taken his place in the Temple. It was a worrisome change. The inquisitors had traditionally been the guardians of the Believer faith, and there had been at most a handful of them. This new group were very different from the Believers he had known, with their emphasis on community, brotherhood and humility before God. *And this will destroy all that they are, inevitably.* He found himself more saddened by that realization than he would have expected.

It also became clear was that inquisitors were a poor army. Their weapons were nothing more than sharpened sticks, most of them didn't even have a bow, and few of those with horses knew how to ride them properly. They didn't have anything that might amount to armor either, and their tactics amounted to rushing an outnumbered enemy in a mob. More importantly they lacked discipline and had little organization. The work on the fortification was haphazard, and it was common enough to see groups of prisoners standing around doing nothing while their masters argued over something. Fights between inquisitors were common. Any of the Earth armies Nikol had studied would have wiped them out with little effort, but they were more than adequate to hunt down and slaughter the hapless Crew. One result of their indiscipline was that they all went to sleep at the usual time, without thought for assigning guards and watches, except around the prisoner stockade itself. Even then the breakfast bell often found the guards asleep. A determined prisoner revolt in the sleeping hours could easily break the stockade and over-whelm the guards. *And if the rest of the inquisitors were caught sleeping . . .*

Except the imprisoned Crew were too dispirited to even make the attempt. They shuffled when they walked, eyes downcast, and only showed enthusiasm for food and for sleep, their efforts directed at walking the fine line between slacking at their labors and avoiding the whips of their masters. The men were completely defeated, none even bothered trying to escape. A few of the women did, perhaps driven by the fear of rape, but they were individual efforts, and the escapees simply vanished into the woods.

There was no attempt at group action, no attempt to free anyone else, no thought to turning the tables on their captors. *The Crew lived life easy for too long, and nobody remembers how to be hard.* The fury that had risen in him when he'd first seen the inquisitors' bestiality had faded, but the images he saw through the surveying lens never left him. One night he'd awoken with a start from a formless nightmare to find Kylie holding him close. "You were crying in your sleep," she said, and when he put his hands to his face they came away wet. The details of the dream wouldn't return to his conscious mind, but he somehow knew their substance—Kylie beaten, Kylie raped, Kylie left on the cross to die. He hugged her tight to him then, rocking her back and forth as much to comfort himself as her. *I can't let anything happen to her, I can't.* Eventually she fell asleep again. He kept holding her, stroking her hair, saying *devuchka* beneath his breath over and over again. He found himself yearning for his long-dead wife. Lynne had given Kylie that name when she was newborn. She had cried constantly as a baby. *But she never cries now.* She had turned that part of herself off, he knew, stored the fear and sadness and loss away for a later time, when it would be safe to take those feelings out again. He lay for a long time, contemplating the wall. *I need to find a way to make her safe.* Eventually he slept.

Kylie was already up when he arose, slicing open mangos for their breakfast with her own shipsteel knife, and he saw her suddenly as if seeing her for the first time, the curve of her budding breasts and the swell of her hips, the practiced way she handled the knife, her easy grace as she moved. She was no longer his *devuchka*, no longer his little girl. She was becoming a woman—*in truth she is already*. It was unthinkable that she go on as they had been, living like rats beneath the feet of the inquisitors. His daughter needed more of a future than that. *We will have to wait, but not too long.* Bishop Nemmer was still securing control, and until he did it would be dangerous to have contact with Believers, but it would not always be so. Bad feelings against the Crew might linger in Charity, but elsewhere they would fade. Sooner or later Nemmer would feel secure enough in his rule that the hue and cry for fugitive Crew would die down. *In those faraway parishes a man with a skill to trade will be able to make a place for himself.* A place for himself, and for his daughter too. He nodded to himself. There would be risk in doing that, but there was risk in everything, and a life of furtive survival was no life at all.

In the meantime watching the inquisitors became even more important, because through their actions they could gauge their mood, which would be the best indicator of when it was time to go. Their work pattern had settled down to a routine now, and each day Nikol and Kylie watched the new defenses grow more formidable. The University was ringed with a semi-circular ditch now, running right up to the forewall on either side and almost as far aftward as the oak grove and the cemetery on the main road. It was three meters deep and full of razor sharp stakes at the bottom. The dirt from the ditch had been piled up to make a steep rampart, and the toiling Crew captives were now working to face it with timber. Behind the rampart a parapet of logs was being started. As they watched and listened they learned the names of the leaders, learned to recognize Nemmer himself, who now came down frequently to supervise the work. The bishop was a man of presence, and Nikol could recognize him even without his improvised telescope, just by the way he stood, and by the way those around him deferred to him. When he was there none of his subordinates dared fight, and he steadily imposed more organization among the inquisitor rank and file.

As time went on fewer struggling captives were being brought in, one or two a day at most, and there were far fewer crucifixions. It seemed that Nemmer had figured out that his labor force was a valuable resource, not to be squandered unnecessarily. As if to compensate for the diminishing number of Crew being added to the stockades the inquisitors began to bring in Believers as well, recognizable by their plain dress, and because they showed no sign of the privations of a fugitive. The new captives gained no advantage for sharing their faith with their captors, the inquisitors worked them just as hard, and applied the lash to Crew and Believer alike to keep the University's new defenses progressing.

As Nikol watched the ditch and wall extend it became obvious that Bishop Nemmer's army wasn't aware that the forewall ledge gave access to the heart of their new citadel from above and behind. *They probably don't even know it's here. That might become important before this is over.* He and Kylie found themselves settling into a routine that echoed that of the inquisitors, watching while they worked, sleeping when they slept. Days slipped into weeks, and they gradually improved their hiding place until it was comfortable, and even almost homelike, using scavenged supplies from the long abandoned store-rooms to make furniture and fixtures. Their part of the University was built over the older, pressure-sealed section that had been used before *Ark* got its atmosphere and, once Nikol was certain the inquisitors wouldn't notice the change, he slipped down three floors and closed the pressure doors, jamming their locking wheels so they couldn't be opened from the other side. He felt more secure after that. Even if the inquisitors discovered their presence they could only get to them by climbing the outside of the structure.

And then they brought in Melany. It was Kylie who was watching through the surveying instrument when it happened. "Father," she asked. "Isn't that Dr. Waseau?"

"Where?"

Kylie pointed, and he saw, then took his daughter's place behind the instrument to see better. The woman being brought in was gaunt and dirty, her hair matted and tangled, but unmistakably it was Melany. She was tied hand and foot, being dragged from a just arrived tithing wagon.

"Quick, get the dish pointed." Kylie put the funnel to her ear and began adjusting the eavesdropping dish while Nikol kept watching. Melany's captors pulled her toward the women's stockade, and he found himself tensing with repressed anger. They were about to throw her into one of the cages used for new prisoners when something happened, and the inquisitors pulling her stopped and looked to the side. He swung the telescope to see what had caught their attention, saw Nemmer himself, gesturing for them to bring their captive over.

"Almost got it," Kylie said, and handed him the listening funnel.

He took it without looking up and held it to his ear while she tweaked the gimbals to line the dish up on Bishop Nemmer and his group. Down below, the inquisitors had stood Melany up in front of Nemmer and were untying her. Evidently their leader wanted to talk to his prize. Melany was angry, and she was saying something, her expression tight and bitter. Nemmer said something back, and then Melany struck him, hard enough to snap his head around. He looked up, slowly, and then cuffed her hard enough to knock her over. He made an angry gesture, and then the three inquisitors who had brought her forward grabbed her and carried her off. Kylie got the dish adjusted, just in time for him to hear Melany's last screamed words. ". . . rot in your hell, *yobany*!"

She might have said more, but one of the inquisitors holding her swung his pole up and around and brought it down on her head. She slumped and was silent, and Nikol felt anger surge up in him like a physical force, and his hand involuntarily went to the handle of his *kukri* blade. There was a scuffle of activity, and then what remained of Melany's clothes were being ripped off. She recovered herself enough to fight back, but she didn't have a hope of getting away. The man landed another pair of sharp blows that left her hanging limp, and then finished stripping her while the other two held her down. He opened his cloak, and Nikol's jaw clenched hard. The man was going to rape her.

"Stop!" The voice was Nemmer's conveyed through the tube at his ear. The inquisitor stopped, and the bishop advanced, moving out of the dish's focus.

"Follow him," Nikol told his daughter, and Kylie

swiveled the dish to follow Nemmer. He finished speaking before he finished moving, so Nikol missed what he'd said, but the content of his words rapidly became clear. The two who had been holding Melany down picked her up again, the one who'd been about to rape her went back the way he had come. Nikol breathed out, long and slow. Melany wasn't safe, but at least for the moment Nemmer had given her some degree of protection. She wouldn't be raped or killed at random. Nemmer was still speaking, and he pointed to one of the crucifixes erected beside the main road, just inside the new barricades. As Nikol watched, the two inquisitors hauled Melany over to it. There was already a body on the cross, rotted halfway to a skeleton, but they just strung her up on the opposite side of it using the loose ends of the ropes already there. She was still groggily defiant, but the pain of her position quickly overcame the anger on her face. One of the inquisitors drew his whip and began lashing her, alternating strokes between left and right while Nemmer watched impassively. Kylie finally got the dish realigned on the group, and her anguished cries came through the listening funnel. He dropped it as if it were a snake. *I have to get her out of there.* The thought came with the strength of instant conviction. *I can't let her die like that.* His throat constricted painfully, in anger and in fear, but his rational brain kept working, assessing the situation.

He couldn't act immediately, he would have to wait until the inquisitors went to sleep. The plan was simple. Sneak down through the lower levels of the University, past his old office, past the classrooms, down through the auditorium and out to the main road, cut Melany loose, and come back the way he had gone down. There would be the stockade guards to contend with, but if they acted true to form they'd be asleep by the midnight bell. He would have his *kukri*, more than a match for sharpened-stick spears, as long as he faced no more than one or two. He felt his belly tighten as he visualized the route he would take, considering how best to avoid the inquisitors, not down the main stairs but down through the faculty quarters, and through the labs, and then out through the auditorium. *And I have to make sure Kylie is safe.* He looked to his daughter and saw, not for the first time, his wife's face in hers. She was entering the stage of her life where a young woman needed a mother's guidance. *Lynne, how I miss you, how I need you.* He looked back to his optics, back to Melany. The inquisitors had stopped lashing her, had abandoned her to hang and suffer. Nikol realized that he was grinding his teeth. *Nemmer is going to pay for this.*

The wait for the evening bell seemed interminable. He spent some of the time talking with Kylie, going over what he was going to do, what she was to do if he didn't come back. She was scared beneath her courage, and he was angry at himself for making her scared. *But I can't abandon Melany, I can't . . .* He pushed down his own fear, and sharpened the blade of his *kukri*.

Nikol woke with a start at the midnight bell, the hazy remnants of another nightmare vanishing as he opened his eyes. Kylie was asleep, curled up beside him, her face relaxed and peaceful and innocent. He kissed her gently on the cheek, and she stirred. He had meant to leave without waking her, but as he was turning to go she yawned and stretched and her eyelids came open.

"Are you going then?"

"I'll be back soon, *devuchka*." He went back to her and hugged her tight. "I'll be back soon."

He went out, went to the stairs to the Crew's quarters and down, into the heart of the University. To move about while the world slept felt strange, and he found himself instinctively seeking the cover of a non-existent darkness, his hand gripped tight around the haft of his *kukri*. *My genes evolved in a world of nights.* On the upper levels dust was beginning to collect on the floors. As he went down he began to see signs of the inquisitors. They had ransacked the place in their first, furious search for Crew. Blood smears marked places where someone had died, most likely impaled on an inquisitor spear. In one classroom the blood was caked so thick and black on the floor that at first he couldn't believe it was blood. *They slaughtered dozens here.* He would have thought himself immune to horror after all the atrocity he'd documented, but his throat tightened at the sight. Farther along he opened a stairwell door and was turned back by a corrupt stench so powerful it made him vomit on the spot. He closed the door, recovered his breath and tried again, driven to see what was causing it, though there was only one possible source of such a smell. *It was here they dumped the bodies.* By holding his breath he managed to get down one flight, but then was driven back, not throwing up a second time only because he had already emptied his stomach. He took another path, his mind struggling to come to grips with what he was seeing. Farther down he came to the flexfab, where massed ranks of the builder's intelligent tools had waited patiently for the return of someone who knew how to use them. The inquisitors had vandalized them, ripped the dexterous manipulators from their mountings, smashed in the control panels, spilled the intricate, delicate mechanisms across the floor like the guts of a badly butchered hog. A new feeling rose in Nikol, a sense of loss that washed over even the sharp, red anger the inquisitors' brutality had kindled. Even the killings seemed less wanton, at least there was some internal logic to the brutality. This was destruction wrought purely for the pleasure of destroying.

He continued down and saw more evidence of the inquisitors' fury, from the simple ransacking of offices and classrooms to the burning of the library. He knew what he would see there before he saw it. The long streaks of soot blackening the steel ceiling and the heavy smell of stale smoke told him all he needed to know. Still he had to go and look, was compelled to. The library doors had been chocked open to let in enough air to feed the flames, and they'd burned the books on the shelves, ripping out the data desks so they could hurl them into the inferno. His stomach clenched and he nearly wept. *All that knowledge destroyed.* He forced himself to turn away. *They don't just want to eliminate the Crew but the entire culture of the Crew.* He steadied himself. The past couldn't be undone, all that mattered was the future. On the floor below he encountered his first inquisitors, sleeping in hammocks in what had been an office. He felt an overpowering urge to slit their throats as they slept, but he confined himself to stealing a red cloak, protective camouflage. He put it on, taking pains to be silent as he did so. There were more inquisitors camped out in other offices. Evidently the conquerors had disdained the bloodstained Crew quarters for the administrative level. Two levels farther down he came to the auditorium hangar. The inquisitors had tried to vandalize the fliers there, but their spears had only managed to flatten the tires, and the fires they built had only charred the paint on the fuselage underbellies. Nikol smiled grimly at this small triumph of civilization over barbarity. He passed the entry to the Temple tower cautiously, but there was neither movement nor sound. *So far so good . . .*

He crossed the hangar doors and went out to the aftward road, looking around cautiously. Ahead of him Nemmer's crucifixes stood in ranks along the roadway. In the warm and humid air most of the bodies on them had already rotted to skeletons, but even so the smell of corruption came to him as soon as he stepped outstide, a fainter echo of the stench that had made him vomit in the stairwell. To his right were the prisoner stockades, heavy log fences topped with thorny vines and ringed by a stake-filled ditch. There were four guards at each compound, carrying out their duties through the simple expedient of having one of their number sleep against the foot of the gate. Their red cloaks were draped carefully to ward off the chill of the mist, and their hoods were pulled down over their faces against the brightness of the suntube shining through it. He couldn't see the prisoners, but he knew from his vigils that they would be asleep too, lacking cloaks they huddled close for warmth. Nikol's skin itched in sympathy as he remembered the discomfort of living perpetually exposed to the damp. He straightened himself from his instinctive crouch, which took more of an effort than he might have imagined, and walked down the road, trying to walk confidently, as if he every right to be there. *Now is the time to be bold.* It seemed to take forever to cover the scant hundred meters to the forest of crucifixes. The stench grew stronger, but he was able to face it and carry on. Once there it seemed to take even longer to find Melany among the strung up bodies, though it was probably no longer than a minute or two. She stood out in being alive, he would scarcely have recognized her otherwise, her face was so gaunt and drawn. She was conscious but semidelirious, her eyes half-lidded, staring at nothing, her expression slack, her lips moving slightly, pronouncing words only she could know. He shook her, shook her again. Her eyelids fluttered, and her eyes seemed to focus on him. Movement caught the corner of his eye and he froze. To his left an inquisitor was urinating in the ditch, one of the gate guards. Melany started to say something, and he held a finger to his lips, as suddenly desperate that she remain quiet as he had been a moment earlier that she respond. Her lips started to move, and he put a hand to her mouth to silence her before she could speak. The other man finished, turned and went back toward the main gate, his slightly uncoordinated movements betraying the fact that he'd been sleeping. There were half a dozen more inquisitors there, sleeping in hammocks strung across the ditch or between the posts of the still unfinished inner fence.

And then they were alone again.

"Melany, it's Nikol." She turned her head in his direction but didn't seem to recognize him. "Melany, it's Nikol. I'm getting you out of here."

"Nikol?" She blinked at him blearily, uncomprehending, then her eyes snapped into focus. "Nikol! Where have you come from?"

"I'll tell you the story later." With swift slashes of his *kukri* he cut her arms free, right and left. She collapsed forward and he caught her, which made it difficult to cut the ropes at her ankles. *I should have cut them first.* It took some awkward jockeying before he could get the knife into the right position, but finally he managed to cut her loose entirely. He held her, steadied her, but when she tried to stand on her own her knees buckled. He put her arm around his shoulder and held it there, so he could support her walking. Now it only remained to get her back up to his hiding place.

"Blessings, Brother. Where are you taking her?" Nikol nearly jumped out of his skin at the voice, and he swallowed hard to steady himself before he turned around. It was the urinating man. He seemed curious rather than suspicious, and he didn't have his spear.

"Blessings." He put on his best Charity Parish accent. If the man recognized him as Crew . . . that didn't bear thinking about. "Nowhere special. Just going to have a little fun with her."

"Are you out of your mind? Didn't you hear what Nemmer said? You get caught with her and he'll put you up there in her place."

"Nemmer's asleep, he'll never know."

"He won't know because you are not going to . . ." He paused, came closer. "What parish are you from?" There was sudden suspicion in his tone.

In response Nikol dropped Melany and drew his knife.

He swung overhand, aiming to split the inquisitor's skull, but the man instinctively thrw an arm up to block the blow. The knife hit home with a solid *thunk*, and Nikol felt it dig into the bone. The man screamed in pain, his face instantly transformed into a mask of fear, and turned to run, blood gushing liberally from his half-severed arm. Nikol swung again, but missed, and then the other was running back to the gate, screaming for help. Nikol took a step to chase him and stopped. There was no way he could catch the inquisitor before he woke his compatriots, no way he could fight them all at once, even with the advantage his knife gave him. Melany had fallen when he'd let her go, and struggled back to her feet. He grabbed her hand, pulling her along. Behind him he could hear confused shouts as the other inquisitors woke up. Ahead of him the guards at the stockade were standing up, looking around, trying to orient themselves as to what was going on. *We don't have much time.* Melany stumbled and he had to stop to pick her up. When he did he saw the group from the main gate already giving chase, spears in hand. They weren't going to get away with it. He glanced up reflexively, to the top of the University, to the forewall ledge and his eavesdropping dish. *Kylie, please be safe. I love you,* devuchka. There were just four in the group ahead, and he was closer to them. He might, with speed, aggression and luck, get past them. He tightened his grip on his knife and charged.

Riverview under the New Prophet was a grimmer place. Red-cloaked inquisitors were always around, poking their noses into every corner of the farm, questioning everything, making sure that God's commands were carried out to the letter, and making sure that the increased tithings demanded by Bishop Nemmer were met in full. Nobody liked them, but nobody dared say so out loud. There was the example of Hosiah Fludd, who had objected loudly to their presence on his land, and found himself tied to the cross in Charity Parish church having a confession to blasphemy extracted under an inquisitor's whip. Nor did his punishment end there, because Bishop Crowley, who had taken over the parish when Bishop Nemmer was elevated, attached his farm, his house and even his wives to the church, and then granted them all to one of the senior inquisitors. Hosiah had been forced to go aft, and no one in Charity or Charity Parish had seen him since. Mary was gone, declared marriageable and placed as a wife to Nemmer himself. Many of the hands and most of the horses were gone too, the hands to take well-paid jobs clearing land in the aft parishes, the horses claimed as mounts for inquisitors. Bishop Crowley came around frequently as well, and every time he did he suggested, strongly, that Jed be given over to train for the priesthood. His father had so far refused, but Jed had taken to hiding in the barn hayloft whenever the bishop arrived. At Thomas's suggestion he kept a pack full of clothing, hard bread, dried fruit and a waterskin hidden there as well. "You might find it easier to go out on your own than stay when the time comes," said Thomas. "This way the choice will be yours, not theirs." His father's mood grew dark and darker, and he would go for days without saying a word to anyone that was not a command or a rebuke. His mother's face grew lined with worry, and Ruth took to avoiding everyone, spending her days hovering over Magda. Magda, insulated by the innocence of youth and her mother's doting, nevertheless picked up on the tension and became stubborn and fussy. Only Thomas's personality seemed unchanged by it all, though the unvoiced concerns he carried were written clearly in his face.

And yet there were still fields to be plowed and grain to be harvested, the work all the harder because of the lack of hands. Once they'd harvested the current set of crops John and Thomas decided to let some of their land lie fallow, a decision that raised the ire of Bishop Crowley, who questioned their ability to meet their tithing responsibility. "Much is expected from those to whom much is given," he said. Jed, remembering the way his father had dressed down Bishop Nemmer over his defiance of the True Prophet, was surprised by the weakness of John Fougere's response. He didn't give in, but there was none of the force and conviction that had been his hallmark for as long as Jed could remember. The change in his father was good in a way, replacing the anger that had characterized their relationship with withdrawn silence, but it made Jed acutely uncomfortable. He worked hard in the fields each day, trying hard to shoulder a man's burden on thirteen-year-old shoulders. The grand plans to raise and breed horses had long since gone by the wayside. It was small compensation that the special focus Bishop Nemmer seemed to have aimed at their family had gone with him to the Temple tower. Under Bishop Crowley it seemed there was no sin too small to escape the inquisitors, and no one was safe from the sudden denouncement of a friend or a neighbor, but he paid no more attention to the Fougeres than to anyone else. Church days became fraught with fear, with Inquisitions happening almost weekly, sometimes with two or even three sinners crucified and whipped into contrition. The Inquisition of Shealah Neufeldt, which had once shocked Jed with its harshness, now seemed a pleasant memory. The inquisitors were now putting sinners on the cross to be put to the test with fire and water, and the Inquisitions could last for days.

The Crew, Jed learned in one of Crowley's fire-breathing sermons, had been cast down as heretics and unbelievers. There was a bounty of a hundred tokens on any Crew turned in and caught, and plenty of people were eager to claim it. Three times now mounted squads of inquisitors had come charging through Riverview's fields in hot pursuit of a fleeing Crew, leaving rows of crushed corn behind them and dragging away their hapless victim. Bishop Crowley preached of the need to reclaim their souls before they were lost to God forever, of the need to reconsecrate the cross in blood to affirm their love of Jesus Christ, and there were nervous rumors that at the Temple itself the crosses were bloody indeed. Jed thought of Kylie whenever the bishop mentioned the Crew, and frequently at other times. *I hope she's safe, wherever she is.* He clung to the hope that she was. Dr. Valori was a smart and resourceful man. If anyone could look after her, he could, and Jed didn't want to think of Kylie on the cross . . . *Anything but that . . .*

And then one day, while he was walking the upper field, assessing the ripeness of the wheat, a group of four inquisitors on horseback came over the crest of the hill in the horse pasture and came toward him. They were trotting easily, not in pursuit of anyone, so he stopped and waited for them to come closer.

"Blessings, young man." The leader's voice was deep, and it carried an aftward accent. His eyes were sharp and piercing, as though they could see right through people to ferret out their innermost secrets.

"Blessings."

"You're John Fougere's boy, aren't you?"

"Yes, sir."

"I thought as much. How long have you been up here?"

"Since last bell, sir. I'm walking the fields for my father."

"We're looking for a runaway Crew. Have you seen anyone come by here?"

"No, sir."

"Well swivel your eyes, and if you see anyone, shout out, we'll be casting around here for a while. It's a girl we're looking for, about your age, dark hair."

"I'll watch, sir."

"Good lad." The man spurred his horse and headed off at a steady trot, and his companions followed him. Jed watched them go, and dared to hope. *A girl my age, dark hair. Maybe it's Kylie. Maybe I'll see her.* Something tugged at his memory, and almost without thought he started walking, up from the upper field, going slowly, carefully not looking over his shoulders to see if the inquisitors were watching him. He got up to the top of the hill, and when he was over the crest he looked back, to see the horses vanishing down the aftward trail that ran along the top of Riverview. He ran then, down the hill and through the cherry orchard, toward the river. The long grass tugged at his legs as he ran, down through the ranks of fruit heavy trees, to the edge of the orchard, into the woods along the river, to a grove of wild oranges, to a willow tree, to the secret hollow beneath it where he and Kylie had sat, side by side, best friends a lifetime ago. He burst through the curtain of hanging willow branches, knowing in his heart that he would find her there.

He didn't. She wasn't there. Disappointment instantly replaced hope in Jed's heart. *I was so sure.* He had, in the brief span of time between speaking to the inquisitor and arriving at the willow, convinced himself that she had to be there, that she could be no other place. In the face of the reality that she wasn't he realized how foolish that really was. The world was big, and he hadn't seen Kylie in . . . *How long has it been?* A year, a year and a half or more, since the fight with Nebiah. There was no reason for her to remember him after that much time still less for her to come to this place that they'd shared only once, such a long time ago.

And yet when he looked in the crook of the log where they'd sat, the grass was pressed down. He looked closer, saw the trail worn into the grass, saw a small pile of orange peels. *Someone* had been there, and hope rekindled itself in his heart that it might be her.

"Jed?"

He jumped at the voice, whirled around, saw a ragged figure, gaunt, barefooted, clothing torn and hair matted, so thin he could barely recognize her. Kylie.

*Kylie!*

"Kylie!" He ran to her. "Kylie!" He reached her, threw

his arms around her and held her tight. She was skin and bones in his embrace, so light he nearly fell over backward when he lifted her. "Where have you been?"

"Oh Jed." There were tears in her eyes all of a sudden, and her voice was tight with emotion. "I've been wishing for you . . ." Her arms were tight around him, holding as if he might vanish if she slackened her embrace in the slightest.

"What happened? Where's your father?"

"They took him . . ." Despite her thinness her muscles were hard beneath the remnants of her dress. She wore a length of rope as a belt, and a heavy steel knife hung from it, ready for instant use. Kylie had grown up in a hurry. "Oh Jed, I've been so scared."

"Who took him? The inquisitors?"

"They took him and . . . and . . ."

"You're safe now." He held her, and she broke down and cried, long and anguished sobs of loss, repressed until now, in the service of survival. Jed held her until she stopped, until she had recovered herself, and then, suddenly conscious that he *was* holding her, he let her go. They stood there for a moment, suddenly awkward. He had always known she was a pretty girl, but when she looked up, even with her eyes red and her cheeks puffy, he realized she was beautiful.

"Come on, let's get you inside and fed." She nodded, and Jed led her back through the fields, keeping a sharp eye out for the roving inquisitors along they way. There was no question of taking her into the house, his father's reaction could only be negative. The barn was a better option by far. Once they were there he took her up to the hayloft, to his own favored hiding place, then went to the house himself to get her some food, leftover lamb stew and bread still warm from the oven. She tore at the food greedily. "You have no idea," she said between bites, "how sick I am of blackberries and oranges."

"Tell me what happened?"

She finished her stew and then told him her story, how she had woken after her father went to rescue the chief engineer, stumbled bleary-eyed to their surveillance perch on the forewall ledge to watch, and from there she had seen the red cloaks take him, beat him, stab both him and Melany to death with their spears. Nemmer himself had come down, incensed at the penetration of his fortress, and ordered a search of the entire University. She had fled before they could get started, first to the forewall forest, where she and her father had hidden for the first weeks after the Crew attack on Charity, and when the mist and rain became unbearable she had moved aftward to the Town. She found it leveled, every building burned by the inquisitors.

"We saw the smoke," Jed said.

"Our house, the forge, it was all gone, except for his steel." She laughed a bitter laugh. "Only because they couldn't set fire to it."

She had stayed for a few days at her secret treehouse, but a patrol of inquisitors had found it and burned it, fortunately while she was away gathering berries for food. They set an ambush for her as well, but the fire warned her, and she came back cautiously, and by a different route. Even then she was nearly caught. One of the horsemen had spotted her and the whole group had given chase, but she ran into a ravine full of dense undergrowth and the horses couldn't follow. The inquisitors had searched hard, but she had crawled into a dense rose thicket. The thorns had torn her clothes and skin, but her pursuers hadn't been willing to fight their way into it after her, and so she had escaped. From there she'd worked her way steadily afterward, skirting Charity. Another inquisitor patrol had caught her in open fields, but they didn't have horses and the plowed furrows had slowed them down. She'd run hard and fast to the river, and jumped in and let it carry her downstream. Again, her pursuers has been unwilling to follow, but for the last three days inquisitor patrols had been searching diligently along the riverbank.

"I remembered that day we spent together, and I knew this would be a good place to hide, where I wouldn't have to go too far for food."

"You're safe now. They won't find you here, if we're careful."

"A hayloft." She looked around, as if assessing the barn for the first time. "It's a better place to live than most places I've been sleeping."

"I'll talk to my uncle Thomas. He should be back for supper bell. He'll know what to do."

"There's more. Look." She took out a sheaf of paper bound in a leather binder and gave it to him. It was prelaunch paper by its fineness, though it was wrinkled and stiff from being soaked and dried several times. "Jed, you're the only person I can trust with this."

The handwriting was somehow familiar, though it took Jed a moment to realize where he'd seen it before, in school, on his work. Dr. Valori. He read. There were dates, people beaten, raped, killed, sometimes with names given, sometimes only with physical descriptions. He flipped forward, saw notes on the construction of the defenses at the University, and diagrams, and then more atrocities, each one carefully documented. At times the writing changed, and Jed realized that it must have been Kylie herself who made those notes. He flipped to the last page, and saw in her own hand the description of her father's murder. The language was precise, detailed, as dispassionate as any of the other entries, but she had put force behind the pen as she hadn't before, the lines were heavy, and deeply indented, as the emotion she had kept out of her words came through in her hand. He looked at her in awe, realizing what she had come through, and suddenly his own troubles under the reign of Bishop Nemmer evaporated to nothing.

He found himself unable to speak, not knowing what to say. He closed the leather binder and handed the book back to her. For quite some time they didn't say anything, just lay side by side in the hay, taking comfort in each other's presence. Eventually Kylie fell asleep, and some time after that, lulled by the darkness and the hay and the shared warmth, Jed did too. He dreamed then, of a city, an Earth city so vast it stretched from forewall to aftwall, the spires of its buildings reaching for the suntube, filling the entire world with their bulk. He dreamed he was flying over it, flying up the curve of the world and around its arch, in a machine that soared and swung, dipping low to wave at the upturned faces below, then soaring high and higher that the world seemed to wrap around him and the heat of the suntube scorched the wings of his craft. He dreamed of Kylie beside him, her face soft and smiling, and then he was yanked to sudden wakefulness by a blow across his face. His eyes flew open and he found his father kneeling over him, fist upraised to strike again.

"Sinner!" The fist came down again, but Jed managed to raise an arm to block it. Pain flared in his forearm, but at least his face was spared.

"Father! No!" Jed scrambled back out of the way, but his father advanced on him, his face was a mask of anger, pulling his belt from its loops to use as a weapon. The commotion had awakened Kylie, who was frozen in the hay, watching the tableau with fear in her eyes.

"You dare to defile my house! You dare!"

"No, Father, I—" Jed kept backing up, felt the barn wall hard behind him. He could retreat no further.

"Heretic!" John Fougere raised his belt and in spite of himself Jed cringed against the blow.

"Stop!" The voice was deep, authoritative. Jed looked past his father, and saw his uncle, just coming off the ladder into the hayloft, his bow over his shoulder. "Stop right there, John Fougere. Hit him again and I swear on our father's grave I'll kill you."

Jed's father turned slowly to face his brother, pointed to Kylie. "He has lain with this Jezebel!"

Thomas unslung his bow and put an arrow to the string, his face hard. "I don't care what he's done. You aren't touching him again."

"After all I've given you—"

Thomas cut his brother off with a sharp gesture. "After all I've given you, John, faith, loyalty and sacrifice. This boy is your flesh and blood and your misfortune is no fault of his. Be a father to him or stand aside for someone who will." He switched his gaze to Jed, not waiting for his brother to answer. "Is this Kylie?"

"Yes, Uncle."

Thomas nodded. "I'm pleased to meet you, Kylie. Jed, get your pack, it's time to go."

"Why, Uncle?"

"Because a dozen inquisitors are searching the house right now, ransacking it. Someone saw you bring this young woman down from the upper field. They'll be here as soon as they're tired of that."

Kylie got up. "I'm sorry. Jed doesn't have to go, I will. I didn't mean to . . ."

Thomas shook his head. "There's nothing to be sorry about, child. There's nothing happening now that wasn't going to happen anyway, and soon. If you hadn't given them the excuse they'd have found another, sooner or later. The thing now is to get you and Jed safe away." He returned his attention to Jed. "Hurry, son."

"Yes, Uncle." Jed fetched his emergency pack from its hiding place in the rafters.

"Now, John," his uncle continued, addressing Jed's father. "You and I have fought for forty years, but we are brothers, and this is our family, and our farm. Bishop Nemmer means to take it, and our women, and our children. We can fight each other, or them. Which is it going to be?"

His father was about to answer when the barn door banged open below, and a voice came up from below. "I heard something. Check up in the loft . . ."

A thrill of sudden fear shot through Jed, and Thomas held his fingers to his lips, drawing his bow. There were footsteps on the floor beneath them, and the ladder creaked as someone put their weight on it, climbing. A red-hooded head appeared at the top of the ladder, a surprised face started to shout, and Thomas put an arrow through the man's forehead. The body fell backward, hitting the floor below with a sickening crunch. Immediately his uncle advanced on the ladder opening, putting another arrow to the string. He saw something, drew and fired. There was a strangled cry and a thud.

"Thomas, you've murdered a man!" Jed's father's face was aghast.

"Two men, John, and there's ten more to be killed if we're to have any hope at all of keeping what's ours." Thomas was moving around the ladder, searching out threats. "I think there were only these two here, but the rest will miss them soon enough. Now, are you going to help me or not?"

Jed watched as emotions warred on his father's face, shock, anger, fear, and resolve. Finally John Fougere's jaw tightened, his eyes hard. "What must I do?"

"Get a bow. Quickly!" He turned to Kylie. "Can you ride?"

"I can. I'm not the best."

Thomas nodded. "Jed, you and Kylie get saddled. Take a mare and a stallion." He was already climbing down the ladder. John followed him, then Jed, then Kylie. "John, get a bow and watch the door."

At the bottom of the ladder Jed couldn't help but stare at the two bodies lying there, blood already pooling beneath them, its color so well matched with their cloaks that it created the illusion that they were melting. "Jed!" His uncle's voice was sharp. "Get saddled."

Jed nodded, and moved to obey, motioning for Kylie to help him. John Fougere had already grabbed a rabbit bow and a quiver of arrows from the rack, and was watching the door.

"They're coming down from the house, going through the toolshed." There was a sharp edge to John Fougere's voice.

"Can you see any of our hands?"

"No."

"We'll wait until they come for the barn, and take them in the open. Take the ones with bows first." John Fougere nodded, and his uncle followed Jed and Kylie into the stalls, where Jed had already led Scarlet and Tannis, the grey mare, out. Kylie was bringing saddles from the tack room. "Jed, you're going to ride aft, all the way aft, to the ocean. Don't take the roads, stay to the fields. When you get deep into the forest it'll be hard going with the horses, but keep them, you'll need them. Once you get to the ocean you're going to stay there."

Jed threw a saddle over Scarlet's back. "Uncle, what about—"

"What about nothing. You're looking after yourself now, and Kylie, and no one else. If something changes here I'll come and get you. I don't know how long Bishop Nemmer is going to last, I suspect a long time. If I don't come for you, it means there's nothing left here for you, so don't you dare come back." He turned to face Jed, looked him in the eye. "Promise me now, and swear it. Don't come back."

"How are we going to live?"

"You're going to hunt. You're good with a bow. Now promise me."

"I promise, Uncle."

"Good. Now, remember that promise when it gets hard, when you long to come home. Remember you gave me your word, as a man, and as a Fougere. Now hurry." Thomas was strapping tools to their saddles as he spoke, an ironwood shovel, an ax and a bucket to Kylie's, a coil of rope, two rabbit bows and a quiver, a second ax and a pair of heavy horse blankets to Jed's. He cinched the straps tight, then boosted Kylie up onto her mare. He turned to do the same for Jed, then paused to hug him, tight enough to take his breath away. "I love you, son. Take care."

"I love you too, Uncle."

Thomas paused, held Jed at arm's length for a long moment, a strange expression on his face. Finally he spoke. "I'm your father, Jed."

"What?"

"You're a man now, and there's no point to keeping secrets any longer. My brother can't sire children, but it's the eldest who inherits and the church will only grant title with his first child. We made an agreement, he and I and your mother, and Ruth too, when she came, so we could keep Riverview in the family."

"They're coming, Thomas." John Fougere's voice came from the main floor, tight with tension.

"Uncle . . . Father . . . tell me . . ."

"There's no time, and you have the truth that matters. Everything else you want to know comes from that. Now ride." Thomas pushed Jed up into the saddle. The stallion whinnied, sensing the urgency of the situation, and Thomas ran to open the main doors, but they opened before he got there, at the hand of a red-cloaked man on the other side. John's bowstring twanged, and his arrow took the man in the chest, throwing him backward. Thomas nocked an arrow and fired as well, aiming at someone beyond Jed's line of sight, and was rewarded with a gurgling scream. He nocked another arrow and jerked his head at Jed. "Ride!"

It was now or never. Jed dug his heels into the horse's sides, and the stallion broke into a trot and headed out the door. He dug his heels in harder and leaned forward, and his mount broke into a lumbering gallop. The suntube was painfully bright after the dim coolness of the barn, but through the glare he could see more redcloaks running toward the barn, spears upraised. One was unslinging his bow, and without conscious thought Jed pulled on the reins to head straight for him. He dug his heels in to keep the stallion in his reluctant gallop, and pulled the reins hard over when he tried to balk. They overran the archer at full speed, leaving him crushed and moaning behind them. He took a single glance back, to see if Kylie was following, and saw Thomas and John at the barn doors, bows in hand, firing at the inquisitors closing in on them. Another inquisitor, farther behind the others, also had a bow and was aiming directly at Jed. A second later the arrow was on its way, and Jed watch in half-paralyzed fascination as it got bigger, and then suddenly it was buzzing past his ear. He pulled the reins left and then right, trying to get established in some kind of evasive pattern. More arrows followed, but they fell wide, and then they were away. He risked a second glance back at the barn, saw John Fougere fall with an arrow through his neck. Three inquisitors were down too, and Thomas was nocking another arrow, but he was outnumbered and there were already half a dozen arrow shafts sticking out of the ground around him. As Jed watched an arrow took in him in the arm. Thomas released his own shaft, but his wound spoiled his aim and it went wide.

"NO!" Jed hauled back on the reins to turn Scarlet around. He couldn't leave his uncle . . . *My father* . . . Sensing their advantage, the inquisitors charged Thomas, spears upraised. Jed dug his heels in to get back into the fight, even as he realized it was too late to save Thomas, and the attempt would likely cost his own life.

"Jed! Look!" Kylie's shout made him swivel around in the saddle to see. She was pointing up the slope, where four mounted inquisitors were galloping down on them. Kylie pulled up and turned with him. He hesitated, saw Thomas go down beneath a hail of blows.

"Jed!"

Decision time, but there was only one decision that made sense anymore. "Just ride, Kylie, follow me," he yelled. He dug his heels in again and turned back the way they had been heading, away from the barn, from the farm, from his entire previous life. *Riverview has nothing left for me now.* There was no time to consider what that meant. The big stallion surged beneath him, now fully committed to his gallop and needing no further urging. Jed headed him for the upper field and the orchards. The fruit trees were spaced wide enough to let him ride through at a full gallop, but were dense enough that perhaps they could lose their pursuers. Kylie followed, but she wasn't the rider that Jed was, and he had to slow his pace so she could keep up. The red cloaks were gaining on them steadily, and he fumbled with the rabbit bow to get it loose. *I can't hit anything from horseback, but they won't know that.* A few arrows loosed backward might do a lot to discourage pursuit. He grabbed an arrow from the quiver, managed to get it on the string despite the jouncing, but before he could shoot the upper field fence loomed ahead. He urged his mount over it, glanced back, willing Kylie to do the same. He saw the fear in her face as she came up to the rails and he realized that she'd never jumped before. He held his breath, but her mare knew what she was doing and leapt the obstacle without breaking stride.

Top field was furrowed and planted, and the soft ground slowed them enough that they were only halfway through when the first inquisitor leapt the fence rail. He was a better rider than the others and a good hundred meters in front of them. The others came over seconds later, as awkward as Kylie, but they all made it. Again Jed twisted in his saddle to shoot at them, and again he didn't quite have time to get the shot off before he had to jump the fence at the far end of the field. Kylie made it over again, though her horse knocked the top rail and nearly stumbled and then they were among the fruit trees. Jed led them on a zigzag course, heading generally aftward and counterspinward, bent low over his horse's neck to avoid the branches whipping past. The world was a blur of green, and he glanced back to see if Kylie was still with him. His blood froze. She was there, and right behind her was the lead inquisitor. There was no way he could shoot at all with the branches in the way. In desperation he hauled back on the reins, slowing almost to a halt. Kylie thundered past, her knife in one hand and desperation in her face, overlaid with surprise at seeing him stop. "Keep riding!" he yelled, and then the inquisitor was coming by, his spear upraised. He thrust it at Jed as he went past, but his target was Kylie and he didn't slow down when he missed. Jed dug his heels in again and the stallion leapt forward. Keeping low he pulled back the bowstring, but he would have to be close to make the arrow count.

He glanced backward again to see if the other inquisitors were close, but they were nowhere to be seen. Lost in the orchard . . . *or riding around it to catch us on the other side.* There was nothing he could do about that, just ride on through the trees until they broke clear, and they'd deal with what they found when they found it. Ahead of him the man chasing Kylie had drawn almost level with her and was jabbing at her with his spear. Jed fired his arrow, though he knew he was too far and saw the shaft go wide. The inquisitor had figured out that a one-handed thrust wasn't going to give him enough leverage to stop Kylie and had switched to an overhand grip, thrusting down so the force of his attack would skewer her against her saddle. She was trying to fend him off with her knife hand, but the weapon was too short and the angle was wrong for her to strike. Jed fumbled for another arrow and caught a branch across the face as the price of his distraction. The lash cut skin and the sudden pain made him drop the arrow. He tasted blood in his mouth and spat it out, fumbled for a second arrow and nocked it. Ahead of him Kylie dodged left into the next lane of trees. It gained her momentary respite from her pursuer, but the inquisitor cut over at the next gap, and when he did he had closed enough distance to be able to grab her reins. Both horses skidded to a stop, and the inquisitor thrust his weapon at her again. It caught her in the chest, knocking her backward and off her mount, and then Jed was on them. The inquisitor turned to face him, spear upraised again, and Jed fired.

The arrow took the man full in the chest. He looked down, his expression transformed from anger to shock in an instant. He dropped his spear and put his hands down to pull the arrow from his chest. It came free with a horrible grating sound, and he screamed in pain. Jed ignored him, reining to a halt beside Kylie and leaping off his horse and kneeling beside her. She was gasping in pain, the front of her shirt soaked in bright red blood. He ripped it open, saw a nasty gash in her left breast, bleeding profusely. He stared dully at it for a moment, unsure what to do. *She's going to die right here and I can't fix it.*

"How does it look, Jed?" There was worry in her eyes and in her voice.

"It's fine," he lied. "There's a lot of blood, but it's just torn skin and flesh. You'll be fine." Behind him the injured inquisitor was moaning.

"Are you sure?"

"Oh yes." Under his breath he said a quick prayer that what he said would be really true. He got up and got the waterskin from his pack, brought it back to clean away the blood, frightened of what he might find. *But at least she'll feel I'm doing something for her.* She winced as he rinsed her wound. There was a lot of blood, but when it was washed off it looked like he was right after all, the spear hadn't penetrated her ribs. He went back to the pack, and emptied a small cloth bag full of dried lamb into a side pouch and returned with it. He folded the bag into a square and pressed it against her wound. "Here, hold this against it."

She did as she was told, and he suddenly realized he was looking at her naked breasts and looked away, unsure of whether it was right or not. She seemed to sense the change and re-arranged her bloody shirt to cover herself.

"Oh Jed, I got blood all over you."

"Blood brothers, remember?" He smiled at the memory and she smiled back. "Don't be worried about it."

She looked down at her injury and seemed about to speak, and then another voice interrupted. "For the love of God . . . help me . . ."

It was the injured inquisitor. He had tried to crawl away, but had collapsed face first in the grass, his breath coming in short, panting gasps. Sure now that Kylie was safe, Jed went over to him. *We should just leave him.* Instinctively he looked around to see if the others were close, but the orchard was still, bees buzzing peacefully from blossom to blossom, the three horses placidly cropping grass, as if they hadn't just been involved in a life-or-death chase. Jed looked at the man. *What do I do now.* The inquisitor was an enemy, personally responsible for Kylie's injury, and there was no doubt in Jed's mind he would have killed them if he could have, or worse taken them back to face the cross. He had not thought twice about leaving behind the man he'd ridden over with Scarlet. *And yet then I had no choice, and this one is right here, and still a human being, and God's creature.* The inquisitor had collapsed in the grass, and a slick, dark pool of blood was forming under him.

"Here, roll over." The man moaned, but complied, and Jed helped him to turn over to lie on his back. As he had with Kylie, Jed washed his wound, but where the spear had only torn her breast and skidded off her rib cage, Jed's arrow had penetrated the inquisitor's ribs on the right hand side. When he'd pulled the arrow out, he'd torn the ironwood arrowhead off the shaft, and Jed could see the head was still lodged inside. The inquisitor was bleeding profusely through the wound, and it was leaking air when he breathed as well. Jed tried to get the arrowhead out, but it was lodged too deeply, and the narrow base of it was too slippery with blood to get a grip on. Every time he tried the man screamed and moaned, which made Jed afraid he'd draw the attention of the others, who had to be somewhere close. *But I can't leave him like this.* Wincing against her pain, Kylie emptied another bag of dried lamb into the side pouch of the backpack. Jed folded it up and had the man press it against his injury. It quickly became saturated with blood, but it reduced the whistle of air through the wound when the man breathed.

"Thank you . . ." The inquisitor seemed only half-coherent, his eyelids fluttering open and shut. "I'm sorry . . . Please God, know I'm sorry." He didn't seem to be speaking to them, but then he reached up and took Kylie's hand, looked directly in her eyes. "I'm so sorry . . ."

"Don't worry, it's fine." Kylie kept holding his hand, and Jed lifted his head and folded one of the horse blankets under it so he would be more comfortable. He thought about replacing the improvised compress with another folded bag, but it was clear that there was nothing they could do to stanch the bleeding. It took the inquisitor a long time to die, though after a while he was mostly unconscious, only occasionally waking up enough to apologize once again, or ask for his mother. Jed found the experience unsettling. *It's strange that we were enemies. It's my arrow that's killed him, and here I am comforting him as he dies.* He felt that he should be the one apologizing, and silently and to himself, he did apologize. *Please God, forgive me for what I've done here today.* Eventually the man's breathing became imperceptible, and then sometime later it stopped. The change that came over him in death was subtle, but unmistakable. *Please God, take this man's soul to the planet of Heaven, so that we can meet him again come planetfall.* Jed felt tears well up in his eyes, and Kylie put her arm around him, and then he threw up. *I have become a murderer today.*

"You had to do it, Jed." Kylie hugged him, awkwardly because of her injury. "He would have killed us, or taken us for crucifixion."

"It's wrong to kill, it's a sin." Jed looked at the body, wondering if there was something, anything he could do that would somehow bring the man back to life.

"No." There was a sudden fierce intensity in Kylie's words. "It isn't wrong, not always. My father told me that nothing is always wrong and nothing is always right. It wasn't wrong this time."

"He didn't deserve to die . . ."

"He's a Believer, isn't he? If he's dead then he's in Heaven. Isn't that a good thing?"

"I don't know, I guess so." Jed took a deep breath. "I feel horrible."

"You saved me, that's not bad." She hugged him,

hugged him again, harder this time and heedless of the pain of her wounded breast. "We should go."

Jed nodded. "The others must have given up, or gone ahead. If they were searching the orchard they would have found us by now."

"Come on." Kylie climbed up into her saddle, wincing as her injured chest took the strain of mounting.

"Shouldn't we do something about him?"

"There's nothing more we can do."

Jed nodded again, but it didn't seem right to do nothing, so he took the horse blanket from beneath the man's head and covered him with it. Then he mounted his stallion, stirred the reins, and they rode off at a slow trot. He felt tired all of a sudden, and hungry too, but it seemed important to at least get out of Charity Parish. The immediate hue and cry seemed to have passed, but he knew from experience that the inquisitors wouldn't give up so easily. In the distance the midnight bell sounded. *I hadn't realized how much time was going by.* They stuck to the orchards and fields, jumping fences when they had to, and they pressed on through the night bells, eating the dried lamb from his side pouch. They were out of Charity and through Blessed before the breakfast bell, and the forest had closed in on them. Finally, exhausted, they stopped in a small clearing in an young grove of ironwood. They hobbled the horses and found a soft, sheltered spot in the tall grass. Jed put his rabbit bow and quiver down within easy reach, and they pulled the remaining horse blanket over themselves. Jed fell immediately into an exhausted and dreamless sleep. His last thought was of Kylie. When he had first met her they had been exactly the same height, but now she seemed so small, cuddled close against him beneath the blanket's warmth.

He awoke to the sound of voices, and feet crunching through the underbrush. The inquisitors were out in force, hunting for them. He froze, not daring to move. He and Kylie would be hard to find where they were, a searcher would almost have to step on them to find them, but he had taken no special pains to hide the horses, and if they were found it would concentrate the search right on top of them. The tree trunks and the tall surrounding brush of the forest had seemed dense enough at the time, but now it seemed scant protection at best. He held his breath as time dragged slowly past. Kylie moved in her sleep, and the slight rustling of the grass seemed to echo. The group hunting for them was large and persistent, and some of them came so close it seemed impossible they couldn't see the horses, who continued to graze placidly among the trees. Somehow no one did. He raised his head slowly, trying to see what was going on. Kylie awoke beside him, and he put a finger to her lips to warn her to silence. Her eyes grew big with fear, but she took her knife in her hand. The inquisitors weren't going to take her without a fight. Stealthily Jed reached for his bow, then drew an arrow from the quiver. Each click of wood on wood, every rustle of grass seemed magnified. He nocked the arrow and waited, heart pounding. The voices seemed to be all around them, searching steadily, methodically through the forest. He wondered for a moment why the inquisitors would bother to put all that effort into finding a pair of runaway children when they already had Riverview, but the question answered itself. *I killed two of them yesterday,*

*Father and Uncle killed more. They can't let that go unpunished.* If they did manage to catch him they would kill him for that, he realized, and they would do it publicly and painfully. Prophet Nemmer would want to send a message to anyone else who might want to defy his desires. The sounds seemed to go on forever, getting closer, then moving farther away but never quite leaving. Eventually the evening meal bell sounded in the distance and the voices started to grow distant. Jed allowed himself to relax, when there was a sudden shout.

"Brother Jacob, I found their horses."

There was the sound of running feet, and Jed traded a glance with Kylie. Her jaw was set in grim determination. Nobody was going to take her alive, to do to her what she'd watched done to so many other Crew. *And I should make the same vow.* He tightened his grip on his rabbit bow and slowly raised his head above the grass, until he could just barely see the horses heads, and the tops of red cowls, one, two, three, he couldn't tell if there were more. They were conversing among themselves, but he couldn't quite make out the words. It didn't matter. They would come soon, and then he and Kylie would sell their lives for the highest price they could extract. Jed could feel the pulse pounding in his ears. His hand shook on the half-drawn string of his rabbit bow, hard enough to make the arrow vibrate where it rested against the bow's curve. It took a conscious effort to ease the tension on the string enough to stop the trembling. He considered popping up and opening fire. The range was twenty meters, no more. He was sure to hit, and with surprise he could certainly take two before they could react, possibly three. *But what if there's more?* Underlying the thought was another one, deeper. *I don't want to kill again, not like this, not in cold blood.* What concerned him was not how hard it had been to kill but how easy. His reaction, as strong as it had been, didn't seem strong enough. *I'll shoot when they come for us, not before.*

They didn't come, which surprised Jed; they didn't even try. Instead they took the horses and moved off, their voices and footsteps fading into the distance. For a long time he and Kylie stayed frozen where they were. Eventually Kylie spoke, just a whisper close to his ear. "I think they're gone."

"They're probably waiting to ambush us."

She shook her head. "The evening meal bell went. They've gone to eat, and then to sleep. They won't be back before breakfast bell."

"That would be foolish, they had to know we were close."

"They are foolish, I watched them for months. They're foolish and lazy and cruel. They sleep when they should watch, and fight each other as much as the Crew. They've got the horses, they figure that's enough for now."

"Are you sure?"

"As sure as I can be. We should move, take advantage of the time."

Jed nodded. It was only when they got up that he realized the sudden enormity of the situation. All their equipment, their food, their water, everything was on the horses. All they had now was Kylie's knife, his bow and seven arrows, and the horse blanket. The forest would provide food, though in the drier aftward lands the fruit trees and berry bushes that populated the foot of the forewall and Charity Parish were less frequent. *And there's nothing to do but keep moving ahead.*

They did move ahead, for how long he didn't know, because at some point the peal of the hour bells grew faint and vanished. They moved until they were too exhausted to walk straight, and then slept again, on the ground beneath the horse blanket, to wake some timeless time later and walk again, keeping direction by the suntube overhead, leading them ever aftward. They found nothing to eat the next day, the ironwood and pine had given way to gnarled oak and beech trees, and the air was noticeably drier. They grew thirsty and moved spinward, hoping to intersect the next river over, but didn't reach it before they had to sleep again. Without hour bells to orient their time sense it seemed to make no difference how long they walked, or slept, or anything else, but Jed's throat was parched when he awoke, and he knew that they hadn't much time to find water, or they'd die. They marched on, slower now, and it was harder to fight their way through the brush and undergrowth. All thought of pursuit was long gone now, but the forest held its own dangers. In a clearing they came upon a clouded leopard, sunning itself on a hillock, its great golden eyes contemplating them with infinite calm, sizing them up. Jed put an arrow to his bow then, and Kylie gripped her knife as they carefully circumnavigated the clearing, on the side away from the animal. When they were halfway through it stood, and with a flick of its tail it vanished into the undergrowth. Whether it had eaten recently or decided they were too big to take they couldn't know. It was enough that it didn't attack. When they were safely away Jed allowed himself to breathe out. *But for every one I see there are ten that see us.*

They were nearly delirious when they reached the river, the name of which they had both learned in school and which neither could remember. They drank from a sandy spot by a clear pool in deep, glorious mouthfuls, heedless of soaking themselves. It was then that Jed understood that something fundamental had changed in him. When he finished drinking he caught sight of his reflection in the water, leaner certainly, and dirty, with his hair in disarray, but it was what was in his eyes that held him. They were hard, and strangely distant, and he felt as though he were looking at a stranger, and a dangerous one. It was a startling realization. *I don't feel that way on the inside.* But there was no denying that he *had* changed. *Perhaps that's what happens when you kill a man, perhaps that's God's mark upon my soul for my sin.* He slapped the water with his open palm to erase what he had seen and got up, looking away from the river as though it was to blame for what had happened. *But I can't erase what I've done.*

They slept again by the riverbank, in a thicket he hoped would be too dense for a leopard to bother with, and walked again when they awoke. They found a small clearing full of strawberry plants, and stopped long enough to strip it bare, but when they were done they were still hungry. Jed kept his bow at the ready, hoping for a rabbit or a chicken—or anything at all, but the game seemed to have vanished as well. There was nothing to do but walk, and it seemed then as if they had been walking forever, but when he looked up he could see the ring of the ocean coming closer overhead, blue against the aftwall. It looked like it was right on top of them, which meant they should already be there, and when it failed to materialize behind each copse of trees, over each rise in the ground, it began to seem more and more like it was a cruel joke, an optical illusion tempting them into a never-ending quest. *Thomas was my father, all those years and I never knew . . .* Walking gave too much time to think, and Riverview seemed like a lifetime away. As for the future, he couldn't even imagine what it held. Thomas had told him to go to the ocean, and so he was going because he had no plan of his own. *And what would he say if he knew I had no plan?*

And then they found it, over a low hill, immensely bigger than anything Jed had ever seen in his life. The ocean was a vast blue ring, ten endless kilometers from the beach to where it encircled the grey aftwall, with the suntube glinting from its waves. *There's so much water even the air smells wet.* Strange that the land should be so dry right next to the world's largest expanse of water. *But what matters is, we're here.* A few hundred meters to spinward the nameless river had built itself a network of channels out into the depth of the ocean, mud and sand carried downstream from above. Kylie came up beside him, and almost automatically he put his arm around her.

"We're here. We made it. We're safe, or as safe as we can be."

She nodded. "The inquisitors will never come here, never." She paused. "Now what?"

Jed swept an arm out over the water, "We'll never be thirsty again. What we need now is food, and shelter."

Kylie nodded. "Food first. Hey!" He jumped at her sudden exclamation, followed her excitedly pointing finger. "Look!"

She was pointing at the expanding ripples where a fish had jumped by the shore, a big fish by the look of it. They ran down to the water, found a wave-carved pool half-sheltered from the ocean itself, steep-banked and still, a tributary of the river, now nearly cut off by the shifting flow of silt and sand. In it was a school of circling fish, big ones. Without thought Jed drew his bow and nocked an arrow, then followed one of the fish until it came almost directly beneath him. He fired and the fish darted, transfixed by the arrow but still alive. He dived in after it, splashing and struggling. The other fish scattered but he emerged, triumphant and laughing, with the arrow in his hand with the fish still on it, flopping and gasping. He threw it up on the bank and clambered out.

"Do you think it's good to eat?"

Kylie nodded. "Father would fish sometimes. It's called a trout, I think. If we can cook it we can eat it." She looked at the fish dubiously. It didn't look like it would be very appetizing raw. "I don't see how we can cook it. Maybe dry it in the sun?"

"I can make fire, if we can find some ironwood."

"How?"

"With friction. I'll show you if we can find some." He frowned. "I wish I'd thought to cut a branch when we were back where there was a lot. I haven't seen any since we came to the river. I just wasn't thinking about cooking."

"Aren't your arrow shafts ironwood?"

Jed brightened immediately. "Perfect, and just the right shape too."

Minutes later she was watching in fascination as he gathered some driftwood, piled it into a cone shape. "Lend me your knife," he asked.

She did, and he split a small piece of driftwood and shaved it with the knife, made a groove to accept the arrow shaft, and minutes later he was demonstrating the use of a fire drill.

"That's amazing," she said, as the tiny ember brightened into a small flame.

"My uncle . . . I mean my father taught me."

Carefully he transferred his hard-won prize into the pile of twigs. They caught fire too, and soon they had a proper blaze going. Kylie split and gutted the trout with her knife, spit it on a stick and started it roasting. It sizzled appetizingly, and Jed suddenly remember how very, very hungry he was. *Funny how your body will forget that, until there's food.* They ate it with their fingers, washed down with gulps of fresh ocean water. After that they sat by the fire, side by side though there was really no need for the warmth.

"Do you think we'll ever be able to go back?" Jed asked.

Kylie shrugged. "I've got nothing to go back to now."

Jed pursed his lips. "No, I suppose you're right. Neither of us do." Jed remembered his uncle's parting words, and the promise he had given. *Nothing to go back to.* It was a simple statement of fact, somehow divorced from any of the emotions that should have gone with his losses. *The future is survival. I have to concentrate on that.* He pointed to the pool where they'd caught the trout. "We could get sticks, make a fence across that and catch all those fish at once."

"Later." She moved to sit beside him, leaned her head on his shoulder. "Let's just rest for now."

He put his arm around her. It was pleasant just to sit there, bellies full for the first time in days, their future suddenly transformed from simple survival into . . . Jed looked out over the ocean to the distant, looming aftwall, up to the suntube, back down to Kylie beside him, and felt the future transform itself. . . . into something more. *Not just survival, something different, something new* . . . She looked up at him, and he leaned forward and kissed her, on the lips for the first time. She kissed him back, shyly at first. . . . *into something beautiful.*

# Finale

*Mother is the name for God in the lips and hearts of little children*
—William Makepeace Thackeray

# SHIPYEAR 261

The old man leaned back in his chair and watched the waves coming into the beach, their rhythm ever constant and ever changing. Out on the water a fishing raft was heading in for dock, sail down and nets up, with its crew pulling steadily on the oars as it slid down the ocean's curve. Another raft was already there, with half its catch already gutted and drying under the suntube. Farther down the coast more wharfs and rafts crowded the shoreline, reaching out from the village like fingers from a hand. It was a tranquil scene, as long as you didn't have to haul fish yourself. *And thankfully I'm long past those days.* He turned his gaze up the beach, to where his granddaughters were trying to build a house with pieces of driftwood. "Come on, girls," he called. "Your mother will be waiting."

They didn't come at once, of course, and so he called them again, and then a third time, and finally they scampered over, six and eight, and to his eye already heartbreakingly beautiful.

"Tell us a story first, *deduchka*," asked the younger girl. She had the wavy dark hair that all fisherfolk had, grown long enough to fall in windblown ringlets to below her shoulders.

"Yes," put in her sister. She was an older, lankier version of her sibling, self-consciously carrying the responsibility of her extra years. "Tell us a good one."

The old man smiled down at the children. The story request was a gambit for more time on the beach, away from home and bedtime. "Well, sit yourself down, *devuchkas*, and I'll see what I can remember." They giggled, because they thought they were getting away with something, and he smiled because he'd called them early in anticipation of exactly that request, and they had just enough time for a good tale. He waited while they made themselves comfortable on the sand, then started. "Once upon a time, a very long time ago now," he began, and he told the old story of Noah, and how he'd built the *Ark* and filled it with two of every kind of animal. He elaborated at length on Noah's adventures, how he'd filled the ocean with his tears for his lost wife and made the land solid with his own clotted blood after he fought the leopard. He told the story of how one of Noah's daughters became the mother of the fisherfolk, and how the other became the mother of the forepeople, who had their own ways and customs quite different from their own, and then he told the story of how Noah flew to the suntube on wings made of beeswax and falcon feathers to set it alight, so there would always be day inside *Ark* even though it was night outside. "And when he was done, he sent it off to voyage through the night to the wonderful world of Heaven, and here we are today," he finished.

"What's night?" asked the younger girl.

"Night is just darkness, *devuchka*. Darkness that's darker than the inside of your eyelids, and with nothing in it, not even air."

She looked at him askance. "How can something have nothing in it?"

The old man shrugged and turned his palms up. "I don't know. I can only tell you what the story says."

"It's only just a story," said the older girl. "It isn't *true*, is it, *deduchka*?"

"Stories like that are always sort of true, and sort of not true."

"So are we going to Heaven then?" persisted the younger child.

"Well, only very slowly. *We* won't get there. Your children's children's children might."

"Don't be silly," said the older girl authoritatively. "We aren't *really* going anywhere." She swept her arms in circles to encompass her world. "If we were you could see us moving."

"Oh we're going somewhere, all right." The old man stood up and offered his hands to his granddaughters. "We're going inside for bedtime."

They protested only mildly, and he took them up the beach to the house, where their mother was waiting. She scooted them inside and closed the door so she could feed them and scrub them and send them to bed. The old man looked out the open window to the ocean, where the first fishing raft had made it back to the dock, with a good catch and their father, and all around them their world sailed silently on.

The Following is an excerpt from:

# STORM FROM THE SHADOWS

## DAVID WEBER

Available from Baen Books
March 2009
hardcover

# ✧ CHAPTER ONE

"Talk to me, John!"

Rear Admiral Michelle Henke's husky contralto came sharp and crisp as the information on her repeater tactical display shifted catastrophically.

"It's still coming in from the Flag, Ma'am," Commander Oliver Manfredi, Battlecruiser Squadron Eighty-One's golden-haired chief of staff, replied for the squadron's operations officer, Lieutenant Commander John Stackpole. Manfredi was standing behind Stackpole, watching the ops section's more detailed displays, and he had considerably more attention to spare for updates at the moment than Stackpole did. "I'm not sure, but it looks—"

Manfredi broke off, and his jaw clenched. Then his nostrils flared and he squeezed Stackpole's shoulder before he turned his head to look at his admiral.

"It would appear the Peeps have taken Her Grace's lessons to heart, Ma'am," he said grimly. "They've arranged a Sidemore all their own for us."

Michelle looked at him for a moment, and her expression tightened.

"Oliver's right, Ma'am," Stackpole said, looking up from his own display as the changing light codes finally restabilized. "They've got us boxed."

"How bad is it?" she asked.

"They've sent in three separate groups," Stackpole replied. "One dead astern of us, one at polar north, and one at polar south. The Flag is designating the in-system force we already knew about as Bogey One. The task group to system north is Bogey Two; the one to system south is Bogey Three; and the one directly astern is Bogey Four. Our velocity relative to Bogey Four is just over twenty-two thousand kilometers per second, but range is less than thirty-one million klicks."

"Understood."

Michelle looked back at her own, smaller display. At the moment, it was configured to show the entire Solon System, which meant, by definition, that it was nowhere as detailed as Stackpole's. There wasn't room for that on a plot small enough to deploy from a command chair—not when it was displaying the volume of something the size of a star system, at any rate. But it was more than detailed enough to confirm what Stackpole had just told her. The Peeps had just duplicated exactly what had happened to *them* at the Battle of Sidemore, and managed to do it on a more sophisticated scale, to boot.

*Honor's been warning us all that these Peeps aren't exactly stupid*, she reflected. *Not that any of us should've needed reminding after what they did to us in Thunderbolt! But I could wish that just this once she'd been wrong.*

Her lips twitched in a humorless smile, but she felt herself coming back on balance mentally, and her brain whirred as tactical possibilities and decision trees spilled through it. Not that the primary responsibility was hers. No, that weight rested on the shoulders of her best friend, and despite herself, Michelle was grateful that it *wasn't* hers . . . a fact which made her feel more than a little guilty.

One thing was painfully evident. Eighth Fleet's entire

operational strategy for the last three and a half months had been dedicated to convincing the numerically superior navy of the Republic of Haven to redeploy, adopt a more defensive stance while the desperately off-balance Manticoran Alliance got its own feet back under it. Judging by the ambush into which the task force had sailed, that strategy was obviously succeeding. In fact, it looked like it was succeeding entirely too well.

*It was so much easier when we could keep their command teams pruned back . . . or count on State Security to do it for us. Unfortunately, Saint-Just's not around anymore to shoot any admiral whose initiative might make her dangerous to the régime, is he?* Her lips twitched with bitterly sardonic amusement as she recalled the relief with which Manticore's pundits, as well as the woman in the street, had greeted the news of the Committee of Public Safety's final overthrow. *Maybe we were just a little premature about that,* she thought, *since it means that this time around, we don't have anywhere near the same edge in operational experience, and it shows.* This *batch of Peeps actually knows what it's doing. Damn it.*

"Course change from the Flag, Ma'am," Lieutenant Commander Braga, her staff astrogator announced. "Two-niner-three, zero-zero-five, six-point-zero-one KPS squared."

"Understood," Michelle repeated, and nodded approvingly as the new vector projection stretched itself across her plot and she recognized Honor's intention. The task force was breaking to system south at its maximum acceleration on a course that would take it as far away from Bogey Two as possible while maintaining at least the current separation from Bogey Four. Their new course would still take them deep into the missile envelope of Bogey One, the detachment covering the planet Arthur, whose orbital infrastructure had been the task force's original target. But Bogey One consisted of only two superdreadnoughts and seven battle-cruisers, supported by less than two hundred LACs, and from their emissions signatures and maneuvers, Bogey One's wallers were pre-pod designs. Compared to the six obviously modern superdreadnoughts and two LAC carriers in each of the three ambush forces, Bogey One's threat was minimal. Even if all nine of its hyper-capable combatants had heavy pod loads on tow, its older ships would lack the fire control to pose a significant threat to Task Force Eighty-Two's missile defenses. Under the circumstances, it was the same option Michelle would have chosen if she'd been in Honor's shoes.

*I wonder if they've been able to ID her flagship?* Michelle wondered. *It wouldn't have been all that hard, given the news coverage and her "negotiations" in Hera.*

That, too, of course, had been part of the strategy. Putting Admiral Lady Dame Honor Harrington, Duchess and Steadholder Harrington, in command of Eighth Fleet had been a carefully calculated decision on the Admiralty's part. In Michelle's opinion, Honor was obviously the best person for the command anyway, but the appointment had been made in a glare of publicity for the express purpose of letting the Republic of Haven know that "the Salamander" was the person who'd been chosen to systematically demolish its rear-area industry.

*One way to make sure they honored the threat*, Michelle thought wryly as the task force came to its new heading in obedience to the commands emanating from HMS *Imperator*, Honor's SD(P) flagship. *After all, she's been their personal nightmare ever since Basilisk station! But I wonder if they got a fingerprint on* Imperator *at Hera or Augusta? Probably—they knew which ship she was aboard at Hera, at least. Which probably means they know who it is they've just mousetrapped, too.*

Michelle grimaced at the thought. It was unlikely any

Havenite flag officer would have required extra incentive to trash the task force if she could, especially after Eighth Fleet's unbroken string of victories. But knowing whose command they were about to hammer certainly didn't make them any *less* eager to drive home their attack.

"Missile defense Plan Romeo, Ma'am," Stackpole said. "Formation Charlie."

"Defense only?" Michelle asked. "No orders to roll pods?"

"No, Ma'am. Not yet."

"Thank you."

Michelle's frown deepened thoughtfully. Her own battlecruisers' pods were loaded with Mark 16 dual-drive missiles. That gave her far more missiles per pod, but Mark 16s were both smaller, with lighter laser heads, and shorter-legged than a ship of the wall's multidrive missiles like the Mark 23s aboard Honor's superdreadnoughts. They would have been forced to adopt an attack profile with a lengthy ballistic flight, and the biggest tactical weakness of a pod battlecruiser design was that it simply couldn't carry as many pods as a true capital ship like *Imperator*. It made sense not to waste BCS 81's limited ammunition supply at a range so extended as to guarantee a low percentage of hits, but in Honor's place, Michelle would have been sorely tempted to throw at least a few salvos of all-up MDMs from her two superdreadnoughts back into Bogey Four's face, if only to keep them honest. On the other hand . . .

*Well, she's the four-star admiral, not me. And I suppose*—she smiled again at the tartness of her own mental tone—*that she's demonstrated at least a* modicum *of tactical insight from time to time*.

"Missile separation!" Stackpole announced suddenly. "Multiple missile separations! Estimate eleven hundred—one-one-zero-zero—inbound. Time to attack range seven minutes!"

✿ ✿ ✿

Each of the six Havenite superdreadnoughts in the group which had been designated Bogey Four could roll six pods simultaneously, one pattern every twelve seconds, and each pod contained ten missiles. Given the fact that Havenite fire control systems remained inferior to Manticoran ones, accuracy was going to be poor, to say the least. Which was why the admiral commanding that group had opted to stack six full patterns from each superdreadnought, programmed for staggered launch to bring all of their missiles simultaneously in on their targets. It took seventy-two seconds to deploy them, but then just over a thousand MDMs hurled themselves after Task force Eighty-Two.

Seventy-two seconds after that, a second, equally massive salvo launched. Then a third. A fourth. In the space of thirteen minutes, the Havenites fired just under twelve thousand missiles—almost a third of Bogey Four's total missile loadout—at the task force's twenty starships.

As little as three or four T-years ago, any one of those avalanches of fire would have been lethally effective against so few targets, and Michelle felt her stomach muscles tightening as the tempest swept towards her. But this *wasn't* three or four T-years ago. The Royal Manticoran Navy's missile defense doctrine was in a constant state of evolution, continually revised in the face of new threats and the opportunities of new technology, and it had been vastly improved even in the six months since the Battle of Marsh. The *Katana*-class LACs deployed to cover the task force maneuvered to bring their missile launchers to bear on the incoming fire, but their counter-missiles weren't required yet. Not in an era when the Royal Navy had developed Keyhole and the Mark 31 counter-missile.

Each superdreadnought and battlecruiser deployed two Keyhole control platforms, one through each sidewall, and each of those platforms had sufficient telemetry links to control the fire of *all* of its mother ship's counter-missile launchers simultaneously. Equally important, they allowed the task force's units to roll sideways in space, interposing the impenetrable shields of their impeller wedges against the most dangerous threat axes without compromising their defensive fire control in the least. Each Keyhole also served as a highly sophisticated electronics warfare platform, liberally provided with its own close-in point defense clusters, as well. And as an added bonus, rolling ship gave the platforms sufficient "vertical" separation to see past the interference generated by the impeller wedges of subsequent counter-missile salvos, which made it possible to fire those salvos at far tighter intervals than anyone had ever been able to manage before.

The Havenites hadn't made sufficient allowance for how badly Keyhole's EW capability was going to affect their attack missiles' accuracy. Worse, they'd anticipated no more than five CM launches against each of their salvos, and since they'd anticipated facing only the limited fire control arcs of their fleeing targets' after hammerheads, they'd allowed for an average of only ten counter-missiles per ship per launch. Their fire plans had been based on the assumption that they would face somewhere around a thousand ship-launched counter-missiles, and perhaps another thousand or so Mark 31-based Vipers from the *Katanas*.

Michelle Henke had no way of knowing what the enemy's tactical assumptions might have been, but she was reasonably certain they hadn't expected to see over *seven* thousand counter-missiles from Honor's starships, alone.

The second attack salvo followed the first one into oblivion well short of the inner defensive perimeter. So did the third. And the fourth.

"They've ceased fire, Ma'am," Stackpole announced.

"I'm not surprised," Michelle murmured. Indeed, if anything surprised her, it was that the Havenites hadn't ceased fire even sooner. On the other hand, maybe she wasn't being fair to her opponents. It had taken seven minutes for the first salvo to enter engagement range, long enough for six more salvos to be launched on its heels. And the effectiveness of the task force's defenses had surpassed even BuWeaps' estimates. If it had come as as big a surprise to the bad guys as she rather expected it had, it was probably unreasonable to expect the other side to realize instantly just how hard to penetrate that defensive wall was. And the only way they had to measure its toughness was to actually hammer at it with their missiles, of course. Still, she liked to think that it wouldn't have taken a full additional six minutes for *her* to figure out she was throwing good money after bad.

*On the* other *other hand, there* are *those other nine salvos still on the way*, she reminded herself. *Let's not get too carried away with our own self-confidence, Mike! The last few waves will have had at least a little time to adjust to our EW, won't they? And it only takes one leaker in the wrong place to knock out an alpha node . . . or even some overly optimistic rear admiral's command deck*.

"What do you think they're going to try next, Ma'am?" Manfredi asked as the fifth, sixth, and seventh salvos vanished equally ineffectually.

"Well, they've had a chance now to get a feel for just how tough our new doctrine really is," she replied, leaning back in her command chair, eyes still on her tactical repeater. "If it were me over there, I'd be thinking in terms of a really massive salvo. Something big enough to swamp our defenses by literally running us out of control channels for the CMs, no matter how many of them we have."

"But they couldn't possibly control something that big, either," Manfredi protested.

"We don't *think* they could control something that big," Michelle corrected almost absently, watching the eighth and ninth missile waves being wiped away. "Mind you, I think you're probably right, but we don't have any way of knowing that . . . yet. We could be wrong.

"*Imperator* and *Intolerant* are rolling pods, Ma'am," Stackpole reported.

"Sounds like Her Grace's come to the same conclusion you have, Ma'am," Manfredi observed. "That should be one way to keep them from stacking *too* big a salvo to throw at us!"

"Maybe," Michelle replied.

The great weakness of missile pods was their vulnerability to proximity kills once they were deployed and outside their mother ship's passive defenses, and Manfredi had a point that incoming Manticoran missiles might well be able to wreak havoc on the Havenite pods. On the other hand, they'd already had time to stack quite a few of them, and it would take Honor's missiles almost eight more minutes to reach their targets across the steadily opening range between the task force and Bogey Four. But at least they were on notice that those missiles were coming.

The Havenite commander didn't wait for the task force's fire to reach him. In fact, he fired at almost the same instant Honor's first salvo launched against *him*, and whereas Task force Eighty-Two had fired just under three hundred missiles at him, he fired the next best thing to eleven thousand in reply.

"Damn," Commander Manfredi said almost mildly as the enemy returned more than thirty-six missiles for each one TF 82 had just fired at him, then shook his head and glanced at Michelle. "Under normal circumstances, Ma'am, it's reassuring to work for a boss who's good at reading the other side's mind. Just this once, though, I really wish you'd been wrong."

"You and I, both," Michelle replied. She studied the data sidebars for several seconds, then turned her command chair to face Stackpole.

"Is it my imagination, John, or does their fire control seem just a bit better than it ought to be?"

"I'm afraid you're not imagining things, Ma'am," Stackpole replied grimly. "It's a single salvo, all right, and it's going to come in as a single wave. But they've divided it into several 'clumps,' and the clumps appear to be under tighter control than *I* would have anticipated out of them. If I had to guess, I'd say they've spread them to clear their telemetry paths to each clump and they're using rotating control links, jumping back and forth between each group."

"They'd need a lot more bandwidth than they've shown so far," Manfredi said. It wasn't a disagreement with Stackpole, only thoughtful, and Michelle shrugged.

"Probably," she said. "But maybe not, too. We don't know enough about what they're doing to decide that."

"Without it, they're going to be running the risk of completely dropping control linkages in mid-flight," Manfredi pointed out.

"Probably," Michelle repeated. This was no time, she decided, to mention certain recent missile fire control developments Sonja Hemphill and BuWeaps were pursuing. Besides, Manfredi was right. "On the other hand," she continued, "this salvo is ten times the size of anything they've tried before, isn't it? Even if they dropped twenty-five or thirty percent of them, it would still be a hell of a lot heavier weight of fire."

"Yes, Ma'am," Manfredi agreed, and smiled crookedly.

"More of those bad solutions you were talking about before."

"Exactly," Michelle said grimly as the oncoming torrent of Havenite missiles swept into the outermost counter-missile zone.

"It looks like they've decided to target us this time, too, Ma'am," Stackpole said, and she nodded.

TF 82's opening missile salvo reached its target first.

Unlike the Havenites, Duchess Harrington had opted to concentrate all of her fire on a single target, and Bogey Four's missile defenses opened fire as the Manticoran MDMs swept towards it. The Manticoran electronic warfare platforms scattered among the attack missiles carried far more effective penetration aids than anything the Republic of Haven had, but Haven's defenses had improved even more radically than Manticore's since the last war. They remained substantially inferior to the Star Kingdom's in absolute terms, but the relative improvement was still enormous, and the gap between TF 82's performance and what *they* could achieve was far narrower than it once would have been. Shannon Foraker's "layered defense" couldn't count on the same sort of accuracy and technological sophistication Manticore could produce, so it depended on sheer weight of fire, instead. And an incredible storm front of counter-missiles raced to meet the threat, fired from the starships' escorting LACs, as well as from the superdreadnoughts themselves. There was so much wedge interference that anything resembling precise control of all that defensive fire was impossible, but with so many counter-missiles in space simultaneously, some of them simply *had* to hit something.

They did. In fact, they hit quite a few "somethings." Of the two hundred and eighty-eight MDMs *Intolerant* and *Imperator* had fired at RHNS *Conquete*, the counter-missiles killed a hundred and thirty-two, and then it was the laser clusters' turn. Each of those clusters had time for only a single shot each, given the missiles' closing speed. At sixty-two percent of light-speed, it took barely half a second from the instant they entered the laser clusters' range for the Manticoran laser heads to reach their own attack range of *Conquete*. But there were literally thousands of those clusters aboard the superdreadnoughts and their escorting *Cimeterre*-class light attack craft.

Despite everything the superior Manticoran EW could do, Shannon Foraker's defensive doctrine worked. Only eight of TF 82's missiles survived to attack their target. Two of them detonated late, wasting their power on the roof of *Conquete*'s impenetrable impeller wedge. The other six detonated between fifteen and twenty thousand kilometers off the ship's port bow, and massive bomb-pumped lasers punched brutally through her sidewall.

Alarms screamed aboard the Havenite ship as armor shattered, weapons—and the men and women who manned them—were wiped out of existence, and atmosphere streamed from *Conquete*'s lacerated flanks. But superdreadnoughts were designed to survive precisely that kind of damage, and the big ship didn't even falter. She maintained her position in Bogey Four's defensive formation, and her counter-missile launchers were already firing against TF 82's second salvo.

"It looks like we got at least a few through, Ma'am," Stackpole reported, his eyes intent as the studied the reports coming back from the FTL Ghost Rider reconnaissance platforms.

"Good," Michelle replied. Of course, "a few" hits probably hadn't done a lot more than scratch their target's paint, but she could always hope, and some damage was a hell of a lot better than no damage at all. Unfortunately . . .

"And here comes their reply," Manfredi muttered. Which, Michelle thought, was something of an . . . understatement.

Six hundred of the Havenite MDMs had simply become lost and wandered away, demonstrating the validity of Manfredi's prediction about dropped control links. But that was less than six percent of the total . . . which demonstrated the accuracy of Michelle's counterpoint.

The task force's counter-missiles killed almost nine thousand of the missiles which *didn't* get lost, and the last-ditch fire of the task force's laser clusters and the *Katana*-class LACs killed nine hundred more.

Which left "only" three hundred and seventy-two.

Five of them attacked *Ajax*.

Captain Diego Mikhailovic rolled ship, twisting his command further over onto her side relative to the incoming fire, fighting to interpose the defensive barrier of his wedge, and the sensor reach of his Keyhole platforms gave him a marked maneuver advantage, as well as improving his fire control. He could see threats more clearly and from a greater range, which gave him more time to react to them, and most of the incoming X-ray lasers wasted themselves against the floor of his wedge. One of the attacking missiles managed to avoid that fate, however. It swept past *Ajax* and detonated less than five thousand kilometers from her port sidewall.

The battlecruiser twitched as two of the missile's lasers blasted through that sidewall. By the nature of things, battlecruiser armor was far thinner than superdreadnoughts could carry, and Havenite laser heads were heavier than matching Manticoran weapons as a deliberate compensation for their lower base accuracy. Battle steel shattered and alarms howled. Patches of ominous crimson appeared on the damage control schematics, yet given the original size of that mighty salvo, *Ajax*'s actual damage was remarkably light.

"Two hits, Ma'am," Stackpole announced. "We've lost Graser Five and a couple of point defense clusters, and Medical reports seven wounded."

Michelle nodded. She hoped none of those seven crewmen were badly wounded. No one ever liked to take casualties, but at the same time, only seven—none of them fatal, so far at least—was an almost incredibly light loss rate.

"The rest of the squadron?" she asked sharply.

"Not a scratch, Ma'am!" Manfredi replied jubilantly from his own command station, and Michelle felt herself beginning to smile. But then—

"Multiple hits on both SDs," Stackpole reported in a much grimmer voice, and Michelle's smile died stillborn. "*Imperator*'s lost two or three grasers, but she's essentially intact."

"And *Intolerant*?" Michelle demanded harshly when the ops officer paused.

"Not good," Manfredi replied as the information scrolled across his display from the task force data net. "She must have taken two or three dozen hits . . . and at least one of them blew straight into the missile core. She's got heavy casualties, Ma'am, including Admiral Morowitz and most of his staff. And it looks like all of her pod rails are down."

"The Flag is terminating the missile engagement, Ma'am," Stackpole said quietly.

He looked up from his display to meet her eyes, and she nodded in bitter understanding. The task force's sustainable long-range firepower had just been cut in half. Not even Manticoran fire control was going to accomplish much at the next best thing to two light-minutes with salvoes the size a single SD(P) could throw, and Honor wasn't going to waste ammunition trying to do the impossible.

*Which, unfortunately, leaves the question of just what we are going to do wide open, doesn't it?* she thought.

✿ ✿ ✿

Several minutes passed, and Michelle listened to the background flow of clipped, professional voices as her staff officers and their assistants continued refining their assessment of what had just happened. It wasn't getting much better, she reflected, watching the data bars shift as more detailed damage reports flowed in.

As Manfredi had already reported, her own squadron—aside from her flagship—had suffered no damage at all, but it was beginning to look as if Stackpole's initial assessment of HMS *Intolerant*'s damages had actually been optimistic.

"Admiral," Lieutenant Kaminski said suddenly. Michelle turned towards her staff communications officer, one eyebrow raised. "Duchess Harrington wants to speak to you," he said.

"Put her through," Michelle said quickly, and turned back to her own small com screen. A familiar, almond-eyed face appeared upon it almost instantly.

"Mike," Honor Alexander-Harrington began without preamble, her crisp, Sphinxian accent only a shade more pronounced than usual, "*Intolerant*'s in trouble. Her missile defenses are way below par, and we're headed into the planetary pods' envelope. I know *Ajax*'s taken a few licks of her own, but I want your squadron moved out on our flank. I need to interpose your point defense between *Intolerant* and Arthur. Are you in shape for that?"

"Of course we are." Henke nodded vigorously. Putting something as fragile as a battlecruiser between a wounded superdreadnought and a planet surrounded by missile pods wasn't something to be approached lightly. On the other hand, screening ships of the wall was one of the functions battlecruisers had been designed to fulfill, and at least, given the relative dearth of missile pods their scouts had reported in Arthur orbit, they wouldn't be looking at another missile hurricane like the one which had just roared through the task force.

"*Ajax*'s the only one who's been kissed," Michelle continued, "and our damage is all pretty much superficial. None of it'll have any effect on our missile defense."

"Good! Andrea and I will shift the LACs as well, but they've expended a lot of CMs." Honor shook her head. "I didn't think they could stack that many pods without completely saturating their own fire control. It looks like we're going to have to rethink a few things."

"That's the nature of the beast, isn't it?" Michelle responded with a shrug. "We live and learn."

"Those of us fortunate enough to survive," Honor agreed, a bit grimly. "All right, Mike. Get your people moving. Clear."

"Clear," Michelle acknowledged, then turned her chair to face Stackpole and Braga. "You heard the lady," she said. "Let's get them moving."

BCS 81 moved out on Task force Eighty-Two's flank as the Manticoran force continued accelerating steadily away from its pursuers. The final damage reports came in, and Michelle grimaced as she considered how the task force's commanding officer was undoubtedly feeling about those reports. She'd known Honor Harrington since Honor had been a tall, skinny first-form midshipwoman at Saganami Island. It wasn't Honor's fault the Havenites had managed to mousetrap her command, but that wasn't going to matter. Not to Honor Harrington. Those were her ships which had been damaged, her people who had been killed, and at this moment, Michelle Henke knew, she was feeling the hits her task force had taken as if every one of them had landed directly on her.

*No, that isn't what she's feeling*, Michelle told herself. *What she's doing right now is wishing that every one of them* had *landed on her, and she's not going to forgive herself for walking into this. Not for a long time, if I know her. But she's not going to let it affect her decisions, either.*

She shook her head. It was a pity Honor was so much better at forgiving her subordinates for disasters she knew perfectly well weren't their fault than she was at forgiving herself. Unfortunately, it was too late to change her now.

*And, truth to tell, I don't think any of us would want to go screwing around trying to change her,* Michelle thought wryly.

"We'll be entering the estimated range of Arthur's pods in another thirty seconds, Ma'am," Stackpole said quietly, breaking in on her thoughts.

"Thank you." Michelle shook herself, then settled herself more solidly into her command chair.

"Stand by missile defense," she said.

The seconds trickled by, and then—

"Missile launch!" Stackpole announced. "Multiple missile launches, *multiple sources!*"

His voice sharpened with the last two words, and Michelle's head snapped around.

"Estimate seventeen thousand, Ma'am!"

"Repeat that!" Michelle snapped, certain for an instant that she must have misunderstood him somehow.

"CIC says seventeen thousand, Ma'am," Stackpole told her harshly, turning to look at her. "Time to attack range, seven minutes."

Michelle stared at him while her mind tried to grapple with the impossible numbers. The remote arrays deployed by the task force's pre-attack scout ships had detected barely four hundred pods in orbit around Arthur. That should have meant a maximum of only *four* thousand missiles, so where the hell—?

"We've got at least thirteen thousand coming in from

Bogey One," Stackpole said, as if he'd just read her mind. His tone was more than a little incredulous, and her own eyes widened in shock. That was even more preposterous. Two superdreadnoughts and seven battlecruisers couldn't possibly have the fire control for that many missiles, even if they'd all been pod designs!

"How could—?" someone began.

"Those aren't *battlecruisers*," Oliver Manfredi said suddenly. "They're frigging *minelayers!*"

Michelle understood him instantly, and her mouth tightened in agreement. Just like the Royal Manticoran Navy, the Republic of Haven built its fast minelayers on battlecruiser hulls. And Manfredi was undoubtedly correct. Instead of normal loads of mines, those ships had been stuffed to the deckhead with missile pods. The whole time they'd been sitting there, watching the task force flee away from Bogey Four and directly towards *them*, they'd been rolling those pods, stacking them into the horrendous salvo which had just come screaming straight at TF 82.

"Well," she said, hearing the harshness in her own voice, "now we understand how they did it. Which still leaves us with the little problem of what we do *about* it. Execute Hotel, John!"

"Defense Plan Hotel, aye, Ma'am," Stackpole acknowledged, and orders began to stream out from HMS *Ajax* to the rest of her squadron.

Michelle watched her plot. There wasn't time for her to adjust her formation significantly, but she'd already set up for Hotel, even though it had seemed unlikely the Havenites' fire could be heavy enough to require it. Her ships' primary responsibility was to protect *Intolerant*. Looking out for themselves came fairly high on their list of priorities as well, of course, but the superdreadnought represented more combat power—and almost as much total tonnage—as her entire squadron combined. That was why Missile Defense Plan Hotel had stacked her battlecruisers vertically in space, like a mobile wall between the planet Arthur and *Intolerant*. They were perfectly placed to intercept the incoming fire . . . which, unfortunately, meant that they were completely exposed *to* that fire, as well.

"Signal from the Flag, Ma'am," Stackpole said suddenly. "Fire Plan Gamma."

"Acknowledged. Execute Fire Plan Gamma," Michelle said tersely.

"Aye, aye, Ma'am. Executing Fire Plan Gamma," Stackpole said, and Battlecruiser Squadron Eighty-One began to roll pods at last.

It wasn't going to be much of a response compared to the amount of fire coming at the task force, but Michelle felt her lips drawing back from her teeth in satisfaction anyway. The gamma sequence Honor and her tactical staff had worked out months ago was designed to coordinate the battlecruisers' shorter-legged Mark 16s with the superdreadnoughts' MDMs. It would take a Mark 16 over thirteen minutes to reach Bogey One, as compared to the *seven* minutes one of *Imperator*'s Mark 23s would require. Both missiles used fusion-powered impeller drives, but there was no physical way to squeeze three complete drives into the smaller missile's tighter dimensions, which meant it simply could not accelerate as long as its bigger brother.

So, under Fire Plan Gamma *Imperator*'s first half-dozen patterns of pod-launched Mark 23s' drive settings had been stepped down to match those of the *Agamemnons*' less capable missiles. It let the task force put six salvos of almost three hundred mixed Mark 16 and Mark 23 missiles each into space before the superdreadnought began firing hundred-and-twenty-bird salvos at the Mark 23's maximum power settings.

*All of which is very fine*, Michelle thought grimly, watching the icons of the attack missiles go streaking away from the task force. *Unfortunately, it doesn't do much about the birds they've already launched.*

As if to punctuate her thought, *Ajax* began to quiver with the sharp vibration of outgoing waves of *counter*-missiles as her launchers went to sustained rapid fire.

The Grayson-designed *Katana*-class LACs were firing, as well, sending their own counter-missiles screaming to meet the attack, but no one in her worst nightmare had ever envisioned facing a single salvo this massive.

"It's coming through, Ma'am," Manfredi said quietly.

She looked back up from her plot, and her lips tightened as she saw him standing beside her command chair once more. Given what was headed towards them at the moment, he really ought to have been back in the shock frame and protective armored shell of his own chair. *And he damned well knows it, too*, she thought in familiar, sharp-edged irritation. But he'd always been a roamer, and she'd finally given up yelling at him for it. He was one of those people who *needed* to move around to keep their brains running at the maximum possible RPM. Now his voice was too low pitched for anyone else to have heard as he gazed down into her repeater plot with her, but his eyes were bleak.

"Of course it is," she replied, equally quietly. The task force simply didn't have the firepower to stop that many missiles in the time available to it.

"How the *hell* are they managing to control that many birds?" Manfredi continued, never looking away from the plot. "Look at that pattern. Those aren't blind-fired shots; they're under tight control, for now at least. So where in hell did they find that many control channels?"

"Don't have a clue," Michelle admitted, her tone almost

absent as she watched the defenders' fire ripping huge holes in the cloud of incoming missiles. "I think we'd better figure it out, though. Don't you?"

"You've got that right, Ma'am," he agreed with a mirthless smile.

No one in Task force Eighty-Two—or anyone in the rest of the Royal Manticoran Navy, for that matter—had ever heard of the control system Shannon Foraker had dubbed "Moriarty" after a pre-space fictional character. If they had, and if they'd understood the reference, they probably would have agreed that it was appropriate, however.

One thing of which no one would ever be able to accuse Foraker was thinking small. Faced with the problem of controlling a big enough missile salvo to break through the steadily improving Manticoran missile defenses, she'd been forced to accept that Havenite ships of the wall, even the latest podnoughts, simply lacked the necessary fire control channels. So, she'd set out to solve the problem. Unable to match the technological capability to shoehorn the control systems she needed into something like Manticore's Keyhole, she'd simply accepted that she had to build something bigger. *Much* bigger. And while she'd been at it, she'd decided, she might as well figure out how to integrate that "something bigger" into an entire star system's defenses.

Moriarty was the answer she'd come up with. It consisted of remotely deployed platforms which existed for the sole purpose of providing telemetry relays and control channels. They were distributed throughout the entire volume of space inside Solon's hyper limit, and every one of them reported to a single control station which was about the size of a heavy cruiser . . . and contained nothing except the very best fire control computers and software the Republic of Haven could build.

She couldn't do anything about the lightspeed limitations of the control channels themselves, but she'd finally found a way to provide enough of those channels to handle truly massive salvos. In fact, although TF 82 had no way of knowing it, the wave of missiles coming at it was less than half of Moriarty's maximum capacity.

Of course, even if the task force's tactical officers had known that, they might have felt less than completely grateful, given the weight of fire which *was* coming at them.

Michelle never knew how many of the incoming missiles were destroyed short of their targets, or how many simply got lost, despite all Moriarty could do, and wandered off or acquired targets other than the ones they'd originally been assigned. It was obvious that the task force's defenses managed to stop an enormous percentage them. Unfortunately, it was even more obvious that they hadn't stopped *enough* of them.

Hundreds of them hurled themselves at the LACs—not because anyone had wanted to waste MDMs on something as small as a LAC, but because missiles which had lost their original targets as they spread beyond the reach of Moriarty's lightspeed commands had acquired them, instead. LACs, and especially Manticoran and Grayson LACs, were very difficult for missiles to hit. Which was not to say that they were *impossible* to hit, however, and over two hundred of them were blown out of space as the tornado of missiles ripped into the task force.

Most of the rest of Moriarty's missiles had been targeted on the two superdreadnoughts, and they howled in on their targets like demons. Captain Rafe Cardones maneuvered Honor's flagship as if the stupendous superdreadnought were a heavy cruiser, twisting around to interpose his wedge while jammers and decoys joined with laser clusters in a last-ditch, point-blank defense. *Imperator* shuddered and bucked as laser heads blasted through her sidewalls, but despite grievous wounds, she actually got off lightly. Not even her massive armor was impervious to such a concentrated rain of destruction, but it did its job, preserving her core hull and essential systems intact, and her human casualties were minuscule in proportion to the amount of fire scorching in upon her.

*Intolerant* was less fortunate.

The earlier damage to *Imperator*'s sister ship was simply too severe. She'd lost both of her Keyholes and all too many of her counter-missile launchers and laser clusters in the last attack. Her sensors had been battered, leaving holes in her own close-in coverage, and her electronic warfare systems were far below par. She was simply the biggest, most visible, most vulnerable target in the entire task force, and despite everything BCS 81 could do, droves of myopic end-of-run Havenite MDMs hurled themselves at the clearest target they could see.

The superdreadnought was trapped at the heart of a maelstrom of detonating laser heads, hurling X-ray lasers like vicious harpoons. They slammed into her again and again and again, ripping and maiming, tearing steadily deeper while the big ship shuddered and bucked in agony. And then, finally, one of those lasers found something fatal and HMS *Intolerant* and her entire company vanished into a glaring fireball of destruction.

Nor did she die alone.

HMS *Ajax* heaved indescribably as the universe went mad.

Compared to the torrent of fire streaming in on the two superdreadnoughts, only a handful of missiles attacked the battlecruisers. But that "handful" was still numbered in the hundreds, and they were much more fragile targets. Alarms screamed as deadly lasers ripped deep into far more lightly armored hulls, and the *Agamemnon*-class were podlayers. They had the hollow cores of their type, and that made them even more fragile than other, older battlecruisers little more than half their size. Michelle had always wondered if that aspect of their design was as great a vulnerability as the BC(P)'s critics had always contended.

It looked like they—and she—were about to find out.

Oliver Manfredi was hurled from his feet as *Ajax* lurched, and Michelle felt her command chair's shock frame hammering viciously at her. Urgent voices, high-pitched and distorted despite the professionalism trained bone-deep into their owners, filled the com channels with messages of devastation—announcements of casualties, of destroyed systems, which ended all too often in mid-syllable as death came for the men and women making those reports.

Even through the pounding, Michelle saw the icons of both of her second division's ships—*Priam* and *Patrocles*—disappear abruptly from her plot, and other icons disappeared or flashed critical damage codes throughout the task force's formation. The light cruisers *Fury*, *Buckler*, and *Atum* vanished in glaring flashes of destruction, and the heavy cruisers *Star Ranger* and *Blackstone* were transformed into crippled hulks, coasting onward ballistically without power or impeller wedges. And then—

"Direct hit on the command deck!" one of Stackpole's ratings announced. "No survivors, Sir! Heavy damage to Boat Bay Two, and Boat Bay One's been completely destroyed! Engineering reports—"

Michelle felt it in her own flesh as HMS *Ajax* faltered suddenly.

"We've lost the after ring, Ma'am!" Stackpole said harshly. "*All* of it."

Michelle bit the inside of her lower lip so hard she tasted blood. Solon lay in the heart of a hyper-space gravity wave. No ship could enter, navigate, or long survive in a gravity wave without both Warshawski sails . . . and without the after impeller ring's alpha nodes, *Ajax* could no longer generate an after sail.

—end excerpt—

from *Storm from the Shadows*
available in hardcover,
March 2009, from Baen Books